2011
10

HONEY OFF THORNS

HONEY OFF THORNS

Anne M Brady

SEVERN HOUSE PUBLISHERS

WB PG5 JL

This first world edition published simultaneously 1988 in
Great Britain by SEVERN HOUSE PUBLISHERS LTD of
40–42 William IV Street, London WC2N 4DF and in
the U.S.A. by SEVERN HOUSE PUBLISHERS INC, New York.

British Library Cataloguing in Publication Data
Brady, Anne M., *1926–*
Honey off thorns.
I. Title
823′.914[F]

ISBN 0–7278–1641–1

Distributed in the U.S.A. by Mercedes Distribution Center, Inc
62 Imlay Street, Brooklyn, NY 11231

Printed and bound in Great Britain

For David, Mark, Davida, Niall and Philippa.

Prologue

The tree was nearly as old as the abbey itself. For nearly four hundred years birds had built their nests in it, children had played with its glossy brown chestnuts and lovers had carved their initials in the bark of its broad trunk, but on this last day of August, fifteen hundred and thirty-nine, a noose dangled from its strongest branch.

They had come from cottage and farmhouse to see the hanging, from village and town, streaming across the sunlit dales since early morning. They sprawled now in the lush grass, talking, laughing, passing jugs of beer and cold meat pies from one to the other while they shouted goodnatured curses at the children – men and women of the dales, bussing each other between gulps of beer and mouthfuls of pie but afraid to go behind the bushes for fear of missing the hanging for something that could be had any night of the week, or any day for that matter.

Beyond the tree a group of monks recited the rosary aloud, and behind them were the beggars, the outcasts, waiting in bitter silence for the death of the one who stood for all they might ever know of charity. A careful distance from the beggars a man waited alone beside his horse, a middle-aged, soberly dressed man with a soft, pale face and the beginnings of a paunch – a man of business, one would have said, more at home counting his money than witnessing a hanging.

Suddenly a shout went up from the crowd for they could see the abbot's tall figure as he stumbled up the hill towards them between two soldiers. He had been taken from the town of East

1

Wooton on a hurdle but now he had to walk, and the people scrambled to their feet as he made his way through them with painful slowness, looking straight ahead. He was no longer wearing his pectoral cross or his ring, and his white habit that had always been immaculate was soiled with vomit.

When he and the two soldiers reached the tree where a small group of the King's men waited he turned to face the chattering crowd who had run forward in order to get a better view, men lifting small children onto their shoulders. He raised his hand in a last blessing, and one of the soldiers stepped forward to blindfold him. The hangman put the noose round his neck, and at a signal from the soldier, pulled on his rope.

It took the abbot nearly twenty minutes to die, his body turning occasionally in the rising wind above the upturned, gaping faces, his dangling feet within reach. His once handsome face had become unrecognisable, the eyes bulging, the tongue protruding obscenely. The crowd had grown quiet but suddenly a woman began to cry hysterically – and then another, and another, until the King's men, listening uneasily, began to wonder if it might not be wiser to leave now, before the mood of the people changed.

The lone watcher, still standing by his horse, both saw and recognised the young man who galloped up the hill soon afterwards and circled the crowd before dismounting to speak to one of the monks, and, as he himself hurried to join the rest of the King's men, he swore he'd have the truth out of the arrogant young pup, and the girl too.

Chapter One

It happened so quickly. One minute they could see the path ahead; bushes, a distant tree, a pile of rocks. The next all but a few yards of stony path was gone, the bushes seeming like a single, great mushroom before disappearing altogether in the fog.

They had left the village behind them by early afternoon of that autumn day, fifteen hundred and thirty-eight, and had followed the path which they had been assured by a boy driving a flock of sheep would lead them directly to the abbey. "Twill be a glave sort o'neet!' the young shepherd had warned them, and John, who acted as interpreter, having made several visits to the dales with Sir William as against Robert's one and only visit, insisted that they should put on their cloaks. He led the way, his flat hat set straight on his big head, his cloak now billowing over the saddle, his booted legs thick as young trees, hugging the white gelding, the packhorse following obediently behind. Robert brought up the rear, but his red, velvet cap was set at an angle. The slashed doublet and breeches under his fashionable short cloak were of red velvet too and had been made for him in London, although his fine boots of Spanish leather and the perfumed, gauntleted gloves that so irritated his grandfather had come from Amsterdam. He had just been thinking that the old tyrant might not be around much longer to criticise and find fault when the fog, that up until then had lain only on high ground, began to creep towards them, and in minutes had all but smothered them.

'Hell and damnation!' Robert swore, reining in his mare. 'We'll be here for the night!'

Suddenly a figure materialised out of the fog – a woman, bulky in a long, black gown, an old-fashioned head-dress covering her hair completely. She was carrying a basket and hurrying towards them as if she herself were a creature of the fog and had no fear of it. She came to an abrupt halt within feet of them and Robert swept off his cap and said quickly, before she could disappear again, 'Good evening, mistress! Can you direct us to Wolden Abbey?'

She did not seem afraid of them either for she came nearer, and there was a look of amazement in her face which puzzled Robert.

'The path is just ahead.' She was quite young, and her voice was soft, educated.

Who was she, he wondered, and what in heaven's name was she doing out alone in the fog? 'If you can just show us – but we must not take you out of your way. I am Robert FitzHugh, and this is John Riddell . . .'

'Robert FitzHugh!' She repeated the name with an odd note of wonder in her voice, scarcely bothering to look at John, while the horses, wanting their oats and a warm stable, began to get restless. The young woman turned away then, beckoning them to follow her as she walked back the way she had come. After a few yards she stopped and they could see the bushes again, and a path behind them, turning to the right.

'Follow the path,' she said. 'It will bring you downhill to the gatehouse.' Her voice was brisk now, matter of fact. She seemed to smile, and then she was gone, hurrying along the path, swallowed up in the fog before he could think of anything sensible to say that would keep her there a while longer.

'What a strange young woman!' he said to John as they moved slowly, cautiously forward. 'Almost like a nun!'

'She *is* a nun!' John's voice was gruff, and Robert was aware of the oddest feeling of disappointment.

'A nun? She can't be! Nuns don't wander about in the fog, all by themselves! Not even in Yorkshire!'

'She is a Benedictine dame, I'd swear, from St. Mary's Convent – though what she's doing out here –' John's voice trailed off. Like the horses he was interested only in the prospect of food and a warm bed.

'I must say I find the whole thing rather intriguing! A young nun, with an attractive voice, who seemed almost to know me –'

'Nun she be an' nun she will likely remain,' John said curtly,

4

'and even the sheep 'ud know a FitzHugh! An' if this bloody path don't improve soon we'll ha' three lame horses!'

And as Robert began to laugh they heard the bells, muffled by fog but unmistakable, becoming louder as they rode slowly downhill.

Suddenly, as quickly as it had come, the fog lifted, and rounding another bend they saw Wolden Abbey. It seemed to rear up against the grey sky. Massive. Arrogant. Like an enormous cathedral set in emptiness. The bells were much louder now, and for a moment Robert forgot the young nun and remembered instead the reason for their coming. He felt guilty that he should have forgotten it for so long. The great studded door with its small grating faced them and as he lifted the massive iron door knocker he wondered if the young Benedictine nun had found her way back to her convent or was still wandering about in the fog. God's wounds, he thought, but if John had not been with him and seen and heard her too, he'd have sworn he'd imagined the whole thing!

Chapter Two

The fog seemed to have found its way into her lungs and Isobel began to cough as she hurried along, wary of rabbit holes, of stones hidden among clumps of grass that might trip her, and nearly falling several times. Yet all of these hazards, her care that she should not fall or lose her way, even the discomfort of coughing, were all somehow remote. It was as if her real self was concerned only with what had happened a few minutes before – seeing not the fog, nor the path, but only a shock of very fair hair, shorter than she remembered it, hearing the voice, deeper now. Everything else – the quick smile, the dark eyes, the look of arrogance – were unchanged, as dearly familiar as if she had been meeting him every day of her life instead of just once, five years ago.

She had believed with a child's belief that she would see him again, but she did not guess that when she saw him next time she would be a nun, a fully professed, Benedictine nun, given to God. And he would be – what he was. The pain of this unexpected meeting was as real as the rough stones that bruised her feet through the thin soles of her nun's shoes.

'I will marry him!' she had told her mother that day long ago when he and his grandfather had ridden out of the yard with their men. 'Some day!' And her mother had laughed at first, and then when she saw that she meant what she had said, became uneasy.

'Isobel child, have sense! He's the grandson of Sir William FitzHugh! *You* marry him? It's not possible, my darling. You must put such foolish thoughts out of your mind.'

'But I *will* marry him! He liked me, didn't you see that? I showed him the puppy and he said he would come back again soon – and – and he's not a bit like his grandfather!' She could hear her voice as if it was yesterday, and her mother's reply.

'I should hope not! His grandfather is a lecherous old man!'

'What does "lecherous" mean, mother?'

But her father had come back into the yard then and her mother had only said, 'When you are older I shall explain.' But she never had explained and Robert had never come back. Until now.

She had put her foolish thoughts out of her mind long ago, at her mother's insistence. 'Learn by my mistakes, Isobel. Do not let yourself be misled. Marriage is – is not what you think – and there are other ways in which to find happiness.'

Other ways. Had it been her mother who had first put the thought into her head that she should enter a convent? Or had it come from within herself, as she had always believed? And had she, as a young novice, been seeking God because her human goal was unattainable and for no other reason? She realised now with a kind of terror, as the abbey bells drowned the shrill clamour of the convent bell, that the questions had lain dormant in her mind for a long time, and she began to wish with all her heart that she had never gone out that afternoon, had never met him. It was God's punishment! She had gone out alone, without asking permission, even if it *was* to bring food to the hungry – and she had broken other rules! She had not kept silence, nor had she observed custody of the eyes! And she had walked on the balls of her feet! She was actually running now, lifting up the heavy skirt of her black habit, through the clearing fog with the convent bell becoming more audible and more insistent. She was going to be late for vespers! Run! her mind screamed at her. *Run!* Forget him! *Forget!*

She was still out of breath when she took her place in the choir, and she saw the abbess turn her head to look at her disapprovingly. In the stall beside her Dame Agatha was smiling to herself – a small, secretive smile of malicious delight that the abbess's pet should be late for vespers with her veil awry and mud on her shoes, and hoarse as a crow when they began to sing the first hymn!

The nuns' voices rose now to the high roof of the chapel,

amazingly strong for a group of elderly women. Isobel could hear her own voice, the first hoarseness gone, rising above them all, singing the Latin of which she, like the rest, only understood a few words. But she took no pride in her voice and it mattered little whether she understood the Latin or not. She only knew that she was praying. Help me to forget him, God. Please help me. I cannot do it alone.

After compline that night she lay sleepless in the narrow bed of the tiny cell overlooking the garden which the abbess had given her as a special privilege because the snoring in the main dormitory kept her awake. Her habit hung from a hook behind the door, over the whip, and her wimple and black veil, together with the rest of her clothes, were neatly folded on the stool.

It was cold, for the fires had not yet been lit in the warming house and she was more conscious of her aloneness than she had been since her first night in the convent. She had cried then for her mother, for the feel of her arms around her, but now the tears slid down her cheeks and she cried for she knew not what. For warmth perhaps, and love. Tangible, human love. For the feel of skin on skin. For someone to hold her, fondle her, warm her with his own flesh – for she had no doubt at all it would be a man, a young man. And she sat up shivering, like a mare hearing the stallion's scream for the first time. I must not! she told herself in an agony of shame. I must not allow myself to think – to think – I must go to confession tomorrow.

But what would saintly old Father Francis think of her? She began to shiver again. How could she tell him that for five years she had remembered a boy, a man, that in spite of her solemn vows she had never succeeded in banishing him from her mind. That in her dreams her memories of him had become confused with her image of God, and now that she had met him again it was not God but only the man that she could see.

I cannot do it! she thought. I cannot tell him that! So, instead, she got out of bed and took off her coarse cotton shift, standing naked and still shivering on the hard green rushes that covered the floor of her cell. Then she groped in the dark for the whip, the twelve-inch long waxed chord with its knotted tails that hung behind the door beneath her habit. Still in the dark she began to beat herself on the shoulders, gently at first and then more strongly until some darkness in her that she could not understand made her want to beat herself on the buttocks, and she threw the whip from her in horrified disgust.

She put on her shift again, got slowly back into bed and, not allowing herself to think or to feel, fell asleep almost immediately, to be wakened for matins by one of the lay-sisters at two o'clock in the morning.

'Benedicamus domino!'

'Deo gratias!' Isobel muttered, turning stiffly on her hard mattress like an old woman.

Chapter Three

They walked together in the long gallery of Whitehall Palace, the brewer's son from Putney and the King of England. Inside the door of the gallery a group of people waited uneasily, men and women of the court, wondering what new mischief was being plotted by the two men, so deep in conversation.

Thomas Cromwell was not a small man, but he seemed dwarfed by the huge, swaggering figure that walked beside him, head bent attentively, for King Henry VIII still listened to what his Vicar General had to say. Soon he would make him Lord Chamberlain and Earl of Essex to repay him for his long and faithful service. But that was still in the future, as was the death to which he would send him not long afterwards.

The two men had been talking earlier about the threat of invasion since the signing of the Truce of Nice which, lamentably for England, had brought together the Pope and the Emperor and the King of France in a joint crusade against heresy at home and abroad. Now, in an attempt to lighten his mood, the minister had just told his royal master that news of the 'disgarnishing' of St Thomas's Shrine at Canterbury was said to have reached Rome and to have nearly caused Paul III to have an apoplexy.

'Ten – or was it twelve? – wagons of precious metals and jewels? You did well, Thomas!' the King said jovially.

The minister bowed his large head in silent acknowledgment, wrapping his sober black gown more closely about him, for it was chilly in the long, ill-lit gallery. To the men and women waiting at the far end he was like a raven of ill-omen beside a gorgeous bird of paradise, and they did not know which of the two they feared the most. Cromwell's small, brown eyes were thoughtful. He was sure there were not even ten wagons – but if it pleased the King . . . The desk in his house at Austin Friars was piled high with documents and accounts relating to the dissolution of the monasteries, but although the monies that had accrued to the royal coffers as a result of the dissolution were already far greater than he had ever envisaged when he first took office, he knew they would not be enough. From the corner of his eye he could see the huge swell of the King's stomach under its satin doublet that was crusted with precious stones. His body was swollen with too much food, too much wine. It had even been whispered that it was being slowly destroyed by the pox. This Cromwell refused to believe, but he could not hide from himself the fact that the King's greed and foolish spending might in the end destroy England. Already the closure of the monasteries had more than doubled the royal income, but money poured through those grasping, bejewelled fingers like water.

'We must finish the job soon, Thomas!' the King said now with sudden harshness and that change of mood to which his minister was accustomed but which never failed to ring a warning bell in his mind. 'We're near bankruptcy! Ireland and our coastal defences have beggared me!'

And your own extravagances, Cromwell thought grimly, but he said only, 'I intend to do so, your grace!' Knowing only too well that more was needed at this moment than just an expression of intent, and remembering with relief a letter that had arrived on his desk the day before, he continued, 'I have been told sire, that the Cîteaux treasure is still in the country. It was taken some time ago from Rievaulx, where it has been for the past hundred years or so, and hidden in Wolden Abbey, close by.'

The King's blond, almost hairless eyebrows were drawn together in a frown. 'The Cîteaux treasure?' he repeated, his interest clearly caught. 'I have not heard of it.' They had reached the far end of the gallery again and they turned together, the King's over-gown, sable edged, swinging from his massive shoulders with an elegance that was not only regal but peculiarly his own.

11

Thomas Cromwell's thin-lipped mouth came close to smiling. It had been like offering a sweetmeat to a fractious child. 'The treasure was given to the monks of Cîteaux Abbey by a Count of Beaune in the 12th century, sire.'

'All right, man, all right!' The royal voice had grown peevish. 'I don't want a history lesson! Is it *valuable?*'

'Immensely so, your grace!' the minister said drily. 'There are seven items, but the most important, the most valuable one is a ninth century jewelled chalice of pure gold, the base of which is a reliquary containing bones from St Bernard's hand. The jewels are said to be unequalled in quality but the fact that it is a reliquary also makes it of *special* value in the eyes of the Old Catholics here, and of course in France.'

'But who owns it, the English or the French monks?'

'There is some doubt. It was brought here for safe keeping, when the French army was pillaging the monasteries in France.'

'Who is your informant?'

'A man called Edward Dutton.'

'Reliable?'

'I have not used him before, but he appears to be useful – a prosperous London wool merchant, originally from Yorkshire. Ambitious, able enough. Has an uncle, now dead, who owned land up there at one time. Wants to be a landowner himself, and has an eye for Wolden.'

'A familiar type.' Now it was the King's voice that was dry. 'Well, Thomas, get this treasure for me! It is not to go back to France! Make the abbot of Wolden hand it over, by whatever means, and if he refuses to give it up, hang him! I'll not be outfaced by any damned priest! Or have that cursed Francis laughing at me either!'

'Very good, sire.' Thomas Cromwell and his master dealt out death as other men dealt out a pack of playing cards and a mere abbot was of little importance. On the other hand, monastic valuables still remained hidden and so were lost to the Crown. 'There is a second man who has an interest in Wolden,' he added slowly. 'Old Sir William FitzHugh. You may remember he wrote asking you to reconsider the closing of the abbey.'

'Good heavens, man, of course I don't remember!' The King's minister knew it was unlikely that he had, but one could never be sure. It was astonishing how much detail that quick, active mind could recall on occasion. 'You say "old"? Too old to be a nuisance?'

'Not so much old as sick, your grace,' Cromwell said thoughtfully. 'There is a grandson, but I doubt if we have anything to fear from him, and of course it is possible that the FitzHughs know nothing of the present whereabouts of the treasure, although that is unlikely since the abbot and Sir William are, I believe, close friends and Sir William is descended from the Count of Beaune – '

But the King dismissed the FitzHughs with a wave of his hand. 'Is there anything else? I'm getting damned peckish!'

Both men knew that there was, and that it was the last thing the King wanted to talk about although it was the main reason for Thomas Cromwell's visit to the palace. The unmaking of a Queen had helped to bring the minister to his present position, for it was his spies who had painstakingly collected the evidence against Anne Boleyn that had put her young head on the block and severed it from her body. Now he was intent on the *making* of a Queen, and he was not to know that in the end this ploy would help to bring about his downfall. After a moment he said in his quiet, stolid voice that still had the flat overtones of his early beginnings, 'Have you given any thought to the matter which we were discussing the other day, your majesty?'

'What matter, man?' The King was determined to bluster evidently, and the minister's heart sank, but he had not got where he was by being hesitant.

'I was referring, sire, to the desirability of a German alliance.'

His royal master grunted deep in his chest. 'You want me to take a pockmarked spinster of thirty-four into my bed, for *wife*? Just to please the emperor?'

'Everybody has praised the beauty of Lady Anne of Cleves,' Cromwell said quickly. 'You have been misinformed.'

'But you haven't actually *seen* her?'

'I have it on the best authority, sire. And her sister is married to Johann Friedrich of Saxony. The alliance would improve our relations with the Schmalkaldic League and make the Baltic ports more accessible to us.'

The King made another dismissive gesture with his hand. 'Why not a Frenchwoman?' he said, his small, sensual mouth under its wispy blond moustache smiling hopefully.

13

'If you remember, the French ambassador said the ladies of his country were not to be inspected like ponies,' Cromwell said coldly, 'as for the Queen of Denmark, she said *she* would only marry the King of England if she had two heads.' As soon as he had said the words he had regretted them, but he was tired after a long day and longing for the peace and quiet of his widower's house and the supper to which he had invited two like-minded friends with literary inclinations. The King's belly laugh rang out, however, causing heads to turn at the end of the gallery.

'The Danish woman sounds as if she might amuse me for a while! 'Tis not all a matter of bedding, you know, Thomas!'

'Of course not, sire,' the minister said relieved. 'But to return to my earlier suggestion – '

There was a royal snort of disgust. 'I'll think on it! I'll think on it! But no more about it for now.'

They were half-way down the gallery and Cromwell knew he would soon be dismissed. 'How is Prince Edward?' he ventured. 'I heard he has been poorly for the past few days.'

'Just a chill,' the King said hastily. 'Nothing more. Nothing to worry about, I assure you.' He was smiling but they both knew that the Prince was a sickly child who might never live to be a man, and yet he was the heir, the only male child ever born to the King after three marriages who had survived. The minister had asked the question deliberately to remind the King where his duty lay. They stopped their walking as if by mutual consent, looking at each other in the flickering light of the wall flares. But the King turned his head away in the first second, for as everyone knew he could not bear for any man to look directly into his eyes. Was he thinking of the child's mother, Cromwell wondered, the gentle, delicate Jane who had died after giving birth? Had he had a fondness for her, as they said he had? Was he capable of it?

'He is very well, Thomas,' the King repeated, no longer smiling, and looking over his shoulder towards the end of the gallery. Someone had opened the great door and in the ensuing draught the nearby flares on the wall were extinguished. As the King, with his minister beside him, began to walk towards the open door, the waiting group, grown suddenly silent, were lost in shadow, only the outline of their bodies visible. Thomas Cromwell caught his breath. He was not an imaginative man, had he been he would not have slept of nights – but now, these dimly seen bodies seemed like ghosts, and as the King roared for more lights and a moment passed before servants of the household came hurrying, the ghosts seemed to peer at them both in silent condemnation. The minister waited by the King's side until the flares were re-lit and in the sudden blaze of light he saw a trickle of sweat run down the side of the great, bloated face that not so very long ago had been firm-fleshed and young, and, it was even said, beautiful.

'See to the Cîteaux treasure,' the King muttered under his breath, and turned away in dismissal.

Thomas Cromwell bowed low but with no hint of subservience, thinking as he straightened that the making of the next Queen might have to wait it seemed, until he could bring the treasure to his master.

Chapter Four

Shortly after midday the abbess of St Mary's Benedictine Convent, Dame Margaret, went up to the small parlour that she called her study and sat down behind the massive table which served her as a desk. Her head ached and she longed to take off her veil and wimple but she dared not. The scandal it would cause, should someone walk in! Besides, how ridiculous she would look, she thought, for try as she might she had never reconciled herself to her cropped head, grey now and rough to the touch like an animal's pelt. She could not even lift her veil higher, for years before the bishops sent a directive that the veil and wimple must be worn well down on the forehead – as if, she had thought scornfully at the time, a group of elderly men had the right to dictate to any woman how she should wear either. Nevertheless she had obeyed the directive and seen to it that not a strand of even her young novices' hair appeared. But she often wondered if that was what God intended.

So she rubbed her forehead instead and gradually the pain eased, becoming merely a dull ache behind her tired eyes. At the side of the table a formidable pile of account ledgers threatened to fall over and she frowned, remembering that she must soon go over them again with Father Francis, although he was not much better at keeping accounts than she was. It was a pity, she thought, that Father Abbot would not send her one of his younger monks to help, but even she and Father Francis could see clearly that the convent's annual income was down. They had taken in no new novices and consequently had no dowries. Nor were there any boarders this year – not that *they* brought in

16

much. Eightpence a week last year, and the two little girls had eaten more than four nuns would have done. If it had not been for the wool sales, and the sales of the ecclesiastical embroidery, they would have been in a bad way, with eight corradies and the poor to care for and all the other unexpected expenses as well – twopence for appearing at the local marshal's court on behalf of one of the tenants, fourpence a year to Convocation, new gloves for the men and women doing the weeding and ditching and hedging. Keeping the accounts was the task that weighed most heavily of all on her, especially since the Act of Suppression had been passed two years before. St Mary's had been granted a respite then when their financial position had been better. Now, she lived in daily dread of the next Visitation, of a messenger bringing a letter to her from the King, or Lord Cromwell, or Dr London or some faceless unknown, saying 'You must leave.'

Where would they go? The convent was their home and, except for Isobel, they had grown old together there. It did not bear thinking about, and anyway there were more immediate problems to be tackled, small but important in their own way for the smooth running of St Mary's. The candlemaker would soon be coming to prepare tallow dips for the dark, winter evenings. She must see to it that there was enough tallow and mutton fat for the rush-lights and cresset-lights – and she really must ask Dame Cecilia if there was anything she could do for Dame Petronilla's rheumatism, her poor old knees were so stiff now she could scarcely walk. And Dame Agatha – she *must* have a word soon with her. She seemed to make trouble wherever she went. She had even upset poor old Petronilla last week, they said. Everyone knew that Petronilla believed Our Lady appeared to her sometimes in the garden. And perhaps She did. Even the chaplain would not commit himself to an opinion either way. But Dame Agatha had no right to tell her that it was wishful thinking. And behind all the clamour of her thoughts the abbess knew that she was still not facing up to what was really troubling her.

Dame Isobel. Her dear Isobel, who was like the daughter she had never had, whose every step along the way since she had first entered she had watched over, whose education she had personally supervised, seeing to it that she had a knowledge of French and even a few words of Latin. What could be the matter with her this year?

17

Isobel had seemed so happy, so content in the past – but recently she had become restless, inattentive, breaking the Rule constantly, endlessly contrite and then breaking it again. For one thing, she was far too prone to leave the convent alone and without asking permission even though she always had some valid excuse – there was an urgent call from the cottages for food, or clothing, or something – and all the nuns who were free to go with her were too old to walk such a distance. But even if the rule of perpetual enclosure *had* been relaxed she herself would be in serious trouble with the bishop for tolerating such behaviour, excuses or not, and God alone knew what the Visitors might make of it if someone told tales.

Was it because Isobel was the only young thing left now in St Mary's with the boarders gone? Or had she not got a real vocation, after all? Dame Margaret thought back to the struggle she had had with the Council to make them agree to Isobel's final profession. 'She is not ready,' they said. Dame Cecilia begged that the decision might be put off for another year. Dame Petronilla agreed with her, but she herself had argued so strongly that Isobel should be professed that year that in the end the Council had agreed. But had she been wrong? Worse still, had she been wrong five years ago? The Council had disagreed with her then, too. Dame Helen Scrope who had just been appointed prioress had been particularly vehement.

'We cannot take a farmer's daughter! It would not be seemly. We are all gently born.'

'Her mother is a Dacres!' she had said, angry with Dame Helen. '*She* is gently born, and she has reared the girl very carefully.'

'Nevertheless, her father is plain Ben Willis,' Dame Helen reminded them in her thin, high voice. 'It will not do, mi'lady.'

'The Willis family have been tenants of the FitzHughs for generations and the FitzHughs gave the land on which our convent stands to the Benedictine nuns . . .' She could remember thinking at the time that it was not really a pertinent argument and had been grateful when Dame Petronilla had spoken up. 'We *need* young blood,' she had said with her usual directness, 'not just for the dowry, but who is going to care for us later on, eh?' She had looked from one ageing face to the other. 'There are not so many novices clamouring to get in nowadays!'

18

And in the end the Council had agreed. But had they done the right thing in taking Isobel, all the same? On the wall opposite the abbess's table the heavy bronze crucifix that had been there when she herself had come to the convent as a young novice, caught the noon sun and she remembered the day when Alice Willis had brought her new-born daughter Isobel to St Mary's to show her to the nuns, and most of all to her old friend, Dame Margaret Fairfax. Alice had ridden across the dale from the farm, a woman servant carrying the baby walking beside her, but Alice had left the woman in the kitchen and carried the baby herself to the abbess's parlour. It had been autumn too then, Dame Margaret remembered, and the mother with the tiny baby in her arms had stood under the same crucifix and been caught in a beam of sunlight – Alice Willis that had been Alice Dacres, younger than herself and like a sister.

The Fairfax and Dacres families were related to one another, and had been friends for generations. Until one day Alice met handsome farmer Ben Willis at a hunt, had fallen in love and eloped with him. Then all the county had shut its doors to her – her own family and the Fairfaxes included. But over the years she had come to visit the convent and her old friend, each year a little thinner, a little sadder.

'Why can't I become pregnant again? Why can't the Lord send me a son?' she used to say. 'Pray, Margaret – please pray for me. It is so hard on Ben.'

But it was harder on her, Dame Margaret used to think, hearing tales of Ben's drinking and affairs with women from the village. And then that last Christmas after Isobel had entered, Alice had come to see her in a state of trembling excitement.

'I am pregnant, Margaret! At last He has answered my prayers! Oh, pray, pray that it will be a boy!'

But it was too late. She was too old for child-bearing and she and the baby boy had died together. Ben had married again within the year, a smallholder's daughter this time – as if he was tired of narrow-hipped gentility – a big, rough, poor creature who had come once to the convent with him to see Isobel. They had never come again and although Isobel had a monk cousin in the abbey she might as well have been a foundling.

Was that what was wrong with her. The abbess wondered. But it should not matter to her all that much, not now. Was it simply that she was not suited to convent life, had no vocation, should never have been accepted?

But how many of us here *have* a real vocation? she asked herself. Dame Cecilia, for all her worldliness, certainly had one, and Petronilla and even Helen, despite her foolishness – but the others? As for herself, *she* had become a nun because she did not want to get married. Men had told her she was beautiful and some had wanted to marry her, but she could not bear the thought of a man's body entering hers. And for women of gentle birth there was no alternative to marriage but the religious life. It was not until that summer, years later, when *he* had ridden across the dales that she had realised what her young girl's decision had cost her. Giacomo Frescobaldi from Florence. Thin and dark and impossibly good-looking. Over to buy wool from the convent's sheep, wool which like the abbey's was carefully graded. He had come into her parlour and bowed, perching himself on the side of her table with an easy familiarity which should have offended her but didn't. They had talked, not only about wool but about Yorkshire and England itself, about Italy, which she had only read about, and occasionally he would smile into her eyes, seeing her womanhood, her very soul or so it seemed to her.

When the time came for him to leave he had taken her hand, her pale, nun's hand, kissing it and for the first time in her life she had felt her body stir and closed her knees in sudden, violent embarrassment. Had he known? Even now she could remember the feel of his lips on her skin. Cool. Smooth as silk and yet burning, so that when he was gone she had half expected to see the mark of them on her hand, like a kind of stigmata, and she had crossed herself, begging forgiveness for such a blasphemous thought.

She had thanked God that he never came back, and yet every spring for a long time afterwards she had watched for him, dreading that he would come and heartbroken because he had not, still hearing the lilt of his Italian voice sometimes when she had shut the parlour door behind her. Well, she was past sixty now and why in God's name did she have to think of him today? Her head was beginning to ache again and she rubbed it irritably. She must be getting senile – and what did it matter if Isobel, or any of them for that matter, had a vocation or not?

20

What else could they do? Where else could they go unless to the little house in York that her family had given her recently fearing the convent would be closed? But St Mary's was their home. They should be left there in peace to do God's work. She must have a talk soon with Isobel and find out what was troubling her.

Chapter Five

They had to wait in the cloister until vespers were over before they could see the abbot, Dom Richard, and they walked up and down wrapped in their cloaks, tired after the long ride up from London, and still chilled by the fog which seemed to have crept into their bones and lodged there. Robert thought of his grandfather, lying in the great four-poster bed in his house on the banks of the Thames, and the old man's harsh, autocratic voice seemed to rise above the distant chanting of the monks.

'Warn Dom Richard! Tell him the King means to have the abbey this year!'

'But the abbot was not involved in the Rising,' he had argued, not wanting to leave London and go up to the wilds of Wensleydale. 'Are you quite sure?'

'Of course I'm sure! I still have friends at court and they write to me. Wolden is lucky to have escaped for so long. But the King's coffers are empty and he wants to destroy the old Catholic ways – he's not concerned with the rights and wrongs of it. And even the FitzHughs can't stop him, although your ancestor Robert FitzHugh gave the land to the Cistercians in eleven hundred and seventy-five, and *he* got it from his father-in-law, Walter l'Espec! And I'd remind you that the FitzHughs can trace their line back to the Count of Beaune, a relative of St Bernard's!' His grandfather had drawn breath and then went on with a rush, as though he had been thinking of what he had to say for hours beforehand. 'We're not like the lickspittle upstarts that surround the King!' His thin, grey lips had twisted. 'One of 'em has gone crawling already to the

22

augmentations men for Wolden – fellow called Edward Dutton, Yorkshire family, owns a few acres but lives in London. Doing well in wool – new money – you know the kind! So Dom Richard must see that the King's Visitors find no cause for closure. He must see to his book-keeping, and there must be no womanising, or anything else. Warn him, Robert!'

'But – but I can't say that to a lord abbot!'

'No, of course not!' The long, bony hands that only a year ago could hold a bolting horse had moved restlessly on the bedcovers. 'You can hint – just hint! Not that Dom Richard is that kind. The man's too good, if anything. But there are twenty monks up there and don't tell me there are not one or two sinners among 'em! That's not to say that the scurvy stories running around the country are all true – far from it! Nevertheless, a hint, Robert. Just a hint!'

'I'll remember.'

'If only I could go myself.' A vein had stood out like a rope on the old man's forehead and his frustration had been terrible to see.

'Don't fret, grandfather. I shall do as you ask.'

The restless hands had become still, but the old voice had gone on, tired now and growing hoarse. 'The convent – St Mary's – will probably be closed soon although it's small and not well-endowed. And there's one more thing. Tell Dom Richard to hide the Cîteaux treasure well. I doubt if the fellow Dutton or the King's Visitors know of its existence but one can't be sure of anything these days.'

Robert had not known of its existence himself until quite recently when his grandfather had told him about it with obvious reluctance. It had caught at his imagination more than the actual closure of the abbey itself because long ago his French ancestor, the Count of Beaune had given the treasure to the monks of Cîteaux and he felt slightly ashamed that this should be so.

'I shall go up tomorrow, don't worry!' Robert could hear his own voice still, humouring, agreeing as always, or nearly always.

But his grandfather had not finished yet. 'Take John with you. He's got a good head on his shoulders and he's been up there a few times already – and remember, you can kill two birds with one stone!'

He had known only too well what his grandfather was leading up to but he pretended ignorance. 'What do you mean?'

23

'Don't try to play games with me, you know right well what I mean! Get yourself to the Nevilles after you've been to the abbey and see the girl. Or don't see her, makes no matter, so long as you come back with the marriage arranged.'

'I don't want . . .'

'Want? What has wanting to do with it? You're twenty-three! You should have been wed years ago! You should be dandling your sons on your knee now instead of wasting your seed on Dutch whores and . . .' The old man had raised himself with difficulty off his pillows. 'If you don't wed soon they'll be saying there's something wrong with you!'

'I've a mind to pick my own bride.'

'Well, you've been mighty slow about it! The girl is the niece of an earl. She has money, *old* money! The Nevilles carried the white rose to victory at Towton with the FitzHughs and we fought together at Bosworth Field, although like ourselves her uncle took no part in the Northern Rising – it 'ud be a good match. He and I talked about it a full year ago.'

'They say she's as plain as a pikestaff – and she's older than I am. Why has she not married long ago if she's such a good catch?'

'I don't know why not!' His grandfather was growing more irritable by the moment. 'What matter so long as she can breed? You can lie with whom you like afterwards so long as you don't foul your own nest!'

His grandfather had lain back against the pillows again, worn out with so much talking and Robert remembered now looking down at him with active dislike, and thinking at the same time that he was right, of course. He should have married long ago and have a son – two sons. It was a duty which had been put before him for as long as he could remember, and it was a miracle he had been able to shirk it until now. Well, some day in the not too distant future he would, by the look of things, be Sir Robert, with estates in Northumbria and Wales and Yorkshire – not as large as his cousins' at Ravensworth but large enough. He would own this house and instead of taking orders from a sick, old man he would be giving orders, able to really enjoy the new England that was emerging from the darkness. He would be his own man. But such freedom, such power, carried its price and part of that price would be marriage. He could not put it off for ever. He had hoped he would find someone to his taste who had all the necessary qualifications of money, noble birth, family influence, but he had never found her. Perhaps he had not looked hard enough.

'Go to it, Robert, and come back to me as quickly as you can.'

The whisper from the pillows had been barely audible but it had echoed and re-echoed in his own head as he strode out of his grandfather's bedchamber and past the waiting footmen in the outer chamber, in search of John. Beside him now, the big man was beginning to grumble. ''Tis hellish cold! Won't they never stop their hymning?'

John Riddell, more friend than servant, who was always there when needed. Years ago he had arrived at the Critley gatehouse in Northumbria during harvest time, a small, forlorn boy who seemed to know only his name and that he had been born near Taunton. He was too young to be of much use on the land so he had been given a job in the kitchens as a cook's boy. Later he had helped in the gardens, and by the time he was eighteen he was a great bear of a fellow with a reputation for honesty and intelligence. Sir William had had him taught the rudiments of reading, writing and numbers and had made him his own personal dogsbody. It was even rumoured that he was one of Sir William's bastards and Robert remembered now with embarrassment that years ago he had actually asked John if this was true.

They had been in one of the small parlours where John was struggling with the estate accounts. He had not replied for so long that Robert had feared he had offended him mortally but at last he had lifted his big head from the ledger and said thoughtfully, ''Tis a wise man that knows his own son , but I'd liefer be John Riddell than a byblow of your grandfather's.' The big head had bent over the ledger again and Robert had felt sure that no more would ever be said on the subject.

They had walked the full round of the cloister and as they turned for what seemed the hundredth time Robert said, 'John, why have you never married again?'

'I had no wish to.' The voice which had never lost its overtones of the west country was curt and Robert knew that John was remembering the year when so many things had come to an end for them both – when the Sweating sickness had crept

25

through the doors of Critley House, killing almost all before it. John's new, young wife, three months pregnant had been the first to die, then Robert's mother and father and his two younger brothers. Many of the servants had died too before the ghost killer had crept across the park to the small manor house where Robert's only uncle had lived with his wife and young family. In a few short days they too were dead and at the last funeral there were only the four of them – Robert, his grandfather and grandmother and John – to walk behind the coffin with the few servants who had survived. And by the end of the year his grandmother had died too, for although she survived the Sweat she was never well again afterwards.

Robert turned his head now to look at John but he could not see his face under the brim of his hat. 'You know that I am to call on the Nevilles?' he said flatly.

'Aye. I heard.'

'You know why, of course?'

'I do!' And now John stopped and looked at Robert full in the face. ''Twas best done soon, Master Robert! For a man like me, it's different. But for you – your grandfather has the right of it.'

They continued their pacing in silence. There was no more to be said.

At last, he came hurrying towards them – not the frail, elderly man that Robert had imagined him to be, but tall, vigorous, still in the prime of life, white habit swinging, pectoral cross gleaming on his broad chest, his cowl thrown back showing a strong, handsome face and tonsured head, an air of authority about him.

'I am Dom Richard,' he said briskly, 'and you are most welcome!' His hand-clasp was firm, his smile reaching his eyes – eyes that assessed them both in one swift, practised glance. 'Come with me! I am sorry to have kept you waiting so long.'

He led them out of the cloister, down steps and into what Robert later discovered to be the Chapter House – a huge, empty room supported by six magnificent marble columns. Stone seats ran all the way round and when they were seated Dom Richard groped for a pocket hidden in the folds of his habit and brought out the letter Robert had given the porter at the gatehouse for him. He read it carefully and then put it down.

'How is your grandfather?'

'Not well, Father Abbot,' Robert replied. 'He had a stroke in the summer.'

'I am sorry to hear it. He seemed to carry his years lightly up to this.' The shrewd eyes appraised Robert again even as he spoke and Robert knew that 'hints', however well intentioned, would be an impertinence. As a priest the abbot would know his sinners and forgive them but as a man he would know what steps to take and would take them without hesitation. 'You say in your letter that your business is urgent.'

'My grandfather has heard that the King means to dissolve the abbey soon, and probably the convent also.'

'I knew that already.' The voice was quiet, without emotion. 'We are lucky to have escaped so far. Three Cistercian abbeys have already been closed in Yorkshire, their abbots executed.' He might have been talking about the weather.

'If there is anything I can do – '

'There is nothing. We can only wait.'

'My grandfather asked me to warn you to hide the Cîteaux treasure,' Robert said after a moment's silence.

'That has already been done.' The abbot's voice was as courteous as ever but Robert was beginning to wonder if his journey had served any useful purpose at all.

'You say it be well hid, Father Abbot,' John said, speaking for the first time. 'Is it still here then, in the abbey?'

Dom Richard seemed to hesitate momentarily. 'It is no longer here,' he said slowly, 'that much I can tell you. It is not that I don't trust you – Sir William was a close friend and one of our benefactors and I know that he has always placed great trust in you.' He looked then at Robert. 'And you are his grandson. But to tell either of you any more would be unwise for your own sakes. The King and his men have special ways for making people talk and they are not pretty, I assure you.'

'How many do know where it is?' Robert asked after a short silence.

'Only myself and one other monk, Andrew Ellerton, my secretary. He is young and strong and I have told him that if the worst happens he is to get the treasure out of the country and back to our mother house in France. Not directly, of course – they will be expecting us to do that – but through the Low

27

Countries. I have written to Abbot Guillaume le Fauconnier of Cîteaux and to your banker kinsman, Cornelis van Ophoorn of Amsterdam, asking him to give any help that may be needed. We met some time ago, in your grandfather's house in London, and I should be glad if you would tell your grandfather what I have done on your return. I hope he will not feel that I have taken advantage of our friendship.'

'Of course he won't!' Robert said quickly, 'But would it not be wiser to get the treasure out of the country straightaway?'

The abbot shook his head. 'No. They are already watching us. Cromwell has his spies everywhere. If one of us leaves, they will follow.'

'But if things come to a head,' Robert argued, 'surely then it will be too late?'

Dom Richard frowned. 'I have thought of that too and it has been a difficult decision to make – whether to wait or risk going ahead. But I must have some reasonable excuse for sending Andrew away.'

'Perhaps I could do it for you,' Robert suggested. 'I often visit Amsterdam – my grandmother left me property there.'

But the abbot shook his head again. 'You would be equally suspect now that you have come up here, and it is well known that your grandfather has interceded for us with the King.' He had a beautifully modulated voice but he had answered too quickly, and Robert knew that he did not trust him completely. But how could it be otherwise? Even though he was Sir William's grandson, they were still strangers to one another. Yet he wanted to help this man, and the thought of setting himself against the King, against Cromwell and Edward Dutton appealed to some part of him that longed for danger as some men long for gold.

Dom Richard reached out and touched him lightly on the shoulder. 'You look very thoughtful, Robert. God will look after us.' He stood up, smiling. 'It will soon be supper-time and you must both be starving. I hope you will stay with us for a few days?'

'We should like to, very much.' Robert said quickly, standing also and ignoring John's suddenly sullen face.

'I'm glad to hear it. I'm afraid I shall not be able to see as much of you as I would like but our guest-master will look after you, and now I must leave you.'

They followed the abbot out of the big room into a stone

passage where a plump, middle-aged monk stood waiting. Dom Richard introduced him as Father Peter, the guest-master and then hurried away. A busy man, and a vulnerable one, Robert thought, as the tall figure disappeared around a corner.

Father Peter fussed over them like a mother hen, showing them first the abbey church with its magnificent rood screen behind the high altar, and then the guest-house, which was separate from the main part of the building. He brought them up to the chamber where they were to sleep, giving them a running commentary on the abbey as they followed him up the stone steps, making sure they had enough blankets and candles, that there was water in their jugs, that their basins were clean and that the floor rushes had been recently renewed, and when he had shown them the lavatory at the end of the passage that drained through a hole in the outer wall, the bells had begun to ring again.

'Supper!' the guest-master cried happily, like a pleased child, and he brought them down the stone steps to a small parlour where they were to eat, hurrying off himself to the main building where his own supper apparently awaited him in the refectory. Soon afterwards a lay-brother brought them a hunk of cold beef and a dish of steaming hot vegetable stew with a bowl of apples, and although they had their choice of beer or wine it was still spartan fare and the guest-house, in spite of Father Peter's housekeeping did not promise any great luxury. Why then had he agreed to stay on for a few days, Robert wondered, knowing that it was not just to postpone his dreaded visit to the Nevilles.

But he knew the answer – it was to satisfy his curiosity. He must find his mystery woman of the fog, and as the wine that he had chosen warmed his throat he knew that it was not just curiosity. He *wanted* to meet her again, and he had still to find a desirable woman who was beyond reach. Yet this strange, sweet-voiced nun was not desirable, or at least not in any way with which he was familiar, but as the wine slid down into his belly a voice inside his mind said, she is more. Much more. And you cannot know how much until you find her, speak to her, *know* her . . .

He put the wine to his lips again, not realising that he was

29

smiling, and John said gruffly, as if he could read his mind, 'Why do you want to stay on here, Master Robert? What's the use of it?'

'Use?' His eyes met John's across the narrow table. 'Not much, I suppose, but then what's the hurry, either? We'll reach Raskelfe and I'll see my bride-to-be soon enough – too soon, dammit! Now, drink up, man! Look cheerful for once!'

John only grunted and Robert knew that he had guessed the real reason for their staying on and disapproved. But he did not care. They went to bed soon afterwards, falling asleep almost immediately, to be woken in the middle of the night by the ringing of bells and the distant sound of chanting. In the days and nights that followed Robert became accustomed to the sound as one becomes accustomed to birdsong when winter ends, but that first night he cursed it, tossing and turning on his straw mattress while John snored lustily beside him. It was nearly dawn before he fell asleep again, to be wakened not so long afterwards it seemed by a monk, standing at the foot of his bed, muttering in Latin.

When he and John had been to Mass on that first day and had breakfasted they were left to their own resources while a meeting was being held in the Chapter House behind closed doors. They wandered aimlessly through the abbey, past the huge refectory with its vaulted ceiling and tall windows and a pulpit in the far corner, reached by steps cut into the immense thickness of the wall. Wooden tables and benches made up the only furniture. The kitchen was another vast room divided in half by two great fireplaces standing back to back in the centre of the floor and carrying a common flue that went up through the middle of the roof. A lay servant with a white apron tied round his middle was stirring an immense cauldron suspended over one of the fires, while a young boy chopped vegetables at a nearby table as if his life depended on it. The smell of freshly cooked bread came from the bakehouse which seemed to open off the kitchen. The cook went on with his stirring as they stood in the doorway looking in but he bade them good morning over his shoulder and the young boy grinned cheekily, waving his knife while the heat from the fires was like a blessing.

They went on down the cold, damp passage until they came to a flight of steps that led them to the dormitory. Here they found the same bleak austerity as in the refectory – two rows of narrow beds, no more than pallets, the coarse grey blankets neatly folded at the foot of each, the floor bare even of rushes. Nearby was the infirmary. They did not go in for fear of disturbing the sick, but instead they went down the next flight of steps and found themselves looking into the warming house with its vast empty fireplaces. The fires would not be lit until the beginning of November, Father Peter had told them apologetically the night before, so they wandered on until they reached a side door and were outside once more.

The air seemed warm and dry compared to what they had been breathing inside the abbey and the atmosphere of harsh self-denial so evident inside contrasted sharply with the aura of peace that enveloped Robert the moment he stepped outside the building. It was as if the place was bewitched, and only man's busyness broke the spell.

They made their way down to the river that meandered its way through rushes and high, spikey grass, disappearing into the distance to turn and twist through the dales. Looking back the abbey seemed less arrogant, as if by some alchemy it had grown out of the earth instead of having been built brick by brick by men dead for nearly four hundred years. Those same men must once have walked by this river, Robert thought, and looked back as he did now, feeling certain that they had built for all time. Yet how much longer would the abbey stand there, he wondered. Would a day come when it was no more than an ivy-covered ruin?

They began to make their way back, saying little, at ease with themselves and with each other, and only when the bell rang out, calling them to dinner did they begin to hurry.

After dinner John rode off with a group of lay brothers to count sheep on one of the granges and as Robert watched them ride away he heaved a sigh of relief, but as he set off to find the convent his good sense told him that he was mad, crazy! He was attempting to do something that could only bring pain and suffering, if not for him, then most certainly for her.

But he set off all the same.

Chapter Six

Robert skirted the main building until he came to the farmyard where several of the monks were hard at work cleaning out the pigstys, their sleeves rolled up and wearing a kind of black apron over their white robes. They were young, active men and as he walked past they stopped to smile at him and talk to each other in the sign language to which he was becoming accustomed. It seemed a strange way of life and he wondered what they knew of women and if they lay quiet in their lonely beds at night. Celibacy surely was too great a sacrifice for any man to make. It was a denial, he thought, of all that men and women had been created for, yet it was said that these men made the sacrifice voluntarily and they seemed content enough. But he had heard tales of men who had not kept their vows of celibacy and of girls having been put in convents against their will. It had all been much simpler, much more natural in the days of the Old Religion. The thought came to him easily, as if it had been lying just below the level of his consciousness and he stopped for a moment wondering at himself. Then he strode on, past the vegetable gardens where more monks were at work and on through the orchards until he was out in open country and could see the hill he had ridden down with John the previous evening.

It was a fine, sunny afternoon and the sweep of the dales beyond the turn of the river was green and lush and infinitely inviting, but he walked up the path that John and himself had followed until he came to the clump of bushes. There he turned in the direction the young nun had taken. He kept on walking, glad to be away from the silence of the abbey – a different silence up here, full of the endless sounds of the countryside, small animals rustling through undergrowth, birds singing, the sudden, angry buzz of a wasp, the distant bleating of sheep. He was on the top of the small hill now, a great, spreading chestnut tree on his right, the dales away to his left and the roofs of what must be St Mary's Convent below him. She had had quite a way to come.

Now that he had found the convent he found himself suddenly unsure of what he should do. Would he knock on the door? There was probably a grating similar to the one in the gatehouse of the abbey, but how could he possibly ask that dehumanised eye if he could speak to someone whose name he did not know, whom he could not even describe properly! Really, the whole thing was madness! He was behaving like a young, lovesick boy instead of a grown man. And yet not so long ago he had done much more foolish things. At least here he would not have to run from an irate husband, or an infuriated father! He decided that he would first reconnoitre.

He could see the river which seemed to run through the convent grounds, and a garden beyond the convent building itself. Perhaps he might meet her there, if she was out and about.

He made his way down the hill, until he came to the garden. Peering gingerly from behind a high yew hedge he noticed there were several elderly nuns walking up and down the paths between the straggling rose bushes, the sound of their voices carrying to him by the gentle breeze, and he quickly withdrew his head. He slipped away as quietly as he could and made his way down to the river, walking along the bank until he judged that he had come to the bottom of the convent garden. There was a small orchard and when he had walked cautiously through the apple trees he saw beehives and what seemed to be a herb garden. But there was no one about and he was on the point of giving up when two nuns came walking towards him from the direction of the convent – one obviously young, helping a much older nun who walked with the aid of a stick. They had not seen him and he stepped hastily back among the trees. When they had come as far as the herb garden they stopped.

'I shall be quite all right now, Isobel dear,' the older nun said, her voice high and clear and only faintly cracked with age. 'You do your weeding if you must and I shall go back and sit down for a while.'

'You are sure you do not need me, Dame Petronilla?' It was *her* voice and Robert held his breath, waiting for the reply.

'Quite sure. It will do me good to walk by myself. I must not become too dependent, you know!'

The old nun walked slowly away from the orchard, her stick prodding the ground tentatively while the young nun, after watching her slow progress for a moment or two, walked over to the herb beds. There was a basket on the ground and she bent down and took out a pair of gloves and a small gardening fork. Then, hitching up the skirts of her habit, she knelt down and began to dig with the fork.

The old nun was out of sight now and Robert watched the girl for a little while wondering how he could announce himself without frightening her. Even under her habit he could see the long, sturdy line of her back and she drove the fork into the earth with quick, decisive thrusts that seemed to hint at anger or frustration, or both.

Clearing his throat and feeling even more unsure of himself he stepped forward and making no attempt to walk quietly, came up beside her. 'Good afternoon!' he said. 'Forgive me for interrupting your work but I just wanted to thank you for – for your kind help, yesterday evening.'

She lifted her head and looked up at him, faint colour sweeping over her face. 'I did not see you – I did not know there was anyone here.' Awkwardly, the habit making her clumsy, she struggled to her feet. He towered over her, reaching out a hand to help. But she ignored it, as if unused to such gallantries, or unwilling to avail of them.

She was even younger than he had thought – no more than eighteen or so – the severity of the wimple and the black veil accentuating her youth, a feather of black hair escaping over one ear. Her cheekbones were too high, her chin above the immaculate white linen too determined for conventional beauty and it was her eyes that held him – grey, black-lashed, huge under smooth dark eyebrows, with a look of intelligence and an innocence in them that he had not seen of late in many women's eyes. He found himself trying to visualise her body under the bulky habit – the same creamy skin and black, glossy hair – and

34

now there was even more colour in her face as if, God forbid, she had read his mind.

They looked at each other in silence, and for once in his life he was at a loss for words. Robert FitzHugh, who could flirt in two, three languages, who had been taught the art of making love when he was fourteen by an attractive Dutch widow – and he could not find his tongue!

The colour had left her face now and she was looking at him with a sudden, new composure. 'You found the abbey then?' she said.

He swallowed. 'Yes. Thanks to you!' At least he could speak again.

'I am glad.'

'I see you are gardening.' What an imbecile thing to have said, he thought, reddening.

But she seemed not to think so. 'Herbs are very important to us,' she said gravely, 'especially to the infirmarian, and the lay servants won't take the time to weed them properly. Anyway, I enjoy doing it.'

There was another silence. You are wasting time, you fool, his mind said. Get on with it!

'What – should I call you?' he managed at last.

'Dame. Dame Isobel.'

'Isobel suits you – but *Dame*? You are far too young, far too pretty to be a dame!'

His tongue was beginning to free itself but her composure seemed to be leaving her. 'You should not say things like that!' she said hurriedly, 'And I am forbidden to talk unnecessarily during working hours.'

'I'm sorry,' he said happily, 'but you see, I know nothing about convent rules or nuns!'

'You must not try to see me again!' The words came in a sudden rush and he could feel his pleasure glowing in his face, spreading like a gentle fire through his whole body, for her words had bypassed hours, days of polite withdrawing-room conversation, bringing them in a few seconds from the status of near strangers to something far more intimate. She seemed to realise her mistake for she said hastily, 'I mean – I – I am not allowed to talk and – and – ' She looked down at the gardening fork that she was still holding as if for inspiration. 'There – there

35

is still a great deal to be done – ' and now her eyes were on his, like great pools of darkness pleading with him to go – or to stay?

'Are you happy?' he asked, the words forcing themselves from him.

'Yes.' She replied too quickly, he thought.

'You want to spend the rest of your life here, in the convent?' He did not even try to hide his disbelief.

'Yes, if it is possible. I have taken my final vows.' Her voice was steady but she was looking down at the fork again.

His eyes were on the curve of her wide, generous mouth and he felt the old familiar excitement beginning to stir in him. 'Surely you must want – other things?' he said.

'What – other things?' She looked up at him quickly and then dropped her eyes again.

'Do you really want me to tell you?' he said very softly, and in the distance he heard the old nun's voice again.

'Isobel! Dame Isobel, can you help me?'

'Go! Please go!' There was a note of panic in her voice, and when he did not move, she threw the fork down on the ground and brushed past him, leaving him standing there.

But he dared not stay for fear of getting her into trouble and he went back through the orchard, walking slowly along the path that ran by the river. Isobel. The name really did suit her, but he would *never* call her 'Dame'! The title had such a ridiculous sound to it, he thought. But in his heart of hearts he knew that it was not ridiculous. He only called it that to prevent him seeing it for what it was, for what it represented. A barrier. A high, unscalable wall shutting him out from a world which he could never enter, a wall that shut her in, imprisoning her. For he refused to believe that she remained in it of her own free will, and he *would* see her again! And again! And again! For as long as he could decently stay in the abbey. He had not yet begun to think beyond that point, and the excitement that had been bubbling inside him slowly died away as he realised he only had a few days, a week at most. After that he would have to go on to the Nevilles and then get back to London where his grandfather would be waiting impatiently for the news of his betrothal.

Betrothal. Hateful word! He put it from him hastily, trying even to stop thinking about Isobel, to concentrate his thoughts on the abbot and the treasure and its likely fate. Where was it

36

hidden, and was it really sensible that he should be told? If the abbot did not trust him now, when would he trust him? And were the King's men really capable of torture? His commonsense told him that they were, and that the name of FitzHugh would do little to protect him.

He was out on the open dales now and he walked on, the breeze lifting his hair, blessedly cool. Sheep dotted the smooth slopes like balls of dirty wool, some of them dozing, seemingly dead, until he got close and saw the narrow jaws working and the open, blinking eyes like round pebbles. He walked until the muscles of his legs began to ache and when he saw a large, flat rock set into the side of a grassy incline he sat down on it and lay back, stretching to his full length and closing his eyes against the afternoon sun. But he was too restless to sleep or even doze and he got to his feet after a while and began to walk back the way he had come until he arrived once more at the abbey.

'I would like you to meet Andrew Ellerton.' Robert turned to see the abbot with another younger monk, 'and this is Robert FitzHugh, Andrew, who is staying with us for a few days.'

Robert put out his hand and after a second's hesitation the young monk took it and shook it without any great enthusiasm. I've seen this fellow before somewhere, Robert thought, and he does not like me. Why, I wonder?

Dom Richard looked from one to the other of them, frowning slightly. 'Andrew is our artist, our one and only manuscript illustrator,' he said quickly. 'Usually we leave such skills to the Benedictines. You might like to show our guest some of your work,' he added, looking at his young companion.

'Of course, Father Abbot.' But the blue eyes, Robert noticed, were still cold.

'Good!' There was an edge to Dom Richard's voice and he took them both by the elbow and drew them into a small alcove opening off the cloister. 'I should like you two to get to know one another. Some day you may have to work together.' It was an order, and Robert saw the colour rise in Andrew Ellerton's face – a countryman's face, broad, strong, with clear skin and sandy eyebrows the same colour as the fringe of hair around his tonsure. A good face, one would say, but without a countryman's slow humour and without warmth. Robert wished the abbot had chosen someone more congenial.

'Have you any idea of when the next Visitation will be?' he asked him now.

'None at all, I am afraid. It could be next week or next year. But I shall send word to you at once, or Andrew will do so if I am – unable to attend to it.' He cleared his throat, then went on in the same level tones. 'The Visitors like to arrive without warning, in the hope, I suppose, of finding some sinner in flagrante delicto. They have of course been told many lies about the conduct of the religious in general, and they hope to find dens of iniquity. What they cannot find they can invent and although the total annual income of all the English monastries taken so far is said to have doubled the royal income they will, I am sure, find a reason to close us, as the king is demanding even more money. But if you and Andrew together can get the treasure safely out of the country, and back to Cîteaux, then you will have saved something of great value to the Church. Now, I shall leave you two to become better acquainted.'

He was gone, the slap slap of his sandals fading as he walked away from them down the wide passage, leaving Robert and Andrew Ellerton looking at each other in an awkward silence. And suddenly Robert remembered. Oxford. The previous year. He had been coming out of a tavern on Ship Street one evening, a girl on either arm, not really drunk but not sober enough to stay properly on his feet. A white-habited monk had been passing and by ill luck the jostling students had pushed Robert and the two girls from behind. They had fallen at the feet of the monk in a heap of waving legs and voluminous, not over-clean skirts, amidst delighted shrieks from the girls and encouraging jeers from the other students. As Robert had picked himself up and attempted to apologise, not very coherently, the monk had looked at him in such silent contempt that it was a wonder he had forgotten about it until now. Drunk as he was it had ruined the evening for him.

How very unfortunate, he thought now. Was it possible that Andrew Ellerton would tell the abbot that Robert FitzHugh was a lightweight, not to be trusted, for he felt certain he had been recognised. Had he done so already? But that was foolish. The abbot would never have brought the two of them together at all in that case. The best thing to do, surely, was to forget about the Oxford incident altogether. What was the fellow saying?

' – if you care to come now? We have just time before supper.'

'Ah – yes! Of course! I would very much like to – ' At least he was trying to be friendly, Robert thought as the monk led the way to what he called his 'carrel', a small study opening off the cloister. There was a drawing-board standing in front of the window overlooking the cloister garth and he removed a sheet of paper from the vellum on which he must have been working. Robert exclaimed aloud. It was an Old Latin manuscript, the script heavy and black against the creamy white of the vellum. Tiny animals in brilliant colours clung to the capital letters with their legs and tails – Robert could identify a turnspit dog, a rabbit, a monkey – while down the entire side of the page, if that was what it was, ran a stem of ivy – not in conventional green but in lilac – with scarlet knots from which the branches sprang, and leaves of gold.

'You did all this yourself?'

'Yes.' The blue eyes were almost warm, the stolid face wreathed in smiles. 'I enjoy it and I take my time. One cannot rush it. If you look closely at earlier manuscripts you will see that the gold was laid last of all and in places overlays the colours. I prefer to lay it before colouring. My problem lately has been to get sufficient gold – Father Hugh, our cellarer, does not place much importance on art I'm afraid – not that I'm an artist, merely a craftsman.'

Robert looked beyond Andrew Ellerton to the table laden with the tools of his craft, pots of paint, brushes, quill pens, a bronze mortar, a curious looking object which seemed to be a dog's tooth set in a wooden handle, a frame which he guessed was used for stretching vellum. 'I shall get you whatever you need in London when I go back,' he said impulsively. 'I shall have it sent up to you by special messenger.'

'Thank you! Thank you very much indeed!' The broad vowels of Yorkshire were very evident now in the young monk's voice and they smiled at each other as if meeting for the first time.

Before long they heard the supper bell and Andrew Ellerton hurried away leaving Robert to make his way to the guest-house. John, hungrier than ever after his long ride over the dales, was

39

waiting impatiently for their meal to arrive. He said little as they ate their frugal meal, looking at Robert suspiciously from time to time under his bushy eyebrows as if he had guessed what he had been up to in his absence. Well, curse it, Robert thought, John was not his nursemaid!

While Robert and John glumly ate their meal, the abbot and his monks ate in silence in the great refectory with its raised dais at the end, where the abbot sat with his principal obedientiares or officials. But the silence here was broken by the monk reader standing in the pulpit, and in the flickering light of the burning tapers the abbot looked down the length of the side tables behind which the rest of the community were seated, not really trying to listen to the reading.

They seemed in a talkative mood tonight, he thought, watching the gesticulating hands as they made their signs, and frowning as he heard the occasional whispered word close at hand, for the reader was old and his voice carried no distance. Earlier the vegetable stew had been taken from the kitchen serving hatch by two lay brothers and brought to the top table first, before being passed from monk to monk until all had helped themselves. It was a good stew, but the abbot was not hungry and he found himself thinking of the young man who had arrived that day.

He was not himself of noble birth, merely a very distant relative of the Fairfax family, but he had rubbed shoulders with those who were and he neither resented nor despised them. He considered Robert typical of his kind but with a special quality all his own that was more than good manners, more than mere charm. But he could sense a restlessness in him, a deep frustration, and he knew that restless, frustrated young men were apt to do foolish things. It would be better for Robert if his grandfather died soon, he thought. There had always been too much of the tyrant in Sir William, even when he was younger. In the meantime, though, Andrew would need help and there was no one else as well placed to give it to him as Robert FitzHugh. Before he left he must see to it that he dined with him in his own chambers – it would be well to try to get to know him better.

Dom Richard's sharp eyes went down the length of the two

short side tables. Only twenty monks left of the thirty-two who had been there when he was ordained, but how many of the twenty could he trust? Andrew, of course, although of late he had begun to show a regrettable leaning towards the New Learning. Was he losing his vocation? Only the previous night they had sat in his study arguing into the small hours so that they had got almost no sleep before matins. He could remember his own voice saying, 'This simple purity that you speak of, Andrew, this classical distaste for the old theology – remember that it breeds a querulous, ultra-clerical temper of the mind. You must beware of it!'

Had he been very pedantic, patronising even? But Andrew had only laughed a little, and he had not dared ask him if he was ready yet to go forward for ordination. But whatever might happen in the future he was still glad he had sent him to Oxford. The boy – he still thought of him as a boy – had so many excellent qualities. A little stolid perhaps, a little insensitive, yet he knew he could trust him absolutely – as he could Father Peter and Father Hugh and of course the prior.

But at the left-hand side table Father Sebastien's face was like a shiny, red bladder. If the man did not call a halt soon to his drinking he would die of liver disease. It was probably quite true that he drank the altar wine although he strenuously denied it. The abbot turned his head to look at the table on his right. He would have to send either Father Godfrey or Father Alexis away – one or other of them would have to go, but where could he send him now with nearly all the other monasteries closed?

It would not take the Visitors long to find the weak ones, he thought grimly, and no matter how many others observed the Rule it would be the weak who would be noted and remembered. Time alone would tell.

At the table to the left of the abbot Andrew Ellerton bent his head over his bowl and ate a good supper as usual, but his mind was busy. Robert FitzHugh did not seem the headless young fool he had imagined him to be – and perhaps it was difficult for a young aristocrat not to live a godless life, especially during his student days. It was generous of him, too, to offer to send materials for his own work and all in all he would himself be lacking in charity if he mentioned the incident in Oxford to anyone.

As he wiped his bowl clean with a last piece of bread and reached for an apple he remembered that he had promised the cook to ask the convent for some of their crop which was always more carefully sorted than the abbey's. He must go over soon, and perhaps the abbess would give him permission to have a few words with Isobel – not that he wanted to but it was his duty. She was his cousin after all, even though there seemed to be little of the Willis blood in her. There was no doubt, he thought moodily, biting into the apple, that she took more after her mother than her father – and her mother was a foolish woman indeed, who would have done better to marry into her own class instead of making a fool of a good, solid dalesman like Ben Willis. And there was something about Isobel recently that made him feel uneasy, not that he had ever felt at ease with her.

He bit into the apple again, remembering the skinny girl-child he had been forced to play with when he was young; who at thirteen had turned overnight into a torment that had driven him nearly mad, like an itch under the skin. Wanting to touch her and afraid to, believing already that the priesthood was the only way for him. Telling himself that what he felt for her was no more than lust, the devil trying to pull him back. Remembering the day when he had gone at last to Dom Richard, asking to be taken as a novice, and remembering even more clearly the day a few months later when he knew the fever had left him. But he had never gone back to the Willis farm and when he heard that she had entered the convent he had been pleased for some reason that he could not understand and that had nothing spiritual about it.

That was all before he had been chosen by the abbot to go down to Oxford, and when he came back, a grown man, the fevers of adolesence long dead, he decided that he must visit her again, that it was his duty. He had been pleased to find that it had been no more than that. But even then he had seen in her that restlessness which made him uneasy now. It was a good thing she was safely inside the convent, he thought, putting the apple core tidily into his bowl.

Chapter Seven

In spite of John's grumbling and his own uneasy awareness that he should have left long since and that his grandfather would be watching and waiting for them, Robert remained in the abbey for nearly a week, and each day he was more reluctant than ever to visit the Nevilles. He spent the mornings riding through the dales but after dinner, when talking was permitted in the cloister, he felt an intruder, unable to join in what seemed to him a childish simplicity. He saw almost nothing of the abbot but he dined with him on one occasion in his rooms and found him pleasant company – a man without prejudice, so well-read that at times the conversation had bordered on an intellectualism far above his own head. But Dom Richard had said nothing about the treasure and when Robert had left after the meal he knew no more than he had at the beginning of his visit.

He saw even less of Andrew Ellerton, for the young monk spent even his recreation time working on his manuscripts. So as soon as he could escape from John's watchful eye Robert would slip away, to lurk in the convent grounds in the hope of meeting Isobel, feeling ridiculous and yet unable to stay away.

'There is a proverb hanging on the wall in the guest-house,' he told her on the day of their next meeting. '"Friends are multiplied by agreeable words, enemies by harsh ones." Is that part of your Rule?'

'No. It's only a proverb.' But she was smiling.

She had been down by the river, alone, and when she tried to hurry on he had caught up with her easily. 'Please,' he said then, 'surely it is not harmful to talk to me for a few minutes? Is this not your recreation time too?'

'It is, but you are not another nun, and – '

'I am a guest, however, in the abbey,' he said, interrupting her before she could finish, 'and the Rule says – the guest-master told me last night – that – '

And now she interrupted him, laughing. 'You don't need to quote the Rule to me! I know it by heart! Tell me about yourself instead. Why have you come to Yorkshire?'

He hesitated, then choosing his words he said, 'My grandfather asked me to come up to see Dom Richard as he is too ill to travel himself. He is concerned about what will happen if the King decides to close the abbey.'

She nodded, as if she had already guessed the reason for his visit. 'Tell me about yourself,' she said then. 'Do you live with your grandfather?'

She seemed suddenly so relaxed, so different to the girl he had tried to talk to the previous day that he found himself telling her about himself as easily as if they had met conventionally in someone's house, and even more easily than that, for there was a directness about her that was unusual.

'So you have three homes,' she was saying now, 'Critley Hall at the foot of the cheviots, the house in London and another in Amsterdam. And yet you are not married?'

'No,' he said quickly, putting the thought of Beatrice Neville as far from him as possible. 'Anyway, two of them belong to my grandfather. Only the house in Amsterdam is really mine, and land outside the town – I've been going there on short visits since I was fourteen. I can even speak the language, although a Dutchman might think my accent strange!'

He said it all so casually that she felt herself reddening, she who had never been as far as York in her whole life. 'Do you have relations there?' she asked quickly to cover her embarrassment.

'My father had a spinster cousin who had the use of the house for her lifetime, but she's dead now and so are all the rest, except for another very distant cousin of some sort whom I've never met, although he once visited my grandfather in London. He's quite old,' he added cheerfully, 'but enough about me! I've been wondering since I first met you how you came to be out alone in the fog!'

'I was bringing food to one of the cottages on the other side of

44

the hill – a hovel really – you can't imagine what it is like – and the fog came down as I was returning.'

'Were you not afraid?'

'Oh no! I was born and raised in the dales and I am used to fog.'

'Forgive me,' he said, 'but you do not speak like a daleswoman. I find the dialect very difficult to understand.'

'Whar's ta cu frae?' She was smiling now. 'I am a daleswoman all right, but my mother was not one, and although my father is a dale farmer, the dialect, as you call it, was never spoken in my home.'

'Do you see your family often? Are nuns allowed – '

'Only with special permission. But I have no family to speak of. My mother is dead. My father married again. He does not wish to see me. I have a cousin also – a monk in the abbey. He comes occasionally.'

'Why does your father not wish to see you? Did he not want you to become a nun?'

'I put it too strongly. He simply has no interest in me.'

What kind of monster must he be, Robert wondered. After a moment's silence he said, 'Which one of the monks is your cousin?'

'Andrew. Andrew Ellerton.'

'*He* is your cousin?'

'You seem surprised.'

'He is certainly not like you.'

She shrugged, as if none of what she was saying was of any great importance. 'He is a distant cousin only, on my father's side. My father's family, the Willises, say I take after my mother. So does Andrew.'

'*Willis*, you said?' At the back of his mind a faint memory stirred. Himself and his grandfather and the old man's bad temper – and a young girl. Little more than a child. What was it? Where? When?

She was watching him. 'You remember now?'

'*You! You* were the girl? And you showed me a puppy? Yes?'

She nodded and he caught her hands in sudden delight. 'Of course I remember! How stupid of me!' He held her away from him. 'Let me look at you again!' He shook his head. 'You have changed so much, it's no wonder I did not recognise you! Except

45

for your eyes. *They* have not changed.' It was true. He had remembered them for a long time – great pools of darkness, that earlier had been happy and full of laughter, looking up at him as he turned to leave.

Suddenly she pulled her hands away, the same note of panic in her voice that had been there the day before and he cursed himself for not watching his tongue. But he had said nothing, nothing at all, and yet she was beginning to walk away.

'Tomorrow?' he called after her. 'Shall I see you tomorrow?' But she did not answer or look back.

The next day he went down at the same time to the river but she was not there and after waiting for an hour he went back to the abbey in a savage temper, half tempted to leave that night. It was too late to make a start, however, and when he woke up the next morning he decided he would not give up so easily.

He found her after dinner, weeding in the convent garden as she had been on the first afternoon. The old nun she had called Dame Petronilla dozed on a bench nearby in the autumn sun, and he waited impatiently among the apple trees, knowing that soon the bell would ring for vespers, willing the old lady to get up and leave them alone. At last he heard her voice.

'I think, child, that I have sat for long enough. Can you give me an arm?'

He watched while Isobel took off her gloves and helped the old nun to stand and then walked a little way with her. Were they going to go back into the convent? A curse on it anyway! He should have gone to the portress and asked for her – but his commonsense told him that she would not have been allowed to see him.

The two nuns were nearly level with the apple trees now and he was afraid Dame Petronilla might turn her head and see him, but she was too intent on not falling and after a few more yards she said that she would walk the rest of the way by herself.

Thank God! Robert breathed, and as soon as the old nun was out of sight he went over to Isobel who was on her knees again, weeding.

'Good afternoon!' He refused to address her as Dame but he did not dare call her 'Isobel' even though that was how he thought of her.

46

Without looking up she said quietly, stabbing the small fork into the brown earth at the same time, 'You will make trouble for both of us, do you not realise that?'

He remained standing where he was, looking down at her, something about the kneeling figure arousing a tenderness in him that he had never felt before for any woman. 'I'm sorry,' he said. 'That is not my intention. What harm is it for us to talk? You talked to me before!'

She sat back on her heels, looking up at him gravely. 'You know the harm. And before I was – foolish.'

'Please!' he said quietly. 'I need to talk to you.'

She got slowly to her feet. 'Just for a moment, then. We can walk a little way.'

But she made no attempt to break the silence as they turned towards the river and after a moment he said, 'Are all the other nuns as old as your companion?'

'Two are older, and the rest are not all that much younger.'

'Don't you miss the company of people your own age?'

'Of course, but the novice who came the year before I did has since asked to be released and another young nun died. We had boarders some time ago but since the Rising parents no longer seem to want to leave their children with us – I used to teach them,' she added.

'And what do you do now?'

'I am assistant cellarer.'

'That sounds very grand!' He was smiling down at her but she gave him no answering smile.

'It does not mean very much. The cellarer is responsible for provisioning the convent and I help her. That is all.'

'*And* weed the herb garden, *and* escort old ladies *and* visit the poor and needy – *and* – '

'I enjoy doing all of those things.' She was looking straight in front of her, frowning slightly and he stopped, taking her by the arm so that he could look into her face.

'Are you ever lonely?' he asked her quietly.

'Everyone is lonely at some time or other. Are you not?'

'Lonely?' He thought about it. 'I honestly can't say that I am.'

'Perhaps you have not recognised it as loneliness?'

The grey eyes looking up at him now were beginning to make him feel uncomfortable. 'You think I'm frivolous, a bit of a waster?'

47

'I did not say that.'

They walked on in silence towards the bend of the river. 'I have not talked to anyone like this before,' he said at last. She barely came up to his shoulder and looking down he could see the dark fringe of her lashes on the creamy curve of her cheek, and the short, straight nose before she turned her head away. It was unthinkable that he would not be able to talk to her again, not be able to tell her all those things that were locked away in the back of his mind and that he had not known were there until now –

But she had drawn away from him. 'I have to go back now. A different way. Alone.'

It was so much like a final parting that he said quickly, 'But we haven't really talked. Not yet!'

'I must go!'

'When can I see you again?'

'I – I don't know! Can't you see that what we are doing is wrong?' It was as if she were pleading with him, and he was deaf.

'What is wrong about it? Just talking? *Please*!' He could not believe that it was his own voice. Robert FitzHugh! The philanderer of all philanderers! Begging a woman, a *nun*, for a few minutes' conversation, when all he could ever hope for was at most a chaste kiss on the cheek – and even *that*, he thought grimly as he watched her face change, seeming to withdraw itself into the folds of her black veil, was a very remote possibility.

'You must find someone who is – free.'

'There is no one who will listen.'

After a moment she said quietly, 'Very well, then. I shall meet you tomorrow, but only for a short time and after that we – we must not meet again.'

'Where? When?' he said quickly – he would argue with her tomorrow.

'The same time as today. Wait in the orchard. I shall know when you are there and come down.'

'How will you know?'

'My cell window overlooks the garden – it is the only one.' She reached out a small hand still tanned with the summer's sun and touched him lightly on the arm, then turned and walked rapidly away, disappearing behind a clump of young trees.

He thought tomorrow would never come and when it did it

48

was drizzling – that fine, Yorkshire rain of which one is scarcely conscious and which wets one thoroughly all the same. Nevertheless he waited in the orchard, watching the single window in the gable, wondering if she would signal to him. But there was nothing, no sign of life at all. He waited twenty minutes, half an hour, growing colder, wetter by the minute. Was it ever warm, ever really dry in Yorkshire he wondered – and then he saw her, hurrying along, a black cloak over her habit so that he wondered how she could carry the weight of so much clothing.

'I'm sorry!' she said breathlessly. 'Lady Abbess sent for me!'

'You have been crying!' he said, looking at the marks of tears on her face. 'What is wrong? I hope I have not caused you any – '

'No! Oh, no!' she said quickly. 'It had nothing to do with you. It's just – that I'm not a – very good nun. That's all.'

They were walking now through the orchard and down a path he had not noticed before, enclosed by a high hedge, which he guessed would eventually bring them out on the river bank. He wanted to take her in his arms and comfort her, yet he dare not touch her for fear she would run away. 'Tell me about it,' he said, instead. 'Was she very cruel, your Lady Abbess?'

'Not at all!' she cried, coming to a stop and looking up at him, her eyelids still swollen from crying. 'She is never cruel, and I'm very fond of her. She has been like a mother to me. It is just that I am not good enough. I cannot seem to live up to her expectations of me – or my own expectations of myself.'

'Not – *good* enough?' he said, suddenly furiously angry. He wanted to shake her, in a rage of frustration. She wanted, really *wanted* to be here then, she actually *wanted* to be the saint this wretched abbess expected her to be, and he had been fooling himself all along. She had made her own prison willingly and he could never reach her. The sooner he rode off and forgot her the better for both of them, he thought grimly.

'You wanted to talk?' she reminded him.

But he couldn't. Not now. Not today. Not ever. He made the rain the excuse but he knew that she did not believe him and a few moments later she did leave him standing there, not knowing if he would ever see her again, not sure that he wanted to.

*   *   *

49

He spent the whole of the following day riding the abbey granges with John and visiting some of the tenants on his grandfather's land whom he should have visited long ago. Before he realised whose farm it was, John was riding into Ben Willis's yard, calling his name.

A big, heavily built man, with a sack pinned across his broad shoulders, came out of the house, a man who must have been a handsome fellow once but now was run to fat, offhand and dour, looking Robert up and down as if to say he was not half the man his grandfather had been. There were two toddlers playing in the yard, and through the open door of the kitchen Robert could see women moving about inside, but Ben Willis did not invite them in. It was the typical long, stone farmhouse of the dales, with a big, untidy yard and it was hard to visualise Isobel in such a setting, yet it seemed to Robert that he remembered coming here before. He could certainly remember the girl who had spoken to him long ago, while he waited for his grandfather to come out of the kitchen, but he was sure the man had not been there, and as he looked down into the small bloodshot eyes of her father, he wondered how such a boor could have fathered Isobel. He left the talking to John and after a few minutes he bade Ben Willis good-day, telling him he would remember him to his grandfather.

On the way back to the abbey he told John that they would leave the abbey at the weekend.

With only one more day left, he woke next morning to cold sunshine, determined not to go near the convent again, but early afternoon once more found him in the orchard. She was sitting on the bench alone, and there was something about the droop of her shoulders that drove the remains of his anger from him. 'Isobel?' he said quietly.

She had not heard him coming but her head lifted quickly now and he saw a flash of pleasure light her face and then die so swiftly he was not sure he had not imagined it. She got to her feet and he took her arm, leading her to the path they had taken on the previous occasion. 'I – I'm sorry,' he said shortly.

'For what?' Her voice was cold.

'For – ' He stopped. What was there to say? They walked on and after a moment he said abruptly, 'I saw your father yesterday.'

'You did not mention me, I hope?' She pulled her arm away.

'Of course not.'

'How – how is he?'

'Well enough, I'd say. The place seems middling prosperous.'

'Did you meet my step-mother?'

'No. We were not invited in.'

She nodded as if that did not surprise her. Then she said quietly, 'Dame Margaret – Lady Abbess – and my mother were close friends.'

It explained at least some of the things that had puzzled him, but not all. 'You seem unhappy. Is there anything I can do to help?'

She shook her head.

'Can you not even talk about it? I don't want to leave knowing that all is not well with you.'

'When are you going?' Her voice was suddenly very young, unsure, as if all her earlier certainties had left her.

'Tomorrow morning, early. I have stayed longer than I should.'

'I shall miss you.' She was looking straight ahead, her voice so low he could scarcely hear her.

'I will come back,' he said slowly, 'if you want me to.'

'I – must not let myself want it,' she whispered. 'I must not – '

'My poor, dear girl, why ever not? *Why?*'

And when she did not answer he took her in his arms and kissed her very gently on the mouth, as if it was the most natural thing in the world to do.

Her body seemed much smaller than he had imagined it to be under the loose, clumsy looking habit and he bent his head and kissed her again. This time, to his astonishment, she kissed him back, her mouth clinging to his with a hunger, a need that seemed even greater than his own, and then as he slackened his hold, afraid that he was hurting her, she slipped out of his arms and stood looking up at him, her eyes dark, huge, the creamy skin of her face suffused with colour, beautiful in the fading light.

'God go with you!' she breathed, and turning, ran from him through the trees.

Chapter Eight

Later that afternoon it grew colder, and, while Dame Margaret fretted over the accounts in her 'study' the older nuns clustered around the charcoal brazier in the parlour as closely as safety and decorum permitted. Isobel sat behind them, holding a book in front of her like a shield, afraid that otherwise they might read in her face all that had happened less than an hour before. She ran the tip of her tongue now over her lips and was surprised to find that they felt no different, and after a while she remembered to turn a page, blinking several times to ease the strain of having stared at the same words for so long. How could she have done it, how could she have let him do it? And if she was never to see him again, could she bear that?

Their meetings had been brief and yet she remembered every word, every nuance of his voice, every change in his expression. Each time they met she had tried to impress the picture of him on her mind, fearing that it would be the last time she would ever see him – the brown eyes, the dark lashes and eyebrows that contrasted so strongly with the flaxen hair, the long, clean line of the jaw, the broad shoulders, the long stride as he walked away from her. Was it a sin, she would ask herself, an especially grievous sin, to think a man was beautiful? And she would look down at her habit, at her clumsy shoes and imagine herself dressed like one of the fine ladies who came occasionally to visit some of the other nuns. Before her dreaming eyes the heavy black cloth became silk and velvet, and tiny slippered feet peeped out beneath the rustling skirts like mice. Surely, for a nun such thoughts were sinful too? And she would pray then for

52

the strength to erase him from her mind, trying desperately to think instead of the day of her profession when she lay prostrate before the altar under the pall, the covering of the dead, while the rest of the community sang the Dies Irae, telling all who listened that Isobel Willis was dead to the world, that her beauty was for the Lord God's and His alone. But His love alone is not enough for me now, she thought bleakly.

In front of Isobel, Dame Petronilla was stitching industriously at a scrap of silk, making one of her purses which afterwards she would embroider and give to some very special friend. She still used an old-fashioned needle of drawn wire, for the new German and Spanish needles had not yet reached St Mary's. The old lady's hands were aching and she was wondering now what she would do in her recreation time when her fingers became too stiff for embroidery, and if the others could finish the last set of vestments without her. Only last week Dame Agatha had hinted that her stitches were not as neat as they used to be. She had had the temerity to say outright that the roses on the black damask on which she had worked for hours did not look like roses at all.

Dame Petronilla wished from the bottom of her autocratic old heart that Lady Abbess would find some reason soon for sending Agatha to another convent. Never a day passed that she did not try to upset her, or someone else. I shall just have to offer it up along with my rheumatism and the cold of the dormitory and the watery beer, Dame Petronilla thought.

Beside her Dame Helen, the prioress, began to read aloud from a letter she had just received from her Neville cousins, and the flush of pleasure that had spread across her pale face as she reminded her listeners of her august connections still lingered there. Dame Cecilia, the youngest of the older nuns, sat opposite, her hands folded in her lap, glad of a chance to rest, her ears shut to Dame Helen's high-pitched voice, thinking about her patients in the infirmary. The two old, invalid nuns were as happy as young children, but the mother from the hill farm that she had taken in after childbirth was running a fever, and the boy's foot that had been caught in a rabbit snare had become infected in spite of her best efforts. There was so little she could really do for them. She shifted on her stool, trying to ease her back. Years ago she could lift a man unaided, but not now. I am getting old, she thought, but in the glow from the brazier her broad, strong face seemed to soften, to grow young again as she thought of the beggar's child, the baby who had died in her arms the previous night. If only it had been mine, even for a few hours, she had thought then. Surely now that she was growing old God would have pity on her and take away that feeling of loss, of deprivation that had haunted her since she first entered the convent years before. She began to pray silently for the baby, for the parents and lastly, as an afterthought, for herself.

And as she prayed, small, bustling Dame Katherine, the cellarer, the busiest nun in the convent, dozed quietly beside her, and beyond them, on the other side of the brazier, Dame Agatha also sat quietly but very much awake, part of the small group and yet somehow, like Isobel, outside it. Her hands were folded in her lap and her red, smooth-skinned face was as bland, as self-satisfied as ever, perhaps even more so, for over the past few days she had become slowly aware that there was something that needed looking into. Her instincts in such matters never failed her, and she felt sure that it had to do with Dame Isobel. She had not missed the swollen eyelids and she could have sworn that she had heard her crying in her cell when she herself was going to the lavatory. *And* the girl had been late for vespers several times during the week. Of course *she* had never considered her suitable in the first place. Well, if there was something afoot it was her duty to find out what it was and report it to Dame Margaret – the thought that it might be the abbess's 'pet' who was at fault made her smile to herself with secret pleasure – and if Dame Margaret would not listen to her, then she would tell the council. She might even mention it at the next Visitation!

At this point in her thoughts Dame Agatha pulled herself up as she realised the enormity of what she had just considered doing. To tell the King's men, the evil creatures who might drive them all out into the world to exist on a tiny pension, and lock the convent gates behind them! Perhaps she should not go so far as that – but if Dame Margaret was her usual high-handed self and refused to listen, and the council refused to listen too, she would at least consider it. Meanwhile, she must keep her eyes and ears open. It was really all much more interesting to think about than Dame Helen's silly letter.

Isobel looked up soon afterwards to find Dame Agatha's gooseberry-coloured eyes fixed on her. I must be careful, she thought, turning a page hastily, and then, with a sinking heart, she heard Dame Petronilla say into the silence that had fallen when Dame Helen had at last finished her letter – 'I saw a most handsome young man in the grounds yesterday – or was it the day before? Did any of you see him?'

Isobel held her breath. No one spoke and then Dame Agatha said, smiling broadly, 'Another vision, perhaps?'

'Do not mock!' Dame Petronilla snapped. 'I know perfectly well what I saw! He was a gentleman, I am sure of that, although he had no servant with him, and quite handsome! It was extraordinary, really. He was just standing there! But when I came around the fuschia bushes he was gone!'

'Someone from the guest-house, perhaps?' Dame Helen suggested soothingly. 'I did hear that young Robert FitzHugh was staying there.' Then she added with a slight lift of her chin, 'The FitzHughs have always been close friends of my cousins, the Nevilles.'

'Indeed?' Dame Agatha's voice was even flatter than usual for she could not claim any connection with a family such as the Nevilles and the fact was a source of great personal bitterness, regardless of what the abbess said to her frequently about envy and plain commonsense. 'I would have thought,' she went on now, 'that someone of his – ah – breeding would scarcely be lurking in the convent grounds – '

'Lurking, Dame Agatha?' the prioress said sharply, 'An unfortunate choice of words, if I may say so! Especially since the FitzHughs gifted the land to the convent – which surely gives Robert the right to admire our grounds occasionally?'

But Dame Petronilla hated bickering. 'Whoever he was,' she said clearly into the sudden silence, 'he was doing no harm and it did me good to see him.' She began to put away her sewing in a linen bag while Isobel prayed the hot colour would leave her face before it was noticed. How could he have hoped he would not be seen, she thought, and why had Dame Petronilla looked at her quickly and then away again? Even Dame Cecilia's head seemed to be turning her way!

* * *

55

It was a clear, fine night and moonlight turned the river into a ribbon of silver. A fox barked in the distance but otherwise it was very quiet. Behind Robert the convent was shrouded in darkness, as was the abbey when he left it half an hour earlier, although a light still showed in the abbot's window. John, like the rest had gone to bed but Robert had known he could not sleep, could not even lie still in bed, and the river had drawn him to it but had not stilled the tumult of his thoughts.

Isobel. Passion and innocence. Strength and vulnerability. I am bewitched, he thought – but *he* to be bewitched! Because he could not have a woman, a young girl who had caught his fancy! He must be losing his wits! But no matter how he flayed himself with words he knew that for the first time in his life the wanting was no whim, to be forgotten in a month, a week's time – it was a hunger, not only of the flesh but of the spirit also, and it was unthinkable that he should never see her again. It was even more unthinkable that he could have given to anyone even the smallest part of himself, his self that he had so carefully guarded – until now he had only taken. He came to an abrupt halt, staring down at the silvery water that scarcely seemed to move. He must see her again, if only to prove to himself that he was still whole.

But they were leaving at dawn.

He was beside the orchard now and in the moonlight the walls of the convent towered above the tops of the apple trees, grey and forbidding. He found himself walking towards them as if he were being led by the hand, until he had reached the far end of the orchard and could see her window. Was she lying awake, thinking of him, or was she asleep? He tried to imagine her head on the pillow, her breasts rising and falling – what did nuns wear in bed, he wondered. His heart was beginning to beat faster and he smiled to himself in the moonlit darkness, already a little drunk with excitement.

He walked quietly out of the cover of the trees, crouching low behind the beehives, then moving forward with infinite caution, taking cover wherever he could find it. When he was in the rose garden with nothing to hide behind he began to run swiftly forward, only to catch his foot in a trailing briar and fall headlong on the stony path. Cursing softly, he stayed where he was, but there was no sound, no sign that anyone had heard him

56

and after a few minutes he got to his feet and moved forward again, more cautiously this time, until he was behind the yew hedge. Peering round the corner of it he found himself staring up at the gable wall and her window, its shutters drawn. There was a ledge of some kind beneath it and from what he could remember of the rough stone walls of the convent when he had looked at them in daylight, there must be footholds – there was ivy too, old and gnarled, but he knew from previous, painful experience that ivy was not always to be trusted.

He took a handful of small pebbles from the ground and began to throw them at her window. Suppose it was not her bedchamber after all, or her 'cell' as she had called it? Suppose she had moved to another one since? What in God's name would he say if some strange nun thrust her head out – how could he explain? What excuse could he give? He had only one more pebble left when he heard the shutters open.

'Isobel?' he called softly.

There was no reply, no sound. He called again.

'Who is it?' It was Isobel, her voice sharp but not nervous.

'It's Robert! Thank God it is you – I was afraid – '

'You're *mad* to come here! And for heaven's sake, keep your voice down!'

'I wanted to see you again before I left.'

'But – but you can't. Not now!'

'We leave at dawn – Can you come down?'

'No!'

'Then I shall come up!'

'Please, please go away.'

He heard the shutters close but he was already beginning to climb. It was even easier than he had thought it would be. The great stones of the wall were unevenly set as he had remembered, and he reached the ledge quickly, holding on to the ivy with one hand and knocking gently on the shutters with the other. But even as he knocked he felt the ivy come away from the wall and he clawed frantically for another hold.

'Isobel, open the shutters for God's sake, or I shall fall!'

She must have been standing just inside the window for the shutters opened immediately and he all but fell into the room at her feet. There was the scrape of flint and tinder as she lit a candle and they stared at each other over the small flame. She

57

was wearing a kind of long, white shift and a white, fleecy shawl draped round her head and shoulders, with feathers of dark hair escaping from beneath it. She closed the shutters very quietly and set the candle down on the top of the small chest beside her, holding the shawl tightly round her face with the other hand. He wondered if she was angry, and the adventure, as he had come to think of it, no longer seemed exciting but somehow childish, undignified.

'I – I am sorry,' he whispered. 'There was no other way.'

She went on looking at him without speaking.

'Can we talk, just for a few minutes?' he begged, 'Then I promise I shall go.'

The 'cell' was small and cold. All that it contained was a bed, the covers thrown back, a chest, and a stool on which there was a pile of clothing. A large, black crucifix hung above the bed, but otherwise the walls were bare and there were only hard, green rushes on the floor. She had nothing on her feet and he found himself staring at the small, straight toes with their rosy, perfect nails, as if hypnotised. She turned away, pulling down the covers of the bed, and sat on the side, motioning him to sit beside her.

'This is madness,' she whispered. 'You can only stay a moment.'

'But sweet madness!' He thought he saw colour in her face and he took one of her hands and held it between his. 'I – I don't know how to say this – '

'Go on.'

'I – have known many women. I make no secret of it.'

She said nothing, only bowed her head, looking down at her hand in his, but she did not withdraw it and he took courage and continued.

'I have never found lasting happiness with any of them.'

'Did you look for it?'

He shook his head. 'I was looking for other things.'

'And what are you looking for now?' The grey eyes were very steady, luminous in the candlelight.

'I don't know. Myself, perhaps.'

She withdrew her hand this time, turning her head away. 'I am a nun, given to God. You cannot find yourself in me.'

He tried to take both hands this time but she folded them tightly in her lap. 'Look at me, Isobel!' he begged. 'You have not

58

really given yourself to God, have you? Not all of you. No one can give all of themselves to anyone, not even to God.'

'Some can.' But her head was still turned away from him.

'Not you, Isobel. You are young, beautiful, made for human love – '

'Please! You should not say such things – ' Her voice was husky as he realised that she was close to tears.

'I *will* say it, since no one else will. You must leave this place and go out into the world.'

'Where can I go? There is nowhere.'

'Then you *have* thought of leaving?'

'Yes,' she whispered, but so low he could scarcely hear her.

'Well then – leave!'

She turned her head to look at him then and somehow the shawl fell. She put her hands up in an agony of embarrassment to cover her head, but she was too late. The small, cropped head was bare. As she groped frantically for the shawl he put his arms around her and held her to him. 'Leave it be,' he whispered against the soft, silky feathers of hair. 'Leave it be.'

He felt her body relax against him and he began to kiss her very gently, covering her face and throat with kisses. Then he laid her back against the pillow and lay down beside her, opening the buttons at the neck of her shift. She put up a hand to stop him but he was stronger than she was and the curve of her small breast was warm now against the palm of his hand. As her eager, hungry mouth found his he began to draw up the shift, to stroke her body. At first she tried to draw away from him, but he stroked gently, skillfully, and she relaxed again, until she began to shiver, to call out his name. Her body was wonderfully rounded, her skin silk smooth, smelling of lavender and his own desire was like a towering wave that carried him on its crest until she cried out in pain beneath him, but he did not really hear her. It was only afterwards, when the wave had receded and he was lying beside her once again, that her cry came back to him like an echo.

'I'm sorry,' he whispered. 'Did I hurt you very much?'

She did not answer, and for a mad, terrible second he thought that she was dead. Half afraid of what he might find he put out his hand to touch her cheek but it was warm and wet with tears. 'Don't cry,' he begged. 'Please don't cry! Making love is the most beautiful thing in the world!'

59

She turned her head at last. 'But not like this.' She was pulling down her shift and her eyes were full of sadness.

'Even like this.'

'We – scarcely know each other.'

'Do you really believe that?'

'No.'

He drew her to him once again and she clung to him like a lost child. 'Shall I ever see you again?' she whispered.

'Yes,' he said, 'I promise.' The words hung between them like jewels in the candlelit darkness and he had bent his head to kiss her when there was the distant sound of a door opening, then closing, and the shuffle of slippered feet coming nearer and nearer.

She had frozen in his arms but now she pulled herself free. 'Go!' she whispered frantically, pushing him off the bed. 'Go quickly! I had not realised it was so late!'

She had blown out the candle, and doing up his breeches he ran to the window. As he threw his leg over the sill he heard the door behind him open.

Chapter Nine

'Benedicamus domino!' The lay sister was standing at the foot of Isobel's bed and in the light of her candle Isobel could see Robert's fingers still holding onto the window sill. Even as she forced herself to say the response the fingers disappeared, there was a slithering sound and then a dull thud. The lay sister turned her head to stare at the open window and then looked back at Isobel while the cold night air seemed to fill the cell. Was the old woman going to go to the window and look out? Don't, please don't, Sister, Isobel's mind cried out and she had to force herself to lie still, but the lay sister only muttered to herself and with a last, puzzled look at the open window, shuffled out of the cell.

As soon as the door had closed behind her Isobel got out of bed and ran to the window, but there was no one below. She thought she could see a shadow moving in the darkness of the rose garden, but the shadow melted into the greater darkness beyond and was gone. It was very cold and an owl hooted derisively in a nearby tree. He's gone! He's gone, it seemed to say, and she closed the shutters slowly, her relief that he had got away tinged with a bitter sadness.

When she had lit her own candle she stripped off her shift, seeing the spots of blood on it before she let it fall to the floor. Then she washed in the ice-cold water from her jug, and as she rubbed herself dry she remembered the touch of his hands. She felt no shame, only a kind of wonder that her own body could give her such exquisite pleasure. She had not *really* known what would follow, but when it happened it was as if she had always known. Now, when she moved, her body was still sore, in spite of his gentleness. Was it always like this, she wondered, was this what love really was? Ecstacy and pain? Pain of the mind as well as of the body? For it hurt that he had come like a thief in the night. She wished passionately that their love-making had not been so hasty, so furtive. That instead it had been unhurried, in some wild and beautiful place with nothing to disturb them but the song of the birds, or, as he was surely used to, in a fire-lit chamber with servants outside the door to guard his privacy. As she thought then of the other women he must surely have made love to, of the many times he must have stroked their bodies as he had stroked hers, the pain of it made her catch her breath – and what if she were never to see him again? That would be the worst pain of all.

The harsh clangour of the bell for matins shattered the silence and she had a sudden, ugly premonition that what had happened this night, what she had allowed to happen, would lead her into darkness and pain beyond even her present imagining. She wanted to drown in sleep, but in a few moments she must go down to the convent chapel and take her place in the choir between Dame Helen and Dame Agatha as though nothing had changed, as though she was the same girl, the same virgin nun who had gone to bed a few short hours before. And now there was not even the memory of ecstacy – there was only a feeling of shame and wonder that she could have let such a thing happen, that she had not told him to leave at once. How could she have behaved as she did? It was her fault. Only hers. He would have left if she had been firm enough. But she had loved him for so long, for five long years, and her body had betrayed her – her body and her ignorance.

As the bell rang out once more she slipped her habit over her head, feeling the familiar roughness of the cloth against her skin. To go on wearing it was blasphemy surely, an even greater sin than the other. I will ask to be released, she thought – and found that she could no longer avoid looking at the crucifix.

'Forgive me,' she prayed aloud. 'Please forgive me.' As she looked up, the black wood of the cross seemed to expand until it loomed over her and the crucified body leant towards her until she could almost touch the blood streaming from His side. 'No!' she whispered in terror, covering her face with her hands, 'Oh, no!' She wanted to run from the cell, from the convent, but when she took down her hands and looked again the crucifix had shrunk to its normal size and she could barely make out the tiny, crucified figure. What was happening to her?

The second bell for matins rang out and she picked up her wimple, but before she put it on she touched her hair. He had not minded that it was cropped, and she found herself suddenly smiling, knowing that she would remember that for the rest of her life. Minutes later, down in the church, she had joined her voice with the others, Deus in adjutorium, the Te Deum, the prayer of the day, and only Dame Agatha noticed the huskiness in her voice.

The days, the weeks went by, the King's Visitors did not come but winter came instead to Yorkshire and still Isobel had not asked to be released. In the abbey and the convent the monks and nuns shivered with cold. In the infirmary one of the very old nuns died of it in spite of all Dame Cecilia's best efforts to keep her warm, but Isobel was hardly aware of the cold, or if she was it was as only a part of her general misery. For her the days were endless now, the discipline unbearable, the nights worst of all. She would lie in the darkness trying not to think of Robert, willing herself to forget him, and yet every thought finding its way back to him, the shame somehow dulled although not forgotten. If only she could believe that she would see him again, but her common sense told her that it was not likely. He had said, 'You must leave'. But he had not said, 'Come to me'. And to whom else could she go? Not to her father nor her stepmother. Not to any of her unknown relations. She had no money, no clothes – those of five years ago would never fit her now, even if the convent had kept them, which was unlikely. And somehow she felt sure that Andrew would never help her. All she could do was to try to find a place in some large household teaching children, or if that was not possible, as a common servant. But to leave the convent would be to throw away all hope probably of ever seeing him again – yet, if she stayed . . . No! It must never happen again! She must never let it happen! And yet she knew that if he came again she would not turn him away.

She would remember then Father Francis's voice in Confession. The unbelieveable harshness of it – the old, gentle voice that she had known for so long changed beyond recognition. 'Fornication! The gravest sin of all! You, a professed nun, a bride of Christ! To allow your body to be desecrated! You have crucified Him again a hundred, a thousand times!'

She had refused to tell the old priest who the man was and she had thought he would have an apoplexy behind the screen of the confessional. 'I cannot give you absolution if you do not tell me.'

In the end she had told him and the pity then in his voice had been harder to bear than its earlier harshness. 'How could you have been so foolish, child?'

'I – I love him, Father.'

'You should love only God. You have given your solemn promise.'

'I want to be released.' Her throat was beginning to ache with tears.

'Do not make a rash decision, child. Think well on it first. Where can you go, if you leave here? What will you do? This man, he can never marry you. He comes from an old, noble family. You cannot expect – '

'I expect nothing, Father.'

After a moment's silence the old priest said slowly, 'You must confess your sin to the community, my child. It is the Rule.'

'I cannot!'

'If you offer your love for this man to God it will be purified, and you will be strengthened for what you have to do.'

He had given her absolution then, and a penance that kept her on her knees half the night, but she had not confessed her sin to the community. That she would not, could not do, and when Father Francis died in his sleep soon afterwards, she wondered if what she had told him had helped to bring about his death. That guilt was one more burden to carry and might have accounted for the strange malaise that seemed to be with her now day and night, so that she no longer wanted to eat and found it nearly impossible to get up in the mornings when the lay sister called her. I will leave in the spring, she promised herself. I will ask for a release and I will find some place to go to then, when I feel better again. He is not going to come back and I cannot stay here much longer.

* * *

Soon afterwards Dame Helen had another letter from her Neville cousins in Raskelfe. She came into the parlour on a cold, wet, afternoon at the beginning of November, waving it in front of her like a flag of victory.

'Good news!' she cried. 'You will all be pleased, I know!'

'What is it, Helen?' Dame Petronilla asked politely, but without any great interest.

'My young cousin, my uncle's niece, Beatrice Neville, has become betrothed to Robert FitzHugh, grandson of Sir William – she was orphaned when she was a child, you know, and the earl and countess reared her. They are to be married in the spring! Is that not good news?'

There was a burst of congratulations and surmises as to where the young couple might live, and through it all Isobel sat as if turned to stone. How could he? So soon afterwards – and knew even as she thought that, that she was being foolish, stupid beyond words. He had told her. She was only one of many. And making love to her might be beautiful but it had nothing to do with betrothal or marriage. Perhaps it had given him some small, extra spice of excitement that she should be a nun – that was all. That was all it had ever been, ever would be to him. He was – who he was, what he was. And she was – less than nothing. Something inside her cringed and died and she found herself hating this Beatrice Neville with a fierceness that frightened her. For a terrible second she thought she was going to faint, and she could hear Dame Agatha's voice coming from a distance.

'Are you not well, Dame Isobel?' The touch of malice behind the words was more bracing than any kindness.

'I – I am all right, thank you.'

Somehow or another she got herself out of the parlour before anyone could say any more to her, but in the days and nights that followed the pain in her heart became part of the malaise that remained with her constantly. She found herself thinking of death for the first time in her life and just before Christmas the abbess sent for her.

'Is there something troubling you, child?'

'No, my lady.' But Dame Margaret knew her too well. They faced each other across the table in Dame Margaret's parlour, both sitting straight, hands folded in their laps. Like most of the other, older nuns all colour seemed to have left the abbess's face years before, but now Isobel was as pale as she was, and Dame Margaret looked at her searchingly.

'You are quite sure?'

'Yes, my lady.' Isobel had to force herself to meet those worried, kind eyes.

'We have all chosen a difficult path to follow here. At the beginning the road seems long and hard. I know that.' Dame Margaret waited and when Isobel said nothing the older woman sighed, lifting her hands from her lap and folding them on the table in front of her. Isobel found herself staring at the silver band on the abbess's third finger. Bride of Christ. Virgin bride. A wave of nausea washed over her and she clenched her hands so fiercely trying to fight off dizziness that she knew her nails had drawn blood.

'We give so much and seem to get so little in return, sometimes,' Dame Margaret said quietly. 'But that is not so. You will see.'

Isobel murmured something. She could not afterwards remember what she said, but the nausea slowly receded and when she looked up again Dame Margaret had drawn further back from the table.

'Dame Cecilia has asked me to increase your allowance of meat after Advent.' The abbess's voice was noticeably colder. 'I have agreed, in view of your age.'

'Thank you, my lady.'

'One more thing. Your cousin, Andrew Ellerton has requested permission to visit you before Christmas. Even though it is Advent I told him he could see you tomorrow, as he is your cousin. But he cannot stay for long.'

'Thank you, my lady.'

'You may go now, Dame Isobel.'

Isobel almost ran from the room. Why had Andrew asked to see her after so long? God in heaven, surely he did not know? Could someone have seen them talking, or worse still, seen Robert that night?

But when he came next day he seemed the same as ever. She sat beside him in the visitors' parlour, trying not to shiver for there was no fire. The freshly laid rushes did not seem dry and the cold from them too seemed to penetrate even the soles of her shoes.

'I have been meaning to come for some time,' Andrew said awkwardly, 'but what with my manuscripts and acting as secretary to Father Abbot – '

'Why did you want to see me?' she said quietly.

He looked at her in what seemed to be genuine surprise. 'It is my duty. You are my cousin.'

So that was all. She let her breath out slowly, smiling with relief. 'You must play with your cousin, Isobel!' She could still hear her mother's voice and her own, answering her. She could have been no more than ten years of age at the time. 'He is only my second cousin and I don't like him, mother. He's bossy and – and he laughs at me, says I "put on airs". What does that mean?'

'It means that you try to appear grander than you are.'

'But – how? I don't understand.'

'Never mind! When you are older you will know what I mean.' How often had she said that? 'Your father would like the two of you to be friends, so try not to fight with Andrew.'

Whenever her mother said 'your father would like you to do it', Isobel always knew that whatever it was had to be done, that otherwise there would be one of those terrible scenes between her parents that used to terrify her, when she would rush in to defend her mother, certain that her father was going to strike her.

'Are you making good progress, Isobel?' Andrew was frowning, his voice, cold and abrupt as usual, bringing her back to the present.

'Progress, Andrew? What exactly do you mean?' Why hadn't she said 'yes' and let it go with him?

'Must you always split hairs?' he said impatiently.

She shrugged. 'One can progress in many different ways.'

'Of course! Of course! I meant in your spiritual life, obviously – '

'How can one judge?'

His face tightened with anger. 'Do you, for instance, feel closer to God?'

'Sometimes,' she said coolly. 'And you? Do you feel closer? Will you soon be ordained?'

The anger left him suddenly and he looked oddly young and defenceless. 'I don't know,' he said slowly. 'I feel I am not yet ready.' And then he added gruffly, 'I – have been reading

Erasmus and – and even Luther. Some of what even *he* says seems to make sense.'

'I know nothing of Erasmus,' she admitted, 'but Dame Margaret told us that Luther is an evil man.'

'Not evil,' he said quickly. 'Oh, no! He sees things differently, that is all. I have always thought myself that it is wrong to sell indulgences – ' He stopped abruptly and she wished that she was more widely read herself and could argue with him, rather than simply repeat parrot-wise what Dame Margaret had told her.

'Could you lend me some books to read?' she said.

He shook his head. 'No, it would be wrong of me. You are lucky, in many ways to be as you are – it is sometimes better to be ignorant – '

And although she did not want to be considered ignorant by Andrew of all people she let it go with him, asking him if he thought the King might close the convent as well as the abbey.

'Yes,' he said. 'I feel sure he will.'

'What shall we do then, Andrew?'

He looked at her as if seeing her properly for the first time in his life. 'I may continue my work outside, but in your case – I don't know. Some nuns have been given pensions and gone back to their families, or have gone to live together in houses in the towns. Has Dame Margaret not talked to you about it?'

'She has told us about a house in York, but I think she does not want to upset the community about something that might not happen. They are all so old, most of them, so dependent on her.'

'Then you should put it out of your mind until she does,' he said. 'And now, I have brought you a small gift,' he added sheepishly, as if to change the subject. She felt suddenly guilty, for she had never in all her life wanted to give him anything.

'Thank you!' She smiled now with real pleasure. I hope it is not something that I must share with the rest of the community?'

'Oh, no! It's not that kind of gift – ' He was unrolling a sheet of parchment, at the same time flushing to the roots of the reddish hair that curled round his broad forehead. But when he handed the parchment to her she could not at first read the thick, black, slanting writing. It was beautifully decorated with tiny flowers in brilliant colours cascading down the sheet.

'Oh, Andrew! Is this your work? It is exquisite!' She touched the flowers with the tip of her finger. 'They are so delicate! So perfect!'

He smiled. 'Can you read it?'

'*Hali Meidenhad* – that is the title? "Hali" means "holy", does it not?' She remembered deciphering an early text with Dame Margaret when she was a novice.

He nodded. 'It means "Holy Maidenhood". It is a quotation from a thirteenth century homily. I thought you might like to have it.'

She tried to swallow and could not, found her hands shaking and had to hide them in her lap, dropping the parchment on the table. Could he know, after all? Was it possible? But when she looked up, the flat, straight mouth was still smiling. It was not in his character to be devious, she thought, merely clumsy. He did not know, she decided. She was becoming neurotic, seeing meanings that were not intended.

'I shall read it for you, if you like,' he was saying. 'I am probably more familiar with that period.'

She heard his voice without taking in anything of what he was saying – until he came near the end. 'Love is a licking of honey off thorns,' he read, his voice without expression or understanding, like that of a child reading its first lesson.

'Honey off thorns?' she repeated slowly.

'Yes!' he said cheerfully. 'Some unknown wrote it, but whoever he was, he had a strange way of putting things!'

'Perhaps it was a woman,' she said.

'Scarcely! But are you feeling all right, Isobel?' he asked hastily. 'You look rather pale.'

'I am quite well,' she said. He had been holding down the parchment flat on the table with his big, freckled hands and now he released it, letting it curl inwards, and she added quickly, 'You must have spent a lot of time working on it, and it must have used up a great deal of your precious paints. I am very grateful.'

'Oh, one of our guests made me a present of new supplies,' he said, handing her the rolled up parchment. 'Otherwise I would not have been so generous.'

'A guest?' She was not really interested in who it was, but she felt she owed it to him to ask.

'Robert FitzHugh.' The name seemed to echo and re-echo and her throat felt suddenly dry. Did she imagine it or had his eyes sharpened? 'He stayed with us in the autumn,' he went on, 'and I showed my work and told him of the difficulty I had in getting paints. So he promised to send me some from London.'

'That was – generous of him.' She knew she should let the matter drop but the urge to talk about Robert was irresistable. 'What kind of man was he, in – in general?'

'Like them all. Not that I've met many.'

She did not need to ask Andrew who he meant by 'them'. She knew. 'They' were the aristocrats. The nobly born. She had a sudden, bleak image of herself and Andrew standing side by side, two small, undistinguished figures, and on the other side of a wide chasm, Robert, with Beatrice Neville, his grandfather and her uncle behind them and the serried rows of their blue-blooded ancestors. How had she ever dreamed she could cross that chasm?

Looking up, she found Andrew's eyes boring into hers, and her throat began to feel dry again. Was he, after all, more subtle than she had thought, and was this gift a homily within a homily, for her alone? She stood up. 'Lady Abbess has only allowed us a few minutes,' she said, anxious now above all else to be rid of him. 'I must go.'

'Of course.' They walked together to the door, and as he opened it for her he said quietly, 'I shall be over again in the New Year.'

Then he was gone, and she watched him walk away from her down the cold, damp passage, his shoulders slightly hunched under the white robe, familiar and yet alien to her in spirit as if he had come from another planet.

That night she hid the parchment in the furthest corner of the bottom drawer of her oak chest. Whatever reason he had had for giving it to her, she never wanted to see it again, and when Christmas had come and gone a fear that had been with her for weeks turned into sick, cold panic. Once again her monthly flow of blood had not come and she knew with certainty that she was pregnant.

Chapter Ten

Months later, on one of the hottest days of July, the baby moved its tiny limbs inside her womb and Isobel rested her back against the wooden stall in the convent chapel. A trickle of sweat ran down between her swollen breasts and she thanked God that vespers would soon be over. It was a day sullen with the threat of thunder, and cocooned as her stomach was in linen bandages to hide the bulge, she was close to fainting. She had been afraid that the tight bandaging would hurt the baby, but the kicking just now had been as vigorous as ever, and if only she did not faint meanwhile she would soon be able to leave the chapel. She willed herself to sit upright, taking deep breaths, sickened by the smell of incense and melting wax, forcing herself to look at the altar and uneasily conscious of Dame Agatha beside her. It had been fortunate for her that the other nun had been ill for so long with the flux, else she would surely have discovered her secret long ago.

In the beginning Isobel had thought of getting rid of the baby. She had been shocked to find that she would even consider it but a persistent voice inside her head had whispered that there were herbs – that there was a woman in East Wooton who did something . . . But in her heart of hearts she did not want the baby to die. It was all she would ever have of Robert. 'Even so,' the voice had whispered, 'it's not a baby – not yet! It's just a thing! Look at your body. There's no change at all! Just think – a few sips – or a few minutes in the woman's cottage and it will all be over. Don't be a fool!'

The voice was lying. She knew that. It *was* a baby, that she and Robert had made together, and the herbs more often than not simply made one very ill without ending the pregnancy. As for the woman, it was said that she lived in a filthy hovel and that whatever she did to them, many of the girls who went to her died afterwards in agony.

She did not want to die, that much she was sure of, but the voice said, '*You* won't die! You're strong! And why do you want his child? If you still love him then you are doubly a fool!'

She knew that this time the voice was speaking the truth but she did not want to hear it, and she closed her mind to it until in the end it went away and left her to her frenzied thoughts. Should she confide then in Lady Abbess after all? But that was impossible. She imagined the kindly face hardening, the shock, the horror in the eyes that had looked so often into hers with affectionate exasperation. Nor could she imagine confiding even in Dame Cecilia. Surely her robust commonsense would condemn her just as quickly? As for Agatha and Helen and the others – it did not bear thinking about. For some unaccountable reason she felt that Dame Petronilla would probably have been least shocked of all, but she was so old, so frail, it would not be fair to burden her with such a secret; and what could she do to help without telling the others? No, she could tell no one. Whatever she did, she would have to do it alone. Unless, by some miracle, Robert came back, and – and helped her. Showed her that he cared about the baby. If she could get word to him, somehow. Find her way to London –

And that inner voice that she had grown to hate so much returned and whispered, 'Fantasies! Madness! Have you forgotten who he is, what he is? Did he say he loved you? Has he not promised himself to another woman? Have you no pride?'

She wanted to kill the voice and then realised that she was, after all, wishing for her own death. Would it not be the answer to all her problems? She knew enough about herbs to make sure of it, and no one would ever know why she had done it. But as she realised that that was not really what she wanted – that she wanted Robert to know why she had done it – her hard, northern practicality came to her rescue and drew her back from the edge of the abyss.

She began instead, that night, to make her plans, if one could call them 'plans'. She would deliver the baby herself in one of the convent stables. But she was afraid. Not so much of death itself, even though her mother had died after childbirth, nor of pain, for she knew very little about that. But of dying – alone. It was a darkness creeping towards her with each passing moment, even though she told herself that women had been giving birth since the beginning of time, often alone, that it was a natural function of the body like any other, that she was healthy and had seen birth on the farm many times – and still she was afraid.

Sometimes she would allow herself to think about the baby, to wonder what it would be like to hold her in her arms. She had convinced herself that it would be a girl – a kind of extension of herself – conceived in her love. She could not rear a child alone. She knew that, but when the time came, would she be able to give her away? And while she thought about the baby and herself and the future she tried to banish Robert from her mind. She even tried to hate him. But it was no use. He had burst into her tiny world like a fiery comet and burned her to her very soul. She could no more forget him than she could stop breathing. She could not hate him either, or at least not for long, and when Dame Helen told them regretfully that the wedding had had to be postponed until September because Beatrice Neville had an illness of the lungs, she knew a moment of happiness that this woman, who already seemed to have so much, would have to wait a little longer before she had everything.

She had only seen Andrew once since the winter. He had come after Easter, when she had only just got over the strain of the Easter ceremonies. He was stolid and calm as ever and, looking sideways at him as they walked up and down the cloister, she had wondered what he would say if she told him, if she said, had been able to say, Andrew, help me. I am pregnant. But she had said nothing, as of course she had known she would, and he had gone back to the abbey soon afterwards with no hint that the visit had been other than an act of friendship, or more likely, a duty done.

Her back was beginning to ache now in earnest. She had to kneel for the suffrages of the saints, but she was so heavy that kneeling was becoming difficult. She was not altogether sure when the baby was due, but it could not be more than another ten days or so, surely? Soon she must leave the blankets and the knife and whatever else she might need in the stable – and she must think of an excuse to cover her absence when – when the baby started to come, and she was – out there, her mind sliding over that as it had done over so many other things lately . . . If only she could sit back on her heels, but of course that was not possible with Dame Helen and Dame Agatha poker straight beside her. Would she *never* get to her bed?

But at last they had sung the final hymn, the new chaplain, a much younger man than Father Francis, had given his blessing, and Dame Katherine hurried out to see that all was prepared for the evening's supper.

As soon as the chaplain had gone from the altar and Dame Helen had left to ring the bell, the abbess got to her feet and, tall and erect, led the other nuns and lay sisters out of the chapel. She had noticed Isobel's restlessness during vespers and it worried her. The girl had changed so much recently she felt she scarcely knew her now. But she is young, she told herself for the hundredth time. And we are all old. Everything is different for her. Everything. I must never forget that. But as Dame Helen rang the supper bell the abbess quickened her steps, resolving to put aside her worries for the moment, her small community following her with hungry obedience into the refectory.

A few minutes later they stood at their places waiting for her to say Grace but as she blessed herself Dame Cecilia stole a quick glance at Isobel, standing opposite. The girl was clearly not well. She had thought so in the chapel but now she was sure of it. Yet what could be wrong with her? She had if anything put on weight rather than lost it. Was she perhaps chastising herself too severely or had some special mortification been given to her by the abbess or the chaplain that was beyond even her young strength? There were times when it seemed to Dame Cecilia that too strict an observance of the Rule was not only un-Christian but downright sinful.

Dame Petronilla had been too taken up with her aching joints, and the other nuns too lost in prayer to notice anything amiss with Isobel during vespers. Not all the other nuns had been so pre-occupied however. Dame Agatha was the exception for she had been pleasantly aware that all was not as it should be almost from the beginning. As she joined now in saying Grace she

watched Isobel from the corner of her eye, promising herself
that she would keep an even closer eye on her from now on. It
was her duty, she told herself, and she was never one to shirk
that . . .

Isobel's back was still aching when finally she got to bed. With
the bandaging off she could feel the baby move strongly. Once
again she worried about the constriction during the day and the
harm it might be causing. Was she going to give birth to an idiot,
or some misshapen horror?

Her shift was wet with sweat and it clung to her swollen body.
The storm had not yet broken and the air was thick and heavy. It
was dark now outside and through her wide open window she
could hear the faint rumble of distant thunder. She was not
normally afraid of thunder-storms but tonight, in her
overwrought state it seemed to carry a warning of impending
doom. She found herself reaching across the empty bed as if
someone lay beside her, someone who would comfort and hold
her, someone who would tell her not to be afraid.

Am I going mad, she wondered. Have I thought about Robert
so much that my mind has gone? And the tears that were never
far off these days began to run down her cheeks once again,
wetting her pillow, mingling with the sweat until the neck of her
shift was sodden.

And suddenly, terrifyingly, it was more than just the neck of
her shift that was wet. Something was happening to her – to her
body – that she could not understand. She was drenched – the
mattress beneath her was drenched. She lit a candle with
shaking fingers and put her hand down, expecting blood. But it
was not blood. Her hand was wet with water. What – what in
God's name was happening to her?

She lay back, her heart thudding against her ribs, trying to
calm herself, trying to remember odd scraps of information that
she had picked up over the years, things she had heard her
mother and the servant girl talking about in the kitchen long ago.
About a neighbour who had given birth, about her 'waters
bursting'. Was *this* it? Was this what had happened to her, and
what did it mean? Was she going to die? Had the baby died? Oh,
why had she not asked to help in the infirmary! She'd have

known then. 'Help me, oh God, help me!' she prayed desperately. If only her mother were here – or *someone*!

She became aware again of a cramp in her stomach that had been coming and going since much earlier in the day and which she had chosen to ignore up to now, blaming it on the apple she had eaten at dinner time. But now it was back again, more severe, disturbing. She lay on her side, then on her back, then on her other side, but the cramp was still there and she knew at last, even as the rumbling thunder came closer and the rain began to slant in through the open window that the baby had started to come.

For the life of her she could not get herself off the bed and the thought of going out to the stable was unthinkable. It had never occurred to her that the baby might come during the night while she was in bed, in her cell. She had always imagined that it would come during the day. She had seen herself forced to leave the church, or the garden, or the refectory even, with excuses ready-made for each situation, disappearing out to the stable while the others were occupied. It had not been rational thinking, but with reality at last upon her she realised that she had not really been thinking rationally for a long time. She should have had the courage to tell Lady Abbess or Dame Cecilia even, not everything, but at least that she was pregnant. The worst that could have happened would surely not have been as bad as this. Now it was too late. Now she would have to face this horror alone.

The pain eased, went altogether and she lay quietly, taking deep breaths, telling herself not to be afraid, trying to pray but no longer able to. She knew she should change into a dry shift but she could not bring herself to do that. Then the pain came back, much stronger this time, hinting at what was to come, and she felt herself drowning in a sea of panic.

She lost track of time as thunder crashed over the roof of the convent and flashes of lightning lit up her cell. The pains were coming much more frequently now, strong, stronger, until they had become unbearable and she was crying aloud, 'Mother of God, help me! Help me, *please!*' She was like a maddened animal, trapped in a cage of pain and she felt herself growing tired, too tired to fight to live. Was this how her mother had died? Had she been too tired to go on living, after they had got

76

the baby out of her body? Oh God, why had she been such a fool! How had she thought she could do it by herself? Why hadn't someone told her what it would be like?

The pain again, tearing at her – stuffing the bedcover into her mouth so that she would not scream, and screaming in spite of herself, her voice hoarse, unrecognisable – and through a red mist of pain, hearing the door of her cell open, seeing candlelight, a face, a red face framed in a white shawl, horrified eyes staring down at her – 'What – what in God's name is the matter with you, Isobel?' Dame Agatha. Her mouth fallen open, the candle shaking in her hand.

'I'm – I'm having a baby! Fetch – fetch – Dame Cecilia – quickly!' The pain gripping her again, her head twisting and turning on the pillow. Why, oh why, had it to be Dame Agatha of all people.

'*What* did you say?'

'Fetch Cecilia – but – be quick – ' Isobel was panting as if she had been running uphill.

The red face disappeared.

It seemed a lifetime before it came back, another alongside – this one under a white cap. Voices. One nearly hysterical, the other calmer. Hands pulling back the covers. Dame Cecilia's voice telling her to draw up her knees. 'Oh, *why* did you not tell me?' And then, before she could reply, 'Go down to the kitchen, Agatha. Fetch hot water – clean cloths from the linen chest – a clean, sharp knife – But be quick, for the love of God! Breathe deeply, Isobel! That's right – now, don't be afraid. It's fear that makes it so hard – Try to relax, girl! *Good* girl!'

Tears of gratitude were running down Isobel's face now, the pain somehow bearable, the panic subsiding. 'Oh, God bless Dame Cecilia! God bless her!'

But still the baby did not come.

She did not think of Robert at all now, although she knew she had called out his name once during the night. Several times she thought she heard the abbess's voice talking to Dame Cecilia but she could not be sure, and towards morning as the pains became worse and the baby still did not come, in spite of Dame Cecilia's encouragement, she gave up hope altogether. She and the baby were going to die and so great was her exhaustion that she did not care.

And suddenly Dame Cecilia was telling her to push even harder, that she could see the baby's head, 'Like a little red bubble,' she said, excitement making her hoarse. 'It's nearly over! *Try*, Isobel, try *harder*!'

Isobel was so tired she could scarcely breathe but she made one last effort, there was a terrible searing pain as if she had been knifed and the baby burst out, helped by Dame Cecilia's groping hands.

She heard a slap and a thin, high, cry and then Dame Cecilia was holding up something that looked like a skinned rabbit, blood on her hands, on her bare arms.

'He's small, but he's a fine, healthy little fellow.' Dame Cecilia's voice was almost young, full of excitement.

But Isobel turned her head away and closed her eyes. So it was a boy after all. She did not hold that against him, but she felt neither love nor hate for her son, only enormous relief that he was out of her body at last.

Isobel woke to find herself in a clean shift lying on a clean, dry mattress. She felt weak as a kitten, and sunlight streamed across the floor of her cell. For the first time in weeks, years it seemed, the bedcovers lay flat on her stomach. The baby was not in the cell and her body, bound and bandaged, still felt sore, as did her breasts, heavy with milk – surely she should be feeding him?

She was beginning to feel uneasy when the door opened and a tired looking, old nun came into the cell and stood looking at her from the foot of the bed.

She realised with a shock that it was Dame Margaret, seeming to have grown old overnight, and she wished that a thunderbolt had struck the convent – anything, rather than have to face her now.

After a long moment the abbess said quietly, 'What have you to say to me, Dame Isobel?'

'I – I am truly sorry, my lady,' Isobel whispered.

'It – it was not forced on you, then?'

'No.'

'I see.' The abbess walked to the window and stood looking out. When she spoke again her voice had changed as if anger, deep, burning anger had taken the place of pity. 'Why did you not tell me? It was your duty as a member of the community to confess your sin to me, at least.'

'I – I could not – and I – I have wanted to be released for some time.'

Dame Margaret turned then, walking back to the foot of the bed. 'I shall request your release at once, but you must tell me who the father is.'

'I – cannot tell you that.'

'Why not?' The abbess's voice had grown even colder. 'Is he – is he a member of the abbey community?'

'No!' Isobel said quickly. 'No, he is not!'

'Thank God for that, at least,' Dame Margaret said shortly. 'Is there any hope of marriage?'

'No.'

'He is already married?'

'No – at least, I am not sure. He is – to marry soon, I think – '

'You are not even sure?' The knuckles of the abbess's hands, which she held clasped in front of her, had whitened, and her voice had risen. 'I cannot – I simply do not understand you, Dame Isobel! How could you break your solemn vows, desecrate everything you should hold sacred, commit grievous sin with a man you seem to know so little about? How could you let him use you in such a – such a way? Do you realise that you have brought scandal and disgrace not only on yourself but on the whole community, and at the worst possible time?'

Isobel's small spurt of returning strength seemed to be leaving her and she closed her eyes, willing herself not to faint, but when she opened them again a moment later the abbess was still standing here, staring down at her.

'Well, Dame Isobel, have you nothing to say?'

'I said I was sorry, my lady. I meant it. I can say no more,' she whispered, turning her head away, looking at the grey stone wall beside her bed and seeing Robert's face as it had been in the candlelight that night. Laughing. Teasing. Loving. Surely, just for that night at least, it had been loving? And suddenly the angry, distraught woman standing at the foot of her bed seemed no more that someone whom she had hurt without meaning to, whom she had thought she had loved but who had failed her in a moment of crisis. Or was the failure all her own? Whichever it was, it no longer mattered.

79

'You must go home as soon as possible.' The abbess's voice broke the silence that seemed to have gone on for ever.

'*Home?*' Isobel sat up, and then fell back, panting. 'I can't go home! My father and my stepmother – they won't want me, or the baby –'

'You cannot stay here, and where else can you go to except back to your family?' Dame Margaret's voice was under control again, as calm, as cool as if she were talking to a perfect stranger about some ordinary, everyday matter and this cold control was worse, Isobel thought, than if she had shouted. 'So that is settled, then.' The abbess turned to go. 'A week should give you long enough to get back your strength. Meanwhile, you will talk to no one except Dame Cecilia, and you will remain here in your room.'

Isobel did not want to talk to anyone, and dreaded that at any minute Dame Agatha would appear, so she merely nodded, wishing that the abbess would leave, and when the door opened and Dame Cecilia came in, her white infirmarian's apron over her habit, the baby wrapped in swaddling clothes in her arms, Isobel nearly cried with relief.

'I am sorry, my lady,' the infirmarian said quickly. 'I should have knocked but I did not know you were here.' Her face was grey with fatigue but there had been a new look of happiness in it which had faded abruptly when she saw Dame Margaret.

'I was about to leave, in any case.' The abbess, without looking again at Isobel, or acknowledging the baby's presence in any way, walked out of the room, closing the door behind her with a quiet finality.

Dame Cecilia remained where she was for a few seconds, the greyness of her face blotched now with colour, looking at the closed door and then at Isobel, who was wiping away tears she had not known she had shed. 'You must not fret too much, child,' she said gruffly, coming over to the bed, ''tis not good for you, so soon afterwards.' Slowly, carefully, she put the baby into her arms. 'You are not the first nun to have a baby, and I daresay you won't be the last,' she added dryly.

'Oh, Dame Cecilia, what would I do without you?' Isobel whispered over the baby's head, and the infirmarian gave her a sudden, warm smile.

'Our Lady would send you someone else! Now, isn't he a fine little fellow?'

But Isobel thought he looked like a wizened old man – an old, man-doll that might break in her arms if she was not very careful. His head was covered with a fine, white-gold down and she touched it gently with one finger, looking up to find Dame Cecilia's faded blue eyes watching her, wise and tired and suddenly sad.

'He has his father's hair,' the infirmarian said quietly.

'His – father's?' Isobel repeated, her voice husky.

'Robert FitzHugh is his father, is he not?'

Isobel bent her head over the baby. How had she found out? Mother of God don't let the whole story be discovered, she prayed. Don't let anyone ever find out that he came to my cell!

'You called out his name during the night, and Dame Petronilla and I saw you talking to him in the orchard last year,' Dame Cecilia said into the silence.

'You saw us!' Isobel's voice sounded strange even in her own ears. 'Yet you said nothing?'

The infirmarian's big, reddened hands began to pleat and unpleat the coarse white linen of her apron. 'We did not want to make trouble for you, but I'm sorry now we did not tell Lady Abbess at the time.' Her hands dropped to her side and she looked directly at Isobel. 'We both thought it could do no harm, that it meant nothing, and you may be sure others saw you too. Not from the convent maybe – very few of the community go beyond the rose garden, not even Dame Agatha likes to leave it – but people from outside – '

People like abbey servants and even Andrew himself, Isobel thought. What a fool I was to think we would not be seen! In the country where nothing goes unnoticed, where anyone or anything out of the ordinary is watched and commented on every minute of the day by invisible watchers –

'Does Robert FitzHugh know?' Dame Cecilia's voice cut across her thoughts.

'No, and I shan't tell him.'

'You should. He's as much to blame as you are. He *must* help you.'

'No!' Isobel shouted the word. 'He is not to know! He is – is soon to be married!' She could not keep the tears from her voice. 'I don't want his pity,' she added in a whisper, 'and Lady Abbess is sending me back to my father and stepmother – I

81

cannot think beyond that point! But please, I beg you, do not tell *anyone* who the father is!'

'I think you are making a mistake,' the infirmarian said slowly. 'However, if it eases your mind I give you my promise not to tell. Now, it is high time to feed your son – '

The tiny, screwed-up eyes had opened briefly and then closed again. Blue eyes. The lids slightly crusted. And then he began to wail, a thin, piercing sound that made Isobel want to clap her hand over the tiny mouth. Instead, Dame Cecilia told her to open the front of her shift and then held the baby's head to her breast until his still wailing mouth had closed over her nipple. The pain was agonising at first, almost as bad as the other. It was as if a knife had been thrust into her breast and she cried aloud, but gradually the pain eased and at last the ordeal was over.

'Will it always be like this?' she asked, as the infirmarian took the baby from her.

'Each time it will be easier, child. Just thank God you have plenty of milk.'

While Isobel was feeding the baby Dame Cecilia had been busy, carrying in a wooden box which she placed on two stools and lined with blankets. She put him on his side in the box that was to serve as his cradle. 'I shall show you how to wash him later,' she promised. 'Now all three of us need to sleep.'

Giving Isobel a steaming hot bowl of broth that tasted unbelievably good, she left her to sleep. But although the baby was sleeping soundly enough Isobel's mind would not rest. To have to go back, in disgrace, to a father who had never loved her, to a stepmother who would certainly have no welcome for her, with a bastard child whom they would want even less than they would want her. How could Lady Abbess do it to her, and yet, in fairness, what real alternative was there? It might have been better, she thought, had she died after all, she and the baby. And yet –

She looked over at the box. From the bed she could see only the tiny mound of his body under the blankets, for his face was turned away from her, the shawl in which he was wrapped covering the back of his head. Pushing back her own bedcovers she got shakily out of bed. Her body was raw and sore under the bandaging but she could walk. If she moved very slowly – it would only be for a minute or two after all.

She bent down and lifted him up, terrified of dropping him, for she had never held such a young baby in her arms before. Gingerly she carried him back to her bed and sitting down, held him against her, rubbing her cheek gently against the soft down on his small head, thinking in spite of herself of Robert. He would never see his son, never know he existed. It was wrong. Surely it was wrong? But she must not look back – or forward. Must think only of now, this very minute, if she was ever to get well again.

Gently, afraid of waking him, she began to unwind his swaddling clothes. He was so small, so thin! The little arms, the legs, almost without flesh and yet perfectly formed. And as she bent over him, the tiny penis erected and a jet of urine caught her full in the face.

'You little devil!' she breathed, and found herself laughing, for the first time in days, months, years, it seemed. As she wiped her face he began to snuffle in his sleep, to move his limbs with small, jerky movements and she wrapped him up again as quickly as she could and put him back in his box. She watched him, holding her breath for fear he would waken, but he settled down, and she climbed shakily back into bed.

She would never give him away. Not now that she had seen him, held him in her arms. Somehow she would look after him. He was hers, as nothing had ever been since her mother had given her the puppy years ago. She had had to leave the puppy behind when she entered the convent and it had nearly broken her heart. To give her son away would be a heartbreak of the same kind but so much worse it did not bear thinking about. And since she could not call him Robert, she would call him Christopher because it would soon be the feast of St Christopher and she had always liked the name. She fell asleep at last, holding on to that thought and banishing all else from her mind.

It was still a day short of the week which Dame Margaret had given Isobel in which she was to recover her strength, when the Visitors arrived at the abbey. An hour later the farm cart creaked out of the convent yard. On the seat Isobel sat very straight, the baby in her arms, beside John, a silent, deaf old man who had worked for St Mary's since he was a young boy. She wore a shabby cloak and an equally shabby woollen gown and her own nun's shoes, for although Dame Cecilia had been able to find some clothes she could not find a pair of shoes that fitted her. The rest of her few belongings were in a satchel – her dowry would be returned to her father directly as had been arranged between him and Lady Abbess, otherwise he had said, he would not take her back. It was Dame Cecilia who told her this and that Lord Abbot, God help him, had been taken away to London for questioning. She had neither seen nor spoken to Dame Margaret since her first brief visit after the birth. It was Dame Cecilia who came out to the yard with her, who hugged her and slipped one of Dame Petronilla's embroidered purses into her hand.

'We were forbidden to see you off!' she whispered, 'but Petronilla asked me to give you this! With her love!' The tears were streaming down her face. 'God go with you child, and if you need help with the baby at any time, send word to me!'

From a window above the yard Dame Margaret watched the cart leave. Her face was stiff and cold, her eyes were dry. 'Oh, Isobel, how could you?' she whispered aloud. 'How could you have been so weak, so foolish!'

And Giacomo Frescobaldi seemed to come from the shadows and stand behind her. 'You hypocrite!' he said, the contempt in his voice cutting her to the heart. *'You hypocrite!'*

Lifting the skirt of her habit she turned away from the window, walking as quickly as she dared out of the room, down the steps, into the yard. But she was too late. The cart was gone and she could not bring herself to look at Dame Cecilia, still standing there wiping her eyes, let alone reprimand her for disobedience.

Chapter Eleven

They came just before vespers – six men with their servants, clattering into the convent yard, and now they faced Dame Margaret across the table in the large parlour where she sat, flanked by the members of her Council, hands folded in her lap, her face as white as the linen of her wimple, not daring to look at her companions.

It was the fat one she feared most of all. He had introduced himself curtly as Dr Thomas Parr – a humourless, overbearing man in his late thirties, his huge paunch forcing him to sit well back from the table, his small eyes almost lost in mounds of pale flesh, but watching her like a cat watching a mouse that it is sure cannot escape. The last time, the other Visitors had gone over her accounts with meticulous care until the figures had begun to dance before her eyes and she had thought she would lose her reason, but this time these men scarcely looked at them, and her initial relief was soon replaced by a cold fear that this Visitation was merely a gesture. They had already made up their minds to close the convent. She felt sure of it.

A somewhat younger man, Dr Richard Whellan, dressed in dark, clerical clothes, sat further down. 'There are only eight choir nuns here, I understand, Dame Margaret including yourself of course,' he said to her now. His tone was courteous enough as befitted a rector, but she had heard he had taken part in the trial of Anne Boleyn and although she could not condone the King's divorce, she felt a shiver of disgust that she should be talking to a man who had played a part in the execution of a young girl.

'There are only seven choir nuns here now,' she said slowly,

85

picking her words with care. 'Dame Isobel Willis has asked to be released, and has returned to her family.'

'Indeed! And what age was she?' His tone, smooth, without expression.

'Eighteen.'

'A *young* nun!' Steepling his fingers he looked at his neighbour Dr Parr, a world of innuendo in his voice. She had heard that he had a reputation for telling salacious anecdotes and for using sly, inquisitorial approaches when Visiting. 'So! A young nun had recently asked to be released! I wonder why?'

'She discovered that she had no vocation,' the abbess said clearly, lifting her chin and hoping that the men had not heard Dame Agatha's sharp intake of breath behind her, or the soft thud of Dame Petronilla's stick as she let it fall on the rush-covered floor.

'No vocation? I see.' He whispered to the man on his other side and the fellow wrote something down – Edward Dutton, she thought his name was – but although he looked like a clerk he still had a certain air of substance about him. He had small, greedy hands and his eyes seemed to have been making an inventory of the parlour ever since he had first sat down, lingering on the tapestry hanging on the wall that she had brought from her own home, the polished oak of the table, the silver candlesticks on the chest beside the door. Now, he bent forward, speaking to her for the first time. 'When exactly did this young nun leave?'

She hesitated, trying to think of a reply that would not be an outright lie but before she could speak Dame Agatha said in her flat voice, 'Today. She left today.'

What had possessed her, the abbess thought in horror. Surely not to make mischief? Surely not even she would do such a thing? Had it been no more than a desire to share the limelight, or a simple inability to keep her mouth shut? But, God in heaven, what mischief might she not have started! Dame Margaret willed herself not to look away, above all not to look at Dame Agatha, and the man Dutton smiled, a stillborn smile that curled his thick lips but never reached his pale, heavy-lidded eyes. 'Today? What a coincidence that we should arrive on the same day!'

'Yes, indeed,' Dame Margaret said calmly, remembering that

86

she was after all a Fairfax and not to be out-countenanced by a jumped-up nobody. 'A coincidence, as you say.'

There was a silence, and then Dr Whellan said with a certain air of impatience. 'Well, it will be dark soon, gentlemen. We must not waste time!'

Edward Dutton looked taken aback and so did Dr Parr, but the others nodded, and the three who had not spoken at all shuffled their papers in front of them importantly. Two were Augmentations men, she guessed, working for the chancellor, Sir Richard Rich, but the third was Sir Anthony Challoner, a local landowner, who was obviously ill at ease. As she was wondering if he could read, Dr Parr broke the short silence, looking down at her along the sloping length of his velvet-covered paunch.

'Lord Cromwell and of course his Royal Highness, have given the matter of St Mary's deep and careful consideration, but after much deliberation I regret to have to tell you that it is the royal wish, the royal *command*, that the convent of St Mary's be dissolved immediately, and all its possessions handed over to the Crown.'

The abbess sat as if turned to stone and there were loud gasps behind her. 'On what grounds?' she asked when she could speak.

'Are they not obvious?' He spread his podgy hands, lifting his massive shoulders. 'Seven elderly women, leading it is true, exemplary lives, but scarcely – productive! Accumulated debts! My dear Lady Abbess, even you must see what a hopeless situation it is!'

'But – ' and as Dame Margaret opened her mouth to argue she knew she was wasting her time.

'Where are we to go?' Dame Cecilia asked coldly.

'Why, that is for you to decide! To your families, or to another convent – or perhaps out into the world.' Dr Parr's voice was beginning to sound impatient, as if he wished the whole tiresome business would soon be settled and he could go home.

'Out into the world, at *our* age?' Dame Helen's scorn was withering.

He ignored her completely. 'We shall of course give you all a handsome pension – three pounds, seven shillings and sixpence a year – more to you of course, Dame Margaret.'

'You wish us to starve to death?' Dame Petronilla said sharply. 'This is monstrous, sir, monstrous!'

Dame Margaret turned to her then. 'There is my family's house in York,' she said quietly. 'It will be all right.'

The men were standing up. 'Then that is settled,' Dr Parr said, running his hands down his paunch with the air of a man well pleased with his afternoon's work. 'We shall have Master Babthorpe here make an inventory of everything.' He had nodded in the direction of one of the men gathering together the papers. 'I do advise you, Dame Margaret,' he added sternly, 'to keep nothing back. Nothing!'

'We have no valuables,' she said in the same quiet, controlled voice.

'We shall see. Master Babthorpe and his helpers are very thorough.'

The immense bulk of the man seemed suddenly to fill the room and she looked at him with loathing. 'How long have we got?'

He hesitated, glancing at Dr Whellan, and then said quickly, 'Two days. No more. It is longer than has been given to most.'

Two days. Only forty-eight hours in which to pull up roots put down forty, fifty, sixty years before. None of the nuns spoke, shocked into a silence more profound than any of them had ever known before, but Dame Margaret said harshly as Dr Parr got to his feet, 'Why has Dom Richard Tyndal been sent to the Tower? He is a good man. Above reproach.'

'It is none of your concern, madame.' Dr Parr bowed briefly and turning, led the way out of the parlour. The others followed him quickly, bowing briefly to the nuns in turn before they walked out of the door.

Edward Dutton was last to leave. Just before he too went through the open doorway he turned to look back at Dame Agatha. Earlier he had wondered if a further conversation with her alone might not be useful, but now, on second thoughts, as he studied her red, frightened face he thought better of it. She had told him enough already. The rest he would find out elsewhere – the boy who had recently been sacked for stealing from the abbey kitchens would be best. He had been lurking in the gatehouse the night the Cîteaux treasure had been smuggled in from Rievaulx – it was the boy who had told him about it. The boy had also said that the monk, Andrew Ellerton, who had been the one who had caught him in the act of stealing, was a very close friend of the abbot's. The boy had overheard them whispering together in the cloister many a time – he was indeed a mine of information, properly handled, and who knew better how to handle a servant with a grievance than Edward Dutton? It was not such a bad thing after all to have the common touch, he thought as he made his way outside to where the others were gathered around their horses.

He nodded to them, trying to catch the eye of Sir Anthony Challoner, but the man was guffawing at some joke of Dr Whellan's and neither saw the nod nor the scowl that followed it. 'A curse on him, anyway!' Edward Dutton muttered, mounting his own horse and gathering his reins, conscious of the fact that he had no servant with him. One of these days fellows like Challoner would have to treat him more civilly – when he owned Wolden Abbey and was *Sir* Edward Dutton! But as he turned his horse's head he had a sudden uncomfortable memory of the morning on which he left London to take part in the Visitation. He saw again his wife's mottled face as she sat up in their four-poster bed, in the bedchamber of their house on Lime Street, her greying hair hanging in greasy plaits over her huge breasts that spilled out from her open shift.

'You're obsessed with Wolden, Edward!' she had screamed at him. 'Why should the King give it to *you*? Especially when the FitzHughs have asked him not to.'

'The FitzHughs!' He had spat the words at her and she had to wipe his spittle from her face. 'The old man is nearly dead, and the young fellow is a fool! Been under his grandfather's thumb for too long! And he's said to have criticised the King. But *I* am loyal, no word of treason has ever passed *my* lips! I've been successful in business too and my family has always owned land – ' His voice had become placating as it always did when she berated him. In one minute, less, she could make him feel like a village idiot.

'It's you who are the fool!' she had screeched at him. '*You'll* not be granted Wolden, whatever way it goes! The few acres your uncle left you don't make you a landowner either! As for a knighthood, you've as much chance of that as I have of lying with the King!' And while he cursed himself, for ever having told her of that particular dream she had lain back in bed laughing, a huge belly laugh that made her breasts shake like bowls of jelly. But he still had not told her of the Cîteaux treasure and his hopes of finding it himself, for fear she would tittle-tattle, and he thanked God that morning that he had kept his mouth shut.

Of recent years the soft feel of her body had begun to revolt him but he had his needs like other men. Afterwards, he would lie beside her, listening to her heavy breathing, fantasising about young breasts, slim legs entwined in his, his body forcing itself in to firm young flesh, and he would wonder if some day he could find enough courage to push her down the stairs or hold a pillow over her wet, loose mouth for long enough.

Even now, thinking about his sexual fantasies had excited him so much that he had to rise in the saddle and stand in his stirrups. He would ride past the abbey on the way back, he decided. That would calm him.

But when the abbey lay before him, its massive dignity mellowed by late evening sunlight, the sight at first failed to soothe him. It would cost him a fortune to dismantle the building, he thought uneasily, for of course he could not afford to live in it. But he would use the stones to build himself a fine house, he told himself quickly, and up on the flat land behind the abbey he would ride his thoroughbred horses, and his sheep would crop the granges and he would be rich beyond his wildest dreams. He would have to borrow at first of course in order to pay the stonemasons – the Italians were the best it was said, but greedy – but he would know how to handle that and no one, no one could stop him, least of all a nearly senile old man or his uppish grandson, with his yellow hair and fancy clothes!

High above him he heard the two-note cry of a curlew and looking up he saw a merlin far below the bird in low-level flight, following every twist and turn of its prey which was as big, if not bigger than itself. He smiled with cold approval as he dug his spurs with deliberate cruelty into the sides of his horse. If he hurried he would reach the inn in East Wooton before sundown, and he would stay there until the trial.

Whellan had told him earlier that day that the abbot would be tried in the town's market-house, when Lord Cromwell had finished with him in London.

They would need as many witnesses as possible, the Visitor had added, putting his finger to the side of his nose, and it was not expected that the abbot would be kept for long in the Tower – Well, Edward Dutton thought now, he himself would not be idle meanwhile. Feeling calm again, all his old confidence restored, he continued on his way.

Chapter Twelve

The singing of the watermen came to the old man through the open bay window, borne on the summer breeze, and the letter that had arrived earlier that afternoon lay on the oak table beside him. They had cushioned the box chair for him but he had so little flesh on his bones now that he still felt uncomfortable, having sat for so long. Yet he was glad to have left his bed at last. If he complained they'd have him back in it and maybe leave him there for good!

'You must rest, Sir William!' He fancied he could hear the physician's unctuous voice again, as if the tapestry-hung walls of the withdrawing-room had absorbed it the previous week and could throw it back at will. 'You are a choleric man. Remember that!'

Cretinous fool, the old man thought now. As soon as he had come out of what he himself called his 'long faint' he had made the fellow take the leeches off – fat and wriggling, swollen with *his* blood! And by Christ, but at nearly seventy a man had not too much to spare of blood or anything else! When he had seen the leeches lying in the dish, he had vomited all over the fool. Serve him right! Just because he had been to Padua and come back with his head stuffed with the New Learning he thought he could lecture his betters!

But under the purple velvet doublet, stained these days with food droppings and spills of wine, Sir William's heart began to race alarmingly. Perhaps the fellow knew something after all, he thought wearily. He leant back, trying to put the urgency of the letter's message away from him, allowing his thoughts to drift.

If only Anna were here – she had always been able to soothe him. Against his closed eyes he could see her now, hair silver-gold against her head-dress, dark eyes watching him gravely. He used to wonder sometimes what she was thinking, but he'd never thought to ask her, and anyway he preferred to remember her as a young bride, chattering in her heavily accented English, laughing.

'She will be big, with yellow hair and bad teeth!' they'd said to him at court. And they had been right, but not about everything. She had been big. Gloriously, wonderfully, big! And her hair had been yellow, but it had been like corn in sunlight, and her teeth had been pearly white and her eyes like brown velvet. His father had done well for him! Anna Hooft! The daughter of one of the richest men in Amsterdam, and a sixteen-year-old virgin to boot! She had soon forgiven him for their wedding night, he remembered, smiling now with a touch of complacency, and the celebrations had gone on for weeks in the Dutch fashion. There had been no honeymoon, as was their way also, and he had got her back to England before winter had come to Critley.

'You were always lucky!' the county had said when they came calling. 'You've the luck of the devil!' Even now, more than fifty years later, he could hear himself laughing, imbecile that he was, but her voice came back over the years to console him.

'I do love you, William! Very, very much!'

How often she had said it in those early days! He'd put his hand into her bodice, or kiss her and she'd cry, 'You must not, William! Not here! The servants! Wait until tonight!' But he had never waited.

When she found out about his other women she cried at first as if her heart was breaking.

'It means nothing, my dear!' he would say to her. 'No more than – no more than an extra bottle of wine. Men must have their little pleasures, you know that – '

'But you are my husband!' she would sob, 'And I *love* you!'

The sudden grunt of the dog sleeping at his feet brought him sharply back to the present and he looked down at his flaccid cod-piece with disgust. So long ago. Another lifetime. And what did love mean, anyway? Whatever it meant it had nothing to do with marriage. Marriage was a business like any other. Anna's dowry had bought this town house and rebuilt Critley, and she had given him two fine sons and a daughter.

They were all gone now, Anna and the children. No one left but himself and Robert, and even though his heartbeat had returned to its normal pace he did not need a fool with a sheep's face and a long gown to tell him that he himself had not much time left. But Robert – what age was the young scamp now? Twenty-two? No, he must be twenty-*three*! High time he was married! I should have seen to it long ago! Sir William told himself – *I* was married at twenty! I should have chosen a wife for him if he would not do it himself. But it was more than just a matter of marrying, the old man thought guiltily. There was the running of the estate as well. I should have given him his head there, he thought. God knows, he'd asked often enough to play a more active part. But he'd been so bullheaded about it all, so sure that he was right.

He could still remember the last scene between them. They had been in the withdrawing-room after supper.

'We need to enclose some of the land, at least,' Robert had said. 'One acre enclosed is worth one and a half in the common field.' He had been standing with his back to the charcoal brazier and his very stance had been galling – arrogant and cocksure. 'Then each tenant should retain his own plot as well as have access to the common.' He had added with a touch of belligerence, 'Some of 'em may need to be rehoused – I remember hovels – '

'Have you lost your wits? Where am I to find the money?' His own voice had risen to a shout.

'We're not exactly paupers, and if you'd take my advice and cross Spanish rams with the cheviots you'd make a deal more from the wool. I could go to Spain for you!'

'You'll stay here! At court! And grow a beard!'

'To curry favour with a King I despise, a murderer and a – '

'Keep your voice down, you fool!' he'd interrupted, in sudden terror that the servants might have overheard them. 'D'you want to end your days in the Tower, like the rest?'

But the young cub would not listen. 'The whole of London knows what I think,' he'd said, making no effort to lower his voice, and his own control had snapped then. He'd got to his feet and they had stood eyeball to eyeball, glaring at each other. 'Perhaps it would be best to bury you in the country,' he had roared at his grandson, 'Maybe the smell of cow dung would bring you to your senses!'

Robert's face had been tight with anger, reminding him suddenly of Anna after one of their quarrels, and he had stalked out of the room, chin up, shoulders well back, hair gleaming in the candlelight, and he himself had had a second's blinding insight into his own heart and seen the truth. He was jealous of his own grandson, jealous of his youth, his virility, the good looks that had once been his, long, long ago. Jealous that Robert and not he would live to see the changes that were coming, that must come if England were to hold her own. And because of jealousy he had hoarded all authority, clutching at every morsel, the least hint of power like a miser hoarding his money.

He had sat down again, staring into the leaping flames of the fire, seeing nothing there but his own death and the ending of all power, all authority. He had been taught to believe in heaven and hell and an intermediate place called purgatory, but he was not really sure that he believed in any of them. In his lifetime he had seen enough corpses to know how soon flesh putrifies. How could one believe in heaven with that stink in one's nostrils, he had asked himself that evening. Easier to believe in hell – and yet some died with a smile on their face, as if they had seen a vision, a sweetness beyond words – as Anna had done. Perhaps death was not the end after all, he had thought. It would be easier to let go, to go, if one could believe that, *really* believe it.

But a few days later when he became ill he still had not wanted to go. In any case he had recovered, and although he knew himself now to be powerless to do many things that would have to be left to Robert whether he liked it or not, he was more determined than ever to expedite the marriage. The wedding must not be postponed a second time.

The old man frowned. The girl might be the niece of the Earl of Westmorland, but a wife needed to be strong as well as willing if she was to bear sons, and he had not known Beatrice Neville had weak lungs – on every other count, however, Robert had made a wise choice, or rather he had made it for him. Still, a man must have sons, and it was only a King who could easily rid himself of a wife who could not bear male children.

Sir William belched weakly. God's truth, but Henry was a King to be remembered! For that and for his greed! What was it the Frenchman had said about him? 'All the wealth of the world would not satisfy the King of England's ambition' – and the new men that surrounded him, overnight rich, they were as greedy as their master! Petty fogging clerks, most of 'em, waiting like hungry curs for a fat monastery to fall into their laps so that they could join the ranks of landed gentlemen and count themselves their equal – men like Edward Dutton. The old man's pale, thin lips with their hint of cruelty tightened over the shrunken gums, and he helped himself to a mouthful of malmsey from the jack at his elbow, wiping a trickle from his chin with the other hand, not able to prevent its trembling. The wine slid down his throat like sweet, white fire and he reached for more, but this time when he attempted to replace the jack on the table it overturned, spilling its contents on the rush covered floor. Damnation! He'd soon be as helpless as a child! He was beginning to feel uncomfortable now for another reason and he rang the handbell for the woman servant who acted as his nurse. She came in at once from her post outside the withdrawing-room where she had been waiting all afternoon.

'Bring me the piss-pot,' he growled, 'and tell 'em to send Master Robert to me!'

When Robert came to him half an hour later Sir William was dozing. The room smelt of urine and dog and Robert went across to the still open bay window to draw in lungfuls of fresh, summer air. Below the slope of the garden he could see their own private landing-place and the barge standing idle since his last foray into the city a couple of nights before. He had had a thick head the day after, and a lean purse and it had all been to no purpose. More than eight months ago and he could still see her, still hear her voice, still feel her skin against his. Hell and damnation but he *was* bewitched! Why in God's name did they ever have to meet, or having once met why had he not stayed away?

It was not even as if she were truly beautiful – or outstandingly witty – or skilled in the art of making love. In his mind he tried to belittle her, to reduce her in any way he could, but it was no use. The stillness that was in her like a deep, deep pool in which a man could drown and find new life, the glorious passion – he could not belittle *them*. And he was still ashamed of what he had done. He had not consciously meant to do it – he told himself that often and knew that he was lying at the same time. He had wanted her from the beginning and everything he had done from that moment on was done with one end in view. It had driven him to climb the convent wall that night, and afterwards, as the ivy came away and he fell to the ground, as he crouched there sure that he had been discovered – even then, behind the shame there had been a wild, triumphant exultation. But it had not lasted, and when it was gone there was only the shame and an abiding sense of loss, for although he had taken, he had, in spite of himself, also given. Was he never then to feel really whole again? He should have persuaded her to come away with him, taken her to London, hidden her where only he could find her, until the fever had burnt itself out.

One thing he was sure of, he would not find peace with Beatrice Neville. Down on the river the wherries and barges made their slow way to and from the city, while inshore a swan lead its flock of cygnets in search of food, but he did not really see any of them. Instead he saw himself and John arriving at the Nevilles' castle in Raskelfe in mid-October, after they had left the abbey. They had ridden through the park, past the fish pond and the bowling green, crossing the moat and entering the great hall as the wall tapers were being lit.

Beatrice Neville had come to meet him immediately, a tall, thin woman with a long nose and receding chin. Her mousey hair was frizzed to cover a too-high forehead and her narrow, slanting eyes were too knowing. She was no beauty indeed, and no virgin either, he judged as he bowed over her hand while a multiplicity of cousins and other relations gathered around them. Afterwards she led him to the top table for it was now supper-time and introduced him to her uncle, Ralph Neville, Earl of Westmorland. He was nearly forty, a tall, commanding figure in doublet of cloth-of-gold with a matching gown edged with fur. It was well known that Raskelfe was his favourite residence and certainly that evening he seemed relaxed and welcoming, as indeed was his wife, the Countess Catherine, grown enormous over the years after bearing him a flock of children.

Robert had been seated beside Beatrice but he could think of nothing to say to her and he had eaten in gloomy silence until it was time for the dancing to begin. He had led her out then to a clapping of hands and shouts of encouragement from the company, most of whom seemed to be more than half drunk. It was a pavan, and she was graceful enough, but he found himself thinking of Isobel, wondering if those small, perfect feet had ever danced, if he would ever dance with her, knowing that he was dreaming of the impossible at the same time. He had led Beatrice Neville back to the table then, and after she had thanked him and he had bowed to her, she said at last, 'Have you nothing to say to me, Robert?' Her voice was oddly hoarse, and he thought grimly of what it would be like when she was older.

'I am sorry,' he said briefly. 'It has been a long journey – perhaps when we know each other better – '

She had smiled, a smile full of promise and he had looked away. By Christ, but when he had done his duty on her he'd leave her alone for good! But he had to sit beside her again, and watch while she settled the skirts of her gown. It was a truly magnificent creation of yellow silk, cascading to the ground from a tiny waist, above which the low, square-cut bodice showed her bony chest and long neck. He himself had changed from the clothes which had got muddied in his fall the previous night and he wore now a doublet and breeches of a green so dark it looked black in the candlelight, relieved only by the narrow collar of his white linen shirt. Against the glowing colours worn by the other men he seemed to be wearing mourning clothes and they suited his mood, if not the occasion.

The Earl sent for the Fool then and while the company laughed at his antics Robert continued to stare sullenly in front of him, until the little fellow sidled up to him and said out of the corner of his mouth, 'For pity's sake, smile, kind sir! Else they'll have my balls for breakfast!'

So Robert had forced himself to smile and the Fool had run out into the middle of the floor and turned a summersault. Later Robert had danced again with Beatrice and forced himself to talk about nothing and at last the interminable evening had come to an end.

A week of lavish entertainment had followed – hunting with her cousins and the other guests – she did not hunt – feasting at night, dancing and playing cards, and occasional walks with her in the rose garden, always heavily chaperoned, and her servant, Walter Clifford, a slightly built, dour man, hovering in the background. Robert had scarcely noticed him in the beginning, but as the days went by he became increasingly aware of the fellow's almost constant presence.

'He follows you around like a pet dog,' he said irritably one day to her.

She had shrugged her bony shoulders. 'He's more than just a servant – a kind of poor relation, I'm told. And he acts as my – my watchdog, on occasions.'

'Watchdog?' He had laughed aloud. 'I could lift him up in one hand!'

She had given him a long look, 'Walter has his own special strengths.'

'Indeed?'

'They are not what you might think!' Her voice was suddenly sharp. 'I am not like the ladies at court.'

'I am sure you are not!' He had bowed, his voice without expression and she had added hastily, as if to try to keep the peace between them, 'When you get to know Walter better you will grow to like him.'

It seemed highly unlikely, Robert thought, although he did not say so, and by the end of the week he did not know even Beatrice any better, nor was he any more interested in getting to know either one of them.

On the last evening her uncle called him into his study. The Earl was dressed in the height of fashion as usual – a doublet of scarlet silk, the huge sleeves slashed like his breeches showing a lining of sky blue, with a long over-gown of a deeper scarlet edged with fur and reaching to the ground. There was a heavy gold chain around his thick neck and an enormous emerald in the ring he wore on his forefinger. Robert was as tall as he was and yet he felt small and insignificant for the first time in his life. Even his grandfather, for all his bullying, had never made him feel like this and he knew that the moment he had been dreading for so long had come at last.

'The date, Robert!' the Earl said as soon as he had closed the door of the study behind him. 'When is the marriage to take place?'

He could have left then, said there would be no wedding, but his sense of duty was too strong to do that and besides, what was the use? It might as well be Beatrice Neville if he could not make his own choice. Dreams were only for fools and poets.

Even so he would not agree to marry before the spring, and in the end it was agreed to have the wedding in the first week after Easter, and the betrothal ceremony that evening. With a great show of bonhomie the Earl had called then for wine and they had lifted their goblets, looking at each other with mutual dislike.

'Robert! Are you there? I've been asleep – can't sleep o' nights and can't stay awake during the day! God's curse on it but it ain't a pleasant thing growing old – '

His grandfather's voice brought him back to the present and he turned away from the window and drew up a stool to sit beside the old man. 'They tell me you are feeling better?'

'Aye, a mite better,' the old man admitted grudgingly. 'But I've had a letter that has put me down.'

'What about?' Robert could not keep the note of hope out of his voice.

'Oh, 'tis not about the wedding,' his grandfather said dryly. 'The wedding will be as arranged, in September. She should be recovered by then. No. 'Tis about the abbey.' He reached for the piece of parchment and smoothed it with a shaking hand. 'I've still got friends at court and they write to tell me that Dom Richard, poor fellow, has been taken to the Tower to be questioned by Cromwell. Since the new act was passed the King can take any monastery he has a fancy to if he can prove treason.'

'But I don't see the abbot as a traitor to the King!'

'Don't be a fool! Anything at all can be called treason these days – any word of criticism. The vultures will be gathering!'

'What can we do?'

'For the abbot? Nothing. I shall write to the King again on his behalf, but 'tis a waste of time. But you can get up there rightaway and see the treasure out of the country. We can do that, at least.'

'If I can find it.'

'You'll have that young monk, what's his name? – to help you, though for the life o' me I cannot see why Dom Richard did not tell you everything when you were there before.'

Robert shrugged. 'I suppose he had his reasons – ' but his mind was not really on what he was saying. He did not want to go back to Yorkshire again, did not want to set foot in the abbey or go anywhere near the convent. He wanted to forget the whole, fog-ridden wilderness! Above all he wanted to forget *her*, otherwise this marriage that he had to endure would be unendurable. But he had given his word. He must get the treasure back to Cîteaux. It did occur to him that should things go badly wrong it was conceivable that the wedding might have to be postponed to an even later date. 'I shall go up tomorrow,' he said more cheerfully, 'and take John with me.'

'Good!' His grandfather peered at his letter again. 'They've closed the convent already, damn them! Sent the good ladies packing!' He gave a dry cackle of laughter. 'I wonder for what reason, eh? Hardly incontinence at their age! Although, come to think of it, there *was* one young one!' When Robert said nothing the old man went on harshly. 'Don't underestimate Edward Dutton, though! He wants Wolden. Marmaduke Constable got Drax last year and 'tis said Roger Cholmley has his eye on Whitby Abbey. Dutton sees himself as landed gentry, poor fool, and maybe with a knighthood some day. *And* he has taken a dislike to you!'

'But I've never even met the man!'

'You have. *And* snubbed him and his family what's more! Last Twelfth Night, it seems. Someone introduced you and you made it clear you were not much taken with his daughter, or himself, or his lady wife!'

'Twelfth Night? But the whole world goes to it! I don't remember.'

'Probably too drunk! Anyway, *he* remembers *you*, unfortunately. Told someone afterwards that you were an arrogant young pup!'

101

Robert grunted. 'Have you any idea what he looks like?'

His grandfather waved a still elegant hand. 'Not a gentleman, of course. Middle-aged, stout body, nondescript, I'm told.'

'No wonder I don't remember him.'

'Well, best mark him well the next time! If he gets to the treasure before you he'll use it to curry favour with the King and feather his own nest.'

The old man's head was beginning to shake which it seemed to do of recent months when he was becoming tired or upset about something. It was time to leave, and even as Robert got up off the stool his grandfather closed his eyes and appeared to doze once more.

Robert had had every intention of setting out for the north at dawn on the following day and John had seen to their horses and baggage for the journey, but that night his grandfather had gone into another of his 'long faints'. The doctor did not hold out much hope of his recovery and Robert refused to let him bleed the old man this time. But on the fourth day Sir William had opened his eyes and demanded wine in a surprisingly strong voice and by the end of the week, to the doctor's disgruntled surprise, he seemed almost to have recovered and Robert judged it safe to leave him.

One week. Seven days and nights. Not a long period of time, although long enough for events to happen that would change his own life and the lives of many others. But Robert sometimes wondered afterwards if his grandfather had not had another stroke and he himself had been able to leave on that first day, would the events that followed have fallen out all that differently.

Chapter Thirteen

They were waiting for Isobel in the doorway of the farmhouse as the cart rumbled to a halt, her father and step-mother, two toddlers peeping around the woman's skirts. Her father made no move to help her down, although she had the baby in her arms, and when old John handed her the satchel she had to put it on the ground at once for fear of dropping the child.

'Thank you,' she said, looking up into the whiskered, wrinkled face under the battered hat, wondering if Dame Margaret had paid him and embarrassed that she could not even mention money for she had not a single farthing to her name. The old man nodded, looking briefly at the group standing in the doorway. Then he lifted his reins and shouted at his mare who looked nearly as old as himself. With a creak and a groan the cart moved forward, and when it was out of sight behind the barn her father came to meet her.

'Whore!' he said, slapping her across the face with his open hand. 'That's all you are. Nowt but a common whore!'

Only her iron resolve not to drop the baby kept her on her feet. There was a ringing in her ears and the side of her face felt on fire. She stepped back, fighting for composure, determined not to cry. 'I did not want to come back, but I had no choice.' Lifting her head, her voice clear now, suddenly under control. 'I will not stay a day longer than I have to, you may be sure of that.'

'I'm right glad to hear it!' he said. 'I had no choice either, in taking you, but I didn't say I'd keep you for long, or t'brat either, for that matter.' For the first time he looked down at the bundle in her arms and she drew the shawl protectively over the baby's

103

face as if she were warding off the evil eye. 'Something wrong with it, eh?'

Over his shoulder she met the eyes of her step-mother, small, hard eyes, over high, bony cheekbones, but with a sudden unexpected look of sympathy in them now. She was heavy with child, and in five years of marriage had aged beyond belief. Her cheeks, that Isobel remembered as apple-red, were now a sickly yellow, her eyes sunk far back in her head, even her hair that had been gypsy black, was streaked with grey.

'The baby is perfectly healthy,' she said coldly, looking now at her father, at the network of broken veins that covered his face, the dirty stubble of beard on his jaw which once had been lean and strong and now was lost in pouches of fat. She remembered the fine-looking man he once had been. What had happened to him?

He grunted, his mouth twisting. 'Who's t'father then, or don't you know?'

She shifted the baby to a more comfortable position on her hip, wishing that she was a man and could hit that twisted, bitter mouth. She said slowly, 'I know who he is, but that is my concern, not yours.'

He took a swift step forward, his clenched fist raised and for the first time the woman in the doorway spoke. 'Leave be, Ben, for God's sake!'

He dropped his fist slowly, the fingers uncurling. 'None o' my concern, is it not? Do you know – ' He came even nearer, so that she could feel his warm, onion-smelling breath on her face. 'D'you know that you've made me, Ben Willis, the laughing stock o' Yorkshire? An' more than that! You've shamed me, disgraced me, you little slut!' It was as if a dam had given way. Through his open mouth there came a flood of words, an incoherent babble of sound only some of which made sense. He mentioned her mother's name once as though for some reason he blamed her for her daughter's disgrace. At last he ran out of breath. 'I'll get the name o' the father yet if I have to beat you for it!' he panted.

She said nothing, just stood there, looking at him, and at last, in disgust, he turned away but over his shoulder he said harshly, 'Go in t'house and make yourself useful. Your step-mother could do with a hand, and if you've any high and mighty ideas of playing t'lady like your mother, you can forget them!'

When she still said nothing he added furiously, 'And you'll not leave t'farm! You stay here, where I can keep an eye on you! No roaming! I'll not have every man in the parish sniffing after you!'

With a grunted aside to his wife he stumped out of the yard, leaving Isobel standing there looking after him, feeling as if he had emptied a pail of dung over her and wondering if she would ever feel clean again.

'Tha's best come in t'house,' her step-mother said from the doorway.

Slowly, reluctantly, picking up the satchel with her free hand, Isobel walked over to her and followed her into the dark passage beyond. How small the house seemed now, even with the lean-tos that had been added on over the years. The woman took her past the parlour, its shutters still closed against the sunlight, and on into the kitchen. And how small *it* seemed, and dirty and untidy as well. She remembered it in her mother's time. The table scrubbed white, the stone floor spotless, the smell of freshly baked bread and everything in its proper place. Now there was a clutter of unwashed bowls on the stained table, there were pools of water on the floor, and instead of the smell of freshly baked bread there was the acrid smell of stale urine. Even as she came in through the door one of the toddlers urinated in front of her and received not a word of scolding from his mother.

'Your father sent t'lass an' t'owd woman away,' her step-mother said. 'Told me I wouldn't need them now that tha's come back!' Her gown, though plain, was of good woollen cloth, but it was spattered with stains and her hair straggled untidily from under her hood. 'I'm nearly killed wi' backwark,' she added, sitting down heavily on the bench beside the open fire over which a pot hung from an iron bar. 'But sit awhile tha'self. Tha must be tired.'

Isobel sat down beside her, pulling back the shawl a little for fear the baby would get too hot, glad to be sitting, glad of even a pretence of friendship when she had only expected hostility.

'Thou little nazzart!' the woman said, reaching out a not very clean hand and touching the baby's cheek. 'What's his name?'

105

'Christopher.'

'So he's been baptised?'

'Yes.' Isobel did not say that he had been baptised twice – once by herself, just in case, since he was so small, and once, later by the chaplain. Dame Cecilia had taken the baby away and returned with him half an hour later.

'A bit on the small side, ain't he?' her step-mother remarked. 'How old is he?'

'A week.'

'Mebbe he'll fill out. Was it hard?' The small eyes bored into hers as the woman waited hopefully for all the details of the birth.

'Hard enough,' Isobel said briefly, letting a silence fall. There was a look of disappointment on her step-mother's face but after a moment she set off at another tangent. 'Your father's been ravin' mad! But no more 'n t'abbess, I reckon?' Open, avid curiosity now in her face.

But Isobel refused to be drawn. 'I prefer not to talk about it,' she said coolly.

The woman tried again. 'What's it like then, bein' a nun?' She stared at Isobel's short hair, revealed since her shawl had slipped back off her head. 'It ain't a natural way to live, surely?'

'Some day I shall tell you about it,' Isobel promised, 'but not now.'

Mercifully the baby began to stir in her arms, the tiny brows puckered in a frown. 'I shall have to feed him soon. When will my father be back?'

'Too soon! But there's time – I'll reckle t'fire up!'

Isobel opened the front of her dress and put the baby to her breast, the heat of the fire warm on her face, reminded her of the feel of her father's hand not so long before. How was she to live under the same roof with him, even though her step-mother, or Joan as she wanted to be called, seemed friendly enough? But if she did leave, where would she go, she asked herself.

She had finished feeding the baby and was about to put him to sleep in the old cradle of woven willow rods that Joan had given her for him, when a young fellow came into the kitchen carrying a pail of milk. He put the pail down and stood there, staring at her and the baby with an insolence that brought the

106

colour to her face, and she bent hastily over the cradle until Joan came back into the kitchen. Only then did the fellow leave.

Straightening, Isobel raised her flushed face and met the other woman's eyes. 'They'll get used to it in a day or so,' Joan said cheerfully. 'Pay no heed!'

But Isobel was still angry when her father came in shortly afterwards demanding his supper. Mercifully he ignored her and scarcely spoke to his wife who sat him down at the table and put a trencher piled high with cold meat, and bread and cheese in front of him. Isobel was soon to discover that the house was usually silent when he was at home, for he spoke to his wife only when complaining or demanding some service or other. Even the two little boys ran out to the yard as soon as his bulky frame filled the doorway, squeezing past him or through his legs. He would try to grab them and put them on his shoulder, but they were afraid of him and he would shout after them as they ran off and take his frustration out on whichever of the two women was nearest, complaining bitterly that the bread had not risen enough or the meat was over-cooked or his ale too warm. Then he would doze by the fire later on, a jug of ale on the floor beside him, until by bedtime he was more than half drunk.

On this, her first night at home, she and Joan ate their supper while he nodded by the fire, as they were to do for the rest of her time there. Half-way through the meal she asked Joan where she and the baby were to sleep.

The woman looked embarrassed and said hastily. 'In – in t'loft. There's no room down here, what wi' the children an ' – an"

'But there are rats up there!'

'No! No! There are no rats – not in t'summer – and 'tis warm, right warm – '

'But – '

Her step-mother nodded towards the snoring figure in front of the fire. 'He's said that's where tha sleeps! Tha's got no choice! But I've put extra blankets up there an 'tis clean enough.' After a moment she added, her sallow skin flushing slightly. 'He's afeared tha might – might go out o' nights, but if tha's up there – ' She left the sentence unfinished, and now it was Isobel's turn to flush, a deep, painful wave of hot colour that swept over her whole body.

She looked at her father's recumbent body with loathing. How could he think – how could he? And yet, was it not what everyone would think, was it not what that yokel had had in mind when he came in earlier and stared at her – that she was a whore, who would lie with any man who came to her, or who would slip out of the house like a bitch in season and go to whoever came. What was it her father had said? Whoever came 'sniffing after her'.

She pushed away her plate, her meat only half eaten. 'I've had enough,' she said dully. 'I'm not hungry.' Suddenly she had to be alone, and if there was no place but the loft, well, so be it. Lifting the cradle she carried it over to the rickety ladder that led up to the loft. After a moment her step-mother came over to help her and between them they got the cradle through the roof hole.

The loft floor was covered with straw, and a mattress had been thrown down on it with a few blankets and a pillow filled with chaff. There was a stool and a jug and basin and an empty pail. That was all.

Long ago, a lifetime ago, in this same house she had had a box bed in a wall cupboard beside her parents' bed, with a shelf for her rag dolls and hooks from which to hang her clothes. She had had sheets and a patchwork quilt and thick, fleecy blankets, and in winter a special cover of budge to keep her warm. But that had been the other Isobel, whose own mother had been still alive – the little girl who should have been a boy and who had not yet lived long enough to disgrace herself and her father and make him the laughing stock of Yorkshire.

When Joan had handed the baby up to her and gingerly made her way down the ladder again, Isobel sat down on the mattress, holding the small, warm body close to her, letting the tears come at last.

But she could not stay in the loft for ever, and in the days, the weeks that followed, she found herself working as hard as any kitchen drudge, and not only in the kitchen. She worked in the dairy, scouring the shelves and the pans and being shouted at by her father if the butter was slow in coming, and in the yard, feeding the calves and the hens and collecting their eggs for Joan's 'stocking' – her step-mother had lost no time in telling her that Ben Willis was tight with his money.

The loft became Isobel's private retreat, and the summer days slipped past in a haze of fatigue and a kind of quiet misery. When harvest time came she was allowed to play no part in it. There was no celebrating this year anyway, but she had to get the food ready for the young farm boy Joseph, and two dour, older men to take out to the workers every day. Joseph's manner had changed from insolence to an easy familiarity which was worse. The two other men, who were also strangers to her, ignored her as her father did, until one day one of them touched his cap to her and bid her good-day. She was so astonished she just stood there staring at him, but the next day he did the same thing and this time she was quicker and returned his greeting with a small, tentative smile. After that his companion followed suit and even Joseph's easy smile became tinged with a new respect.

At night she was so tired that she fell asleep the moment her head touched the hard pillow, to be wakened a couple of hours later by the crying of the baby. She was used to being wakened in the middle of the night, but somehow this was different, and life in the convent seemed now to have been one of leisure compared to her present existence. She would pick up the baby and put him to her breast with a feeling of anger and near dislike that frightened her. What kind of mother was she to feel like this? He could not help it, but oh, for a whole night's sleep! And sitting up on the hard mattress as he sucked the milk that came freely now, she would will herself not to fall asleep, not to lie on him.

Then she would find herself thinking of Robert. Was he sleeping now beside his new wife, making love to her, perhaps? And did he ever think of her, ever remember? But although the pain never left her, she had begun to distance her memories of him from reality. Reality was a hungry baby who constantly needed to be cleaned. Reality was working from sun-up to sundown. And reality was her father's anger, of which she was always uneasily aware, as one is aware of a bubbling pot that is about to boil over.

Gradually, however, the baby began to sleep for longer periods. In turn she began to feel stronger, to know the pleasure of feeling hungry again, able to enjoy the mutton, the rabbit pies, the fresh green vegetables, the hard, pale cheese that went so well with Joan's fruit cake. For her step-mother was a good enough cook, even if she was a bad housekeeper, and she was generous too in an off-handed way that maddened her penny-pinching husband. But although Isobel's breasts were swollen, her stomach was as flat as though she had never had a baby and her face had grown thin, her eyes looking back at her from Joan's hand mirror with a kind of fearful intensity that made her throw down the mirror.

And yet, although she did not realise it herself she had brought a kind of gentleness home with her to the farmhouse. The shutters were put back now in the parlour at her request and sunlight flooded the house, even if sometimes they still had to be shut because of the smell from the midden, and there were no longer hairs and bits of straw floating in the milk. Her two little step-brothers, Matthew and Simon, adored her – she had only to raise her eyebrows for them to obey her. There were no more pools on the kitchen floor, and if they had a tantrum it was to her they ran, not to their mother.

Joan was so heavy now, so tired most of the time that she did not seem to care. She made no secret of the fact that she had not wanted Isobel or Christopher in the beginning. But once they had actually come she had changed her mind. She seemed delighted now to have someone to talk to, someone who listened, for "t'owd woman was deaf, an' t'lass was simple! An', well, tha knows thy father, an' he wants no folk to coom to t'house!' Joan did not seem to realise that after the first day Isobel did not listen either and had soon found a way to let her step-mother rattle on with just the occasional interjection to reassure her. As a result there was peace in the noisy, busy kitchen.

Towards the end of the month Ben Willis went into East Wooton to the market, leaving at dawn with the pigs he was to sell, silent as ever but in no worse a humour than usual. There was more than enough work to keep Isobel fully occupied, but she managed to find a half hour in the evening, after the supper dishes had been cleared away in which she could relax. Her father had not yet returned, and she brought the baby out to the last of the day's sun.

She sat in the meadow beyond the barn, the baby lying on his shawl, kicking his legs and crowing with delight as she

110

tickled his cheek with a blade of grass. His eyes had gradually changed from blue to brown – Joan had told her that all babies' eyes were blue when they were born – and he had a tiny curl of corn coloured hair on the top of his head, like the curl on a duck's tail.

'Bless you!' she whispered, gathering him up in her arms and hugging him. 'Oh, bless you!' And for the first time, the very first time, she thanked God most humbly for the gift He had given her.

She laid the baby gently down on the grass again and turned back the shawl so that the sun could warm his bare skin. He gurgled with joy, smiling his toothless smile. One day, she thought, God willing, he would be a man – the fruit of a few moments' madness, that she had carried for nine weary months, that had burst from her womb in pain and agony – the memory of that agony blurred, forgotten.

Her father's shout was like a blow to the heart. He was walking towards her, hatless, from the cart which she had not heard returning, and even at a distance she could see that his face was mottled with rage. 'Come here!' he shouted again.

Slowly, protectively, she picked up the baby, holding him close to her and began to walk across the meadow to meet her father.

'Is it true?' He was beginning to bellow like a maddened bull when she was still a few yards away from him. 'Is it true what they're saying – that Andrew Ellerton is t'father of your child?'

'Andrew?' she repeated, when she had come closer. 'Of course not! It's a stupid lie!'

'They're saying that he came to see you in t'convent.'

'He did. Twice this year. But only for a few minutes each time. What are you suggesting?' Her voice was hard with incredulous anger.

But he did not answer her directly. 'Where did you see him?'

'In the parlour, once, and the next time, in the cloister.'

'Was there anyone else with you?'

'No! Of course not! I had permission from Lady Abbess – and he was my cousin.'

'So you were alone?'

111

'Yes, but what you are suggesting is – is not only obscene – it is impossible!'

'Don't play t'high and mighty with me, lass! I am a plain man as you well know and when I hear what they be saying about you it makes me want to vomit!' He took a deep breath as if fighting hard to control himself.

'Why don't you ask Andrew if you don't believe me?' she suggested coldly.

'He's disappeared,' her father said heavily. 'The King's men are out looking for him, and they've taken t'abbot away and closed t'abbey and t'convent.'

So it has come at last, she thought, trying to imagine the convent empty, abandoned. And feeling nothing. 'Why do they want Andrew?' she asked after a moment.

'They think he's hidden t'treasure – a chalice and God knows what else that came from France years ago.'

'And has he?'

'I don't know,' her father growled. 'I hope he has and that he gets it away to some safe place, but I wish to Christ – ' He broke off to glare at her and added viciously, 'They're saying too that t'abbot let the abbey be turned into a whorehouse – all because of you and Andrew – '

'But I told you, it's a lie! I don't even *like* Andrew!' It was childish, but she had had to say it.

'What has liking to do with it?' her father roared. 'I'm talking about lust and stupidity and – and a good man's weakness!' He lifted his clenched fist as if to strike her and then dropped it as she drew quickly back out of his reach. 'Andrew has been like t'son I never had,' he said hoarsely. 'I used to hope that he and you – but he got religious and your mother packed you off t'convent. Dom Richard thought t'world of him – when he chose him out of all t'others for Oxford 'twas t'proudest moment of my life!'

Isobel felt a sudden, unexpected twinge of sympathy for this ageing, unhappy man who was her father but who might have been a total stranger for all he meant to her. She could think of nothing to say and he went on hoarsely, dropping his voice almost to a whisper. 'Can you imagine what 'tis like for a man like me, for a family like ours, to have a scholar, a man of t'church that we can call our own? But of course you don't! No more 'n she does!' He jerked his head backwards in the direction of the house. 'But your mother would have understood,' he added, as if speaking to himself. '*She*'d have understood.'

'I do understand,' she said quietly, 'but you must believe me. Andrew is not the father of my child. He could not be.'

'Then who is?' He was beginning to roar again. 'By God, if you don't tell me – ' Again he raised his fist, and terrified that he might hurt the baby, she said between her teeth, her chin up, all sympathy gone, 'All right! I shall tell you – not that the truth will do you any good. Robert FitzHugh is Christopher's father.'

He let his arm fall slowly to his side, staring at her as if she had two heads. 'Robert FitzHugh?' he said, and then he began to laugh, an ugly sound that was worse than any shouting. 'The FitzHughs have taken half t'women in t'dales, but not t'Willis women, not till now!'

She looked him in the eye. 'Robert is not like that.' She tried to say it with confidence.

'I doubt that he's any different! But I'm talking about his father, and his grandfather and his great-grandfather and all t'others before 'em who took their rights.' And then he added with a look of cunning in his face, 'But there was never a woman that was not left with a bit o' gold in her hand. Does he know?'

'No,' she said shortly, 'and I won't tell him, either.'

'Then you're an even greater fool than I thought! You expect me to bring up his bastard for nowt?'

'No, I don't,' she said coolly. 'As soon as I can, I shall leave here and find work.'

'Who'll want an ex-nun with a brat, eh?' he said grimly.

She looked at him with cold dislike, but she could think of no answer that would carry conviction, for had not her own common-sense been saying the same thing for some time?

'Where – how – did you meet him?' he asked at last.

'He was staying in the abbey guest-house,' she said dully.

He nodded. 'Of course! I remember hearing – And you went to him there?'

He had said it as if she were a mare that had gone to be served. With a small, choking sound she ran past him, back to the house, climbing the ladder to the loft before Joan could say anything to her.

* * *

113

In the loft she knelt and put the baby back in its cradle with shaking hands, covering him, her own body as cold as if it was mid-winter instead of only the end of summer, the poison of her father's words not only in her mind it seemed, but in her blood as well. It was as if evil possessed him, spilled out from him through his mouth. How could her mother have loved him enough to elope with him? How could she have believed he loved her? Had he been so good-looking, had she been so lonely that she could not see him for what he really was? Was love always blind then, so that one did not see the thorns for the honey?

But maybe she was wrong about her father. Maybe he was, after all, capable of finer feelings, maybe he had in his own way even loved her mother once and found his own thorns, had bled and was still bleeding? And if he was angry now, could she really blame him? Had she not indeed brought disgrace on him and on the convent, and it would seem on the abbey too. But how could he believe that she and Andrew – how could anyone believe it?

Sitting down on the stool she began to go back over what he had said, pushing the hurt into some dark corner of her mind. He was repeating gossip surely but who were 'they'? The men he met at the market, who helped him during the year as he helped them, who used to dance with their wives in the Willis barn at the harvest festival? Or were 'they' the wives themselves who used to come visiting, when her mother was alive, sitting in the tiny parlour while her pretty, smiling mother tried desperately not to seem 'uppish' as they filled the small room with their noisy, boisterous laughter? Or were 'they' the men from East Wooton who drank with him in the tavern there, or men from the village over the hill?

Gossip. Feathers in the wind, impossible to catch, let alone hold. She looked down at her hands, folded in her lap, at her feet, close together in the straw, and thought, I still sit like a nun. Her thoughts turned to the convent. They must have had so little time to get ready, and where had they gone to? The house in York was said to be small and not all had wanted to go there anyway. And how had they managed to move out the old, invalid nun from the infirmary, Dame Ita, who had nearly died of cold with her companion the previous winter? Dame Cecilia would have had her hands full! She smiled, remembering the

114

infirmarian's kindness, her compassion. She had thought she felt nothing when her father had told her the convent was closed, but she was wrong. Did one always then leave some part of oneself behind, whether one wanted to or not, she wondered, and looking down at her bare, ringless finger she wondered too if the abbess would ever forgive her, or she the abbess. Life would be much simpler, she thought bleakly, if one expected nothing from anybody.

For once she could hear the murmur of voices from the kitchen below and she guessed that they were talking about her. She would not go down again tonight – she did not want to go down ever again, but the morning would come, and all the other mornings.

Slowly she took off the gown that she had had to ask Joan for in order to wash the one Dame Cecilia had given her. It was an ugly shade of blue and far too big for her, but she had not had the time or the energy up to then to alter it for herself, so that it hung drearily to her feet, not touching her body at any point. She laid it carefully nevertheless across the stool and got under the bedcovers in her shift, lying back and closing her eyes. Soon she would sleep as she always did now, and the present and the past would recede and leave her in peace for a few hours at least.

But she did not sleep for a long time. She found herself thinking of Andrew. Had he found friends to shelter him, another monastery, perhaps? How angry he would be if he heard the gossip – and suddenly the fear that had been with her since her father had spoken to her, unrecognised until now, grinned at her from the darkness like one of the gargoyles that she had seen in paintings of ancient cathedrals. It was not a fear that she could put a name to, and it was not fear certainly of Andrew, but it stayed with her even in the sleep that eventually came to her, so that her dreams were feverish and she woke the next morning with an aching head.

Chapter Fourteen

The men came for her early next morning, riding into the yard with a clatter of hooves, two of them coming into the kitchen through the open door without as much as a by-your-leave, the third remaining outside to hold their horses. One was middle-aged, prosperous looking, like a townsman, his face as pale as if it was mid-winter. The other was younger, rough-looking, wearing a blue sash and carrying a pike.

'What – what does tha want?' Joan gasped, looking up from the table where she and Isobel were kneading dough.

'We have come for Mistress Isobel Willis, ma'am,' the older man said curtly. 'Are you she?' He looked directly at Isobel with colourless, yet sharp eyes that drifted slowly from her face down to her feet and seemed to pierce the shapeless cloth of her gown. It was like being touched by a corpse.

She felt herself begin to shiver and pushed the hair that had grown a little in the past few weeks off her face. 'Yes' she said curtly. 'I am Isobel Willis. Who are you, and what do you want with me?'

He did not answer her for a moment, and now his eyes were on her mouth, and he ran the tip of his tongue over his own thick, rubbery lips, smiling slightly. Then the smile faded and he said in a voice as curt as her own, 'You are required today as a witness in the trial of Abbot Richard Tyndal, in East Wooton.'

'But – why me?' she said, her voice rising. 'I know nothing – '

'Oh, dear!' He smiled again, the same contortion of the thick lips. 'I do hope you are not going to be difficult! You see,

116

you have to come, my dear!' There was an unctuousness in his voice now that was more unpleasant than his previous curtness.

'Best go wi' him, lass!' Joan muttered. 'Best go!'

'You have not said who you are,' Isobel said coldly, ignoring Joan.

He bowed slightly. 'How remiss of me, but the occasion did not seem – ah – conducive to formal introductions. My name, Mistress, is Edward Dutton. I am a commissioner appointed by Lord Thomas Cromwell, and my friend here is a soldier of His Majesty's government. There is another outside in the yard.'

Soldiers! A royal commissioner! His Majesty's government! It was a dream, a nightmare! It could not be really happening! For the first time in her life she found herself longing for the sound of her father's footsteps, to see him come in from the yard, but he was up on the fell with the men, counting sheep and he would not be back for hours.

'Your name means nothing to me,' she said slowly, 'and I cannot understand why a good man like the abbot should be brought to trial, but if there is any way in which I can help him – '

'Help him?' he interrupted. 'Well, that is up to you! And now, if you are ready – We have to be back in East Wooton on the hour. And if I may say so, I think a day will come when my name *does* mean something to you! Yes, I think I may safely promise you that!'

They looked at each other across the big wooden table and she saw and recognised the overweening pride in his face and behind it the lust that had been there from the beginning. She knew that she hated this man, would always hate him, but not with the hatred that she had thought she felt for her father. That had been a sudden spurt of emotion born of hurt and rejection that might once have been love. This hatred was different, for it was born of fear.

'I must bring the baby with me,' she said coldly, into the silence. 'He will need to be fed later.'

She thought he was going to say she must leave Christopher behind, for he looked over at the cradle for the first time, frowning, but then, as if he had thought better of it, said quickly, 'Yes, by all means, bring him!' – smiling broadly now, his teeth yellow as a sheep's. He moved round the table, taking her by the arm. 'Come, girl, we are wasting time.'

117

She drew back, rubbing her arm still clammy with his sweat, and he followed her over to the cradle, standing close beside her as she lifted the baby and wrapped the shawl round him. Mercifully, Christopher remained asleep and she held his head against her shoulder, unpleasantly aware of that silent figure beside her. Out of the corner of her eye she could see the dark cloth of his doublet, the thick legs in the wrinkled black hose. 'I thought you said we had to hurry?' she said, stepping well back.

The pale eyes flickered. 'You are ready?'

'Yes.'

Ignoring Joan who stood with her mouth open, he led the way out of the kitchen, but Isobel stopped in the doorway and looked back, smiling at the little boys who ran forward from behind their mother's skirts.

'I shall be back soon!' she said. 'Very soon!'

'I – I hope so, lass!' Joan muttered, twisting and untwisting her hands, still covered with flour, and the older of the two boys, Matthew, said doubtfully, 'Promise, Is'bel?'

'I promise!' but she found it hard to smile at him now, and she went out into the yard where they waited for her. Edward Dutton gave her his hand to mount the cob that the second soldier was holding – an old, fat animal whose broad back was like a bed. She sat astride, her skirts rolled up to her knees, holding the baby to her with one arm, the reins in her free hand, and slowly, awkwardly, she followed Edward Dutton out of the yard, a soldier on either side of her.

Chapter Fifteen

The warm air of late summer lay thick with the smell of un-washed bodies and food that the crowd had brought in to eat during the trial – the big man sitting behind the table holding what seemed to be a sprig of rosemary to his nostrils and the din indescribable – the market-house packed to its open doors with more people trying to force their way in and still more coming. It was an occasion that would be talked about for years to come, for never before, in the history of East Wooton, had an abbot been brought to trial. Isobel, unused to crowds and noise felt strangely unnerved, and wondered how Christopher could sleep through it all.

The two soldiers had brought her up to the front, to a bench at the extreme end of which she now sat, beside a man who looked like a merchant and a woman she took to be his wife. Both of them drew back from her as far as they could, nudging their neighbours to have a good look at the girl with the baby who had been brought in under guard, until she felt her face begin to burn and turned sideways, with her back to them. But mercifully like the rest of the crowd they did not seem to know who she was.

The abbot sat alone on another bench to the side of the table which faced the crowd. He was unshaven, ashen grey, his tall body drooping as if he had been sitting on the bench all night. She had only spoken to him on a few occasions in all the years she had been in the convent but she had always been conscious of the strength of his personality. Today she felt she was looking at a shell, that the real Dom Richard was far away.

She became aware of Edward Dutton staring at her from where he sat beside the big man holding the rosemary, and again she felt her face grow hot, and looked away quickly. She recognised his other neighbour, Sir Anthony Challoner, who had come to the convent a couple of times to visit his aunt, the old nun who had died during the winter. There were four other men sitting at the table but she did not know any of them – all were prosperous looking and well dressed. The big man, whom she thought might be the Judge, had a jewelled ornament in his flat, grey cap and there was a richness about his grey silk overgown and blue, slashed doublet. His other neighbour, grossly fat and sweating visibly wore a gown thickly edged with wolf fur which even as she looked at him he pulled off, handing it to a servant who stood behind him.

Further back a row of men sat on benches, their shabbiness contrasting oddly with the men at the table, silent and yet somehow seeming aware of their importance. Were they the jury, she wondered – the men who would decide the abbot's fate? They looked hardly competent to judge the value of a sheep, she thought, and wished that there was not so much noise. It was in fact some time before she realised that the proceedings had actually started, and she wondered if trials were always conducted in this casual fashion. Surely not? Then why this one? As if it were of no importance – or the verdict had already been agreed on beforehand.

The big man called suddenly for silence, bringing his clenched fist down hard on the wooden table, and beginning to read, in spite of the continuing noise, from a parchment that he had unrolled and spread out in front of him. He had a strong, resonant voice that carried well, and she caught some of what he said.

' . . . did search and did find a treasonable manuscript in favour of Queen Catherine and against the royal divorce and the beheading of Queen Anne, which examined upon by Lord Cromwell did show Abbot Tyndal's cankered and traitorous heart . . . the abbey to come to His Majesty by right of attainder and the monks dispersed . . . Abbot Tyndal has permitted incontinence and homosexuality among his monks . . .'

There were shouts of 'Lies! Lies!' He held up a long, white hand for silence and began again. ' . . . the additional charge of robbery is brought today against Dom Richard Tyndal, abbot of Wolden Abbey, by this court on behalf of His Gracious Majesty, King Henry the Eighth . . . on the thirtieth day of August, in the year fifteen hundred and thirty-nine, and – '

He could not go on. The crowd was in too much of an uproar. 'Robbery?' the man beside Isobel said to his wife. '*Robbery?* Did tha hear that? They're all mad!'

There must be some mistake, Isobel thought, but the booming voice rolled on. ' . . . that Dom Richard Tyndal did withhold treasure from His Gracious Majesty with the help of the monk, Andrew Ellerton and did refuse to give information as to its whereabouts or the whereabouts of Andrew Ellerton, wherefore he is now on trial . . . Witnesses will be called . . . to show how the two plotted together . . . Andrew Ellerton, leaving the abbey in great secrecy . . . with a sack . . .' The rest of what he said was drowned by the shouting of the crowd and this time he had to stand up before he could get silence again.

'I call on James Turner!' one of the men behind the table said harshly.

A tall, shaggy-haired youth stood up at the back of the hall, looking as if he might run away at any second.

'Your name is James Turner and you were employed until recently in the abbey kitchens, when you were unfairly dismissed you say. Is that correct?' The fat man sitting beside the Judge seemed to have taken over the questioning.

'Aye, sir, tha's t'truth!' the youth mumbled.

'And you confirm that what His Lordship has just read out is what you have already told an officer of the court?'

'Con – con – what, sir? I'm a bit hankled – '

'I am simply asking you to state again that you – ah – happened to be in the gatehouse one evening in January of this year when two monks came from Rievaulx Abbey with a laden pack horse, and that when Dom Richard Tyndal and Andrew Ellerton came out to talk to them you heard one of the other two monks say that they had brought the treasure for safe-keeping. Then you heard the abbot say to Andrew Ellerton that indeed the treasure would not be safe for much longer in Wolden either and that they must find some other hiding place for it. And that you even saw Andrew Ellerton leave the abbey one night – '

121

'Oh, is tha' what tha meant?' the youth said cheerfully, interrupting. 'Aye, I did hear 'em – an' – '

'You also saw Master Robert FitzHugh talking privately many times to the monk, Andrew Ellerton, while he was a guest in the abbey, did you not?' the fat man went on quickly.

'Aye, sir! Tha's t'truth!'

'You may sit down, James Turner.'

There was a buzz of conversation among the crowd and little as she knew of legal procedure it seemed to Isobel to have been a very strange examination of a witness, but the Judge, if that was what he was, had begun to speak and she strained to hear him above the noise.

'Since Andrew Ellerton cannot be found for questioning, the court can only assume his guilt as charged.' He cleared his throat. 'I now call on Isobel Willis to come forward.'

Her name was repeated a second time as she remained where she was, frozen, unable to move. 'ISOBEL WILLIS! Come forward and take the oath!'

She got slowly to her feet, holding the baby tightly against her breast as if she were trying to draw courage from the tiny body, the man beside her moving even further from her as if he had just discovered she had leprosy. She walked the few steps to the table and one of the men behind it handed her a bible. 'Repeat after me,' he said, 'I do swear . . .'

'I do swear . . . by Almighty God . . .' her mind only half taking in what he was saying, racing ahead. The youth had not been asked to swear on the bible – what were they going to ask her, what trick was this? How could she possibly help the abbot or Andrew?

'You are Isobel Willis, daughter of Ben Willis, farmer, and his late wife, Alice?' The fat man was still putting the questions.

'Yes.' There was a murmur among the crowd, but fortunately she was not facing it.

'What age are you, Isobel?' His voice was kindly enough but patronising, as if she were simple-minded.

'Eighteen,' she said coldly.

He shuffled the parchments lying in front of him and

cleared his throat noisily. 'You were a nun until recently in the Benedictine convent of St Mary's – is that correct?'

'Yes.' Behind her the crowd had begun to chatter like magpies.

Edward Dutton whispered behind his hand to the fat man and she held her breath, waiting for the next question.

When it came the small eyes sunk in their mounds of flesh bored into hers. 'Please tell the court why you left the convent!'

She felt the blood rush into her face until it seemed to be on fire. 'I – I had no vocation and – and the abbess agreed to release me.' There was a burst of laughter from the back of the hall that was quickly followed by other guffaws and the man interrogating her held up a podgy hand for silence.

'Oh, come now, girl, surely you are splitting hairs? If not actually lying! Remember that you are on oath! Is not the real reason for your leaving the convent asleep in your arms at this very moment?'

She could hear the silence of the crowd, waiting for her to make her shame public. The abbot was looking at her now, the dazed expression gone from his face, his thick dark eyebrows drawn together in a frown. She saw Edward Dutton smile and remembered his eager agreement that she should bring Christopher with her, and she promised herself that some day she would repay him in kind – but the court was waiting for her answer, and at last she lifted her chin and said huskily, 'Yes, I left because I had a baby.'

'A *baby*?' The fat man looked round the hall. 'A fully professed, Benedictine nun had a – *baby*!' He waited for the crowd to respond and he was not disappointed. Cat-calls. Jeers. Shouts of 'whore!' followed.

'Silence!' he cried, when he considered the crowd had enjoyed themselves for long enough, and the big man beside him hammered the table with his closed fist. 'If you do not keep silent I shall have the court cleared!' he thundered. 'Dr Parr wishes to continue with his questions!'

Eventually, the crowd became if not silent at least quieter and the fat man cleared his throat again and said sternly, 'Now, Isobel Willis, will you please tell the court who is the father of your child.'

She ran her tongue over her dry lips, praying for strength. 'I cannot see how that is relevant,' she said at last, her voice hoarse.

'You refuse to say? You know that that is contempt of court?'

When she still remained silent the big man beside Dr Parr said curtly, 'I am the Judge of this court, appointed by His Majesty, and I must warn you that if you refuse to answer Dr Parr's questions you may find yourself in prison for a long period of time. Is not the monk, Andrew Ellerton the father of your child?'

She had been half expecting such a question, yet to hear the words actually said in public made her feel weak, and she hoped she was not going to faint. 'No!' she said quickly. 'That is a lie! We are only cousins, nothing more! Never anything more!'

But her words were lost in the shouting of the crowd and this time, although the Judge called for silence several times he was ignored. In the end he had to stand up. *'Silence! Or you will all be sent home!'*

After a moment, when the worst of the noise had subsided he sat down again. 'Isobel Willis,' he said weightily, 'you are doing yourself and the accused no good. Will you please tell the truth!'

'I have told the truth,' she said clearly, anger overcoming every other emotion. 'Andrew Ellerton is *not* the father of my child. He could not be.'

'You deny that you have fornicated with him, that you came to him in the abbey and were let in to him with the abbot's knowledge and consent?' Dr Parr's voice was surprisingly high-pitched for a man of his size, but it carried to every corner of the hall and the crowd worked itself into a frenzy of excitement.

'I do deny it, absolutely,' she shouted above the din.

'Then who *is* the father?'

Her throat felt very dry and there was a sudden, eerie silence. At last she said slowly, 'Robert FitzHugh is the father of my child.' She had to say it. She had to tell the truth. There was no choice.

The crowd was in an uproar. She turned for a second and saw the red faces, the round 'o's of the open mouths, row upon row of them. They don't believe me, she thought dully, listening to the derisive laughter. They think I am lying.

Then she heard her father's voice come suddenly from the

124

back of the hall. 'It's t'truth she's saying, sir! She's speaking t'truth!'

But no one paid any attention to him and when the laughter had died away at last Dr Parr said, sweat glistening on his moon face, 'You have named Master Robert FitzHugh as the father of your child – are you referring to the grandson of Sir William FitzHugh, of Critley?'

'Yes,' she said shortly.

The Judge had leant forward. 'But how could *you* possibly know such a man?'

'We have established already, my lord,' Dr Parr said quickly, 'that Robert FitzHugh was staying in the guest-house last year.'

'So you went to the guest-house, no doubt with the abbot's knowledge?' the Judge said, frowning, while the crowd, nearly beside itself, roared and shouted.

The Judge called for silence and when the hall had grown a little quieter, he repeated his question.

'No!' she said, her voice hard with sudden anger as the abbot turned his head to look at her again. 'I did not go to the guest-house.'

'Then where did this – this coupling take place?'

Edward Dutton was leaning forward now, his pale eyes fixed on her face, the tip of his tongue showing between his lips as it had done in the farmhouse kitchen. 'I – I – ' But she could not go on.

'Why not admit it?' Dr Parr said smoothly. 'You went to the guest-house, just as you went to the abbey to fornicate with Andrew Ellerton! Why not admit it, girl!'

'No!' she said hoarsely, 'No! He – came to the convent. One night. Just – one night.' Her voice died to a whisper as the crowd began to stamp its feet in an agony of enjoyment.

'So! One man came to you in the convent, and you went to the other in the abbey!' Dr Parr was smiling for the first time like an obese cherub, while the crowd had lost all control. The abbot's chin was sunk in his chest.

Isobel stood, holding the baby, afraid again that she was going to faint. 'It is not true!' she said, trying to force her voice so that it could be heard above the din, but it was a waste of effort. She could scarcely hear it herself, and in any case, who would believe her? The men at the table seemed to be holding a conference and at last the Judge raised his hand for silence. This time the crowd, anxious for more tit-bits, became quiet of its own accord.

'Isobel Willis,' Dr Parr began again, his voice controlled, almost friendly. 'This court is not sitting in judgement on you or the true paternity of your child. What I have been attempting to do has been to show that you were on exceptionally intimate terms with the monk, Andrew Ellerton.' He stopped, hoping perhaps that the change in his tone of voice would have disarmed her, shooting his question at her with arrow-like swiftness. 'What do you know of the whereabouts of the treasure? Tell the court all you know and then you can go home and forget you have ever been here!'

'But – I know nothing,' she said hoarsely, seeing the abbot lift his head again and stare at her.

'Speak up, girl!' the Judge said irritably. 'So that the whole court may hear you.'

'I know nothing about the treasure,' she said loudly. 'Nothing whatever!'

'Yet you do know that your cousin has disappeared and that the abbot refuses to tell the court of his whereabouts? Do you know where your cousin is?' Dr Parr was beginning to shout.

'No!'

'Do you realise that you, as your cousin's lover, can be charged with being an accessory? Do you know what that will mean for you?'

'We were never more than cousins,' she said dully, not even trying to raise her voice any longer, 'and I know nothing, only what has been said in court today. And I believe none of that.'

'You do not believe – God above, was there ever such stupidity!' The Judge passed a weary hand over his high forehead. 'You deny that you know where the treasure is hidden – you deny that your cousin told you, and you say you have no idea where he is? Do you really expect this court to believe that, girl?'

'It is the truth,' she said flatly, 'whether you believe me or not.'

There was a low buzz of talk among the crowd, disappointed that there were to be apparently no more exciting revelations and the men at the table put their heads together again. She was beginning to feel very tired and was turning to go back to the bench to sit down again, whether they were finished or not when Edward Dutton spoke for the first time.

'One last question!' His voice was as bland as ever. 'I would like to ask the witness if Master Robert FitzHugh ever mentioned the treasure to her?'

'A good question, sir,' Dr Parr said. 'Well, Isobel Willis, what is your answer?'

'He never mentioned it to me,' she said quickly.

'He did not even say that the treasure should not go to the King, something like that?'

'No!'

'I find that hard to believe, my lord.' Edward Dutton turned to the Judge.

'You are quite sure?' Dr Parr said.

'I am quite sure,' she said clearly, with a lift of her chin.

There was another coming together of heads at the table while the crowd chattered and she put the baby on her hip in order to rest her arms.

'You may sit down,' the Judge said curtly at last, and she went back to the bench, turning her back as soon as she could on the staring eyes that devoured Christopher and herself. If only she could leave now – but after a shockingly brief summing-up by the Judge the jury were asked to consider their verdict, and as they remained seated she guessed the verdict would not be long in coming.

The abbot seemed so alone, she thought, looking at his bent head with pity and wishing she could go to him, try to comfort him. But perhaps he would not want her near him. Perhaps he believed what had been said about Andrew and herself. She wondered if he was praying.

Dom Richard was not praying, although he felt closer to God than he had done in all the years of his priesthood, and the voice of the crowd did not really reach him, reminding him only of the waves breaking on the shore at Whitby. He was thinking of the Tower, to which they had taken him by road, while a clutter of boats were conveying other prisoners to Traitors' Gate. He had spent one night in the large chamber on the middle floor of the Beauchamp Tower with a dozen strangers, all men. There was one other priest but little or no conversation, for two guards stood inside the door and suspicion and fear hung over the sour-smelling, cold, ill-lit chamber like a pall.

When the sun began to slant in through the slits of windows early next morning he had been able to read one of the names scratched into the weeping stone of the wall nearest him. 'Thomas FitzGerald.' He was an Irishman, he had remembered. 'Silken Thomas' they had called the poor devil, and he had been executed with his five uncles at Tyburn the year before. How had he ever thought an Irishman could defy the King of England and men like Thomas Cromwell, he wondered. Or had FitzGerald known what the outcome would be and still not cared?

Close by he had seen another name and a date. 'Adam Sedbar Abbas Jorevall, 1537' – his old friend, the abbot of Jervaulx had been there before him. And he too must have known what the outcome would be, just as he himself had come to know it during the long, quiet hours of that night, while he wished with futile regret that he had not forgotten to destroy the notes he had made for a sermon concerning the royal divorce.

Yet, a few hours later, when they had let him out to walk on the 'leads' between the Beauchamp Tower and the one next to it, he had thought, for a little while, that there might yet be hope. In his heart he knew it was unlikely – all that really mattered was that he should not betray Andrew or lead them to the treasure –

Nor did he. And later, when they found he would not weaken, Sir Edmund Walshingham, Lieutenant of the Tower, acting no doubt on Thomas Cromwell's orders, instructed that he should be brought down below. After three days and nights without sleep in the small, dank dungeon beneath the Beauchamp Tower, with relays of men coming in to question him and make sure he never even nodded off, without food or water or even one blanket to keep out the petrifying cold – after all that, he knew he too would soon die. But he still had not betrayed Andrew or told them where the treasure was.

And now he was running a fever, after what must have been surely the shortest ever imprisonment in the Tower for a prisoner of his kind. But it was his mind and his heart that had suffered the most, for they said that he had permitted 'incontinence' among his monks. They even inferred that his relationship with

Andrew was sinful, and that a letter he had received long ago and kept, from his dear friend Robert Joseph Beecham of Evesham showed signs of immorality. He had tried to explain to them that phrases in the letter like 'thine beyond all flattery' were merely ironic, but they would not listen. As for his relationship with Andrew – what could he do but deny that it was ever more or less than it was? He could not, however, deny that over the years there had been men in the abbey who *had* sinned in this regard, but he had qualified that and said that they had not been made like other men, were not truly sinners, and needed help rather than condemnation. He had had to say it, but they had turned that against him too.

As for the girl, it seemed to him wildly unlikely that Andrew had ever been more than a friend to her, and now that he had listened to her in court he believed her. It seemed far more likely that Robert FitzHugh was the father of her child, but of what use was his belief in her to either one of them? He himself had already been tried and convicted and whatever punishment was meted out to him would surely be meted out to Andrew too if they could find him, regardless of his relationship with the girl. But if Andrew could get the treasure out of the country to Amsterdam then the banker would help to get it the rest of the way. Now Andrew must surely need Robert FitzHugh's help. The pity of it was that FitzHugh did not know – or perhaps he did but was not to be trusted, if what the girl had said was true. But they would go after him too . . . His mind that had lost its fine edge since they had taken him to the Tower began to drift once more, and he thought he could hear the waves crashing on the beach at Whitby again as the now familiar dizziness threatened to overcome him . . .

The men behind the table were standing now, their spokesman coming forward to speak to the Judge, then going back to his place. Isobel, like everyone else in the hall, was holding her breath. Not a sound was to be heard except the snarling of the town curs as they fought over the scraps of food that littered the ground. The Judge was writing, raising his head at last, clearing his throat –

'Dom Richard Tyndal, you are found guilty as charged. The

129

sentence of this court is that you will be hanged by the neck until you are dead . . . the execution to take place tomorrow the thirty-first day of August, fifteen hundred and thirty-nine, on the hill known as Wolden Hill, at noon . . . the body afterwards to be drawn and quartered . . .'

The roar of the crowd rose to the roof in a mighty crescendo so that the rest of his words were lost. Isobel found herself suddenly on her feet.

'Murderers!' she shouted. 'You cannot hang an innocent man!'

But her voice was lost in the tumult and only the man and his wife beside her heard. The woman leant across and spat in her face, and as she wiped it clean with a shaking hand, the woman said viciously, 'Murderers they be, but who's calling names? Whore, that's what tha is! Ruinin' a man o' God an' t'abbot blamed for it!'

A woman sitting beyond her pointed a bony finger. 'Jezebel!' she hissed. 'Wearin' t'habit an' offerin' thyself to any man that cooms! Thou wilt suffer fer it, lass!'

'Aye!' growled the man. 'Tha should hang instead of him!'

Isobel stared at them for a few seconds, unable to speak, then turning and holding the baby tightly to her breast, one hand over his head to protect him, she got to her feet and burrowed her way through the crowd like a terrified animal.

She could not see her father anywhere and at first they did not notice her, but when she had almost reached the door a shout went up and hands clutched at her, tearing the shoulder of her gown. She was quick on her feet and through them before they could catch her, but she was not in time to turn down the lane that ran behind the market-house before a stone clipped her on the side of the head, and something soft and foul-smelling splattered her skirt.

She flew on, her scalp stinging where the stone had hit her, feeling dizzy, her breath coming in short gasps. Her legs were beginning to turn to jelly but they had not come after her, and soon she had reached the houses that made up the town proper. The place appeared to be deserted, yet she could not be sure, and she turned at the first lane and made for the rising ground behind, not able to run any longer. The baby began to whimper as she stumbled through the neat, cultivated strips behind the houses, on up to the scrublands where a few children tended flocks of goats. She turned at last in the direction of the farm and sat down to feed him. Firstly, however, she tore away the part of her skirt which the human faeces had splattered, but even with it gone the smell seemed to remain, half suffocating her.

She was still some distance from the farmhouse, and when the baby had had enough she wiped a trickle of milk from his mouth, shivering in the sudden chill, for the sun had gone in. His skin was very fair, rosy with health and she hugged him to her. 'Oh, Christopher my love,' she whispered, 'what would I do without you?'

But what of tomorrow, she thought, and all the other tomorrows? How was she going to look after him, what sort of life would he have? If only she could get away from this place – far, far away. Those women – she could not live among them, but neither could she and Christopher hide away on the farm for the rest of their lives. And yet she knew it was possible, could see herself growing old there, and strange. Mad Isobel, her son running wild, less than his step-brothers, less than the lowest paid labourer on the farm.

She got to her feet, unable to bear her thoughts any longer, and thought she saw movement in a clump of bushes nearby. An animal, she told herself. Maybe even just a bird – but her heart had begun to thump, nevertheless. She began to walk on, not daring to run, the house still out of sight. There was a small wood a few hundred yards on, that her grandfather or her great-grandfather had planted years before – not really a wood, more a windbreak, but it offered cover of a kind. When she came to it she turned sharply right, and went and hid behind the broadest of the trees. Nothing moved. No sound broke the late afternoon's quiet.

And then she saw him. Coming out from behind the bushes, and up to the place where she had been sitting, crouching behind a nearby rock, looking up the way she had come. A man, thick-set, seeming young from the speed of his movements. Wearing a hat and rough-looking clothes. Who was he, and why was he following her? She looked round for a weapon but there was nothing. No heavy stick, not even a stone. Remembering what her father had said about the men who might come looking for her, remembering the jeers of the crowd – and the trees would not hide her for long. He had only to walk among them and sooner or later he would see her. And if she screamed no one would hear her –

He was walking rapidly towards the trees now, the hat well down over his face, and she held the baby tightly to her. Now he was coming up to the trees – was level with them – was turning in! Had he seen her already? Oh, please God, don't let him – please save me, *please!* Why hadn't she run for the house while there was time, why hadn't she? Her heart pounding so hard he must surely hear it – He had reached her tree, was looking round it, and she was staring into his eyes.

'Andrew! Oh, Andrew! You gave me such a fright!' she breathed, scarcely able to speak.

'Isobel! I wasn't sure it was you and I had to be sure! I'm sorry if I frightened you. I've been hiding up on the fell since they closed the abbey.'

They looked at each other without speaking. Under the brim of his hat his face was sunburnt but thinner, and his moleskin breeches and leather jerkin were old and worn. It seemed strange to see him in ordinary laymen's clothes yet she was so glad that it was he she could have wept for joy. But he looked at her with a kind of horror in his eyes, staring at her torn, shapeless gown, her shaggy hair, glancing swiftly at the baby and then away.

'If I smell like a kennel,' she said, 'it's because they threw filth at me.'

He frowned. 'Who?'

'Women – someone – It was after the trial.'

But he was not listening. 'Tell me,' he said harshly, gripping her arm so tightly that it hurt. 'What was the verdict?'

'They said he was guilty of treason, then they tried him for robbery – for witholding the treasure, and they – they found him guilty.'

'Robbery! God above!' Then he asked quietly, 'What was the sentence?'

'He is to hang,' she said slowly. 'I am very sorry.'

He let go of her arm and turned away, standing with his back to her for what seemed a long time. 'When?' he asked, turning to her at last.

'Tomorrow,' she said. 'On Wolden Hill, at noon.'

'Oh, my God!' he whispered, taking off his hat and putting a hand over his eyes. The tonsure on his bent head looked oddly out of place and she thought, her mind skipping ahead, that will surely betray him.

'They are searching for you,' she said into the silence, 'but you know that. You must go away, Andrew, far away, else they'll hang you too.'

He lifted his head then, looking at her with eyes that she knew did not really see her. 'I've been up there on the fell, waiting for the trial. I could not leave before I knew the verdict but I was afraid to go into the town, so I hid behind the houses, hoping I'd see someone I could trust. I saw your father but he was with others and then I saw you, but I was not sure if it was you or not. I will leave tomorrow – when – when it is over.' His voice was without expression, only the big hands turning his hat round and round by its brim giving any hint of the tension within him.

'Where will you go?'

'Out of the country.'

After a moment she said, 'Is it true that you hid the treasure?' He hesitated, and she said quickly, 'They are convinced that you did.'

'You were at the trial, then?'

'Yes. I was called as a witness.'

'Why?'

'They thought that you might have talked to me about the treasure because – because of the baby.'

He frowned and his mouth that had always been hard, became even harder. 'I don't understand.'

She laughed shortly. 'They asked me if you were the father of my child.'

'They've minds like sewers,' he grunted. 'What did you say?'

'I said that Robert FitzHugh was the father.' She found she could say it easily, as if the time she had spent in court had burnt away all reserve, all shame.

He grunted again and she said quickly, 'You do not seem surprised.'

133

'I'm not,' he said briefly. 'I thought as much, when I first heard about the baby – I'd heard them talking about you in the kitchen – some of them had seen you with him down by the river last autumn.'

'And you brought me the homily afterwards,' she said quietly.

'The homily?' he said, frowning, as if he had forgotten. 'Oh, yes – I knew it was no use saying anything to you – ' But she guessed that his mind was not really on what he was saying, that he was thinking of what was to happen next day, and she felt deeply sorry for him. He was more subtle too than she had given him credit for. She wanted to touch him, to put her hand on his arm but she did not dare and they looked at each other in silence until he said abruptly, 'What happened afterwards? You said the women – someone – '

'It does not matter,' she said. 'It's over and done with, but I think I shall go mad if I have to stay here much longer. My father never speaks to me except to abuse me, yet I work all day for him.'

'Where could you go?'

'If I could find work somewhere – '

'Don't be a fool!' he said curtly. 'You'd be no better off, worse in fact. Your step-mother – how does she treat you?'

Isobel shrugged. 'Well enough, better than I expected.'

'Well, that is something, isn't it?'

'Yes, but – but – Oh, Andrew, I can't live the rest of my life like this!'

'You brought it on yourself, Isobel,' he said heavily. 'You made your bed. Now you have to lie in it.'

It was as if he had hit her, and yet he was right, of course. She felt suddenly very tired. 'You'd better go, Andrew,' she said. 'They will be looking for you.'

But he did not move. 'Does FitzHugh know about the child?' he said.

'No!' Her voice was bleak. 'I do not intend to tell him, ever.'

'Maybe you should.'

'No!' she said again, her voice rising.

He still did not move. 'I'd like to help you, but what can I do?'

And looking at him, at the broad, honest, worried face, the angry mouth, the idea came to her. 'Take me with you, Andrew!

please! I'd be no trouble – I might even be able to help you!' Her words came tumbling out. 'They will be looking for a man on his own, not someone with a woman and a baby – oh, please!'

'You mean – bring the baby too?' He looked down in horror at the child in her arms.

'I won't leave him behind!'

He stared at her without speaking and then the horror faded, giving place to anger and finally to surly resignation.

Chapter Sixteen

This time Robert and John reached the village just after noon, slowing their horses to a walk. They might just as well have galloped through, for the place was deserted. The last time there had been a group of children playing a game of handy-dandy in the middle of the lane that divided the two straggling rows of cottages. Women had gossiped in open doorways, and smoke had curled from holes in the thatched roofs. But today there was not even the smell of smoke in the hot, still air and nothing stirred – until they came to the end of the village and saw the man in the stocks, his bare feet sticking out through the holes in the wooden structure. The man lifted his head as they came near and Robert could see flies clustered around sores on his face.

'Water! For t'love o' God – water!' The hoarse croak was barely audible. He could have been any age from thirty to fifty, thin to the point of emaciation, in rags of clothes, his face fiery red from the sun which had been beating down all morning. Dismounting, Robert took his water bottle out of his saddle bag and held it to the man's mouth for the thin wrist seemed too weak for even such a light weight. 'What has you here?' he asked when the fellow seemed to have drunk enough.

'I stole a loaf of bread,' he replied hoarsely. 'I was starving.'

Was he telling the truth, Robert wondered, but what did it matter anyway? He hated these infernal contraptions in which a man or a woman could be confined for days on end for the most petty of crimes. He was struck once more by the silence of the place, as if a plague had struck it.

'Where is everyone?' he asked the man.

'Gone to t'hanging!'

'A hanging? What poor fellow is it?'

'Abbot Tyndal! And shame it is too!'

'Dom Richard is to be *hanged*?' Robert did not recognise the sound of his own voice. 'When? Where?'

'Up on t'hill, by t'abbey! Today – sometime today – '

'God in heaven! John, we must hurry!'

Leaving the water bottle and a handful of coins with the man, Robert swung himself into the saddle and before the fellow had finished thanking him he had galloped out of the village in a cloud of dust, while John's horse was still trotting.

He looked for the hill since it could be more easily seen from a distance than the abbey and he had forgotten the way, but he could not see the hill anywhere. The lane that was now only a path was pitted with holes and hard as rock, and bushes caught at his clothes as he galloped past, John far behind him. Then he heard the voice of the crowd and at last saw the hill itself. It was minutes more before he actually reached it, and saw the limp body in its white habit hanging from the tree, with the gaping crowd beneath. A red mist gathered before his eyes and he circled the crowd, shouting and cursing, unaware of what he was saying, until he came to the group of monks. He reined in then and dismounted and the monk nearest to him turned his head. It was Father Peter, the guest-master, his plump cheeks fallen in.

'How did it happen?' Robert tried not to shout. 'Surely someone could have stopped them?'

Father Peter moved away from the others. 'No one could have stopped them. Lord Abbot was convicted yesterday of robbing his own abbey because he would not hand over the treasure to the King.'

Looking into the man's deepset eyes Robert realised that he was ill with shock. 'I just can't believe it!' he said. 'It's insane, grotesque!'

'Be careful!' the guest-master muttered. 'You should not have come here – they have their spies everywhere. Any hint of treason – '

'My opinion of the King is already well known,' Robert said drily, but Father Peter frowned.

'It's more than that. They think you are involved in hiding the treasure.'

'I don't even know where it is!'

A nerve began to twitch near the guest-master's mouth and he made a move to rejoin the other monks. 'Where is Andrew Ellerton?' Robert asked quickly.

'No one knows,' Father Peter muttered. 'The abbey is closed, – the gates locked against us. The King's men tore it apart.'

It was unbelievable now that it had happened, and yet was it not what his grandfather had feared would come about sooner or later?

'Is it possible that Andrew Ellerton might have left a message for me with someone?'

'No,' Father Peter said with cold finality. 'He would not have done that.'

It must be shock, Robert thought. Nothing else could have changed a man so completely, and yet who could blame him? He himself was well used to the sight of corpses hanging from trees and gibbets, but the poor, limp body in its white habit was different. This was a sight that sickened him and he had hardly known the man. What then must it be like for his fellow monks? And what was he to do if Andrew could not be found and had left no message for him?

Father Peter had rejoined the other monks and Robert saw that the body of the abbot was being taken down. He watched, cold with horror as the body was stripped naked and laid on a kind of trestle table. There was the flash of steel in sunlight and suddenly great spurts of blood splattered the bare arms, the leather aprons, even the faces of the men who bent over the table.

Butchers! he thought. A curse on them all! He could feel vomit rise in his throat and there was a deep, throbbing roar from the crowd. As he turned to look for John he felt a hand on his shoulder.

'Master Robert FitzHugh?'

He swung around to find two men behind him, one middle-aged, pale-faced, the other younger, grossly fat, and on either side of them soldiers wearing blue sashes and armed with pikes.

'Yes! What do you want with me?'

'We are the King's commissioners. This is my colleague Dr Parr – ' It was the older man speaking, his voice with its faint hint of northern roots unpleasantly unctuous. 'You and I have met before, but I see you do not remember – '

Robert looked from one to the other, at the pikes pointing at his stomach, and said harshly, 'No! I do not remember! And I would like to know the reason for this – this stupidity! Will you please tell those men to lower their weapons?'

He was not conscious of any fear, only of an overpowering anger but the fat man said waspishly, 'It is not "stupidity" as you call it. The Cîteaux treasure has disappeared and the monk, Andrew Ellerton, along with it. The abbot refused to give us information as to their whereabouts. Had he done so he might have lived. But *you* are here, and *you*, Master FitzHugh, are known to have been a friend of Andrew Ellerton's, as your grandfather was a friend of that foolish abbot's!'

Robert laughed shortly. 'But I don't *know*, man! I know no more than you do! And now, if you will excuse me – '

'I am afraid the matter cannot be settled as quickly as that,' the older man said smoothly. 'We have our instructions from Lord Cromwell himself.'

For the first time it occurred to Robert that he might actually be in real danger. He looked hard at the pale face in front of him. They had met before, he'd said. Robert frowned, trying to remember and as if he had read his thoughts, the man said softly, 'Edward Dutton. At the last Twelfth Night.'

'I don't remember you,' Robert said slowly, 'but I know who you are.'

There was a fleeting look of pleasure in the colourless eyes. 'Good! Then you will know too that it would be in your best interests to tell us the truth.'

'But I have told you the truth,' Robert said curtly. 'I know nothing! I have had several conversations with Andrew Ellerton during my few days in the guest-house, but we were not close friends.'

'You were more than close friends, however, it would seem, with his cousin, the nun, Isobel Willis – is that not true?' The fat man's words were once again like the sting of a wasp.

Damn them to hell! Robert thought. How did they know? And how dare this fat pig of a fellow say it to his face! 'I don't know what you mean,' he said flatly.

139

'It is quite simple.' Edward Dutton's voice was smooth as silk and yet Robert felt he was the more dangerous of the two. 'You see, we know all about your amorous adventures in the convent! And what is more likely than that you would have told the young woman of your fancy what you are unwilling to tell us? After all, is she not the mother of your child – your son?'

'The *mother*?' But Robert could not go on. Isobel had had a child! His night of madness had resulted in this – God in heaven, what had he done to her?

'Indeed, yes! A fine, healthy boy too! There is of course the possibility that Ellerton is the father – ' Edward Dutton stepped hastily back as Robert swung his clenched fist at his face.

'Now, gentlemen, please!' Dr Parr cut in impatiently. 'Did you or did you not tell the girl, FitzHugh?'

Robert swallowed. It no longer mattered how they knew or what they said. But they must not go after her too. 'I swear I never mentioned the treasure to her! I will swear it in court, if necessary,' he said harshly. 'She knows nothing about it – nothing at all!'

'You know nothing. She knows nothing, and Ellerton cannot be found. It is not good enough, I'm afraid.' Edward Dutton looked at Dr Parr and the two men seemed to come to an unspoken agreement. 'I must ask you to go back to London, to the Tower, with these soldiers,' he said bleakly, the smoothness gone from his voice.

The Tower! Robert felt suddenly cold. 'And if I refuse to go?'

'You have no choice,' Dr Parr said, 'we have a warrant for your arrest. Of course, if you can remember – '

'I told you – I do not know!'

'Well, in that case – ' Edward Dutton signalled to one of the soldiers behind him and gave an order, then turned back to Robert. 'These men will take you to London and I strongly advise you not to try to escape. It would not only be – undignified, it would also be very foolish.'

'I will see that you suffer for this!' Robert's voice was grim but Edward Dutton only pulled at his lower lip, looking at him consideringly.

'I doubt if you have the power to do so,' he said slowly, 'from what I hear they say about you in court.'

Robert stepped forward and his clenched fist came up again,

140

but one of the soldiers deflected it so that the blow glanced off Edward Dutton's shoulder. The man was trying to appear calm, but he was shaking and there was a cold malevolence in his eyes.

Dr Parr had moved his obese body out of range as quickly as he could and Edward Dutton went and stood beside him, rubbing his shoulder while the soldiers moved closer to Robert. Over the head of the man in front of him he could see the men gathered around the trestle table, still engaged in their grisly task, and a long time afterwards he heard that the body had been hacked into four parts and the head struck off. The quarters had been sent to four different Yorkshire towns, and the abbot's head was fixed that same day above the gates of Wolden Abbey.

But now the monks were chanting their lament for the dead and five minutes later Robert found himself back in his saddle, surrounded by armed guards, on his way to the dreaded Tower of London. In the distance he could see John hastily mounting his horse, but then he lost sight of him in the crowd.

Chapter Seventeen

They had agreed in the end to meet at dawn on the morning after the hanging, for Andrew felt he could not leave before it. Isobel had been afraid to go to sleep when she went to bed the night before for fear she would not waken in time. She lay on the mattress fully dressed, wearing the green, woollen gown that Dame Cecilia had given her, one of Joan's white cotton hoods pulled well down on her head, covering her hair completely, the cloak of worn brown velvet that the infirmarian had also given her beside her with the satchel and the sack in which she had put a blanket for the baby and an extra shawl and food – a cold chicken and a lump of mutton, a round of cheese, two loaves of bread. She wished she could have taken money but her father always kept it in his pockets or so well hidden that no one but himself could find it. Anyway to have taken his money would have seemed like stealing. A day would come when she would regret her scruples, but that day was still a long way off and now she could hardly contain her excitement. To be leaving! To be able to see a world beyond the farmhouse, beyond the village, even beyond the town! To be free!

But suppose Andrew changed his mind about taking her and Christopher? Only the fear that sooner or later they would come after her again, and this time force the truth out of her, had made him agree in the end. The journey would be too long, too hard, he said even after he had seemed to have resigned himself to it. The child was too young, too liable to get sick. But each argument he put up she knocked down. Yet now, waiting, she knew he could still change his mind. And if she fell asleep she might sleep on and he would go without them.

And should she not leave a message for her father? But what could she say in it? He would believe only one thing anyway – that she had gone to a man. Some man. Robert himself perhaps, and in the darkness her mouth twisted suddenly with bitterness. As if that were likely, or even possible.

In the end she did fall asleep, but not heavily, and when the baby began to whimper it was still pitch dark. She lit the candle and put him to her breast and when he had had enough and was dropping off to sleep again she wrapped him in his shawl and got up. Even if she had to wait it was better than to risk missing Andrew.

She had to go down the ladder twice, first with her satchel and the sack, and then with Christopher. The second time, before she blew out the candle she looked around the loft for what she hoped would be the last time, and yet even as she put on the cloak and gathered up the baby in her arms she found herself suddenly loathe to leave what had become a kind of sanctuary for her in the past few weeks. Sanctuary – but prison also, she told herself firmly, blowing out the candle and putting her foot on the top rung of the ladder, going down slowly, step by step until she was in the kitchen, the only sound her father's snores coming through the leather screen dividing the kitchen from the small alcove where he slept with Joan.

The night before he had come in late, drunk by the sound of him, knocking over a stool on his way across the kitchen. She did not know if he had gone to see the hanging or not. He had been in a frenzy of rage over the verdict when he had returned after the trial, and she had fled to the loft to get away from him, staying there until she heard him leave the house again. At breakfast he had forbidden Joan and herself to go – not that she had any wish to see the abbot hanged, but Joan was bitterly disappointed and complained all morning so that Isobel had to go out to the dairy and pretend to be busy there for even longer than usual in order to get away from the sound of her stepmother's voice.

Now as she reached for the latch of the kitchen door she knew she might never see her father or Joan again, but she felt nothing. Her only regret was that she might not see the children until they were grown men – or maybe never again either – and then she was out in the cool darkness, the door closed quietly behind her, the hooting of an owl the only sound to be heard.

She got to the trees in less than fifteen minutes and already the sky was beginning to lighten, the tip of the orange ball showing above the horizon. But Andrew was not there and the silence was absolute.

'Oh, God make him come!' she prayed. 'Please make him come!' It was growing lighter by the minute but she did not dare ask herself what she would do if he did not come, and the sack of food and her satchel beside it mocked her as she waited. Suddenly she heard the distant creak of wooden wheels and saw a farm cart coming towards her, a man hunched on the seat, urging the horse forward hoarsely.

She ran to meet it and Andrew said gruffly, pulling in, 'I'm sorry I'm late. There was much to be done.'

'I'm so glad to see you!' she said, looking up at him and laughing with relief. 'I'm so very glad!'

'Best get up quickly, then!'

His voice had no welcome in it, no hint of warmth and he let her put the sack and the satchel in the back of the cart beside the sacks of turnips and piles of cabbages without offering to help her. She had to hand the baby to him before she climbed up and she watched his face with bitter amusement as he took the small bundle awkwardly from her, holding it far away from him as if it might give him the plague. He gave it back to her as quickly as he could and as she settled herself on the seat cuddling the baby, he looked straight ahead, flicking the horse with the reins. She found herself wishing in a second of madness that it was Robert, not Andrew who sat beside her. With Robert it would have been an adventure. There would have been excitement, even laughter – but I'm fantasising, she thought. What do I really know of him? And I cannot even tell him that this is his baby. If he knew, is it likely he would be here? But Andrew is here. Andrew is reality.

'Best watch your speech,' he said curtly, breaking the silence. 'And forget your convent manners.'

Why was he so boorish, she wondered, not bothering to say anything. Why was he so determined to keep her at arm's length? As the cart rolled bumpily along the track she found herself thinking of him as a man, not just her cousin Andrew, for the first time, trying to imagine what it would be like if Christopher were *his* son. It was what her father had wanted for them both. Was this then her fate that had caught up with her at last – to be with Andrew? She felt suddenly cold, even though there was only the gentlest of breezes and she pulled her cloak tightly about her.

'We'll head north west,' he said, turning to look at her and flushing slightly beneath his sunburn as he met her eyes. 'We'll cut through the hills and across the moors to Whitby. With luck we'll get a boat there that will bring us to Kingston-upon-Hull, and maybe if we're lucky there too, another to get us to Amsterdam.'

'You have it all worked out, then?'

He frowned, giving her that familiar, patronising look she remembered so well from long ago. 'Don't be foolish, Isobel. How could I? I've been advised to go to France through the Low Countries and there is a man in Amsterdam, a banker called Van Ophoorn, who will help us, but there are many problems. This cart, for instance. We can't take it across the moors. Could you ride, with the baby?'

She thought for a moment, determined not to let him irritate her. 'I shall have to,' she said slowly, 'I can see that, but I'll think of some way to carry him.' After a moment she added, 'I have brought food, but we shall need more, and money for our passage.'

'I have money,' he said. 'Just enough, I think.'

'And we have plenty of vegetables!' She tried to strike a cheerful note.

'They're not all vegetables!' he said drily.

It took her a few seconds to catch his meaning. 'The treasure?' she said.

He nodded, and at that moment they saw them. Two men riding rowards them, carrying pikes and wearing blue sashes. She heard Andrew draw in his breath and begin to curse softly.

The two soldiers were much closer now, and she recognised one of them as the man who had come into the kitchen the previous day. She bent her head over the baby, thanking God for Joan's hood and the loose folds of the cloak. The men slowed to a trot, reining in as they drew level. "Alt there!' the man whom she had recognised called out. Andrew pulled up the cart horse.

"Ave you seen the monk, Andrew Ellerton?' the soldier asked, unpleasantly.

'Nay, sir!' Andrew mumbled, touching his hat.

'Wot you got there, then?' the other soldier said, thrusting his pike into one of the sacks.

'Turnips! Nowt but good turnips for t'market!'

The fellow grunted, pulling out the pike and Isobel held her breath, waiting for him to say that whatever was in that sack it was not turnips, but he said nothing, grinning at her instead, running his eyes over her face until the other fellow growled at him. 'Come on, Jack! We're wasting time!' Kicking his horse into a gallop the second soldier left them in a cloud of dust and with a last, lingering look at her the other one followed him.

As the dust settled behind them Andrew said grimly, 'We've a long way to go and if we're caught, we'll both hang. You know that, don't you?'

She nodded, holding the baby close to her, feeling colder than ever.

Silence still came naturally to both of them and for a long time afterwards the cart lurched along the rutted path without their having said a word to one another. Earlier Andrew had heard the distant lowing of cattle waiting to be milked but that was long before, and now there was only the twittering of the birds and the occasional bleating of sheep. The sun had climbed higher and it was a fine, bright morning. If the weather holds, then we have some hope, he thought, not much, but some.

But he should never have followed her, never have spoken to her, he told himself for the hundredth time, the reins loose in his hands, the horse finding its own way. As for the baby, he did not want to even think about it. It – he still could not think of it as 'he' – was a hidden, private shame for him as if she had been his own sister. A nun. Professed. Thought highly of by Lady Abbess and all the nuns in spite of her giddiness. And she had

146

allowed herself to be – his mind shrank once more from what his thoughts had conjured up.

His adolescent fever had burnt itself out long ago through prayer and fasting and mental discipline, and he was still a virgin himself, not only physically but mentally as well. He had cleansed himself, but she was unclean. Not even churched, probably.

From the corner of his eye he looked at her profile. With her hair concealed under the white hood she might still have been a nun – and then, in spite of himself, his man's eyes saw the straight, perfect line of her nose, the softness of her mouth as she looked down at the child asleep in her arms, and the old, familiar itch under his skin came back, faint but unmistakeable. I should never have taken her with me, he thought in sudden terror. I should have left her to take her chance – maybe they would not have looked for her again.

'You took her with you because you wanted her, didn't you? You've always wanted her,' a voice whispered inside his head. 'No!' he told the voice. 'No! It was never more than a young boy's bad thoughts – the devil's tempting! Nothing more than that, ever! I took her with me only for her own sake.'

The baby had opened its eyes and was beginning to cry and she was fumbling with her cloak. He realised that she was putting the child to her breast and although he was used to seeing women suckle their babies this was altogether different, so different he could feel the sweat break out on his body. In his mind's eye he could see the white curve of her flesh, the baby's mouth closed on the nipple, and he wanted to pull back her cloak, to look. To touch. To take away the baby from her and put his own mouth – it would be so easy to do, and after all another man had done much more than that. And she had not minded, it seemed.

But only a short while ago he had seen a man die for his principles. He had sat among the beggars so as to be close to his friend until the end, and when it came he had been shocked to find his face wet with tears. He who despised emotion. A grown man. To *cry!* He had had to leave before they took the body down from the tree for fear of discovery and his grief itself had been like a wound, as he tried not to think of the mutilation that would follow. And now, so soon afterwards, this torment of – of

147

lust! He felt bitterly ashamed of himself, and shouting at the horse he slapped it with the end of the reins forcing it to a trot while the cart lurched from side to side. After a few moments, however, he slowed the horse to a walk and Isobel said coolly, 'When shall we eat?'

He dared to look at her. She was holding the baby to her shoulder. 'Soon,' he grunted. 'When we find some place that will conceal us from passers by.'

Half an hour later they found what they had been looking for – a thick, high clump of bushes. She got the food out of her sack and when they had climbed down from the cart they sat down behind the bushes while the horse cropped the grass nearby and Christopher gurgled happily in the sun.

'Tell me more about the treasure,' she said when they had finished eating. 'Where has it been all this time?'

He hesitated before replying and then wondered why she should not know. Even though she is a woman, and a foolish one at that. It was fortunate, he thought, that neither he nor Lord Abbot had taken Robert FitzHugh into their confidence since he had proved to be what he had first called him in his own mind – a dissolute, godless man with no sense of responsibility. He hoped he would never lay eyes on the fellow again.

'Well, Andrew, where has it been?' There was a touch of impatience in her voice.

'I hid it in a disused lead mine,' he said reluctantly.

'The one we used to play in?'

'Yes.'

'Did anyone else know, besides the abbot?'

'No one. And I promised to see it safely to Cîteaux.'

She was quiet for a moment, taking up the baby and wrapping the shawl more closely about him. Then she said slowly, 'Is the treasure so very valuable?'

He wanted to shake her. 'A fine man has died for it.'

'I know.' Her voice was cold. 'But you've not answered my question.'

'In terms of money it's worth a fortune,' he said gruffly. 'But its value for many people lies in what it stands for.'

'I know that too.' Her voice was still cold. After another short silence she said, 'Is it easily carried?'

'I wrapped everything in cowhide and put it in a sack.'

'A sack?' She began to laugh and as he felt his face redden with anger she said quickly. 'You did all this last night?'

'Yes. But first I went to the abbey and took one of the last carts – I already had a horse.'

'Were you not afraid of being seen?'

'The Visitors have gone. There's no one there at night and I can find my way around blindfolded. The looters come in daylight only.'

'Looters?' She was frowning now and he said sadly, 'Aye. They've stripped the place already – there will be precious little left to auction. I saw piles of books still burning outside – and some of my own manuscripts too – not that they are of great value – '

'I'm sorry!' There was sudden warmth in her voice and she touched him on the arm.

He felt himself go rigid. 'I still have my paints and brushes,' he said shortly, 'and I have some of my paintings too.'

'I'm glad.' Her voice was still warm but she had withdrawn her hand. 'I hope it won't be long before you can paint again.'

He looked past her, over the lush green land sloping gently away from them, saying nothing.

Isobel looked at the hard, straight line of his mouth and fell silent, trying to imagine the convent empty too and Dame Margaret and whichever of the nuns had chosen to stay with her riding through one of the gateways into York. She had an image of the town built on what she could remember her mother telling her years before. It would not be Micklegate surely, for was not that the gateway to the south? So it must be one of the others – and Lady Abbess had said the house was not a very grand one, on a lane near the Shambles, where meat was sold on open stalls. It was difficult to imagine Dame Margaret Fairfax in such a setting, but Dame Cecilia would make her own of wherever she went. Somehow Isobel felt sure she would have gone to York, for she had no family of her own now, and as she held the baby close to her she thought again of the night of his birth and Dame Cecilia's strength and kindness. Would she ever see her again?

Andrew broke the silence at last. 'Would you go back to the convent if you could?'

'No,' she said quickly. 'I was going to ask for a release anyway. Will *you* return to the religious life when all this is over?'

'I – don't know,' he said slowly. 'I am no longer sure. About anything.'

For a second they looked at each other over the baby's head and she wished that she could somehow get through the armour of his defences. If she had succeeded in doing so, would she have found a more vulnerable Andrew, she often wondered afterwards, and would the future have turned out very differently for them both? But he said briskly now, as if he could read her mind and was determined to maintain a barrier between them, 'It is time to be moving. We must get to Whitby before the weather breaks.'

In the days that followed they passed other carts like their own, laden with farm produce. The drivers would wave a cheery 'good mornin'' and pass a comment on the day's weather – ''t'sun's varra glishy today!' or ''tis a varra loun day for time o' month!' and Andrew would shout back and she would smile and the other cart would roll on. There were children picking blackberries and old men shuffling along with dogs as old as themselves. There was the occasional shepherd making his way home from the fells, but that was all. Until it began to seem that their fears were needless, that the world had forgotten Andrew Ellerton and Isobel Willis and the treasure.

At night they stopped wherever they could find shelter – once in the ruins of an old church, another night in the open behind a cluster of rocks – taking it in turns to sleep, lying on either side of a fire that Andrew sometimes had had difficulty in lighting. They spent another night in a kind of cave, in the side of a hill, and at last they came to a market town. Even Andrew was not sure what town it was for he was relying on his memories of a journey he had made more than two years before to Whitby with Dom Richard.

They needed to buy more food and if possible, two ponies, and Isobel desperately wanted a pot in which to heat food and water for washing the baby. She did not mind cold water for herself but the tiny, pink body seemed to cringe when she washed it with ice-cold water from whatever stream or lake they passed on their way.

It had seemed to them both that they would cause less comment in a crowded market than if they approached an isolated farm house and although many might be disposed to help them, no man's loyalty could be trusted absolutely either to withstand pressure from the King's men or the temptation to rob them of the treasure. So Andrew left Isobel sitting in the cart among their own wilting cabbages while he went to barter with a fellow standing nearby, holding several shaggy looking ponies by their halters. She watched the crowd, looking at the women picking among the vegetables, comparing the cheeses unfavourably with their own, a pedlar weaving his way among them, crying his wares. She felt like a gypsy, and a stall of second-hand clothes caught her eye but she had no money of her own to spend and would not ask Andrew to give her any, at least not for clothes.

At last he came back, leading two ponies, looking pleased for once. 'Fellow didn't want to sell – said 'twas not a horse fair – but I bid him and he sold them to me for three pounds each! Now, you go and get the rest!'

He gave her two silver testers and while he stood guard she went and bought eggs and cheese and more meat and loaves of bread and a bag of apples, and her greatest find – an iron cooking pot. She had bought so much that she could not carry it all back and she gave a young boy an apple to help her, but when he had run off she saw that Andrew's face was tight with anger. 'For God's sake, what kept you? Every second man has been trying to get into chat with me! And to bring that young fellow back with you!'

She was stricken with remorse and yet he infuriated her. 'I only bought what we needed,' she said coldly, 'but I could not carry everything.'

'All right, all right!' he said irritably. 'Get up, quickly!'

She had left Christopher lying in the back of the cart but he was awake now and crying to be fed, and she put him to her breast. As they set off for the hills that rose gently behind the town, the two ponies trotting behind the cart, their halters tied to the back of it, the usual silence fell between them once more.

* * *

151

That night they slept in the open again for there was no cave, no place in which they could shelter. They lit a fire and she made a stew with the meat and vegetables and they had their first hot meal in days. Afterwards, when she had washed the pot she bathed the baby in warm water and herself as best she could, while Andrew sat with his back to her, staring morosely into the fire.

Later they took it in turns to sleep as always, but Isobel nodded off when her turn came and woke to find the young boy from the market standing there, looking down at them.

'Don't tha ha' nowhere to sleep, then?' he said.

Andrew woke with a grunt. 'Aye, but 'tis a long way from here,' he said quickly coming to his senses and, throwing aside his blanket, he reached for his hat and put it on quickly. Isobel wondered fearfully if he had been quick enough, for though his hair was beginning to grow the tonsure was still clearly visible.

'Where is it?' the boy asked.

She smiled at him before Andrew could think of a reply. 'Gaa tet' stream,' she said, 'an' bring me a pot o' water, please!' She held out the pot and when he was gone she said sharply to Andrew, 'We'll have to humour him – and get rid of him quickly at the same time. I am afraid he may have seen your tonsure.'

'I hope not! If he talks – ' But the boy was back already carrying the pot full of water and they could say no more.

He stayed with them for nearly twenty minutes, eating the food they had to give him, while he plied them with questions. He was thin and scrawny, in patched breeches and a torn shirt – like a stray mongrel dog, although his home was nearby, he said, a small farm. When at last they succeeded in getting rid of him, he ran off on his skinny legs as if he had a tale to tell and would waste no time in the telling of it.

Ten minutes later they were on their way, and when they saw a path which intersected the one they had been following and which led to a wood that seemed a mile long, they turned up it. As soon as they reached the wood Andrew led the cart horse in among the trees and the green, dark silence closed in on them. But he soon became restless and leaving her to nurse the baby, he walked out to the edge of the wood again. It was cold under the trees and she could not help but worry for Christopher. Suppose he got a chill, became ill, what would she do? He was still so small, so vulnerable. In a passion of tenderness she held him to her, and he put up a chubby hand and pulled her hair with astonishing strength.

Andrew's voice, cold and harsh, was like a whip across her shoulders. 'I saw a group of soldiers riding along the path we were following earlier.'

Her arms tightened around the baby. 'They may not be looking for us.'

'True.' There was a heavy growth of reddish hair now on his upper lip and on his chin and it occurred to her that with his hat on few would recognise him. 'They could have been going to Mount Grace Priory or even to Whitby Abbey,' he said slowly. 'There has been talk of closures there too, or maybe they were on some other business altogether.' He looked at the cart, and then back at her. 'But we can't assume anything. That boy may talk, and we're moving too slowly.'

'Then we must ride, both of us, from now on. We can leave the cart here – it won't be found for a while.'

'What about the baby?'

'I shall carry him. You'll see.'

She unwound the shawl and wrapped Christopher in a blanket instead, making a kind of pouch from the shawl and tying the ends of it round her neck. Then she took one of the swaddling-bands that Joan had given her and tied it first round the baby and then round her waist so that he was held firmly against her.

Andrew had been standing watching her, frowning, but now he gave a grunt of relief and began to unload the cart. He slung the sack which contained the treasure on one of the ponies, hiding the vegetables as best he could under branches pulled off the trees – but keeping some back for their own use. When he had pulled the cart in as far as he could among the more thickly growing trees they were ready, and although it was not yet dark they set out, keeping in the shelter of the wood for as long as they could, then cutting quickly across the main path further on and heading north west, making for the hills and the moors that lay beyond.

She sat astride her pony, her skirts rolled to her knees, her legs white against the pony's shaggy coat, the baby bound securely to her body and her satchel slung over her shoulder, the rest of their few belongings carried by the second pony. It was years since she had ridden any great distance and she knew that she would be stiff and sore when she dismounted, for she had been stiff enough even after the short ride into East Wooton. But they moved so much faster now, and were so much better able to make use of any cover there might be, that she did not let it worry her. All she wanted now was to get to Whitby as quickly as possible – she tried to imagine what the sea must be like and found that she could not – following Andrew with a kind of reluctant gratitude, and a determination not to show fatigue or pain or fear of any kind, praying only that the pony would not stumble and fall and Christopher be injured.

But the ponies were sure footed and soon they had skirted Mount Grace Priory set below steep, wooded hillsides, riding on until even Andrew felt they had ridden enough for the first day.

They spent that night in the shelter of more trees, taking it in turn as usual to keep watch, Isobel promising not to fall asleep this time, as stiff and sore as she had foreseen but saying nothing of it. And next morning they set off, riding up the steep incline of a high bank and finding the moors spread out before them when they got to the top of it. But she saw none of their beauty, only their vastness, their emptiness.

They lost their way several times in the days that followed and the weather was becoming colder. They had to ration their food too, for although Andrew had long since taken to milking a cow or goat when he could do so unobserved, she found herself perpetually hungry and worried for fear she would not have enough milk for Christopher. Everything about them seemed stunted, petrified by the thin, cold wind and it was hard to believe that grouse had ever fed off the scraggy clumps of bilberry or that the heather had ever been purple, or above all that the sheep could find grazing. Yet they did, as of course they did too on the moors further south. Occasionally they would meet a shepherd and he would stop to talk and ask where they were going and Andrew would tell a different story each time.

They lived in constant fear of a break in the weather, for September was more than half over, spending the nights in the

154

shepherds' huts or behind one of the grassy mounds that Andrew said had been burial places years ago, or behind the rocks that sprouted occasionally from the moors and could be seen for miles, one sleeping, one watching. And sometimes it rained – soft, fine rain that lay lightly on their clothes and could not be considered a serious threat but which nevertheless chilled their bodies. They would have to wait until night-time to dry out before the fire and she would pray again that Christopher would not catch a chill, but he seemed as healthy as ever.

Once they met a packhorse train, making its way south – thirty or forty horses with three drivers, shouting at the beasts who carried their loads in panniers slung on either side of the saddle. The men raised their whips in salute but they did not stop to speak and although that should have been a relief she looked after them with a feeling of regret as they disappeared into the distance. She and Andrew had grown no closer in all the days and nights of being alone together and she was lonelier than she had been even in her last year in the convent.

Soon after they met the packhorse train they came to a river. It was the Esk, Andrew said, and when they came to a bend he said it would lead them straight to Whitby. A few days later they found themselves in rolling countryside and when they had climbed a steep hill, wooded on one side, she got her first glimpse of the sea – flat, unreal, stretching into the distance, becoming one with the sky.

'When we reach the cliffs we shall see Whitby beneath us,' Andrew was saying. 'The abbey is bigger than Wolden with six granges, but there are only eighteen monks there now, and the Chomley family are badgering the King for it.'

'Could we not stop there?' she asked, her stomach clamouring for a proper meal, her whole body aching for a full night's sleep, and enough hot water to wash herself properly.

But Andrew shook his head. 'It would be too risky. Abbot de Vall was a close friend of Father Abbot's but there are lay servants as was the case in Wolden too, and elsewhere.'

And although she knew he was right, she knew too that it was also because of her and Christopher that he would not stop there. How could he explain their presence? Would even the abbot believe that the baby was not his, that she was not his woman? And what must she look like? Her cloak had been dried too often at the fire and the velvet was matted and hard, the skirt of her gown was torn and muddied and she had lost her hood long ago on the moors. She knew too that she smelt of horse and smoke from crouching over the fire and her hair that was at last beginning to grow was a tangle of black curls. She found herself thinking suddenly of Robert, seeing him as he was that night – the rich, red silk of his doublet and breeches, the fine linen of his shirt, his hair thick and clean-smelling, white-gold. He would not recognise me now she thought, even if he wanted to. Her mind shrank from the image of Beatrice Neville, and yet some perverseness in her made her conjure it up as if she wanted to torture herself – perfumed and powdered, in rustling taffeta and lace and glossy furs, jewels in her hair, around her neck, between her breasts – or in nothing at all –

'There's the abbey,' Andrew said brusquely, 'and St Mary's church.' She raised her head, looking in the direction of his pointing finger and saw ahead of them and far to their right a massive stone building bigger indeed than Wolden, with another, smaller building beside it. 'The abbey is built on the clifftop,' he added. 'At night you can hear the sea. I thought I would never get to sleep.'

But she was not listening to him, or even looking at the abbey, her eyes drawn instead to the immensity of the North Sea that had beaten against the Yorkshire coast since the beginning of time. And soon, she thought, if everything went according to plan they would be in a boat on that great expanse of water – a tiny dot, a smudge on the horizon.

They had reached the cliffs now and Andrew had found the way down. She followed him cautiously. It was a narrow, winding path that eventually led to a group of cottages and as they rode slowly past, women and a few children watched them curiously from the open doorways, but there were no men. Not until they came to the shore and the pier alongside, where a few of them were gathered.

'Wait here,' Andrew said, dismounting and giving her the reins of his horse to hold. A little way out from the pier a boat rocked at anchor, its sails furled and she watched while he went from one to the other of the men. But each in turn shook his head until he came to the last, a burly fellow in leather jacket and long boots, a woollen cap pulled down over his ears. They drew apart from the others and she could hear Andrew's voice and the growling tones of the man, but she could not make out what they were saying. Suppose no one could take them, what would they do then? She waited uneasily, sitting on her pony and holding Christopher close to her while the salt laden wind tore at her cloak and she heard the raucous cry of seagulls for the first time in her life.

He came back at last. 'I've found a fellow who will take us, but he drives a hard bargain. Four pounds only for the ponies, and my horse against our passage to Kingston-upon-Hull.'

She thought about it for a moment. It seemed that they would soon have spent all their money for they had been hoping to sell at least one of the animals at a profit, but at least they wouldn't have to waste time looking for a buyer.

'We leave in an hour's time,' he added more cheerfully, 'and he's throwing in food for the journey as well – says his wife's a good cook.' All the time he had been speaking to her he had been scanning the clifftop behind them as if he expected to see a row of pikes along it, and the thought was absurd and frightening at the same time. But when he gave her a hand to dismount she took it. She stood in the sand, looking down at it in wonder.

'I'd like to walk,' she said. 'Just a little way.'

Andrew watched her go, the baby in her arms, thinking that she had come through the journey better than he had thought she would – she did not take after her mother in every respect then. He had been afraid she would chatter as she used to do when they were children, but she rarely spoke now and she seemed to have forgotten her teasing ways altogether. He did not ask himself if she might be happy, or even less unhappy, and he found this new, grave Isobel a much more congenial companion than the other. But he found the baby a continuing irritation. When he saw her kiss and cuddle it he wanted to pull the child out of her arms and throw it to the ground. He never thought of it as a person, however small, merely as a nuisance and even more as living evidence that she had sinned. At least, that was what he told himself in the darkness of his mind, and if he was jealous he was not aware of it, for he was not used to examining his own emotions.

She was coming back towards him now, her head down, kicking the sand up with the broad toes of her shoes like a child herself, and he wondered uneasily if she had really changed after all and how she would react when she heard what he had to say.

'I – I told the boatman that – that you are my wife,' he said shortly. He did not know what he had expected but it was certainly not the bitter amusement that twisted her smile and made her suddenly seem older than her years.

'Poor Andrew!' she said quietly. 'You need not have done that. I would not have minded what he thought.'

'But I would!' he said even more shortly. 'And I'm afraid we shall have to keep up the pretence for the present, at least.'

She shrugged, and he felt the old familiar surge of anger and desire to hurt her. 'Such things are not important to you, I know, but they are to me!'

'Don't worry.' She was beginning to untie the shawl from around her neck and her voice was very cold. 'I shall not embarrass you for a moment longer than is necessary, I promise you that.'

The boatman called to Andrew and he walked away while Isobel bit her lip in fury. Why did he have to be so hateful? She had finished untying the shawl and she held Christopher against her shoulder, staring blindly out to sea, but he had soiled himself and she knew that now she would have to clean him and feed him and then clean him again, and she was tired from too much riding, too soon after the birth. Tears of anger and fatigue ran down her cheeks but she brushed them away impatiently. If she no longer laughed then she would no longer cry either.

They left within the hour on the turn of the tide, sails belling out in the wind, and she sat with her back to their baggage. The boak stank of fish as did the owner himself and his two helpers, and the smell and rise and fall of the sea made her feel ill. Andrew sat opposite her, staring morosely out to sea. And so it was for hour after hour. She was not sick all of the time but it seemed afterwards as if she had been. Sometimes she dozed. Sometimes she simply stared at the heaving mass of green-grey water which never ceased to terrify her. The boat was small and yet it rode the waves smoothly enough, sinking down into the deep valleys but riding up the other side just when she thought they were lost. Then, finally, they were in sight of the mouth of the river and the long, thin neck of land that ran out into the sea.

And at last they sailed into the harbour of Kingston-upon-Hull, their boat small and insignificant among the much bigger vessels moored there. There was a stone jetty and Isobel could see the town walls with their many towers and the town itself within, although to her it seemed a city. Some said it had grown out of the trade with Iceland in stockfish, Andrew told her now, and there were monasteries, he said, and hospitals and fine stone houses and the streets were paved with Icelandic cobbles which had been used as ships' ballast. He told her all this in his usual patronising way although he had only been there once before himself, but she did not resent his tone this time, so interested was she in this 'city'. But when she stepped ashore, her legs unsteady, she felt alien and lost in the bustle of activity and the babble of foreign tongues of which she could only recognise French.

Their boatman arranged for their passage to Amsterdam. The Dutch boat was returning home on the next tide laden with wool, he'd said, the Frenchmen had only just docked and were not going back for a week at least – as for the Spanish they seemed uncertain when they would return. 'But the Dutchmen – they always know to the hour!' he had added, laughing as he took the money from Andrew, not only for their passage but for the forged papers which he had got in some devious way that they did not want to know about, even if the fellow had been willing to tell them.

'We shall have very little money when we get to Amsterdam,' Andrew said gloomily when he had gone. 'The abbot gave me enough money for one, but there are two of us now.'

'Three,' she said coldly, 'but I will teach English when we get there, and see that I am well paid for it!'

He opened his mouth to say something and closed it again, and she turned her back on him, wondering if she really could teach English when she could speak no Dutch, and how long they would be in Amsterdam anyway before they left for Cîteaux. Above all she wished that she was a man and could look after herself without help from anyone, but as the baby stirred in her arms and began to whimper the burden of her womanhood lay on her, heavy as lead.

They waited, cowering behind the wall of the jetty, afraid even now to go into the town for fear they might be recognised, but they left at last on the evening tide in a galley bound for Amsterdam.

Thomas Cromwell's men, who had followed them as far as Whitby, arrived in Kingston-upon-Hull only one day later. The scrawny young farmer's son had been afraid to ask the King's men for any money for his information but there was a man in Whitby who was willing to tell them where the fugitives were going for half a crown. The sailor in Kingston-upon-Hull, however, who had watched them going aboard the Dutch galley told what he had seen for only one tester.

Chapter Eighteen

They kept Robert under close guard all the way to London, armed men with him always, eating, sleeping, even when he relieved himself. Dour, taciturn fellows, well disciplined and with none of the camaraderie between themselves that up to now he had thought was usual among soldiers. He tried to reason with them, to tell them they were wasting their time, that he knew nothing, but they did not even bother to reply. He offered them money to let him go and they laughed at him. He had seen John in the distance only once, flogging his already tired horse in an effort to make it gallop faster but he had not seen him after that for the soldiers had given him a fresh animal and they rode their own hard. And as the miles flew by he tried to put out of his mind the stories he had heard about the Tower, about the men and women who had gone there to be questioned and had returned to their families broken in mind and body, or never returned at all.

The day came at last when he could see the spires of the city and it did not seem long before he could hear the clip-clop of their horses' hooves on the cobbles and houses closed in around them, the smell from the open sewers suffocating after the clean air of the countryside. It was now almost dark, but vendors still called their wares. No one called a greeting, however, and other parties of riders drew quickly to the side to let them by as they approached the river, staring at Robert with a ghoulish curiosity that made his blood run cold.

There had been no sign of John since they had left York and soon the great pile of stone buildings that was the Tower of

161

London loomed over them. It seemed inconceivable that he, Robert FitzHugh, was to walk across the small bridge that spanned the moat and enter that massive doorway as a prisoner of His Majesty the King. Yet it seemed only minutes later that he was standing staring into the gloom, the great door shut behind him, a soldier on either side of him holding his arm, another shouting the name of the new prisoner as shortly before he had shouted the password.

As the wall flares were being lit, they brought him to a small chamber in the lieutenant's lodgings. A man sat behind a large desk and looked up at him with small, expressionless brown eyes. He was well into middle age, dressed in dark, old-fashioned clothes, with a humourless, heavy face under a black cap set squarely on bushy, iron-grey hair. He did not invite Robert to sit, leaving him instead to stand in front of the desk while he continued to look up at him, his face as impassive as that of one of Robert's oriental chess-men. Robert wanted to relieve himself and said so harshly, furious that he should be treated like some village dolt.

'In a moment. When you have answered my questions.' The voice went with the man himself. Toneless. Uncultured.

'Who are you?' Robert asked coldly.

'You do not know?'

'No!'

'I am Thomas Cromwell, and it would be in your best interests to be civil, Master FitzHugh.'

The thin lips had tightened ominously and Robert felt his heart miss a beat. He should have guessed who the man was although he had never seen him before and had had no idea what he looked like. But he had not thought himself to be of sufficient importance to be brought to Cromwell, and even if he were he would have expected to find a man with more presence. Yet the longer he remained standing in front of him the more he became aware of a kind of aura of power emanating from him – the King's right-hand man. Feared and hated by Catholics. Despised by the aristocracy, but respected by bureaucrats and intellectuals.

The small brown eyes seemed to have become hypnotic. 'Why have I been brought here?' Robert asked, as coolly as he could.

The minister looked down at his hands, folded in front of him

162

on the table, the skin pallid, a heavy gold ring on the forefinger, and then he looked up once again at Robert. 'Where is the Cîteaux treasure?' he asked curtly.

'I don't know. I have already told your – minions that. I simply do not know.'

'And the monk, Andrew Ellerton – do you know where he is?'

'I do not know that either! He had gone before I went back to Yorkshire.'

'Why *did* you go back?'

'To visit my future wife.'

'Ah, yes. Mistress Beatrice Neville.' So he even knew about *her*, Robert thought, shocked, but the cold voice went on inexorably. 'Yet you broke your journey to Raskelfe to be present at the execution of the abbot of Wolden. Why so?'

'I heard of it on the way, quite by chance, and I hoped that I might be able to speak for him, to ask that the sentence of death might not be carried out.'

'You sympathised with him? You consider then that the treasure should not have been handed over to the King?'

'Be careful,' a voice said inside Robert's mind. 'Be very careful.' And slowly, picking his words he said, 'I felt that a fine man like the abbot should not be executed for guarding what was given to him for safe keeping – '

'Not even if the King himself says he must hand it over? You are speaking treason, Master FitzHugh, and the abbot was a traitor. He was hanged for that as much as for robbery. As others of his kind have been and will be.'

Robert felt suddenly cold and the need to relieve himself had become even more urgent. 'I have to go to the jakes,' he said quickly.

'In a moment.' The minister's voice had become hard as stone. 'Do you still refuse to tell me where the treasure is, or where I can find Andrew Ellerton? Think well before you answer.'

'I don't need to think!' Robert was beginning to shout. How many times did he have to say it? 'I tell you again, I simply do not know! I had nothing to do with the hiding of it! Nor do I know where Ellerton is or even if he is still alive!'

'You have reason to believe he may be dead?' Thomas Cromwell asked with sudden, new sharpness.

163

Robert shook his head, conscious that he was tired and hungry as well as being acutely uncomfortable. 'No, I have no reason to think so, but surely it is a possibility? And I can stay here for the rest of the evening, tonight, tomorrow, and I still won't be able to tell you what I don't know.'

There was a grunting sound from the other side of the table and then the minister signed to the soldiers standing on either side of the door as motionless as if they were made of wood. The two men came forward, taking Robert by the arm and he was hustled from the room before he could say another word.

Unlike the abbot he was not taken to the Beauchamp Tower dungeon and its squalid discomfort which would in fact have been the height of luxury compared to what was in store for him. He was taken instead to the White Tower, then to a dungeon beneath it that seemed to have been hewn out of the bowels of the earth. The roof was so low he could not stand upright, and in the light of the candle held up by one of the wardens he saw that there was not only no window but there was not even a slit in the walls, although what seemed to be the end of a pipe jutted out from one of them. There was no pail and not even a single blanket or a wisp of straw and the horrible, evil-smelling place was so small he could not have lain full-length had he wanted to. He began to protest furiously but a heavy hand pushed him inside and the door clanged shut behind him with a rattle of heavy bolts being drawn on the other side, leaving him in pitch darkness.

He had to relieve himself on the floor and afterwards, without thinking, he tried to stand upright, only to bump his head against the stone roof. It was bitterly cold but he was no longer hungry; when he shouted no one came, and although he knew it was a waste of time, he threw his weight against the door but it did not budge. He crouched down on his hunkers then, and found himself thinking of Isobel for the hundredth, the thousandth time – and of his son. If it was his son. And if it was not, whose then? Andrew's? Someone else's? His commonsense told him that both possibilities existed. But he could not bring himself to believe that either was the truth. She had been a virgin. He was sure of that, and he was just as sure that she would never have given herself to that cold fish of a cousin – as for another man, he could not believe that either. For a second he saw her as clearly as if she were beside him. Saw her eyes, her mouth, the lift of her chin, the soft, dark hair short as a boy's. Shorter. He should have gone back. But perhaps she had left the convent long since? Still, sooner or later he would have found her if he had tried hard enough. And she would have welcomed him, would have forgiven him – women always did, in the end. But for all his adventures he had never given a child to a woman before, and perhaps she hated him now. Besides, she was not like any other woman he had ever known. And yet he had turned his back on her and promised himself instead in marriage to someone he could not abide.

The cold of the stone floor was in his bones but he was hardly aware of it so lost was he in the bitterness of his thoughts. Marriage had always seemed to him to be a sordid business, a commerce in human bodies, and he scourged himself now with the fact that in spite of all his promises to himself that he would do better, he had traded in the end, like all the rest – and he had never even thought of Isobel as a wife. But now, suddenly thinking about it, just imagining the delicious folly of marrying a beautiful, penniless girl of no family seemed to bring a blaze of light into the dark, coffin-like dungeon.

If only he could turn back the clock! Yet he knew that even if he could he would still not have gone after her, let alone thought of marrying her. Given the same choices he would still have become betrothed to Beatrice Neville and to think otherwise was foolishness – at least he must be honest with himself. And as he saw himself clearly for the first time in his life, not liking what he saw, he realised to his horror that the drip-drip of water from the pipe had become louder and the entire floor was covered with water.

Soon it was up to his ankles. Gradually it rose higher and higher until it was up to his knees, and still it was rising. He knew then that what he had subconsciously feared the moment he had seen the pipe was a reality. The pipe was connected with the tidal moat and would let in water at high tide. If enough water came through the pipe he would drown. Unless they came for him before that.

He began to shout again, throwing himself against the door that never budged, until he grew silent at last, knowing they would not come and determined to die with at least a show of

165

courage. The water was up to his hips now, the smell indescribable, and he knew by the soft, dead feel of the small bodies that he had the corpses of the river rats for company. He threshed about like a madman trying to keep his blood circulating, no longer caring that from the growing stench he knew there must be human faeces as well as dead rats in the water.

He tried to pray. But he could not remember the words of any prayer and he found himself instead just saying the Lord's name over and over like a child, or an old, old man – saying Isobel's name sometimes too. Once it seemed as if she was with him, and he wondered if he was beginning to lose his reason or if she really had come to him, and if that meant he was going to die. And just as the roof of the dungeon seemed no more than a few inches above the level of the water and, he had to lift his chin to keep his mouth free of it, he became aware that the water was no longer rising.

It seemed like hours, a lifetime before the water began to subside noticeably and another lifetime before it had crept down to the level of his hips again, then to his knees and at last, to his feet. He was lying in a sodden heap when they came and took him, shivering and retching, up the stone steps, out of the White Tower, and back to the room in the lieutenant's lodgings.

This time Edward Dutton was with Thomas Cromwell. They gave him a stool to sit on, while the water dripping from his clothes formed an ever widening pool on the floor and filled the room with its stench.

'Well, have you remembered where the treasure is?' The minister's voice was as toneless as ever.

'No!' Robert said, through chattering teeth. 'How could I? I told you I don't know!'

'Have you remembered where Andrew Ellerton might be?' Edward Dutton said, leaning across the table.

'I don't know anything about him either.' Robert hardly recognised his own voice. It sounded like that of a dying man, and he tried to force some life into it. 'If you think trying to drown me will make me remember something I don't know, then you are a fool!'

Edward Dutton's pale face flushed an ugly red but the minister said almost gently, ''tis you who are the fool, Master

166

FitzHugh. It matters little to us whether you drown or not. All we want is the truth. Then you can return to your home.'

Robert felt himself begin to shiver even more violently, not from fear but from the cold that seemed to be melting his bones, and then as through a fog he heard Edward Dutton's voice again. 'The girl – Isobel Willis – where is she?'

He shook his head wearily. 'I don't know.'

'My men will find her, sooner or later,' the minister said evenly, 'and they will bring her here. You know what will happen to her then. If you speak now you can spare her that. Have you no care for her or for the child?'

'She has nothing to do with any of this!' Robert's voice broke in spite of himself. 'Leave her alone! For pity's sake, leave her alone!'

'When we sent to the farm for her she had gone,' the minister said with sudden impatience. 'Her family did not know anything about her nor the nuns, either. Yet her father had taken her back to live on the farm. Why should she suddenly leave?'

Robert shook his head like a crazed animal, trying to clear his mind, but he could think of no answer, nothing that would not put her in greater danger than she was in already. The minister and Edward Dutton got up from the table and went to the end of the room, talking in low voices. He could not hear what they were saying and he felt as if he were becoming lost in a thick, white fog...

'I think the young fool is telling the truth,' Thomas Cromwell said irritably. 'There's nothing to be gained by keeping him here.'

'You are surely not thinking of letting him go free?' The other man could not keep the disappointment out of his voice. 'Perhaps the rack might persuade him to talk?'

The minister frowned. 'If I am right and we try further persuasion then he will either waste our time with a pack of lies or he will die, still protesting that he does not know. And he does have connections.'

'But what makes you think he is telling the truth?'

'Experience. I have questioned a considerable number of

people in my time, Dutton, and I have come to recognise the ring of it.'

There was a new curtness in the minister's voice and Edward Dutton said hastily, 'Of course! Of course! I was only just – '

But he was not allowed to finish. 'I shall have him watched, however,' the curt voice went on. 'Sooner or later he will try to get in touch with either Ellerton or the girl. It is our only hope now.'

'How wise of you, minister!' Edward Dutton was smiling now but his eyes were watchful. 'That would certainly be our best course and perhaps you will keep me informed – you can, of course, call on me at any time. And now, if you will excuse me, I shall take my leave.' It was growing dark and even with his servant beside him he found the Tower an unnerving place. Who knew what demented creature might not escape and leap on him from some dark doorway?

Thomas Cromwell watched him leave the room with relief. The fellow had his uses, but he was a sychophant of the worst kind, and, he suspected, a sadist. He did not himself take any pleasure in the torture he inflicted on so many men and women. To him it was merely a means to an end, a part of his never-ending commitment to King and country and thereby the furtherance of his own career. But for Dutton he guessed that it would be different, and that he felt a personal animosity towards the young man, crouching now on the low stool, and filling the room with his smell.

Going back to the table he sat down, drawing a sheet of parchment towards him, and the scratching of his quill pen was the only sound in the room for the next few minutes as he wrote an order for the release of the prisoner, Robert FitzHugh. When he had sanded it he gave it to one of the guards.

'Give this to the Chief Warden,' he said, 'and take the prisoner to him.' He drew a pile of documents towards him as the two guards half lifted, half carried their prisoner from the room, but as soon as the door had shut behind them, he pushed the documents away and leant back in his chair, frowning. The pity was that the whole matter of Wolden Abbey and the treasure had dragged on for so long. Wolden should have been closed months ago, and he should have interrogated Dom Richard himself – he knew better than anyone how to break a priest. But he had been still ill with the flux when the abbot had been brought to London, and some fool had hurried things along too fast. He'd had no choice then but to order the trial and arrange for the sentence to be given and carried out – and there had been other pressing matters too to take his attention at the time – the larger monasteries to be closed, and the King's continuing reluctance, under the influence of Norfolk and Gardiner, to commit himself fully to Protestantism.

There were, too, the never-ending intrigues of Reginald Pole and his aunt the Countess of Salisbury. At least the pestiliential old woman was now safely lodged in the Tower, he told himself, not foreseeing the manner of her death later, on Tower Green, when the headsman would bungle his job and would have to chase her round the block like a terrified chicken trying to escape from the farmer's knife – not that in any case he himself would have cared. She had caused him too much trouble at a time when there had been trouble abroad too, aggravated by the fear of Scottish intervention.

But the minister consoled himself now with the thought that the King had agreed at last to marry Anne of Cleves, and her brother, Duke William, had given his assent. But he himself was not looking forward to her arrival in England in December. A recent report from Germany had described her as a plain-looking woman of little charm, and the King was sure to be bitterly disappointed and blame him for having encouraged the marriage. If only he could have found the treasure in time he could have presented it as a peace-offering . . .

'I want the chalice on the altar for the wedding ceremony!' Henry had said recently, 'And all the rest as well! I want them to be *seen*!' He had been like a spoiled child remembering a long-promised treat, eating supper alone with him in a small parlour in the palace. It was his own, private continuing regret that he could never entertain the King in any of his houses because of his humble birth and he had wished that evening that he could have said with truth, 'I am only a brewer's son but I know where the Cîteaux treasure is. I will bring it to you in time for the wedding.' But he had known no more about it then than he did now. Well, he would set someone who knew his job to watch FitzHugh.

* * *

169

A week later, while Robert was still in bed with fever in his grandfather's house, word was brought to Cromwell from Kingston-upon-Hull by special messenger – Andrew Ellerton and Isobel Willis with her child had left for Amsterdam. Thomas Cromwell sent two of his men with Edward Dutton to follow them and set men to watch the house of Sir William FitzHugh, knowing that Robert's Dutch grandmother had left him property in Amsterdam which he frequently visited. But his men found that Robert never seemed to leave the house in Chelsea for more than an hour or so until the day, now fully recovered from fever, when he left for Yorkshire for his marriage to Beatrice Neville, accompanied by John Riddell. Nevertheless, Cromwell's men followed at a discreet distance, in case he should plan to leave the country from some northern port, hoping that if he did he would lead them to Andrew Ellerton and the treasure.

Chapter Nineteen

They had got off the galley ten minutes before and now they pushed their way through a chattering, laughing crowd. Andrew went ahead, laden like a packhorse, Isobel following, carrying Christopher and her own satchel, and some of Andrew's paintings in her one free hand, so glad to be off the boat that she never once turned to look back at it. Her cloak was caked with sea salt, her hair thick with it, the skin of her face roughened by sea winds, her empty stomach craving properly cooked, hot food, her unwashed body craving hot water and soap.

As she elbowed her way past one broad, uncaring back after another she began to think that she was invisible. They seemed so big, these Dutchmen in their baggy breeches, and heavy looking clogs, so intent on one another that no one seemed to exist for them outside their own group, their belly laughs ringing out, their incomprehensible language flowing over her head.

She had seen no women as yet but as they left the jetty behind, she saw them – big like the men and seemingly full of the same boisterous good humour, reminding her strangely of Yorkshire women. When she attempted to speak to them first in English and then in French, however, they had stared at her blankly, before turning away. Dame Petronilla had taught her French – they were the only two nuns in the convent who could speak the language and she had always been rather proud of the fact. It must be her accent, she thought, or perhaps her appearance.

Andrew, ahead of her, had obviously fared no better and her first joy in having set foot on land became tempered by the fear

171

of rejection. They walked on slowly, leaving the harbour with its myriad of galleys and smaller vessels behind them, until they came to the walled town, going through one of the gates like two pilgrims, seeing their first canal, their first sluice, forgetting their hunger, lost in wonder at the strangeness of it all.

'But we must find some place to stay,' Andrew said. 'It will soon be dark.' They had come to a narrow street where the houses leant towards each other like gossiping women, and lines of washing ran across the street that had been hung from top windows. There was an inn on the corner, its doors wide open, its tables packed with noisy, laughing men and women, the smell of beer heavy on the cool, autumn breeze. Andrew thought they should lodge there, but she persuaded him not to go in, for she could not imagine herself in such boisterous company. So they walked on a little way while she put the baby on her hip to rest her aching arm, and it was then that they saw the couple coming towards them.

The man was bearded, unlike most of the Dutchmen she had seen so far – a magnificent brown beard that contrasted oddly with the dark severity of his clothes. The woman's dress was of grey woollen cloth, severely cut too, and with tight-fitting sleeves, quite unlike the bright colours and billowing skirts that Isobel had seen on the other women. Her cap of plain white linen was neater also, more close-fitting, although wisps of blonde hair escaped behind her ears. But it was more than just their clothes that was different. There was a kindness, a gentleness in their faces that had certainly not been in any of the other faces she had seen since she got off the boat. They knew no English either, but when Andrew asked about cheap lodgings in his halting French they smiled, nodded and beckoned him to follow them.

The couple led the way down the street, turning left to follow a path that ran by the side of a canal, whose dirty sluggish water seemed scarcely to move, until they left the path and turned left up a narrow lane, stopping in front of a house. It was a timber house like the rest, with staggered storeys facing the lane, its roof running up into a peak but seeming even narrower than its neighbours. The man opened the green painted door and let the woman in, beckoning to Andrew and Isobel to follow her. When the door had closed behind them they found themselves in darkness until the man opened back the window shutters and let in the evening half-light.

There was a smell of cleanness, a glow of warmth, and Isobel saw that they were standing in what seemed to be the living room. There was a bed built into one wall like a cupboard, an oak table and chairs and a massive chest standing in one corner, and plaques of painted porcelain on another wall. Through the open door at the back of the room she could see the gleam of copper pans hanging on the wall of what seemed to be the kitchen.

'You are welcome to our house,' the man said, in slow, careful French, taking off his hat for a moment and pushing his dark hair off his forehead. 'My wife will show you where you are to sleep. It is not very grand but you will be safe, at least.'

While Andrew remained below with their host the woman led the way up narrow stairs to an attic. It was tiny in comparison to the loft in the farmhouse in Yorkshire but, although there was straw too on the floor, there was a proper door and a window. The bed was a huge mattress, laid on the straw but there was a chair and a small chest and in one corner, a large chamber-pot. Isobel found herself staring at the mattress and the pot. Where was Andrew to sleep? And then she saw that there were really two mattresses, one on top of the other, and they were more like feather bags than any mattresses she had ever seen before. Well, Andrew could have one and she would have the other. But all the same she shrank from the idea of sharing a room with him.

She realised that the woman was beginning to look at her anxiously and she smiled quickly and said that it would do very well if she could give her something in which Christopher could sleep and blankets for themselves, and while the woman hurried off she sat down on the chair with the baby in her arms, dreading the moment when she would find herself alone with Andrew.

Yet she thanked God they were off the galley. There had been a forced intimacy of a different kind on the journey over from England. They had been cooped up with the rest of the passengers on the high stern or below deck, all of them men, merchants for the most part, some English, some Dutch, one or two Frenchmen. Christopher had been fretful, sleeping for only short periods, crying as soon as he wakened and she had had to walk up and down carrying him, trying to soothe him and ignore the irritated faces, the muttered curses. Worst of all she had had to squat behind the shelter of their baggage. Even thinking about it now brought the colour to her face.

And Andrew, engrossed in his painting, had been no help. A sea-gull which he had painted on wood with meticulous care, caught the eye of an elderly Englishman who had bought it for a few testers. She had thought it worth more. Sitting now on the chair, she found herself thinking ahead, worrying about how they would find the money to pay for their lodgings.

The woman returned soon afterwards with blankets and a wooden box – not unlike the one Dame Cecilia had given her in the convent – for Christopher, and when she left again to prepare a meal Isobel made the box as comfortable as she could for the baby and put him down to sleep.

She combed her tangled hair and looked at her muddied gown. There was nothing she could do about it, torn at the hem by brambles and spiky bushes on the long ride to Whitby and she was too hungry now to care about such things anyway. When the woman called her to eat she hurried down, determined to forget about their lack of money and all their other problems for the moment.

There was a hot, steaming soup of minced meat added to stock and flavoured with nutmeg, fried red herrings with cabbage, and black, sticky bread, dense and indigestible, followed by mouth-watering fruit pie and cheese as good as any Wensleydale. The Dutch couple called the meal their dinner, even though by now it was late in the evening and they all ate together at the table in the living-room. There had been milk and beer to drink but neither the man nor the woman drank any beer although Andrew and Isobel helped themselves.

The Dutch couple were man and wife, Pieter and Saskia Eisinga, whose families had come from Friesland, although they themselves had been reared in Amsterdam. They had spent a year in the south, where they had learned to speak French. They said they were Mennonites, which meant nothing to Isobel, but she thought that Andrew looked taken aback. After a moment he said hesitantly that he and Isobel were Catholics. Pieter had frowned, looking down at the table, and then glancing briefly at Saskia. 'It makes no difference to us,' he said slowly, 'but the

174

situation in Amsterdam is difficult at the moment. How long are you planning to stay?'

'Not long,' Andrew replied. 'I am an artist and I have come to Holland to learn what I can. We shall move on soon to some other town.'

'You have come to the right place then, and if you are only planning to stay here for a short while, then perhaps there is no problem.' But Pieter was still frowning a moment later while Andrew brought the sack and the rest of their baggage up to the attic and Isobel wondered what new problem had been added to all the rest, for she was reluctant to ask the Dutch couple what Mennonites were.

Later, when she had fed Christopher, Saskia gave her hot water in which to wash him and even enough water in which to wash herself from top to toe. Then she dried her hair in front of the peat fire in the kitchen while the two men talked in the living room.

When it was time for bed she went up the stairs alone, and when she had undressed and lain down on the mattress, pulling the blankets up to her chin, she lay in the dark, the candle blown out, dreading the sound of Andrew's footsteps on the stairs. She told herself not to be foolish – that he wouldn't – that he was her cousin – a monk still, surely – that in all of their long journey he had never as much as taken her hand in his – And yet –

Half an hour later he knocked on the door and when she said, 'Come in', he entered slowly, and she sat up and lit the candle as he closed the door awkwardly behind him.

'I'm sorry,' he muttered. 'I couldn't tell them that we – that we are not – '

'It's all right,' she interrupted him quickly. 'I've made up a bed for you.'

He looked at the other mattress spread out on the straw, blankets thrown on it and one of the pillows Saskia had given her afterwards. 'So I see.' His voice was without expression of any kind. 'You can blow out the candle now,' he added.

She did so, lying back and turning to face the wall. She could hear him groping about in the dark and then all was quiet. Her eyelids were beginning to close, in spite of her earlier fears, when his voice, sharp and cold, brought her back to full wakefulness.

'We can't stay here.'

'Why not?'

'They are Mennonites! You were there when they told us.'

'I – I did not know what they meant.' She hated to admit it, to him of all people.

She could hear his sigh in the darkness. 'They are a religious sect,' he said after a moment as if he were her teacher and not a very patient one at that. 'The sect was founded by a man called Menno Simons. They are like the Anabaptists, in that they affirm the Scriptures as their final authority and believe in adult baptism, but unlike the Anabaptists they are passive, opposed to violence, and they do not take part in civil government or swear oaths. In a sense they are secluded from the world.'

'What is wrong with any of that?' she asked, not having any very clear idea of what Anabaptists were either.

'In many ways, nothing,' he replied with the same note of forced patience in his voice. 'But they have broken away from the Catholic Church which is all-powerful here in Amsterdam – Simons was a priest himself once – and many people think of them as Anabaptists, not knowing the difference. Anabaptists were responsible for a terrible massacre at Münster some years ago and only last week stones were thrown at Pieter in the street. He and his wife have no animosity at all towards us, as you saw, but he told me it might not be safe for us to stay here, or I suppose for them to keep us, although he did not say that.'

'Just when I'd thought we had found new friends,' she said sadly.

'Pieter is well educated,' Andrew went on, as if she had not spoken. 'He even has a knowledge of Latin and we discovered that the Friesian dialect is similar in many ways to some of our Yorkshire dialects!' His voice had become warmer, almost excited but she was tired and knew that she would not be able to go to sleep all the same. Why could he not have waited until morning to tell her his bad news?

'When do we leave?' she asked shortly.

'As soon as possible. Tomorrow I shall try to sell some of my paintings in the market and I can change what is left of my English money there for Dutch. Pieter says too that I might be able to find work in what he calls the Old Church, repainting altar panels, and perhaps someone there can direct us to other lodgings.' His voice changed, became hesitant, as he added, 'I have been thinking – '

'Thinking what?' she asked warily.

'That – that we ought to get married.'

'*Married*?' She nearly choked on the word and then lay silent, cold with shock, and yet with a feeling of inevitability creeping over her, as though she had been waiting for him to say those words to her for a long time.

'We cannot go on like this,' he said curtly into the silence. 'You must see that.'

'Of course I do,' she said quickly. 'But we don't have to get *married*! I shall tell the Eisingas the truth, and when we leave here I shall – shall – '

'What will you do?' he interrupted harshly. 'On your own, with a child to look after. Find another lover? Is that it?'

She was too angry to answer him at once. 'I shall find work as a servant if necessary,' she said quietly, after a moment. 'Or I can teach English.'

'You would need to have at least a smattering of Dutch for that.'

'I shall soon have that – but to talk of *marriage*!' She went on hoarsely, 'You don't love me, nor I you! You don't even *like* me, nor any woman, I sometimes think!'

'Love! Like! I'm not talking about that kind of foolishness,' he said coldly.

'But – but the Church – don't you want to go back to it?' She said it as if she were begging him to say 'yes', but his voice when he answered her was bleak.

'That is over for me, and I would look after you and – and the baby. To the best of my ability.'

But all she could think of was the horror of lying with him. It would be like incest, as if he were her brother, a brother whom she did not even like. All I have to do is to say 'no', she thought frantically. Just a firm 'no!' Why have I not said so already? What is wrong with me?

'Will you at least think about it?' His voice now was suddenly so hesitant, so almost gentle that she could not find it in her heart to refuse to do that much.

'All right,' she said slowly. 'I shall – think about it. But that is all.' Later I shall tell him, she thought. Later.

177

She could hear him throw himself on his side with anger or impatience, and she lay listening now to the rattle of the night-guard, afraid that their talking might have disturbed Christopher, but there was no sound from him and she turned on her side, praying for sleep.

Andrew, too, lay awake for a long time, his thoughts chasing each other in endless circles. She was impossible, he told himself. He had offered marriage and she had not even considered it seriously. Not really. He knew her too well to believe her when she said she would think about it. Yet her father had wanted it for her and so had his, and he had no vocation. The certainty had come during the long hours of their journey together, saddening him at the time. But now he looked to the future. And he was honest, sober, diligent. What more could she want? Unless she was still dreaming of FitzHugh? Could a girl, a woman as she was now – be so foolish, so full of – of *evil*?

Tonight, when he came up the stairs, before he even saw the outline of her body under the blankets, he was sweating, and every time he heard her turn on her mattress it was as if his adolescent yearnings had returned to torment him, in spite of all the years of self-discipline. But after a while she lay more quietly, scarcely seeming to breathe and he began to think of the treasure and his undertaking to bring it back to Cîteaux.

Where was he going to find the money for the journey? Already he owed the Eisingas for a day's lodging. Soon – tomorrow – he must go to see the banker, Cornelis van Ophoorn, although he hated the thought of being beholden to a relative of Robert FitzHugh's, however distant. Perhaps, he thought, we should have gone directly to France since no one seems to have come after us. And as his thoughts began to drift again he saw her face behind closed eyelids.

He had had doubts about his vocation even before leaving Wolden but she had played no part in the losing of that vocation. Women were necessary for child-bearing and for some men. Until tonight he had not thought that he might be one of them. He had asked her to marry him out of a sense of duty – at least he had believed so at the time. Now he was not so sure and her unwillingness to say 'yes' seemed, as the night hours drifted slowly past, to be not only irritating but in some strange way, hurtful.

When at last he fell asleep, he dreamed they were children again, playing in the old mine where he had hidden the treasure. Yet in his dream there was no treasure and it was she who hid herself from him. He found her at last behind an old rock-fall and she laughed in his face, the girl-child turning into a woman as he pulled her furiously to her feet, his hand on the soft roundness of her arm, burning hot. He woke to silence and the knowledge that she lay within arms' reach, and it was a long time before he could get back to sleep. Mercifully, this time he did not dream.

Chapter Twenty

The Eisingas rose early and the noise of the window shutters being opened woke Isobel. Andrew had already left the attic, to her great relief, and when she had fed Christopher and gone downstairs herself she found the other three at breakfast in the living room. It was a simple meal of milk and cheese and the bread which did not seem quite so awful this time. She wondered if she might eventually even grow to like it. After breakfast Pieter left the house and Andrew left soon afterwards, carrying two of his paintings.

'I have some gowns that are too small for me,' Saskia said later, as Isobel washed Christopher in the kitchen. 'Perhaps one might fit you? It seems a pity not to use them, although they are not of the latest fashion and you may find them not to your liking.'

The gowns were grey, all of them, and severely plain, like the gown the Dutchwoman was wearing at the moment, but one of them fitted better than the rest.

'It is the same colour as your eyes!' Saskia said, smiling with pleasure. 'Your husband will like it, I hope!'

Her own blue eyes were so honest, so kind that Isobel said quietly, 'He is not my husband, and he is not Christopher's father.'

'I know.' The Dutchwoman's voice was very gentle. 'Can I hold the baby now?'

Isobel gave her Christopher to hold, watching while she cradled him in her arms. 'How did you know?'

'The way Andrew looks at you, at the child. His voice. The way he never touches either of you.'

180

'I see.' Isobel felt tears sting her eyes for no apparent reason. 'He is my cousin. That is all.'

'You need not tell me about it,' Saskia said, 'not if you don't want to, but you are very lucky to have a child. Pieter and I have been married for five years and we have never been blessed. I feel such a failure. The main purpose of a Mennonite marriage is to have children, and in Holland anyway a woman is expected to have a child every year. They hang a wooden plaque covered with red silk and trimmed with lace on her door after a birth.'

She spoke French so fluently that Isobel had to ask her to speak more slowly and then she said herself, frowning, 'I would not want to have a child every year.'

'Not even if you were married to the man you loved?'

The two women looked at each other. 'Giving birth is not easy,' Isobel said, 'and I can't imagine myself married to – '

'Christopher's father?' Saskia interrupted her gently.

Isobel nodded, and then went on quickly, 'But you are young still and so is Pieter.'

'I am twenty-nine,' Saskia said sadly. I am getting old. Pieter says it does not matter, that we have more love to give each other if we do not have to share it with children. But he is just saying that to console me, I know.'

Young as she had been at the time Isobel could still remember her mother's face as she prayed for a child, a son. It had had the same look of hopeless longing that she could see now in Saskia's, but her mother had not had a husband like Pieter and when God had granted her wish in the end He had taken back His gift and her life with it. 'I wonder if you know how much you have already?' she said into the silence.

Saskia gave her a sudden, brilliant smile. 'Yes! I do know! I have loved Pieter for as long as I can remember! My father brought three men to me from whom I was to choose a husband, as is the Mennonite custom and one of them was Pieter. It did not take me long to decide!'

'Did your father know you loved him?'

'I am not sure. I think so. I was lucky I know, luckier than most, but usually Mennonite marriages are happy enough. Mennonite men are taught to be kind to their wives and families.'

Isobel felt suddenly terribly alone. Perhaps it showed in her face for the Dutchwoman handed the baby back to her saying with another smile, 'I think he needs his mother! His is getting restless!'

Isobel took the happy, contented baby in her arms and tried to hold back tears as Saskia pretended not to notice and talked instead about her family in Friesland and how they worried about Pieter and herself, and of the goodness and courage of Menno Simons. The moment passed, and the other moments of that quiet, uneventful day, and years later it was its tranquillity that Isobel remembered, when the horror and tragedy had begun to fade from her mind, and her only regret was that she had not told Saskia everything, for she of all people would have understood.

The two men returned in the evening darkness. Pieter said nothing about his day, but Andrew told them one of the stall holders in the market place had taken his paintings, and he had been promised a few days' work in the Old Church. He had asked about other lodgings and the priest had said he would surely have an address for him when he came back again, and he had bought himself a pair of baggy, black Dutch breeches and a black, tight-sleeved doublet in the market, for his own clothes were not only filthy he said, but made him feel conspicuous. With his beard which he had not yet shaved off, he looked not unlike a Mennonite himself, Isobel thought, but although he glanced at her grey dress he passed no comment on it and she was glad Saskia was not with them at the time, guessing that he merely felt relieved that he did not have to give her money to buy a new one.

When she told him, after Pieter too had left the kitchen, that he was to sleep downstairs his face hardened and he looked away. 'Saskia knows now that we are not married,' she said. 'I told her you are only my cousin and that Christopher is not your son.'

'What did she say?'

'She said she had guessed already that – that we were not husband and wife.'

He was silent for a moment and then he said, looking her full in the face, 'Have you given any thought to what I said to you last night?'

'There has been no time. I – I shall think about it – I – I told you.'

His eyes were full of cold anger but Saskia had come back into the kitchen and he could say no more. From that night on, however, he slept downstairs in an alcove near the Eisingas' tiny bedchamber that was itself little more than an alcove, and he seemed to avoid being alone with her.

Next day, on his way back from the Old Church, Andrew called to see the banker, Cornelis van Ophoorn, in his house on Kerkstraat, the address and the letter of introduction which the abbot had given him long ago, in the pocket of his breeches. It was a difficult interview. The man was older than he had been led to believe, clean-shaven, grey-haired, with the manners of what Andrew thought of as the 'gentry'. There was no physical resemblance of any kind to Robert FitzHugh and he knew the man was trying to put him at his ease, but there was such an air of unobtrusive wealth about the house, about the banker himself, that he felt out of place – even the servant who had admitted him had looked him up and down as if he were a beggar. They spoke in French which Andrew was only able to follow with difficulty, for he was not as fluent as Isobel but he had already picked up a few words of Dutch and the banker had a smattering of English, so they could understand one another after a fashion. The Dutchman was clearly distressed to hear of the abbot's death and the manner of it, but then he began to ask about the treasure, his face sharpening, becoming secretive, becoming a banker's face.

'How valuable is it? Can you name a figure?'

Andrew shook his head. 'All I can say is that it is truly magnificent, and Father Abbot told me it was unique and of great historical significance.'

'Where is it now?'

'In the house where I am staying, in the Doutsteeg.'

Cornelis van Ophoorn raised bushy, grey eyebrows. 'That rabbit-warren? The sooner you get it out of there the better! And you say you brought it over on the boat from England, alone?'

'I had no choice.' Then as offhandedly as he could, Andrew added, 'My cousin travelled with me. She is in my charge.'

'Your cousin?' The man sitting on the other side of the small table raised his eyebrows again and Andrew felt his face grow hot, cursing himself for having mentioned Isobel at all. But the

183

banker went on matter of factly as if a travelling companion, cousin or otherwise, was of little importance. 'I suggest that you lodge the treasure in the bank's vault as soon as possible, because it is far too late in the year to set out for Cîteaux. You should wait until the spring and you will need an escort, otherwise the treasure may be stolen on the way and your body left lying somewhere. I shall help you with all of it. My promise on it – and now, if you will excuse me, I have matters to attend to.'

Andrew left soon afterwards, not sure that he liked Cornelis van Ophoorn and knowing that he had no alternative but to trust him. He told himself that it was not the man's fault that he was related to the FitzHugh family, but he was glad Isobel did not know of the relationship and he was not going to tell her, as if somehow her ignorance of it might help to maintain a distance between herself and Robert.

As he hurried back to the Doutsteeg, anxious to get there before dark, he thought about what he would say to the Eisingas about the treasure in case anything should happen to him before the following spring. But to tell Pieter, to ask him to act for him might place the Dutchman, as a Mennonite, in an impossible position. No. He would have to leave it to the banker and to Isobel, even though she was only a woman and easily led astray. But as he came into the lane that led down to the Doutsteeg he told himself he was worrying unnecessarily. What could possibly happen to him?

He brought the treasure to the banker's house the following day, Isobel walking beside him, carrying the baby, as they had done so often before, but he told her to go home as soon as the servant had opened the door, and she walked away down the street leaving him to go in alone. He saw nothing odd in this and she did not argue with him. An hour later, protected by two brawny bank servants he lodged the treasure in the vault of the bank house that was near the Damrak, having given them a note from Cornelis van Ophoorn. They in turn gave him an official bank receipt for a sack of 'valuables'. It was the best, the only thing he could do.

A few days later he found another house where they could lodge, but the woman could not take them immediately as her daughter was soon to be married and she would be busy preparing for the wedding. When he told Pieter this, on his return that evening, the Dutchman assured him it would be all right for them to stay a while longer, his narrow, intelligent face alive with interest as he listened to Saskia's efforts to teach Isobel the Dutch language. He appeared to be a man of some standing among the Mennonites of Amsterdam and Andrew knew he would be sorry when the time came to leave, for he enjoyed their discussions together.

Isobel was in no hurry to leave the Eisingas' house either. Saskia had become like a sister to her, the sister she had never had and always wanted. For her the days slipped past unnoticed, the two men out all day – Pieter busy with his own, private business and Andrew painting wherever he could find work. The painting of the altar panels in the Old Church was now finished and he painted front doors, canopies, anything at all that would bring in a few guilders. She had nothing to do except look after Christopher and help Saskia with the housework, and Andrew, to her relief, had not talked again about marriage.

Sometimes she would take the baby with her to the canal nearby and watch the boats go up and down with their air of lazy purpose. Most of the time, however, she stayed in the house, and when Saskia went to the market she would come back to find everything even neater and cleaner than it had been before she went out and Isobel playing with Christopher or sitting by the fire while he slept.

And then one night Isobel woke to hear the sound of voices below and some time afterwards, the soft thud of the front door closing. It was just before dawn and she soon dropped off to sleep again but when she went down to the kitchen next morning Saskia was there alone, dark shadows under her eyes. 'I heard voices during the night,' she said to her. 'Is anything wrong?'

Saskia shook her head. 'It was just a – a friend who called. He is gone now.'

Chapter Twenty-One

A week later an air of sadness hung over their evening meal with Pieter and Saskia, for the woman had sent word that the wedding festivities were over and she was free to take them. They were to leave the following day and now, after the meal, while the two men sat talking Isobel helped Saskia clear the dishes away and asked her if she would come and visit her in the new lodgings.

'I shall come,' Saskia said slowly, 'If I can.'

Isobel had taken the baby up to the attic then, wondering if she really would see Saskia again after they had left, and why there should be any doubt about it. She sat down on the chair, the baby in her arms, listening to the sounds from below – Pieter laughing, Saskia saying something to him and laughing herself – and suddenly, like a crash of thunder there was a loud, heavy knocking on the front door.

She heard someone, Pieter surely, go to the door and open it, heard men's voices, talking, shouting in Dutch. She did not yet know enough of the language to understand what they were saying, but she was horribly aware of the threat, the violence of the tone and she held Christopher to her, standing now just inside the doorway of the attic, trying to see down the stairs without being seen.

There seemed to be five or six men standing at the table, their backs to her, men in leather jackets carrying pikes. One of them was holding Pieter by the arm, the others staring down at Andrew who was still sitting. And then she saw Saskia being led, dragged rather, from the kitchen. Her cap had fallen off and her

186

blonde hair had come uncoiled and hung below her shoulders. She tried to pull away from the man holding her and he struck her across the face, sending her spinning across the room. There was a burst of laughter as Pieter struggled like a madman to free himself, and Andrew tried to get up from the table and was prevented, and then a deathly silence until one of the men began to speak. He seemed to be the leader and Saskia was staring at him as if she could not believe what he was saying.

What in God's name was going on, Isobel wondered – and realised then that another man was making for the stairs. She drew back and slipped behind the door, holding the baby close to her and giving him her finger to suck, praying he would make no sound. The man came into the attic and stood in the middle of the floor. He was turning around when there was a shout from below. She scarcely dared to breathe, and if the light had been better or the door not so wide open he would surely have seen her. As it was, he walked out through the open doorway and she heard his heavy footsteps going down the stairs again. There was what sounded like a command and then she heard Andrew's voice.

'This is an outrage! I am an Englishman, a Catholic!'

Pieter said something then and there was another burst of jeering laughter from the men that made her whole body feel cold. Someone knocked over a chair and Saskia screamed. A single, terrified scream, and but for the baby in her arms she would have gone down. There was more shouting, a crash that sounded like the table being turned over and then all noise gradually died, until there was total silence.

When at last she dared to come out from behind the door the living-room was empty and the front door stood open. It was growing dark but she knew there was no longer anyone in the house besides herself and Christopher. They were quite alone.

She went slowly down the stairs half expecting that someone might yet come from the kitchen or through the front door, hoping against hope that when she looked up the lane a moment later she would see Andrew and Saskia and Pieter walking back to tell her that it had all been a mistake. But the house was silent as the grave. Nothing stirred, not even a board creaked and the memory of fear and violence lingered on, destroying the feeling of peace that had always been there until now. When she had righted the table and picked up the chair she went to the door and looked up the lane. There was nobody there and the doors of the other houses were all closed, shutters over the windows. For the first time it occurred to her that the Eisingas had always seemed aloof from their neighbours, or perhaps it was the other way around, and she closed the door very quietly and locked it. If anyone was going to offer help they would have done so long ago.

She stood in the pitch darkness of the living room listening to her heartbeat, wondering why they had been taken and what would happen to them. It must surely be because they were Mennonites, but why Andrew also? Had they thought he too was a Mennonite? He looked a little like one, but he had only to explain. Surely they would believe him? She went into the kitchen and lit a candle from the dying fire.

The smell of cooking hung in the air and the smell of smoke, for, as Saskia had explained apologetically that evening, the wind had been in the wrong direction. Her gleaming pots hanging on the wall reflected the candlelight, and a bowl of apples made a splash of red on the scrubbed wood of the table. She felt her presence as if she were standing beside her and she wanted to promise that she would look after the house for her, but how could she promise anything? Suppose they never returned, or were kept in prison for weeks, months, what would she do? She had no money for food, not a stiver, not a single farthing. At least she had a roof over her head but if she remained in the house and was known to be there, might they not come for her too? What would happen then to Christopher?

But if she left, where could she go? She became aware of hot wax dripping onto her hand and thought in panic, I must save this candle. There may not be any more and then I shall have no light.

She went back to the living room and up then to the attic and stood looking down at Christopher. He was fast asleep, lying on his side as usual, sucking his thumb, his lashes, that like Robert's were dark in spite of his flaxen hair, thick and silky on his flushed cheeks. Tomorrow, she thought, she would find out exactly how much food was left in the kitchen and ration herself accordingly and know – know what? How long before she and Christopher starved to death?

But that was nonsense. She would wait a while and if they did not come back she would go to the Old Church. Andrew had said it was not far away. She would find the priest who had employed him to paint the altar panels and tell him what had happened. Surely he would try to help? But he was a Catholic! And it was Catholics who were persecuting Mennonites! How stupid she was! Of course she could not go to him! She would go instead to the banker – Cornelis van Ophoorn. That was what she must do! Having reached a decision at last she went and lay down on her mattress, fully dressed, the candle carefully extinguished, and when she had pulled the blankets over her she drifted off at last into an uneasy sleep.

Christopher's hungry crying woke her next morning. She opened back the shutters of the window to a grey sky. The attic was very cold and she pulled her cloak around them both while she fed him. Afterwards she went down to the kitchen and tried to light the fire, but the peat was damp and she could not get the fire going. She forced herself to eat some bread and an apple, but the milk was sour and Saskia had warned her not to drink the water. She saw now in daylight that there was enough food to last her for several days and she found three candles, but she felt more anxious than ever about the others and the walls of the small house seemed to be closing in on her. The kitchen itself was little more than an alcove and she went back to the living room to wait, not daring to open the shutters on the front of the house, for fear that someone would report that it was still occupied.

She waited all of that day and most of the next night until she fell asleep. She woke just before dawn the following morning and knew that she could bear to wait no longer.

When she had fed Christopher, she put her few possessions in a small sack with as much food as she could carry. Then she went through Andrew's bits of clothing in the hope that she might find some money, but there was not a single coin. She did find the bank's receipt for the treasure, and this she put carefully away in a pocket of her gown, thinking that to leave it behind for anyone to find would surely not be wise and refusing to think beyond that point. Wrapping the baby then in

189

an extra blanket and putting on her shabby cloak she was ready to leave.

When she opened the door inch by inch a few moments later there seemed to be no one about and the shutters of all the houses were still drawn. Closing the door very quietly behind her she set off up the lane in the direction in which the others had been taken. No door opened, no one called after her and yet she held her breath until she was safely out of the lane. She had to force herself then not to run but she walked on as rapidly as she dared, not knowing where she was going, wanting only to find a place where she could shelter until it was time to call at the banker's house.

In the end she found an old, empty church with its doors mercifully open, and she went and sat in a dark corner until the people began to arrive for Mass. No one paid any attention to her and she waited until the Mass was over before setting out to look for Cornelis van Ophoorn's house on Kerkstraat.

It was a dry, cold morning and as she left the church she came into a wide street where women hurried along in their wooden clogs with baskets on their arms, sometimes in pairs chatting comfortably to one another, some of them leading small children by the hand and all of them staring at her and the baby in her arms before looking away quickly as if she were a vagrant. Was it in her face then already – the look of hunger, of despair? Or was it only the shabbiness of her foreign clothes that caught their attention?

She held Christopher even more closely to her, wishing foolishly that she was a part of those women's secure, matronly world, and hurried on until she came to a huge square dominated by a massive church standing in the far corner of it. The tall, ramshackle building close by with the bell tower on top of it must surely be the Town Hall that Saskia had told her of, and she remembered her saying too that the bell was rung whenever the Schout wished to read out a new law, which was often apparently for he was a strict disciplinarian, quite unlike his easy-going predecessor. There were rows of market stalls in the square but most of the people seemed to have gathered around a large wine barrel not far from the Town Hall – men as well as women, lifting up small children so that they could look in, and then walking on after a few minutes.

She was level with the barrel now and she found herself walking over to it too and looking down. It was filled with water and there was what seemed to be pale sea-weed such as she had seen on the beach at Whitby, floating in it. She stood, unable to drag her eyes away, vomit rising in her throat, for it was not sea-weed. It was human hair, and it was Saskia's face, the drowned features swollen from long immersion, and they were Saskia's blue eyes that stared blindly up at her.

She could not move, could not free herself from that dreadful, blue stare. They had put Saskia into a sack first, she realised now, for she could see the open neck of it below the fronds of blonde hair. Had she known then what was going to happen to her? Had Pieter known? And where was he? Where was Andrew?

'The others!' she said, turning to a woman standing beside her. 'Two men – where are they?'

The woman shook her head in bewilderment, clearly not understanding Isobel's strange sounding Dutch, but when she repeated what she had said more slowly, fearful at the same time that by asking she might somehow be putting Andrew and Pieter into danger, the woman seemed to understand. Taking her by the arm she hurried her towards the Town Hall, making for a courtyard on the far side of it.

And there Isobel saw the gibbet and the two bodies that hung from it and knew she need look no further, that nothing anyone could do would harm Andrew or Pieter now. Their lifeless bodies hung like broken dolls, their faces mottled, tongues protruding. The woman was saying something but she could not hear, could not speak. Had Pieter had to look on Saskia's dead face before he died himself or had he been spared that, she wondered. They must surely have died because they were Mennonites, but Andrew – why had he to die?

She began to retch while the woman held Christopher and watched her with curious eyes. But no one else paid any attention to her, least of all the three men who hurried now into the Town Hall, after having spent some moments looking down into the wine barrel. One of them, plump and middle-aged, had looked down for even longer than the others.

Isobel, straightening at last, took the baby from the woman.

She saw the man's face, but was too shocked still to be even conscious that she had done so.

The woman left her and she walked slowly away, stumbling now as if she were drunk, until she came to a bench and sat down. The cold autumn air began to revive her, but she was horribly aware of the danger of her own situation. Andrew must surely have died either because they thought he too was a Mennonite, or was at least helping them. Then beginning to shiver, not because of the cold but of fear of what might yet happen to her, she saw the man's face again in her mind recognising it this time with horror. Edward Dutton was in Amsterdam.

She told herself he was over merely on business – but what if she was wrong? Suppose he was still looking for Andrew, for the treasure? Since he would surely find out that Andrew was dead would he not soon come looking for her? But then how could he know she had been with Andrew in the first place? For a few brief seconds the thought was consoling, until another question presented itself. How could he know that Andrew was in Amsterdam, unless they had been followed after all? If that were so he would know they had come away together.

Christopher was stirring in her arms, beginning to whimper and she put him to her breast, aware suddenly of her own hunger. But when he had had enough she still did not eat, afraid to deplete her small store of food until she had to. At last she got to her feet and set off to find the house of Cornelis van Ophoorn, determined not to let herself think of what might happen if she could not find it or if he would not help her.

Chapter Twenty-Two

Andrew had spent the night before their so-called trial with Pieter and Saskia in one of the city's gate-towers, with its six-foot thick walls and narrow, barred windows. There had been others with them – a young girl accused of killing her illegitimate baby, an old man who admitted to stripping the corpses in the Carthusian cemetery, a husband and wife accused of receiving stolen goods, two young boys who could have been no more than twelve and were too frightened to talk to anybody, so that no one knew why they were there.

The stench was indescribable and Andrew kept his spirits up during the long night by telling himself that they would surely believe him and let him go free when he explained in court that he was not himself a Mennonite, in spite of the fact that he was lodging in a Mennonite house. The men who had arrested them had not been able to understand him, but surely in court they would be able to find someone who could? The fact that the men did not listen to Pieter, whom they must have understood and whom he knew, even with his scanty knowledge of Dutch, had spoken in his defence, was something he did not want to think about. Fortunately for his peace of mind he did not know that recently several people who had had no connection whatever with Mennonites or Anabaptists had been executed along with them, simply because they had been with them at the time of their arrests.

Pieter and Saskia had spoken very little after the gate-tower door had been closed and locked and they sat together, Pieter's arm around her, her head resting on his shoulder. Once or twice

193

he kissed her – not as a man should kiss a woman, especially his wife, in front of other people, Andrew had thought uncomfortably, wondering if Isobel would agree to marry him in the end. But he did not think of her very often.

They were left without food or drink until the following morning when the three of them were brought to the court room to be tried before the magistrate for harbouring the Mennonite, Menno Simons.

Half an hour later, after he had shouted who and what he was in French, Latin, and finally, hopelessly in English; shouted that he knew nothing of Menno Simons and had never seen him in his life; knowing by now that, whether they understood him or not, they did not believe him, Andrew was led out for execution with the other two. Pieter and Saskia held hands until they were separated in the market square. She was taken away, sobbing quietly, and the two men were brought to the yard behind the Town Hall. Andrew could hear Pieter praying aloud beside him, but the last thought in his own mind, before they bandaged his eyes and fear took over absolutely, was that he had failed the abbot.

That same morning the clerk in the Town Hall recorded laboriously that Pieter Eisinga and his wife Saskia, self-confessed Mennonites, of the Doutsteeg, Amsterdam, had been tried for the crime of harbouring their leader, Menno Simons, of Witmarsum in the province of Friesland, in their home on the night of sixth October, fifteen hundred and thirty-nine, and for refusing to give information as to his present whereabouts. They had been found guilty and been sentenced to be executed – the man by hanging and the woman by drowning – the executions to be carried out at once.

At this point the clerk leaned back in his chair and began to chew the top of his quill pen. Then he started to write again. He was very proud of his writing which was clear and easily read in spite of the little curls and squiggles with which he liked to adorn his capital letters. Others who might be interested would no doubt have little trouble in reading what he wrote next. ' . . . an Englishman, Andrew Ellerton, had been tried with the others, and convicted of the crime of aiding and abetting them, and had also been sentenced to be executed by hanging.'

The clerk had a certain amount of trouble in transcribing Andrew's name but even that had been done to his satisfaction, and now that he had finished the entry he sanded the page and leaned back again in his chair.

He recalled then that a man called Tyaard Renicx had been executed in Leeuwarden for the same crime only the previous week. The Mennonites seemed to him to be harmless enough, even if foolishly devoted to their leader, and he considered the penalties for helping him rather severe, although he would not have dreamed of saying so to anyone for fear of finding himself up before the magistrate too. But the woman Saskia had been pretty, and good for another ten or fifteen years. It seemed a waste.

At this point the clerk's stomach began to rumble and he put away his pen with relief, thinking of the hutsepot his wife had promised him for dinner. He was not at all pleased to find the same Englishman in front of his desk who had been bothering him with questions every other day of the past week. The man and his two companions were trying to find an English friend of theirs, who owned a house in Amsterdam and who might be travelling with a woman and child.

The clerk had begun to regret admitting to his knowledge of English. He had only acquired that knowledge because of his late father's ambition to have a son in business rather than in a lowly clerkship, an ambition alas, that had never been realised. But all that was neither here nor there, he thought, as he suddenly remembered the name he had just written. Looking up a little nervously he said, 'Tell me again the name of your friend.'

This time Edward Dutton spelled it out slowly and the clerk looked down at his own handwriting. He cleared his throat. 'Your friend is dead, meneer.'

'Dead? What do you mean? He can't be dead!' Edward Dutton had raised his voice and people standing about turned to stare.

'He was hanged this morning for helping two Mennonites. I was told he even looked like one of them.'

'Mennonites? Anabaptists?' Edward Dutton repeated dully.

195

'But he was a Catholic! A monk! There must be some mistake!'
He knew next to nothing about Anabaptists or Mennonites but
he did know they belonged to some Protestant sect.

The clerk thought again, regretfully of the hutsepot, surely
ruined by now. 'That is the name. Read it for yourself.'

Edward Dutton bent down and looked at the writing, unable
to read a word of the Dutch, but the English name seeming to
jump off the page. He began to curse then, very quietly, and the
clerk, looking at him thought he would have an apoplexy and
then he would never get to his dinner, curse him!

'Where is the body?' Edward Dutton asked at last, the ugly
red flush gone now, leaving his face as pale as ever.

The clerk jerked a thumb towards the window. 'Out there, in
the yard.'

'Had he any baggage?'

With a sigh of impatience the clerk began to turn over some
papers until he found what he was looking for. 'No baggage,' he
said curtly, reading from what seemed to be a short list. 'Just a
few coins, and a paint brush that were found in his pockets.
That is all, meneer, except for his clothes.' He added then with
a sneer in his voice, 'They were not worth much!'

'One more question,' Edward Dutton said quickly. 'Can you
tell me where he was living in Amsterdam?'

'I have only the address of the house where he was arrested.
But I understand he was living there – Number 9, the
Doutsteeg.'

They went out to the courtyard while the clerk hurried off on
short, fat legs. Although by now Andrew's features were so
distorted, Edward Dutton was sure it was he – the colour of his
hair and the general shape of his face was evidence enough.

The other body did not interest him and he thought bitterly of
the days and nights he and his two companions had spent here
looking for Andrew Ellerton and the girl. They had taken it in
turn to watch Robert FitzHugh's house, which they had found
with the clerk's help, but although an old couple, obviously
servants, were to be seen coming and going there had been no
sign of their master and the clerk could not find anybody who
could tell them anything about him. They had stood for hours in
the market place, looking at faces, deafened by the cries of the
pedlars and the chatter of the crowds. They had drunk beer in

every tavern in Amsterdam until the stuff threatened to come out of their eyes. They had walked up and down the Kalverstraat twice, three times a day, had gone to Mass and watched the people coming out, had walked by the canals staring into the faces of strolling lovers, had enquired nearly every day at the Town Hall – and never found him or the girl. And all the time he had been there. With those cursed religious fanatics! But the girl – where was she now, he wondered. Had she been with Ellerton and if so how had she escaped? Was she still perhaps hiding in the house, and was the treasure there too?

The cold wind blowing up the Ij estuary whipped his black woollen cloak against his rotund body – a man one would not notice in a crowd, or even in a group. But in the past hour a cold, dogged ruthlessness and an evil that had always been latent in him seemed somehow to have surfaced. The two men with him were suddenly aware of a change in him and looked at him with new respect and a shade of uneasiness. 'What do we do now?' one of them asked. 'We can't stay in Amsterdam for ever. My orders were to be back within the month.'

The other man nodded, hunching his shoulders against the cold, big, heavily-built fellows both of them, useful in their way but bored long since with this assignment that seemed to be leading nowhere.

'We shall search the house,' Edward Dutton said. 'After that we can decide.'

It took them an hour to find the Doutsteeg and they approached it cautiously, but the lane was deserted and the door of the house ajar. A man came down the lane staring at them curiously but he walked on in his heavy clogs until he got to the bottom of the lane and turned the corner. They slipped inside then and Edward Dutton knew at once that the house was empty. He could feel its emptiness as if it were a physical substance he could touch with his hands, and not only was the house empty but it had been picked clean as a whistle. A broken chair lay on its side but otherwise not a stick of furniture remained, not a scrap of clothing, not a morsel of food. The walls were bare, even the shutters had been wrenched off the tiny windows. Some of the floor boards had been taken up and those that had not been touched they themselves prised up now with their knives. And found nothing.

It was growing dark and as they walked back to the tavern where they were staying Edward Dutton wondered with cold anger if someone else had been looking for the treasure and found it. Or had common thieves merely seen their opportunity in an unoccupied house and looted it? But whichever it was, like his two companions he would now have to return to London, for he could not abandon his business any longer for what was beginning to seem like a hopeless quest.

Chapter Twenty-Three

It took Isobel a long time to find the house again. Her arms were aching now with the weight of the baby and she half expected to feel a heavy hand on her shoulder and to hear Edward Dutton's unctuous voice in her ear. She had thought she was free of him for good but it was beginning to seem that in some horrible way their lives were linked and only the death of one of them would break the bond. Or was that just a sick fancy born of shock, fear and loneliness? Nevertheless, she looked nervously behind her every few minutes, beginning to stumble now with exhaustion but seeing only the men and women of Amsterdam going about their business, wrapped in layer upon layer of heavy clothes against the cold, clumping cheerfully past her in their heavy clogs.

At last, near a huge church, the one probaby in which Andrew had worked for a few days, she found the street she was looking for, Kerkstraat, and the name she was looking for above a huge, varnished front door – van Ophoorn. The house itself towered above her with its painted canopy and steps leading up to the door, its narrow pointed roof higher than any of the neighbouring houses, the rope that apparently well to do Dutch householders used to haul up bulky goods and chattels from the street hanging idly from the pole that projected below the eaves.

Andrew had said that it was the house of what seemed to be a very rich man, and certainly the little house in the Doutsteeg was a hovel by comparison. But as she put out her hand to lift the heavy knocker she wished she was back there now. What would he think of her, this wealthy banker, in her shabby clothes, with a baby in her arms and her only other possessions in the whole world hanging from her shoulder in a small satchel? She lifted the knocker all the same, and let it fall, and after a few minutes the door was opened by a manservant who stared down at her with a look of supercilious surprise on his broad face.

'I wish to see Meneer van Ophoorn,' she said in her careful Dutch that she had rehearsed a hundred times.

The man frowned, his eyes sneering at her shabbiness, at the baby in her arms, ready she knew to shut the door in her face, but behind him she saw movement, and raising her voice she said quickly in English, 'I am a cousin of a friend of the meneer's.' The servant stood blank-faced, the door still open, not recognising the language let alone understanding it, and uncertain what to do. And then a man's voice spoke behind him in rapid Dutch, and the fellow opened the door wide.

'You are to come in,' he said ungraciously, stepping back as if she had the plague.

There was a man standing in the middle of what seemed to be a kind of entrance hall – a man in his late sixties or early seventies, of middle height, elegant in a black velvet doublet under a jacket of dove grey, with breeches of the same colour. His pale, hooded eyes appraised her in one swift glance, not offensively as the servant had done but missing nothing nonetheless, she felt sure, and lingering for a second or two on the baby in her arms. Then, in heavily accented English he said, 'I am Cornelis van Ophoorn – please come!' He led the way into a room that opened off the hall – big and spacious, with several windows and polished mahogany furniture, and a peat fire blazing on the open hearth. There were paintings and squares of coloured porcelain on the walls and a damask cloth covered the small table.

'Do you speak Dutch?' he said in that language. 'I speak only a few words of English, I am afraid.'

'Not very well.' She tried to remember what Saskia had taught her. 'But – but I speak French a little better.'

'Then we shall converse in French!' he said briskly, pulling forward a cushioned chair for her. 'Now, sit down and tell me why you have come to see me. Who is our mutual friend?'

'Andrew Ellerton,' she replied, pushing back her hood,

afraid suddenly that she was going to cry. 'He came to see you recently, to ask you to – to place some valuables in safe keeping for him.'

'I remember.' The long face with its high cheekbones had become suddenly wary. 'You say you are a friend of his?'

'I am a cousin, a distant cousin.'

'Yes?' He waited for her to go on.

'Andrew – Andrew is dead,' she burst out. 'He – he was hanged this morning, in Amsterdam.'

'In God's name, why?' His voice was like a whiplash.

She told him the story then, starting with the day of their arrival in Holland. He waited for her to finish and then the tears came at last, streaming down her face as she cried for the waste of life, for Pieter and Saskia who had loved each other, for Andrew whom she could not love – for that now most of all. Until there were no more tears to come, and then the banker clapped his hands and when the servant came running he told him to bring wine and food for the young lady.

She had been sure she could neither eat nor drink but the wine slid sweetly down her throat, and she found herself reaching out for a leg of cold chicken like a starving dog. She had to force herself to eat slowly and the man sitting on the other side of the fire waited until she had finished before speaking again. 'I cannot tell you how sorry I am about the whole business,' he said, 'but there is nothing anyone can do to bring them back, unfortunately. Had your cousin told me he was staying in a Mennonite house I would have advised him to leave at once. However – ' He shrugged shoulders that were only slightly stooped. 'You will have to try and put it all behind you, and I will see to it for you that the Cîteaux treasure gets safely back to France. I give you my word.'

For the first time she realised that the responsibility for the safety of the treasure lay now on her and she wanted no part of it. But this man would help her and surely she could trust him? Before she could say anything he went on.

'But what is to become of you, eh?'

'I – I don't know. I – can't go back to England.' She looked down at Christopher, fast asleep, his face turned towards the warmth of the fire, and her host poured more wine for her. 'Why don't you tell me the whole story?' he suggested. 'I am terribly old, you know! Nothing shocks me!'

201

To her surprise she found herself telling him everything then, everything except the name of Christopher's father, words coming slowly at first and then in a torrent. When she said she had been a nun his eyebrows had lifted a fraction, and he reached out once again to pour more wine for her. Perhaps it was the wine that loosened her tongue, or his air of sympathy, or her own exhaustion, but in the end she found herself giving him the name that she had at first been so careful to withhold, thinking in any case that it would mean nothing to him.

But she had been wrong, as she realised at once to her horror.

'Robert FitzHugh.' The name as he pronounced it seemed strange, but there was no doubting the sudden sharpness of his voice.

'Yes,' she said reluctantly.

'Is he related to Sir William FitzHugh?'

She nodded uneasily. 'He is his grandson, but please, please, if you know him forget what I have told you! All of it! *Please!* She leant towards him in her agitation and he put up a long, white hand.

'My dear young lady, we are speaking in confidence, the strictest confidence.' He looked down at the sleeping baby with a frown on his face and a sudden hardness about his mouth. 'A cousin of my father's, Anna Hooft, married Sir William FitzHugh,' he added slowly.

For a moment she forgot everything except that this man was a relative of Robert's. She wanted to reach out and touch him as if in some way it would bring Robert close to her and she had to force herself to sit very straight in her chair, hands folded in her lap, telling herself to remember instead all that Dame Margaret had once taught her in that long-ago convent life about Discipline of Self – And as if she could actually hear the abbess's voice, sanity returned. 'Please forget what I said,' she said stiffly. 'I cannot imagine what happened to me.' – And at the same time she thought, why did Andrew not tell me they were related? Surely he must have known?

'I am very glad you told me,' Cornelis van Ophoorn said, settling back in his chair, smiling now as if to put her at ease again. 'I shall make it my business to see that you are looked after and that this man – Dutton? – does not bother you in any way. You must consider yourself welcome to stay in my house for as long as you wish. We shall say – let me see – ' There was a ghost of a smile on his face. 'Ah, yes! We shall say that your husband was lost overboard in a storm when you and he were crossing over from England, and that all your baggage was lost too. How is that for a tale, eh?'

'But I can't stay just because – because you are related – '

Crossing his still fine legs in their grey stockings, he said cheerfully, 'Then stay because I need someone to teach me to speak English more fluently! You would be doing me a great favour and I am sure you are an excellent teacher. Did you not say you taught in the convent at one time?'

What could she say? And more to the point, where else could she go? Was something like this not what she'd had in mind when she set out to find his house?

'May I take it that you will stay then?' he said, smiling, his teeth discoloured but very even, and when she nodded at last, he lifted his goblet. 'Let us drink to the future!'

But as she sipped her wine, fearing at the same time that the dead might think she was already forgetting them, she wondered if he would ask more of her than lessons in English.

Chapter Twenty-Four

Robert had been more than half drunk on their wedding night. Next morning he had wakened to find his new wife's long, thin, naked body pressed against his, her head on his chest, the dry frizz of her hair against his chin. The air inside the drawn curtains of the giant four poster bed was thick and stale and he tried to pull away without waking her, hoping to get up and take his horse out for a gallop in the park before breakfast. But Beatrice was already awake. 'Was I as good as the others?' she said, her voice still husky with sleep.

He grimaced into the darkness. What was he to say? Tell her the truth? That she had been no better, no worse, that it had been a night like the rest – except for the one night, the one girl, who had been different. 'One's wedding night is always best,' he said at last.

She lifted her head and kissed him, open-mouthed, but there was not even a flicker of desire in him. 'Who was he?' he said idly.

Now it was she who drew away. 'Who?' Her voice was suddenly sharp.

'Your lover. Or was it lovers? I was not all that drunk, you know.'

She pressed herself to him again, laying her cheek on his bare chest. 'Robert, you must know I am not that kind of woman! It was only the one time – I was young, inexperienced, and – and he took advantage – I – I did not realise – I was so innocent. But I can't tell you his name! It would not be fair to him!'

It had in fact been her tutor, and the countess had discovered

204

their secret and had had him thrown out of Raskelfe, but she did not want to admit that to Robert. Let him think it was someone far grander, she thought – and of course the last time had been much, much better! But even she had not known who *he* was! She had drunk too much wine at the masked ball which her uncle and aunt had given two months before and that Robert could not attend, and she had gone walking in the garden alone, since no one had wanted to dance with her. And in the darkness this man had appeared like a masked satyr and taken her in her aunt's summerhouse.

'Are you jealous?' she said hopefully, nuzzling his shoulder. 'I shall make it up to you, my darling, and anyway, I've heard tales of a lady-in-waiting and a young widow in Cheapside and – '

'What man's a virgin?' he said, interrupting her and yawning again. The lady-in-waiting he remembered had been very beautiful, a few years older than himself but so terrified of being caught up in Queen Anne Boleyn's troubles that she had told him in the end they must not see each other again. He had thought of her for a long time afterwards with gratitude, but the widow in Cheapside had been no more than a passing fancy, like all the others except the one, and as if Beatrice had read his mind, she said into the silence, the teasing note gone from her voice, 'Of course, there was the nun too, Isobel Willis.'

He had wondered if she knew, but then, he thought sourly, everyone in England seemed to know. Pushing her away from him almost roughly he sat up in bed and reached out to pull back the bed curtains. 'I prefer not to talk about her,' he said curtly. 'Not ever.'

'Why not? Because she gave you a son? Because you love her? Is that why?' Her voice had become shrill and she pulled the covers up to her chin. In the cold morning light she was a plain, unattractive woman with puffy eyes and yet he felt sorry for her, for both of them, bound together for the rest of their lives.

'Please,' he said gently enough. 'I'd rather not talk about it. It's over. Finished. Long ago.' He got out of bed then, and walked across the rush-strewn floor to the windows that he had left unshuttered the previous night, hoping that some air might find its way into the stuffy, over furnished bedchamber.

Beatrice Neville watched her husband from the bed as he put a robe over his nakedness, thinking that he was the most beautiful man she had ever seen. She had loved him since the first night he had come to her uncle's house, surly and ill-tempered, guessing even then that he did not want to marry her, that he would never love her in return – she was too tall, too thin, too plain-looking. Only a man like Walter would ever love her, and he did not count. But she was Robert's wife now. He was hers for life. And she was safe. No one could say anything about her, whatever happened.

As he pulled the bell for the servants she snuggled down under the fine linen sheets of their bridal bed. Soon they would leave her uncle's house for London and go to live with her old grandfather-in-law on the banks of the Thames, whom Robert had said was determined to remain alive until he had a great-grandson to carry on the name. She did not much fancy living with a cantankerous old man, but he could not be much worse than her uncle, she told herself now, and at least she would no longer have to fetch and carry for her aunt. And she would bring her maid Sarah with her, and of course Walter – with Robert still in disgrace they would not be going to Court but she did not really care about that. And when the old man died she would be mistress of the house – *Mistress!* Giving orders! Receiving calls! Returning them! Just thinking about it made her smile with pleasure.

Robert was in the ante-chamber dressing and she could hear his voice as he talked to the man servant. Dear Robert, she thought. She would let him have a certain amount of rope of course – wives always had to do that – but she would set Walter to keep an eye on him all the same, in case he strayed too far. And before she drifted off to sleep again she found herself wondering where Isobel Willis was now, and the child. But it didn't matter now, she told herself. Not any more.

They left for London a week later, and if Sir William was disappointed in his new daughter-in-law he took care not to let Robert know. He did say to John rather wistfully that he liked women with a bit of flesh on them, and that beauty wasn't everything, but when she announced a few weeks later that she was pregnant he nearly had another 'long faint' from pure joy.

Even Robert was pleased to hear the news, for it meant he

need not do his duty on her so often – sometimes he would wait until she was asleep before going to bed himself, telling her next morning that he had not wanted to waken her.

There were times when he would think of the other child with a strange new feeling of guilt that had nothing to do with Isobel herself. Rumour in the city had it that Andrew had slipped out of the country with the treasure, taking Isobel and the child with him. If this other child was his, then the boy was his rightful heir in the eyes of God, if not in the eyes of the Law. But where was he now? Was he being fed, would he be properly educated, given some start in life? And lying beside his wife, listening to the distant sounds from the river and the opening and shutting of his grandfather's door as the nurse went into him during the night, Robert resolved that one day he would look for Isobel's child. If he was satisfied that he was the father he would see that the boy was provided for.

Then he wondered if Isobel had married Andrew, since she could surely never return to a convent. It would seem to be a solution for her of sorts, but she deserved better he knew, much better, and the old, familiar ache of regret would return. He would wake up next morning irritable, having to watch his wife retching into a bowl, for she was often sick now in the mornings – indeed, she had been sick after waking up, long before she announced that she was pregnant.

Had Isobel had to go through this, he would wonder, steadying the bowl before Sarah came to help her mistress. Isobel would have been so alone in the convent, trying to hide it all from the other nuns. Sometimes he felt that Beatrice knew he was thinking of her and he would feel doubly guilty as she bent over the bowl – God in Heaven, but he deserved to have no luck, he would think unhappily.

By Christmas Beatrice's health seemed to improve, with Sarah fussing over her and Walter like a dark shadow always in the background. She was no longer sick in the mornings and by that time many other things had happened as well. Cromwell's men had long since given up the task of watching Robert, and Edward Dutton was back in London, even though he had remained on in Amsterdam for a week after the other two men had left, looking for Isobel Willis and not finding her. When he could not stay away from his business any longer he had gone back to England morose and ill-tempered.

Soon after his return his wife had died in strange circumstances, falling down the stairs of their house on Lime Street and breaking her neck. Shortly afterwards a business rival committed suicide and it began to seem that a black cloud of what some called ill luck was following him. But although his clothes were even more sombre than usual and he took care to wear a mourning face on most occasions, his heart was lighter than it had been for years, despite his failure to bring back the Cîteaux treasure to the King.

The same could not be said for Thomas Cromwell, however, or his royal master.

On 27 December the King met his bride-to-be for the first time when she arrived in England, and was so sorely disappointed in her that he could not bring himself to present her with the sables he had brought with him as a wedding gift. 'She's got a face like a bloody horse, and not a word of English!' he roared afterwards at Thomas Cromwell, walking with him once again in the long gallery at Whitehall. 'You have tricked me, man!'

'I fear she is indeed plainer looking than I was given to believe, sire, but she will soon learn to speak English.'

'I doubt it! She has no more wit than she has beauty – and the wedding date set for 6 January! 'twill be a heavy yoke I enter into on that day, Thomas.' The King's voice was bitter.

'Perhaps not as heavy as you fear,' the minister began soothingly, only to find himself looking at the royal back. The audience was clearly at an end, and as he made his way out of the palace Thomas Cromwell cursed the German woman who had failed so signally to charm, and his own bad judgement in encouraging the marriage.

The making of a Queen, however, could not wait any longer, either for a reluctant bridegroom or for the finding of the Cîteaux treasure, and the royal wedding took place on 6 January as arranged. But eight days afterwards the new Queen was still a 'maid' it was said, for her husband the King could not 'stir himself to the act.' He called her 'the Flanders Mare' among his intimates and Cromwell began to fear that he himself might one

208

day follow in the footsteps of Cardinal Wolsey whose head, in the end, had rolled like all the others.

Yet his royal master made him Earl of Essex and Lord Chamberlain of England in April, and by manipulating Parliament and the convocations the new earl collected three million pounds for the royal coffers, plundering the property of the Knights of St John as well for good measure. But Henry still asked about the Cîteaux treasure, and had been bitterly disappointed he had not been able to flaunt it on the altar at his wedding ceremony.

'God's curse on it,' he had shouted the day before. 'You promised me, Thomas! You promised I'd have it! But where is it, eh? You say it was brought to Holland – why didn't your men catch 'em there? A few acres of land as flat as the back o' my hand – they could have seen 'em a mile off!'

He had been at his most unreasonable. Nothing pleased him, but then nothing short of the news that the wedding had been postponed would have done so, his minister had thought grimly, or better still, that Anne of Cleves had dropped dead. And he could not even tell him anything more about the treasure, except that it had not yet been returned to Cîteaux, according to the latest reports from France.

By the end of April, little more than three months after the wedding, the Duke of Norfolk and Stephen Gardiner, Bishop of Winchester, were trying to lure the King into a new marriage, to Norfolk's niece, Catherine Howard, no more than twenty-one, nicely rounded with auburn hair and hazel eyes. A marriage with her would favour the Catholic interests and by now it was common knowledge that the King had no liking for the second Queen Anne. Sir Thomas Wriothesley, his new secretary who had got his appointment, which he shared with Sir Ralph Sadler, through Lord Cromwell, although no friend to him, begged the newly made earl and Lord Chamberlain to devise relief for the King. If he did not, he warned Cromwell, 'they would both smart for it.'

But there seemed little that Thomas Cromwell could do. If he somehow contrived to make it possible for the King to rid himself of Anne of Cleves, of whom he himself had been such a strong advocate, then he cleared the way for Catherine Howard and his own enemies. And since he could find no alternative to Catherine, his only hope seemed to be in discrediting the Queen makers. In desperation he had the Bishop of Chichester and Dr Wilson, a royal chaplain, arrested as papalists who had denied the King's supremacy. He even introduced a new treason bill, and there were rumours that he was to arrest five other conservative bishops. But he knew that in spite of his recent honours which counted for nothing with the aristocracy, he was on the edge of a precipice and the smallest push could send him into the abyss.

Neither his problems, however, nor the King's, directly affected, as yet, the household of Sir William FitzHugh living together uneasily in the big, draughty house on the banks of the Thames.

In March Robert had had to go to Northumberland to see the old house, Critley Hall, which was falling into ruin, and to collect rents. On his way home, at the end of April, his wife Beatrice was delivered prematurely of a baby boy, two months before her time. The baby was stillborn, after a difficult birth, so difficult that the doctor said she could never have another child. The baby had been already buried when Robert returned, finding her still in bed and his grandfather in such a rage of anger and disappointment it seemed he would surely die this time.

Chapter Twenty-Five

For Isobel the months that followed her first meeting with the banker slipped by like a strange, twilight dream, lit by odd flashes of happiness. It was not in her nature to become plump but she did become sleekly rounded as the result of good food, plenty of sleep and not enough exercise, for she had nothing to do except look after Christopher and try to improve Cornelis van Ophoorn's knowledge of the English language.

She took the luxuries of his house now as much for granted as if she had been born to them, but she knew the servants still talked about her behind her back – about the young English girl and her baby whom their master had taken into his house on the pretext of teaching him English, for she soon realised that none of them really believed the story about her drowned husband. But they were civil enough to her face, partly because they knew they might be dismissed if they were not, and partly because her own natural reserve coupled with her old-fashioned convent manners soon quelled any insolence.

The housekeeper, Griet, however, kept a careful distance between herself and Isobel. She had once been lady's maid to the banker's wife, who it seemed had died fifteen years earlier, and was in her late forties, born and bred in Amsterdam. She was tall like most Dutch women, her brown hair drawn smoothly back under her white linen cap, her pale, unlined face giving nothing away, although her still red mouth hinted at a sensuality as rigidly controlled as the full breasts under her tightly laced bodice. Isobel guessed, with the wordly wisdom which seemed to have come to her recently from nowhere, that the woman might have been

211

Cornelis van Ophoorn's mistress at one time, although now, in her presence at least, they treated each other with the formality of master and servant. Griet seemed fond of Christopher and liked to play with him, but Isobel knew the housekeeper did not like her.

Her relationship with the banker had its own, different formality, at least to outward appearances. They had their evening meal together in the big living-room unless he had guests, when she would eat alone in a small antechamber at the back of the house. Then her food would be served to her not on silver or even pewter dishes, as was the case in the living room, but on kitchen earthenware, some of it slightly cracked, as though to say, You are no better than a servant really, even if the master does eat with you when he is alone. It always irked her, but not so much that she wanted to make a fuss about it, and after all, was it not true? She would touch the wings of her own cap then, for she dressed now in the Dutch fashion. She would smooth her billowing skirts, puff up her huge sleeves, tie her little mock apron more tightly about her neat waist and think, I am nothing. All that is mine is Christopher, and one does not really *own* one's child. Everything else of any value that I have has been given to me by Cornelis van Ophoorn. She would resolve then to take her teaching even more seriously and try at least to earn their keep.

Although the old man's fluency in the English language improved enormously, his accent remained the same – unmistakeably Dutch.

'I am too old, Mejuffrouw Isobel,' he would say when she corrected him, smiling as he said it, but his eyes seeking reassurance. And she would tell him then that he must not be foolish, he just must try harder, and *really* listen to her. She would repeat the word for the tenth time, and he would look at her mouth shaping the word and she would know he had not been listening.

Sometimes he would touch her. On her shoulder, on her bare arms, or her hand. She did not draw away from him because she had grown fond of him, and when his eyes lingered on her bare throat, or the tight bodice of her dress it was like being touched by a flame that has no heat in it. Once, she had had the absurd wish that they could have met when he was young, as though, by wishing, she could juggle with the past and present, but leave the future be. She did not know that he had begun to dread the day when she might leave him.

212

When she first came he would not let her outside the house, fearing that Edward Dutton might see her, and she used to take the baby to the courtyard at the back in order to get fresh air. But he had discreet enquiries made about the Englishman, and when he could find no trace of him and it began to seem that the fellow had left Amsterdam, he allowed her to go out with Griet and two of the menservants for short walks while Christopher was sleeping. It was still winter and she had had to wrap herself in the long, fur-lined cloak he had had made for her against the bitter cold, but she enjoyed these walks in spite of Griet's unyielding formality and the taciturnity of the two men.

After a while she even forgot to look out for Edward Dutton and even though she was determined not to think of him, she found herself wondering where Robert's house was and if they would ever meet, should he chance to come to Amsterdam. She would look at tall, very blond young men who in the distance might seem like him, and as they came nearer they would smile hopefully at her, but none of them was Robert, none of them was even English and she would walk on, crimson-faced, aware that her three escorts had noticed and were probably thinking, What more could you expect?

In mid-winter the canals were frozen over for a few days and she liked to watch the skaters gliding past – men, women and children, on long, wooden skates twice the length of their feet, the metal blades curving upwards in front like the prow of a ship, while among the laughing, talking crowd, plumed horses drew sleighs of painted wood, and even old folk were pushed along in armchairs on runners. Once she stayed so long watching, in spite of Griet and the two men, that when they got back they found Cornelis van Ophoorn pacing up and down the hall.

'I was afraid something had happened,' he said, angry with her for the first time since she had come. 'What kept you?'

'I'm sorry,' she said, ashamed. 'I was watching the skaters. I had no idea you were waiting for us.'

'It doesn't matter,' he said, turning away. 'Come and warm yourself at the fire.'

One evening, when they had finished their meal, he said to her across the cluttered table, 'I intend to make a new will.'

She looked up at him, startled. 'Why?'

'Mejuffrouw Isobel, I wish to provide for you and Christopher.'

'But I – but you have already given us so much.'

He made a dismissive gesture with his hand. 'I have to work out the best way in which it can be done – tomorrow I shall talk to my legal advisor about it. My son and daughter are more than amply provided for and since I only hear from them when they want more money – ' he shrugged and laughed a little grimly. Both of his children were long since married and lived in Antwerp. There were grandchildren, of whom he was clearly very fond, but he had not seen them since they were infants. She did not know what to say and he added quickly, 'Some day you may wish to marry, and you will need a dowry.'

She shook her head violently at that. 'I will never marry.'

'You think that now, but you may meet someone – '

'No,' she said with quiet finality, and he frowned. 'Well, I shall talk to this fellow tomorrow and make arrangements – but there is another matter which has begun to weigh on me of late. The Cîteaux treasure. I had planned to return it to the monks myself, but it is a long journey and somehow I don't seem to have the energy now that I had last autumn.'

It was the first time he had ever alluded to his health, and she had noticed recently that he often seemed short of breath. 'Perhaps you should see a doctor,' she suggested uneasily.

'The fellow would only try to bleed me, or tell me to give up my banking business and stay at home, twiddling my thumbs. That would kill me off more quickly than anything else!' She tried to smile, and he said quickly, 'I shall be all right when the sun comes out again and I can get some heat into my bones!' He stood up then a little stiffly. 'And now, my dear, if you will forgive me for leaving you, I shall retire. It has been a long day full of small annoyances. One man told me I was only a money-lender, not a banker! As if one could lend money to a fool!'

'Such a man is not worth thinking about,' she said.

'I know, but it is good to hear you say it.' He stood for a moment looking down at her. 'I am glad you came to me,' he said quietly before turning to leave the room, his back not quite as straight as usual, the limp that was noticeable only when he was tired, worse than she had ever seen it.

* * *

214

The sun came out early next morning and bathed the house on Kerkstraat in a warm glow of heat, but Cornelis van Ophoorn had gone far beyond its reach, for he had died in his sleep during the night in the Dutch bed that was so like a coffin.

It was Griet who found him and who told Isobel, and Griet who with her usual efficiency sent off a messenger to tell the people in the bank house on the other side of the canal and the burghers and the townspeople of Amsterdam.

When Isobel went into his bedchamber she found the bed curtains had not yet been drawn, nor the top bed-sheet pulled over his face, but the hooded eyes were mercifully closed and there was a look of startled surprise on the grey, sunken face. Death had come unannounced, then, she thought, and mercifully, hopefully, without pain. Bending down she kissed him on his forehead, for the first and last time, the skin still warm, and realised that Griet had followed her in. She moved aside but the woman seemed unaware of her presence, her face twisted out of recognition by grief. Isobel went out of the bedchamber, leaving them alone together, closing the door quietly behind her. But as she made her way back to Christopher, blinded by sudden tears, she wondered how she was going to look after him now and what would happen to them both. With all his good intentions Cornelis van Ophoorn had left it too late, and all she had to show for the treasure was a small, square piece of parchment with a few lines of writing on it.

When she opened the door she saw that Christopher was still asleep in the cradle that had been brought down from the attic when she first came, and would soon be too small for him. She closed the door quietly behind her, dreading that he might wake and demand her attention, and went and sat down on the stool. Her face was still wet with tears and for a second, as thought rather than time is measured, it seemed that Cornelis van Ophoorn stood beside her. She was not afraid, not even surprised, and when he left her – not leaving her in the conventional sense of the word but rather withdrawing his presence – she felt strangely comforted and less alone.

Chapter Twenty-Six

The bedchamber smelt abominably and his grandfather's voice had not lost its familiar bitter harshness, although his face seemed to have shrunk in the few weeks Robert had been away, so that the old man looked now like a grey-faced gnome peering over the top of the soiled top sheet. I'll get that nurse to wash him and change his sheets this night if I have to stand over her myself, Robert thought grimly, hard put to it not to pinch his nostrils against the smell.

'Your wife's no good!' his grandfather barked at him for what seemed the tenth time. 'She can't breed! You should have her put away! If the King can do it, there must be ways and means – '

'I wouldn't do it even if there were,' Robert said shortly. ''Tis not her fault, and they tell me she suffered greatly.' He would never rid himself as long as he lived of the memory of his return earlier that day and the hysterical creature that had clung to him, sobbing. He had done his best to soothe her, to reassure her that he would not in fact try to do what his grandfather had just suggested. And in the end she had believed him. 'I love you, Robert!' she had whispered. 'I could not live without you!'

He had freed himself gently from those clinging arms, wishing that he could have said the same to her, and meant it. As it was, he could not honestly say he even liked her, and they were bound together for life, with no hope now of children to make the union tolerable.

'But there is no one to carry on the name!' The old man in the bed tried to raise himself from the pillow and fell back panting. 'When you die everything will go to that spindle-shanked nonentity up north who's not even a FitzHugh! And if he dies before you and has no issue it might all go to some whey-faced Dutchman! And her dowry was not as much as was promised either! Think on it, Robert! Think on it!'

'I have done so.'

'Well, then – '

'There is one thing I could do,' Robert said slowly, watching his grandfather warily, afraid that what he was about to say would bring on a last and fatal seizure.

'What's that?' It was like the bark of a dog.

'I could try to find the other boy. Fine out if he's mine.'

He had expected outrage, anger, but there was not even surprise. Only a familiar look of cunning on the grey face. 'The nun's brat? I'd thought of that. But how can you be sure he's yours, and would she give him to you?'

The two men looked at each other, eye to eye, in sudden, total accord, a brief period in time when they drew close to one another. 'I will know if he's mine,' Robert said flatly, 'but she may not want to give him to me even if he is.'

'Don't be a fool!' the old man snapped irritably, the drawing together destroyed as if it had never been. 'Give her enough money and she'll part with him, quick enough!'

'Money means very little to Isobel.' Robert's voice had an edge to it now.

'Then she's a rare woman indeed,' his grandfather said dryly. 'But how will you find them?'

''Tis known they left for Holland, and they were most likely on their way to Amsterdam, to Cornelis van Ophoorn as the abbot advised.'

'Van Ophoorn?' the old man grimaced. 'I remember him well. Full of airs and graces and too cursed mean to lend a fellow even a few hundred! Still, he might know where they are. Or the monks in Cîteaux might know, if they got that far – '

'I shall start in Amsterdam – I doubt if they'd have travelled on to France so late in the year.'

'Best leave at once, then, and take John with you. Maybe you'll need to see the treasure home yourself, after all. But I'll miss his ugly face – and with that bloody man of your wife's creeping round the place – what's his name? – Walter? – I don't feel easy in my own house. Came in here the other evening and stood there staring down at me as if I was coffined already – can't abide the fellow.'

'Nor can I,' Robert said grimly. 'However, I can see no way of getting rid of him. I must see that you are made more comfortable before I leave, though.'

But in the end Robert had to dismiss the elderly nurse and hire a new one that same afternoon, a relative of the cook's – young, fresh-faced, like a pouter pigeon with the bib of her white apron stretched tight across her breasts. As soon as the old man saw her he stopped screeching that he'd be damned if he'd let anyone near him with soap and water – he'd catch his death o' cold – he'd die that very night – and lay back instead, smiling his gummy smile as she rolled her sleeves up over dimpled elbows.

Walter Clifford stood behind the screen in the withdrawing room later that evening, peering round it every so often to look at his mistress lying on the day-bed before the fire. He was a man of middle height, with a dark, secretive face and lank, black hair falling to his shoulders, and he was quieter than the mice that scuttled behind the wainscot; but Beatrice FitzHugh knew he was there. She had in fact told him to go behind the screen for she liked to think he was within call, but yet did not want the burden of his company. So he stood in the fire-lit gloom calling her names as he often did, and unable at the same time to stop loving her. It had been like that since their early childhood – two plain-looking, unattractive children of much the same age, playing together in the great park at Raskelfe. No one seemed able to remember even then how Walter had come to be part of the Neville household. He just seemed always to have been there, like herself, ignored by everyone, and so they played their children's games, and others that she invented, always with her as the leader. Sometimes, too, they explored each other's body, like two small animals, and even in this she took the initiative, telling him to open his breeches before she lifted her multi-layers of skirts. Then one day the countess realised they would soon be thirteen and packed Walter off to help in the kitchens, telling Beatrice she was not to play with him any more.

Yet, when her first flow of blood came it was to Walter she went for reassurance and information – not that he knew much more than she did – and as the years went by it was always to him she went in times of trouble. And he always did what he could to help her, for he loved her as he loved no other person, no other thing. She knew it and teased him about it. Even on the day she told him she was going to marry Robert FitzHugh she teased him. 'You can come with me, Walter! Won't you like that?' And then, becoming serious. 'I shall need you. They say his grandfather is a horrid old man and I shall be all alone down in London, miles away from everyone!'

'You'll have your husband.'

'But he's not like you, Walter dear. You've known me all my life. And you love me, don't you? I don't think Robert loves me one little bit!'

'Do you love him?'

He could still hear her laugh, a little too high pitched. 'I must do my duty, Walter. You know that.'

But he had seen her looking at Robert FitzHugh, seen the hunger in her eyes. God in heaven, if only she would look at him like that! Just once. Even once. Not that she was a great beauty or had great wit or even charm, he would tell himself, over and over. But it was no use. She was Beatrice, and she owned him, body and soul, even though he had known about the tutor, and had come within an ace of killing the fellow. But the countess had got rid of him instead.

There was no way, however, of ridding Beatrice of Robert FitzHugh, although he wished he had the courage to smash his smooth, good-looking face. She had wanted the fellow for husband and he had wanted her connections and her dowry. But now that she could give him no heir what would happen to her? Earlier he had listened outside the old man's bedchamber and heard him talking to Robert. He had rushed to tell her what they were planning and she had been bitterly angry, calling the nun names that shocked even him. 'If he goes near her again – ' She began to pant at the end, running out of breath, and he interrupted her before she could finish, sickened by the flow of filth that had come from her twisted mouth.

'He may find that the child is not his.'

She had become suddenly silent, staring up at him and he

knew she was thinking, as he was, of the tiny, dead body he had taken from the midwife – the body of a full-term baby, with perfectly formed limbs, a fuzz of dark hair and small, perfect finger-nails. Why could it not have lived, he thought now, as he had thought so often before. The midwife had said it would have grown to be a strong, fine man. Why then did it have to die?

'You won't ever tell, Walter?' She was whispering now. 'I was so stupid that night and a little drunk, I'm afraid!' In the end she had told him about the night in the summerhouse, when she was beginning to fear she was pregnant, running to him as always with her troubles, but he had not scolded her, only turned away as if unable to meet her eyes, and shortly afterwards she had married Robert.

'Have I ever told,' he said now reproachfully, 'about anything?'

'No. Of course not.' She put out her hand, touching him lightly on the arm. 'And Sarah is loyal too! But the midwife – I had to give her money.'

'That was foolish,' he muttered. 'She'll come back for more.'

'If I refused she might have told.'

He had been bending down over her, but now he straightened slowly, thinking of the small coffin he had stayed up all night to make, thanking God for her sake that the doctor had not been there at the end, although he had cursed him at the time. 'The child may not be his,' he repeated. 'What then?'

She seemed relieved at the change of subject. 'I don't know. But leave me now please. I wish to rest.' He had obeyed, as always, and now he could hear her sobbing. He wanted to comfort her, but he knew better than to go near her again unasked. Love, hate and grief seemed to tear his own body apart.

Robert was surprised, when the time came to tell her, that Beatrice seemed already to have some inkling of his plans, but he did not waste time trying to find out how she knew. 'I don't want another woman's child in my house,' she said, clinging to him tearfully in bed that night.

'But if the child is mine,' he said levelly, 'then he is my natural heir anyway. Surely you must see the sense of it?'

220

'The child could be anyone's,' she muttered, drawing away from him.

'Not anyone's,' he said in the same level tone, determined not to lose his temper. 'Mine, or possibly, just possibly, Andrew Ellerton's.'

'How will you know? Would you take the word of that – '

He put his hand none too gently over her mouth before she could say the word. 'Enough. I shall leave for Holland in the morning, and when I come back, if I have the boy with me, I hope that you will make him welcome. Remember he is still only a baby.'

She knew him well enough already to know it was useless to argue against the hardness in his voice. 'I will try,' she whispered. 'I promise.'

He felt a great pity for her suddenly, and turned his head on the pillow, kissing her gently. 'You must sleep now, and regain your strength. I shall return as quickly as I can and perhaps I shall have found the Cîteaux treasure that I told you about before.'

But she cared nothing about the treasure and turned on her side without another word.

When she woke next morning he was gone. She lay for a long time staring at the still drawn bed curtains, seeing them together in some other bed. The nun slut and *her* husband – her golden, handsome husband and the girl who had been able to give him a son, for she had no doubt in her own mind that the child was his. It was as if she knew this girl as well as she knew herself, knew that she still loved Robert as much as she did, that it was his child she had carried in her nun's womb for nine months and given birth to in an agony almost as terrible as her own, and this knowledge was like an unwanted intimacy making her hate her all the more.

The girl was pretty, they said, and years younger than herself – surely that in itself was enough for her to have to bear? She found herself writhing in actual physical pain at the thought of them together, making love, making another child perhaps, which she herself would never be able to do again. She wondered drearily if it was God's punishment for her sins, and especially for that night in the summer house, when she had given herself to a stranger, whose face she could not even see

221

but whose passion had matched her own, so that for those few moments it was as if they had known each other all their lives.

But these were foolish thoughts, she told herself impatiently. She was no young girl shivering in the Confessional, and when the bed curtains were drawn slowly back and she saw Walter's face looking down at her, like a genie – Walter, who rarely came into her bedchamber – she smiled her slow, unwilling smile. It was as if the plan her subconscious had worked out while she was asleep had surfaced and become a reality, without need of further help. But would her genie obey her this time?

Her eyes were like slivers of jet in the cold morning light as she willed him to be her slave.

Chapter Twenty-Seven

Isobel stood on the top step of the short flight of steps that led down into the living room, for the house on Kerkstraat was built on many levels. She had Christopher in her arms and for once he was quiet instead of constantly pulling away from her. The coffin had been placed on trestles, and the people of Amsterdam came in single file through the green-painted front door to pay their last respects to Cornelis van Ophoorn. He lay in his coffin with his feet pointing towards the same door, for in Holland only suicides and criminals were borne to burial head first.

From where she stood Isobel could see the sharp beak of his nose and his hands that a weeping Griet had placed together on his chest. There were to be more days of mourning before the coffin lid was finally closed, and it would be several more days too before his son and daughter arrived, but with the weather as hot as it was, the funeral might well have to take place before they came. Already there was an unpleasant sweetish smell pervading the big living room, in spite of the open door and the bunches of herbs that Griet had placed around the coffin. After her mother's death and the many deaths in the convent infirmary, Isobel had thought the smell of death an insult to the newly dead, the ultimate sadness beyond all tears, in spite of the other nuns' determined cheerfulness. But now, older and wiser, she wondered if it was not even more a cruel reminder to the living.

There was the subdued murmur of talk from below but no one even glanced up at her and for that she was grateful, for she was reluctant to have to return to her small bedchamber. She

223

seemed to have spent a lifetime in it since the death. She even ate her meals there now, for she found that the servants were no longer willing to bring them to her, and she had to go down to the kitchen and forage, not only for herself but also for Christopher who was already weaned. She would take what she could find and retreat to the privacy of her bedchamber with the scraps of food and a jug of milk, wondering when someone, Griet perhaps, or the long expected son and daughter, or a lawyer, would say, 'You must go. Now.' She knew that she would have to leave, and if she could have found a position in teaching, or any employment at all, she would have left at once, but although she had asked the housekeeper about the possibility of finding work, the woman had only frowned and said after a moment, 'It won't be easy. You speak the language fluently enough but you are not known to anyone here. It would be best to go back to your own country.'

Griet was right, of course. Although she had not actually said it, eyebrows would be lifted she knew, if she admitted to prospective employers that she had lived for nearly eight months in Cornelis van Ophoorn's house with no one but Griet to chaperone them. They would not believe the story of the drowned husband any more than his servants had done. But she had no money for the fare back to England, and even if she had, where could she go? Nothing would induce her to go back to the farm or to the nuns – and now she was afraid to go to sleep at night. While the banker was alive she had soon realised she had nothing to fear from any of the men living in the house. But last night Jan, the big countryman from near Vollendam who worked in the kitchen, had come to her door and begged her to let him in. She had heard his drunken footsteps on the stairs and managed to drag her chest across the door before he got there but she knew he would come again, and next time the chest might not keep him out. She had spoken to Griet about it, but the woman had only shrugged. 'What can you expect?' she said curtly. 'You'd best leave. Soon.'

That had been hours ago and she still did not know what she was going to do. If only poor Cornelis van Ophoorn had made his new will even a day earlier, she thought – but what was the use of wishing? And then, just as Christopher was beginning to get restless she saw him.

He was wearing a short cloak of tawny coloured frieze over a doublet of rich, dark green velvet with jacket and cap of the same colour, and he was talking to one of the menservants standing by the door. She thought she was going to faint and she had to lean against the wall beside her. Robert turned his head as if he felt her looking down at him and their eyes met briefly – then he looked away. He had not recognised her, or perhaps had forgotten her very existence.

Everything below her became blurred, indistinct, and she did not see him look up at her again, frowning this time. She wanted to fly to her room but she could not move. It was as if she had been turned to stone, and when she looked down again, she could not see him anywhere. A moment later she saw his broad back as he talked to a group of men on the far side of the coffin. What had brought him to Amsterdam, she wondered, trying to force herself to think clearly, telling herself that of course he would not recognise her. The last time he had seen her she had looked quite different. She thought of the last time and the probability that not only had he not recognised her, but had simply forgotten all about her. She told herself that she was insane to waste a second glance at him. Go! her mind screamed at her. 'Go! *Now!* But still she stayed, as if waiting. And then she saw him walk away, stride out through the open door into the summer sunlight and the fresh air, as if glad to be going.

Moments later she found herself back in her bedchamber, the baby on the floor crawling busily after the pieces of wood he used for toys. She sat down once more on the stool, hand to her face. Was she never to be free of Robert FitzHugh? Why had she had to see him? It had been as if a scab had been torn off a nearly healed wound and she was bleeding again, and she refused to listen to the small voice that said, 'Why don't you go and look for him? He might help you. He *should* help you.'

After a while, unable to stay where she was any longer, she picked Christopher up and carried him, screaming lustily for his pieces of wood, out to the courtyard at the back of the house. She watched him listlessly for a while as he distracted himself with a pile of loose tiles that someone had left stacked in one corner and when he had broken some of them and was becoming bored she brought him in again, and retreated once more to her bedchamber. The night loomed ahead of her, and when darkness fell she barricaded her door with everything she could move – the chest, the stool, even Christopher's heavy wooden cradle, letting him sleep with her for once, slipping the knife she had found in the kitchen under her pillow. But although she remained awake for what seemed most of the night, no one came to the door, and towards dawn she fell into an uneasy sleep.

She went into the courtyard again in the morning after she had fetched food from the kitchen, but for the rest of the day she stayed in her bedchamber, determined not to go down in the living room again where the vigil was still in progress. She felt dull and stupid from lack of a proper night's sleep, and she thought at first she had imagined the knock on the door. Then she heard Griet's voice.

'Isobel?' She no longer called her 'mejouffrouw'.

She opened the door.

'There is an Englishman downstairs who wishes to see you.' The woman's eyes were bright with curiosity. 'He asked me who the young woman was that he had seen here yesterday, and when I told him he did not seem surprised. Then he asked if he could speak to you for a few minutes.'

'What – what is his name?' Isobel whispered, scarcely able to speak.

Griet shrugged. 'I cannot pronounce these English names.' Then she added reluctantly, 'but he speaks our language quite well – '

It must be Robert – it had to be – but she was afraid to believe it in case she was wrong, and equally afraid she was right. Picking up the wriggling baby who did not want to be parted again from his toys, she followed Griet down to the ground floor, to the small antechamber where she used to eat her meals when there were visitors. And she found Robert there, looking as arrogant and impatient as ever, but older, harder, pacing up and down like a caged animal.

She could hear Griet close the door behind her, but it was as if such ordinary sounds belonged suddenly to some other world. All she was really conscious of was the man standing in front of her, looking down at her and then at Christopher, grown miraculously quiet, with a kind of wonder in his eyes.

'You've changed so much,' he said slowly, and his voice was

quiet and deep as always, but gentler than she remembered it. 'Yesterday, I thought it could not possibly be you, but I had to come back, had to ask. And now I still find it hard to believe.'

'You've – changed too,' she said, but her voice sounded strange and harsh in her own ears. 'Why did you ask to see me? What do you want?'

He did not answer immediately, but drew up a stool for her. 'Please sit down,' he said then, drawing up another for himself, so that they were facing each other, knees almost touching. The baby was warm and solid and comforting in her lap, quiet as a mouse now, his eyes that were so like his father's fixed unblinkingly on him.

'I have wanted to talk to you for a long time,' Robert said then, 'but I did not know how to find you. A very – unpleasant man told me about the baby and I wanted to say that I was sorry, that I bitterly regret what I did.'

She could think of nothing to say, and he reached out and touched Christopher's rosy cheek with his knuckles. 'Now that I've seen him, however, I can't say that that is altogether true. But I'd rather have heard about him from you. Why didn't you get word to me?'

'How could I?' she said, her voice even harsher than before. 'And if I had succeeded in doing so, what difference would it have made?'

He flushed and looked away. 'I would have helped you. In every way possible. You must know that.'

'I know nothing about you,' she said flatly. 'Nothing at all. But it's past – all done with.'

'You're wrong,' he said, his face flushing again, but with anger this time. 'You have a child, now. Our child.'

'Ours?' She could not keep the bitter irony out of her voice. 'You seem very sure. At the trial they asked me if it was not Andrew Ellerton's.'

His mouth tightened, but after a moment he said quietly, 'I considered the possibility, but not seriously. And as soon as I saw him I knew he was mine. He has a look of me but even more of my grandfather, poor child! What have you called him?'

'Christopher.'

He was smiling now and she had had to smile back, a small, wintry smile that did not reach her eyes and he went on evenly,

227

'A good name. I shall provide for his future of course. You need have no fear about that.'

She rested her cheek against the top of Christopher's head, his fine, white-gold hair like silk against her cheek, no warning bell sounding in her mind, feeling nothing but an enormous sense of relief. 'I am glad to hear that,' she said after a moment, forcing herself to look him in the face.

'I will do whatever I can for you too,' he added stiffly, and then before she could say anything, 'but where is your cousin, Andrew Ellerton? It was believed you came away together.'

'He was executed. Here in Amsterdam. Months ago.'

'Executed!' he repeated, looking at her as if he thought she must be losing her mind. 'But for *what*, in God's name?'

'It – it was all a terrible mistake,' she said slowly, suddenly tired beyond belief.

He leant forward, elbows on his knees. 'You'd best tell me everything,' he said grimly.

She began to tell him, halting at first and then the words tumbling over each other like a river in flood. And yet there were things she did not tell him about herself, at which he could only guess – the humiliation, her fear of the future, her loneliness, and when she had finished at last he looked down at the floor. 'It's even worse than I feared,' he muttered, 'and the smell of Edward Dutton is everywhere.' It was as if he were talking to himself.

After a moment she said quietly, 'There is the matter of getting the treasure back to Cîteaux. I feel it should be done at once. I have the receipt – '

'Good!' He got to his feet and stood looking down at her. 'You are quite right. We must see to it together. And you cannot stay here. That is obvious. It's a great pity that Cornelis did not attend to his legal affairs a bit more promptly.'

'He was very good to me while he was alive,' she said quickly. 'I was a total stranger, not even Dutch. Why should he have even thought of providing for us?'

'You liked him?'

'Very much.'

'Did he ever ask you who Christopher's father was?'

228

She shook her head. 'But I let it slip. I – I am sorry. I did not know you were related at the time.'

He shrugged. 'It's not important. Perhaps it was one of the reasons for his letting you stay. If so, then I'm glad he knew.' But his voice sounded as if he was thinking already of something else.

'You have not told me about yourself,' she said evenly.

He began to walk up and down the small room with a sudden, new restlessness. 'I was arrested,' he said curtly, 'and taken to the Tower for questioning. About the treasure. When they found I knew nothing, they let me go.'

'Was it very bad?' she said quietly.

He shrugged again. 'It's not something I want to talk about.'

His voice was still curt and she said into the silence, the words seeming to force themselves from her. 'Is – is your wife here with you in Amsterdam?' She had to know if he was married.

'No,' he said shortly. 'She's not here. She gave birth recently. A boy. Stillborn. Premature. She was not well afterwards.'

'I'm sorry' – the words like stones falling, the taste of ashes in her mouth. So he *had* married Beatrice Neville in the end and she had had his baby. She got to her feet holding Christopher to her shoulder trying not to feel glad the child had not lived. He stopped his pacing and came and stood looking down at both of them, the new lines about his mouth and eyes more noticeable than before.

'You must come with me,' he said abruptly, 'you must leave now.'

'I – I can't,' she began and he took her by the arm, his fingers digging into her flesh.

'Don't be a little fool! Do you not know what it's like for a woman left without a protector, without even her own servant?'

She shivered, remembering Jan's voice outside her door and he went on brusquely, 'They'll throw you out into the street, sooner or later, and only the brothel owners down by the harbour will be willing to take you in.'

'But – '

'Go and pack' he said tersely. 'I'll wait here for you.'

229

Chapter Twenty-Eight

For Edward Dutton the months had slipped by pleasantly enough. After his wife's death – he always called it that, even in his own mind, blotting out all memories of the night he had tied the rope across the top step of the stairs, removing it quickly afterwards – after the death of his wife he had found an accommodating woman friend. An elderly housekeeper saw to his other needs and he had finally got rid of his daughter, marrying her off to a wealthy old widower, a corn merchant in the city. When his daughter later came to him to complain bitterly that the old man was impotent and wet their bed he sent her home at once, telling her to count her blessings. So he had a quiet, pleasant, relaxing house all to himself – not that he meant to live alone for long. Already he had set his sights on the seventeen-year-old daughter of one of his neighbours. He could not count on a large dowry, having outwitted the girl's father in several business deals, but she was pretty, plump and clearly terrified of her middle-aged suitor. With such a combination of circumstances he felt the marriage could not fail to be a success.

So, in spite of his earlier near-obsession with it, he was not altogether pleased to be reminded of the Cîteaux treasure by the FitzHughs' footman whom he had long ago paid to tell him if and when Robert FitzHugh left for Holland, although as far as he had been able to discover, the treasure had never reached the French monks. But sitting alone over his mulled wine in the front parlour of his house he could not but remember the grandeur of the abbey, the sweep of the green pastures behind it, the river winding its way through the dales. Edward Dutton of

Wolden. Maybe even *Sir* Edward! How well it sounded, he thought, licking the wine off his thick lips with a furred tongue, especially now that he could hope again to have a son. I will go to Holland, he decided. I will follow him, and who knows, he may yet lead me to it.

But FitzHugh might not be going over about it at all, he thought then. The fellow might indeed be looking for his bastard son as the footman had said. Well, in that case there would be no harm done. His business had been going well and could look after itself again for a short while. But if his luck still held and FitzHugh *was* going with the treasure in mind, then it should be a simple matter to follow him. He would need help though for that, someone who spoke the language and someone else with muscle as well as brains. Not like the two clowns he had had with him the last time –

As the hot, spicy wine slid down his throat all things became suddenly possible and he saw himself returning in a few weeks' time with the treasure, servants bowing before him as he walked through the palace, the King himself thanking him with tears in his eyes . . . granting him the abbey of Wolden and its land at last . . . and afterwards, a small brown-haired girl waiting for him in the big, four-poster bed, shivering . . .

A burning log sent up a shower of sparks on the open hearth and brought him back to reality. It might not be so easy to get permission to see Lord Cromwell this time, but he would have to have his authority and help behind him if he himself were to succeed. He stared into the dregs of his wine, the feeling of elation leaving him like water disappearing into sand. All the same, when he went up to his cold bed to lie alone in the stuffy darkness, his mind was made up. Whatever the difficulties he encountered on the way he was going to make one last effort to find the treasure.

In the end he had to wait several days before he could speak to Lord Cromwell, and first he had to talk to what seemed an endless number of minor Tower officials. The fact that he was anxious to avoid all mention of the treasure for fear someone else would go after it made it all the more difficult to catch their interest. But at last he was brought to Sir Thomas Wriothesley, and *he* was certainly not to be fobbed off with a vague request for a few minutes' private conversation with the Lord Chancellor.

'Unless you tell me what you want to see his lordship about, I can do nothing for you,' he snapped irritably, but when he was reluctantly told that it was in connection with the Cîteaux treasure he changed his tune. 'Who *really* owns it?' he asked then, lowering his voice. 'The French monks?'

'They would try to claim it, certainly.' Edward Dutton was choosing his words even more carefully now.

'I see,' Sir Thomas said thoughtfully, thinking that although this paunchy, middle-aged man might be no King Arthur searching for the Holy Grail – if he went after the treasure it would surely be for material gain – there was still a force about him that was not to be gainsaid. 'I shall see what I can do,' he added briskly.

An hour later Edward Dutton faced Lord Thomas Cromwell across a cluttered table. The table and the room itself were both larger and grander than when he had last been granted an interview and the man facing him across the table seemed to have grown in stature, his clothes still sober in colour but made of velvet now and silk, edged with fur, a huge, gold ring on his forefinger, even a jewel in his cap. But the heavy, sallow face seemed to have fallen in and there were pouches of loose flesh under the small eyes. Whatever his new honours had brought him it was not peace of mind, Edward Dutton thought as he launched into his story.

'So you want to go to Holland again, in the hope that Robert FitzHugh will lead you to the treasure?' the minister said, leaning back in his chair.

'Yes, my lord. I have been told the treasure had not reached the monks in Cîteaux – '

'That is true – at least according to the last report – but is it not more likely that Robert FitzHugh has in fact gone to look for his natural son, as you say he claims to be doing?' There was a note of impatience in the minister's voice and Edward Dutton said quickly, 'There is some doubt that the child is really his.'

The footman had told him too that his mistress could bear no more children but he had thought it wiser not to mention that fact, and the minister grunted, leaning back in his chair, his eyes beginning to wander over the untidy table. 'Perhaps you are right,' he said at last. 'But remember, Robert FitzHugh is not as soft as I was led to believe he was.'

'I shall remember, my lord.' Edward Dutton's voice was smooth as silk now that he had won his point. 'But I shall need better men with me this time, and one of them must be able to speak Dutch.'

'When do you want to leave?'

'As soon as possible. FitzHugh has left already.' And then, his voice not quite so smooth Edward Dutton added, 'I have plans to marry in the near future.'

'Indeed?' The minister's voice was dry as dust. 'We must see to it quickly then. I shall ask my secretary to find you a suitable man, and a bodyguard as well. Good day to you.'

The big, clumsy looking hand reached out for the handbell, and bowing from the waist Edward Dutton left the room.

The minister watched him go with cold eyes, wondering if the stories about his wife's death were true. The fellow seemed to have got himself an unsavoury reputation, he thought morosely, and he disliked having to have dealings with him. But if he succeeded in bringing back the Cîteaux treasure – that would be a different matter, he told himself. God knows he needed a sweetener to give the King more than anyone, it seemed, and he must see to it that Edward Dutton did not get all the credit if he *was* successful.

It took Isobel no more than twenty minutes to pack for herself and Christopher, stuffing their clothes in two large canvas bags that she found in one of the attics, and when she was ready she went down to the living room where Robert waited for her impatiently, holding Christopher tight to her with one arm, dragging the baggage behind her with the other. When Robert had taken it from her she led the way towards a side door, but in one of the short passages they met Griet. The woman blocked their way.

'You will be glad to hear I'm leaving,' Isobel said.

'Yes, I'm glad.' The woman spat the words out. Then she looked over Isobel's shoulder at Robert. 'I see you do not waste time,' she said bitterly, and turned and walked away.

'Not a friend of yours I'd say.' Robert moved ahead to open the door.

'No,' Isobel said shortly, her face still flushed with anger. 'She never trusted me.' But as she stepped out into the street she forgot all about Griet, forgot everything except that Robert FitzHugh, whom she had never expected to see again, was actually beside her, his shoulder brushing hers.

Later that same day, after he had brought her to his house off Kalverstraat – big and rambling like Cornelis van Ophoorn's, but older – they went together with John to the bank to retrieve the treasure. They were sent from one pompous official to another, each in turn staring at Isobel as if to say he was not accustomed to dealing with a woman and certainly not a woman with a child in her arms, and Andrew's sheet of parchment was scrutinised from every angle.

'Your cousin met with an unfortunate accident, you say? But we have only your word for that, and alas, Meneer van Ophoorn is no longer with us.' And while Isobel sent up a brief but fervent prayer of thanks for the bank's apparent lack of knowledge of what went on at the Town Hall, Robert put her case pleasantly but with that hint of arrogant authority that was second nature to him, until the officials began to weaken and gave the order at last for the sack of 'valuables' to be brought up from the vault. A few minutes later it lay at their feet and one of them looked down with raised eyebrows as much as to say, Is this what all the fuss is about? But there were still signatures to be taken and pompous words to be said before Isobel found herself ouside the bank house at last, Robert and John carrying the sack between them.

When they were back in the house Robert led the way into the living room, closing the door carefully behind him.

'I think it is time we saw the Cîteaux treasure,' he said grimly, heaving the sack onto the table and breaking the seal. The other two watched in silence – Christopher sound asleep in Isobel's arms – as he thrust his arm into the sack and began to pull out objects of varying size, and Isobel, looking at the cowhide wrappings, remembered another sunny day when she and Andrew had had to hide behind a furze bush with Christopher and he had told her how he had saved the Cîteaux treasure. It seemed so long ago.

She gasped suddenly, for Robert had unwrapped one of the larger objects and a gold monstrance blazed like a sunrise against the polished wood of the table, the centre of it circled with jewelled finger rings set into its own gold. He began to unwrap the rest with hands that were beginning to shake with excitement – twin candlesticks of bell-metal, richly guilt, a bronze book shrine, beautifully enamelled, an exquisitely wrought silver-guilt censer with silver chains, a gold ewer and flagon and finally the chalice itself of purest gold, standing about

234

nine inches high, the rim and the base studded with precious stones – rubies like splashes of blood spilling onto the blue of sapphires big as pigeons' eggs, the vivid green of emeralds, and jewels that she could not put a name to.

'No wonder the abbot did not want to part with it,' Robert said softly, breaking the stunned silence.

'The whole lot must be worth a bloody fortune!' John muttered.

But Isobel said nothing. The treasure seemed to her to belong to a world of pomp and ceremony and intrigue that she had never known and about which she had only read, or been told by Dame Petronilla. A world of popes in tall hats and cardinals in scarlet robes. The world of Rome and the Vatican, as far removed from the Last Supper as it was possible to be.

'You're very quiet, Isobel,' Robert said. 'What do you think of them?'

'They are – magnificent,' she said. 'But not worth dying for.'

'It was for what they represent.'

'I know.' And then she added as if the words had been put into her mind to say, 'They will cost more than one life.' She began to be afraid of what was happening to her.

'I hope you are not gifted with second sight?' he said, frowning.

'I – don't know.'

He looked at her, still frowning and then picked up the chalice and held it against the light. 'Bones from St Bernard's hand are in the base I believe, but I won't disturb them.'

She watched him put the chalice carefully down on the table and begin to wrap it in cowhide again, feeling strangely depressed.

'You'll come to France with me, won't you?' he said quickly. 'I must go there rightaway! Now that I've seen it I know there's no safe place for the treasure anywhere else, but I can't stay away from England indefinitely.'

And because she could hardly remain on in his house without having been invited to do so and because it seemed only fair that he should see something of his son, she agreed to go. But she knew, in her heart of hearts, that she was really going because she wanted to be with him, in spite of all her resolutions to put him out of her life for ever.

Chapter Twenty-Nine

They had told Isobel apologetically that it was an unusually hot June for Holland and she had laughed and said she did not care. She loved the warmth of the sun as she had loved all the good things of the past few days – the big house that had once belonged to Robert's grandmother and was mercifully free of the smell of death; the kind old husband and wife who looked after it for him and had seemed to take to her and Christopher on sight; her new maid Brechtje, who helped her with Christopher; Robert's unfailing care for her and the baby that seemed to ask for nothing in return; and above all, her own inexplicable feeling of belonging.

At the end of each day he would walk her to the foot of the stairs and bid her a grave 'good-night', and afterwards lying in bed she would wonder if he was thinking, perhaps, even for a moment or two, of her. They were friends now, surely they were that, even if never lovers again – or had they ever been lovers? And she did not really belong, of course. She was a waif, a stray that he had taken pity on, who would, sooner or later, have to go on her way with Christopher while he went back to his wife. But this was something she refused to think about, clutching instead at the thought of the 'good things' to ward off the sadness that was never far away, and she would go to sleep at last, thinking only of tomorrow, which she hoped would slip past in another golden haze of warmth and comfort.

Even when they set off on the big, flat bottomed boat that was to take them south she was almost happy. The boat itself seemed not to move, in spite of the sweating efforts of the men on the tow path. Only the lazy water sliding past, and the sails of the distant windmills against the sky line moved. She had not realised until then how truly flat the country was – after the hills and dales of Yorkshire it seemed unreal – yet it had its own, strange beauty.

But even the easy contentment of those first weeks had its hidden pain. Robert had made a harness for Christopher from an old leather belt and he seemed to delight in holding it and watching the baby climb and crawl within the limited confines of the boat. When he lifted him up he held him in front of him like a wooden doll, legs and arms dangling, as if terrified he might break in two. She would look at them both, then, with an ache in her heart, thinking that a child needed its father as well as its mother, and a boy especially.

One very hot day Robert stripped to his breeches and jumped into the canal, swimming alongside, his hair sleeked wetly to his head, his teeth white against his skin as he laughed up at her, treading water. She found herself wishing with all her heart that she could be in the water with him, and as if he had read her mind his smile faded slowly, his eyes holding hers. Then someone shouted that there was a boat coming in the opposite direction and he had to scramble aboard, his breeches clinging to him like a second skin.

'The meneer is very handsome, isn't he?' Brechtje had whispered behind her hand and Isobel could only nod her head, unable to wrench her eyes away from the long, clean lines of his body, longing to touch him, to be touched by him. And yet she had discovered that she was no longer in love with him. Somewhere, at some point in time, the fever had left her, along with her young girl's fantasies. Instead, she had grown to love him, for all that he was, good and bad, and although she felt old and wise and strangely comforted by the discovery, she knew now that she would never be free of him and she was haunted by the prospect of a second parting. Not that he ever talked to her about the future – but then they seemed never to be alone. Even when the boat was moored for an hour or two by the side of the canal John seemed always to be within earshot, and although the big man was never openly hostile to her, there was a look of cool speculation in his eyes when they spoke to one another which reminded her unpleasantly of the servants in Cornelis van Ophoorn's house. She longed to hit him, to scream, 'I am not his mistress.' But what was the use? It was part of the price she had to pay for that night of madness – unless she found some poor fool, or some doddering old man willing to make her his wife. But I will never marry for that reason alone, she swore to herself. Never! I will never marry at all!

In all the growing tumult of Isobel's mind she never once thought of Edward Dutton, or Lord Thomas Cromwell, or least of all, of His Majesty, King Henry VIII of England. But if the King and his minister had too much on their minds to think about her either, Edward Dutton thought of her constantly, and of her baby. He thought too of the dead Andrew and the living Robert with an even greater malevolence, and it was a wonder that his fury did not reach across the distance that still separated them from him.

Once in Amsterdam he had met the young Dutchman who spoke some English, as had been arranged by Cromwell's secretary. He had already brought with him from England a man who called himself simply 'Colby', a young, dour giant of a fellow with a reputation for being faster than most with his knife. He never smiled and rarely spoke, but he remained close as a shadow to Edward Dutton throughout the voyage, so that the older man became restless and ill at ease and was glad to get off the boat when they reached Calais.

He would have felt even more ill at ease had he known that on 10 June, when he had at last reached Amsterdam, luck had finally run out for Lord Thomas Cromwell. The new Earl of Essex and Lord Chamberlain of England was arrested and brought to the Tower, on a trumped up charge of treason against the King whom he had served so faithfully and with such devotion. Two days later he was allowed to write to Henry. In his letter he denied that he had ever divulged the King's confidences, and at the end of his letter he made a plea for mercy. But the plea fell on deaf ears. Under the influence of Norfolk and Gardiner, whatever the King might have thought of his minister in the past, he now saw him only as a witness who could substantiate the royal claim that the marriage to Anne of Cleves had never been consummated. Apart from that he had no further use for him.

But Edward Dutton, of course, knew none of this. It had taken his Dutch colleague, Klaas Groot, a fluent linguist, a very short time to find out that Robert FitzHugh had left Amsterdam for France some days earlier. He had gone by boat, taking an Englishwoman and her

238

baby with him, and it seemed to Edward Dutton a near certainty that he was making for Cîteaux with the treasure.

He lost no time in hiring a boat so that he could follow, and the day after he arrived in Amsterdam he set off with his two companions like a clerk taking an unwanted holiday in a foreign country, sitting bolt upright on the wooden boat seat in his dark, nondescript clothes. Nevertheless, there was something in his pale, soft face which made the other men wary of him – the look of evil, had they but recognised it. He soon made it clear that there were to be no delays on the way, no lingering at wayside taverns, no late starts. Occasionally they would hear of the Englishman and his party who had gone ahead of them, but most of the time they simply went on as fast as they dared hoping to reach Cîteaux first, and be waiting when Robert arrived.

Ahead of them now by only a few days, Robert continued to keep a wary eye on the treasure, on the lookout for common thieves whenever they moored the boat or went ashore, but never giving a thought to Edward Dutton or the King's men whom he was sure would have long since given up the hunt. He would look at the flat, empty countryside and the distant windmills, at John's bulk and Frans, his muscular young Dutch manservant, and tell himself that he had nothing to fear; and he would look at Christopher, like a naked cherub, laughing up at his mother and pulling her hair with small, chubby hands, and tell himself that such innocent happiness could not be destroyed.

Isobel's face and throat and arms were a smooth, golden brown now and her hair, freed from the cap which she had long ago discarded, curled thick and dark to her shoulders. Sometimes he would wonder if this poised, beautiful girl could ever have been the ghostlike creature he had met in the fog, or even the young nun with whom he had spent one strange and wonderful night, and yet her eyes, her voice, the turn of her head, the tantalising moments of withdrawal were the same. It was as if a statue had come to life, and he longed to live that night again – but he was afraid that by making any false move he would lose her, and Christopher.

He had not yet told her that he wanted to take him from her, and now he was sorry he had not done so in the very beginning, for with each day it became more difficult to say anything, as he saw how close they were to one another. He would tell himself that it was not good for a mother to be so close to her son – that it was bad for both of them, that as his acknowledged heir Christopher would have a future, a name, a place for himself in the world. But a child needed a mother – he knew that only too well – and Beatrice was not likely to show Isobel's child any love.

And always, at the back of his mind there was the picture of a small, quiet house on the outskirts of London that he would buy for Isobel, where she could live with dignity. He would bring Christopher to see her there and if for a while he could forget that he was married, if she allowed him to, could they both not snatch a few moments of peace and happiness now and then? Was it not as much, if not more than came the way of most people? But would she agree to any of it?

The golden days, the moonlit nights slid past, becoming even warmer as they travelled further south. They had had to leave the canals and continue their journey by river in a sailboat, but the day came when it was faster to ride, sometimes sleeping out under the stars or in rough, country inns, so hot now they had to rest during the middle of the day.

It was already July when they skirted the Ardennes, following the Meuse for a while and riding until they were no more than eighteen miles or so from Cîteaux. The end of the journey was in sight at last and yet, for all the friendship that had grown between them like a delicate sapling that had become a sturdy tree in a matter of weeks, he still had not asked her for Christopher, still had said nothing, done nothing, that would have made that quiet house in London a reality. For the first time in his life he felt awkward, clumsy, unsure of himself. But when they stopped for their midday break, having spent the previous night in the inn at St Auguste, a small village a couple of hours' ride from Dijon, he knew that he could wait no longer.

They had made their stop near a wood and when they had eaten, he said quietly to her, 'There is something I want to talk to you about. Will you walk down to the river with me?' She got up with only a second's hesitation, and he said quickly, 'Brechtje will look after Christopher. Don't worry about him.' He had somehow found her hand and was holding it – it felt as if it belonged there, he thought, like a bird settling into its nest.

Neither of them heard, or even sensed, the three men who had ridden up the track and saw them disappear among the trees.

Chapter Thirty

On a warm, sunny mid-June afternoon Beatrice FitzHugh sat on the wooden garden seat staring out over the river. Sir William used to sit there often before he became bed-ridden, his dog lying across his feet, but no one else had sat there until now. She could see the FitzHugh landing-stage and the private barge which had been moored there since Robert had last taken her out on the river, and she wondered fretfully where he was now and what he was doing.

A pair of swans swam inshore, followed by their flock of brown cygnets and further out two wherries passed each other, the boatmen's singing drifting up to her on the breeze, their oars flashing wetly in the sunlight. But she saw and heard none of it, so lost was she in her own bitter thoughts. How long had he been gone? Five, six weeks? It felt like a year. And if he found the girl in the end and the child, what would he do? She did not doubt that Isobel Willis would hand over her son for what woman would refuse such a future for her bastard, but would he leave the mother behind? And if he did not –

She did not hear Walter coming down the steps until he was almost level with the seat, and then she looked up and saw him. He was carrying one of her shawls, frowning down at her. 'I thought you might be cold,' he said.

'I'm not an invalid!' she snapped, 'And it is quite warm.' Then, as she remembered that she would need him in the near future, she said more kindly, 'Thank you all the same. Sit down and talk to me.'

But he looked back at the house without moving and she said impatiently, 'No one will see you, for heaven's sake! Do as I say!'

He sat down then, well away from her and she laughed sourly.

241

'Are you afraid to be seen talking to me? You used not to be, in Raskelfe.'

'It's different now,' he said. 'You are a married woman.'

'I don't feel it! I've been married nearly a year and it seems my husband has been absent for most of it!'

'You exaggerate.' His voice was harsh with jealousy. 'You've not been married as long as that, and he's only been away a few weeks in all.'

She shrugged. 'We won't argue about it, but I have a feeling he will be away this time for quite a while.'

When he said nothing she moved a little closer to him, touching his hand briefly with her own. 'Walter,' she began, looking sideways at him, 'I have been thinking –'

He knew from previous experience that she was about to ask a favour of him, that she was going to put forward a plan, of which perhaps he might not approve, but a plan whose success nevertheless would depend on his co-operation, and he said quickly, his eyes suddenly wary, 'Remember this is not Raskelfe, Beatrice.'

'I know, I know!' The impatience was back in her voice. 'But what I have in mind would – would not happen here –' And then putting her hands over her eyes, she said huskily, 'You don't know the hell I've been through, thinking of that child that I shall have to pretend to welcome – and he may try to bring her back here too!'

'Nonsense!' he said quickly. 'Sir William would not allow it.'

'He'll be dead soon,' she said bleakly. 'But even if Robert does not bring her here, he'll bring her back to London and make her his mistress. I am sure of it.'

'She may be dead or he may never find her – ' he began, but she was no longer listening to him.

'She's alive! I know it! And she'd come away with him if he asked her! There's only one thing to do, Walter!' she said, sitting up straight. 'We must get rid of her for good!'

'We?' His eyes had narrowed.

She hesitated and then went on with a rush of words, 'Both of us really, but – but I've thought of a way and – and it will all depend on you! But if you do what I tell you, if you succeed, I shall not forget it, I promise!'

She touched his hand again and felt it quiver. He would do it, she thought exultantly. He was still hers! But she must make sure – and when he said nothing she went on, her voice grown husky, 'If my son

242

had lived, I might not feel as I do, but as you know, I can't have another child.' Her voice broke in sudden, real grief and she put her hands to her face. 'I feel useless, degraded. I could not bear to be humiliated further!' Her voice was so muffled he could barely make out the words and his pity and love for her were like knives turning inside him. He moved closer, putting an arm tentatively round her shoulders but he knew she was not even aware of it and he withdrew it slowly, feeling the old, familiar pain of rejection. At last she raised her head. 'It's hard for you to understand, Walter,' she whispered, 'but if you'd ever had a child you'd know what I feel – oh why, *why* did my son have to die?'

'*Our* son,' he said quietly before he could stop himself, stung into indiscretion by her lack of response, by her words even more.

'*Our* son?' she repeated stupidly, drawing away from him. 'What – what do you mean?'

He wished that he had kept his mouth shut but it was too late, and after all what difference did it make now, and she deserved to know, he thought with a touch of malice. 'I was the man in the summerhouse,' he said, and heard her gasp of horror with a kind of twisted pleasure.

'*You?*'

He nodded.

'How dared you! How *dared* you!' And you let me think –'

'That it was some blue-blooded gallant? Why not? If it gave you pleasure –'

'I could kill you! *Kill* you! Oh, how I *hate* you!' But after a few minutes, when he said nothing, she laughed shrilly. 'No wonder I felt I knew him.'

'I'm sorry,' he said, and then added quickly, 'No, that is not true, I have no regrets. But now you know that I *do* understand what it is like to lose a child – and if he had lived, my son, *our* son, would one day have been heir to the FitzHughs, with a title and all the other things I have never had myself, could never have given him.'

She got up from the seat and walked a little way from him, leaving him sitting, lost in thought, but when she came back a few minutes later, although her face was still pale, she was smiling. 'We have shared more than I realised,' she said evenly, 'and it makes it that much easier to tell you of my plan.'

But he would not look at her, his narrow shoulders stooped, his slight body gathered into itself like a hedgehog and she knew that if

243

she touched him now he would pull away from her – and she must not lose him.

'Please forgive me!' she said softly. 'It is not in my nature to be tactful, you know that! But I would not hurt *you*, of all people! I sometimes think you are the only friend I have in the whole world!'

He turned to her quickly, like a dark flower turning towards the sun, and she smiled again, her cat's smile of secret satisfaction – but he saw only forgiveness.

'Come,' she whispered. 'Come with me, old friend!'

She brought him into the house, and when she had sent Sarah out on an errand with one of the menservants and made sure there was no one else about, she brought him up to her bedchamber and led him over to the enormous four poster bed. He followed her like a man that has been drugged, and she had to open her bodice herself and put his hand on her breast. She felt more like a mother than a lover, and to her disappointment it was Walter, not the man in the summerhouse, who entered her, for he was afraid of hurting her so soon after the birth. Indeed, her body was scarcely ready and she was glad when it was over and he had rolled over on his back with a deep sigh.

She began to tell him of her plan then, and when she had finished he said only, very quietly, 'I thank God that our son will never know.'

'But you will do it? For me? For us?'

'Yes,' he said. 'I will do it.'

She smiled her cat's smile again, but he lay staring at the drawn bed curtains, a bitter taste in his mouth. It had all happened before, but this was the first time she had asked him to commit murder, as it was also the first time she had given herself knowingly to him. Would he never be able to refuse her anything? For a second he saw the other side of love, saw hate, saw the colour of it, felt its cold heat, and then she put her bare arm across his naked chest, kissed his shoulder and there was nothing left but his love for her.

He rode away the following morning, telling everyone else that he was going up to Raskelfe. He had cut his hair, as she had told him to do and in the new clothes that she had told him to get he looked different, elegant, not the Walter she knew. She had given him more than enough money and it would not be his first time to leave the country, for he had been abroad already with the earl and even had a scanty knowledge of French. But he knew no Dutch, and although she had told him how to find the house in Amsterdam, remembering all that Robert had told her about it, she began to have misgivings about her whole plan as soon as she heard the front door of the house slam shut behind him.

So many things could go wrong, and if Robert found out afterwards that Walter had done it, he would surely kill him – not that that would mean very much to her. But Robert might guess that she had been behind it, or Walter might even betray her under pressure, and then it was *she* who might be killed, or put away at the very least. Alone in the creaking house with no one to talk to except Sarah and the old man in his evil-smelling room, who looked at her now with undisguised disappointment verging on contempt, with nothing but her fears to think about, she began to wish that she had gone with Walter. At least then she would have known what was going on, could have stopped him doing anything foolish, for it was always she who in the past plotted and schemed and he who put her plans into action.

I should have gone, she told herself, tossing and turning in her lonely bed in the small hours. I should have gone with him. I am well enough now. I could have thought of some excuse – said I was too lonely to remain behind alone – that the doctor said I needed a change – anything!

And in the end, a week later, taking Sarah and a new manservant that she had insisted should be found for her to replace Walter, she set out on horseback for Dover. After the first day's riding she was stiff and sore and so tired she thought she would never ride again – but she forced herself to get out of bed early next morning, and after she had walked about for a while in the yard of the inn where they had stayed overnight, her muscles ceased to scream at her, and she was able to mount again.

'You be mad, mistress!' Sarah scolded, but in fact she was pleased enough to see Beatrice determined to continue the journey. She had never expected to ride even as far as London in her lifetime and yet here she was, Sarah Applegarth, born and bred in the Yorkshire Dales, riding for the boat that would carry her across the sea to Amsterdam!

Walter found himself in Amsterdam a few weeks later, the sun not much warmer than in London, but the air fresher, and the town itself only a fraction of the size of the English city. He looked what he was, a foreigner – his clothes, his walk, his very expression different – and yet he succeeded in finding the house quickly enough. Even spoken with his English accent someone eventually understood that he was looking for Kalverstraat, but although no one understood him when he tried to say Begijnhof, he found it himself when he left the Kalverstraat. Beatrice had said it was a kind of convent, where women lived who were like nuns, and there it was, bathed in sunlight, with a group of women in long, blue woollen gowns with white, winged wimples on their heads, talking together in the central courtyard. And in a street nearby, that ran alongside a canal he found the house, with the name Hooft on the wall plaque that had never been changed since Robert FitzHugh's grandmother had lived there.

It took some time to find the courage to raise the door knocker, but when he did it was opened by a small, apple-cheeked woman who looked at him cheerfully and said something in rapid Dutch. When she discovered that he was English she beckoned him in, and later he found that in her eyes and in the eyes of her husband, all English people were welcome. He had only to mention Robert FitzHugh's name and claim to be his friend for their old faces to light up. He had not believed such simple trust could exist, but it made his task that much easier. They fed him, and then with much laughter and sign language and the few English and French words that they knew, he was given to understand that their young master had left by boat for France.

At first he wondered why Robert should have gone to France, remembering then, with a quickening sense of interest, what Beatrice had told him about the Cîteaux treasure and its link with the FitzHugh family. But it was only while he and the old fellow were negotiating with the boatmen for a boat in which he could follow, that he discovered for certain that Robert FitzHugh had had an Englishwoman and her child with him. He forgot about the treasure then in fear and horror at what he must now do, and not for the first time he cursed the fates that had sent him to Raskelfe as a young boy. Nevertheless, he left Amsterdam that afternoon, heading south by boat like a mindless puppet, and he was well on his way when Beatrice FitzHugh arrived in Amsterdam.

As Robert's wife she got an even warmer reception from the old couple than he had done, but later, when she made no secret of the fact that she found Dutch ways strange and uncomfortable, and the food uneatable, they shook their heads as soon as they were alone.

'How could he have chosen such a one for wife?' the old housekeeper said. 'She is not a good woman. I can see it in her face.'

'What's worse, she's too thin,' her husband growled, 'and ugly too. She must have had a very large dowry – but I do not think we should tell her where he has gone. Maybe he came over to get away from her?'

'I think you are probably right.' His wife's plump, wrinkled face looked wise. 'But I would not care to lie to her.' She smoothed her hands down her immaculate white, embroidered apron. 'Mejuffrouw Isobel would have suited much better.' She whispered, although Beatrice was not in the kitchen with them, and the old man nodded his head in agreement as he picked up the jug of wine and one of the best goblets for their unwelcome guest, who waited impatiently in the living room.

But even if they did not like her they still had to be civil to Robert's wife, still had to try to understand her English and her occasional words of French, even her sign language, which was showing more and more signs of barely controlled irritation. She did, however, eventually find out from them that Walter had been there before her and had set off by boat to follow Robert south, although they could not tell her the reason for Robert's journey. She guessed, however, like Walter, that it must be to do with the treasure. And she did find out in the end, after much probing, that an Englishwoman and her child had been with Robert. The old couple watched her turn white, then fiery red at that point and looked at each other like two guilty children, fearing that their beloved master would be angry that they had told her, but what else could they have done?

Next day the old man had to bring her too down to the boatmen and arrange for her to hire one of them to take her and her two servants south. She had looked at the flat-bottomed craft and the sluggish canal, biting her thin lips with disgust, but there was no alternative. It had all turned out as she had feared it would. The convent slut was with him and Walter could not be far behind.

That same afternoon she, Sarah and the manservant began their long journey. The old housekeeper and her husband stood unsmiling on the canal bank, wondering uneasily what Robert would say to them when they saw him again, whilst in England, Lord Thomas Cromwell sealed his own fate by giving intimate details of the revulsion which the King felt for his 'Flanders Mare'. The minister's royal master had no further use for him now and the date for his execution was set for 29 July.

247

Chapter Thirty-One

It was much cooler under the trees, and they walked for a few minutes in silence, the only sound the rustling of Isobel's silk gown. She could have walked for ever with Robert, with no need of speech, his hand holding hers, but he said at last, 'I have wanted to talk to you alone for a long time, but I've always been afraid –'

'Afraid?' She looked up at him, startled. 'Of what?'

He shrugged. 'Of saying the wrong thing – or – or using the wrong words.'

'Tell me what it is you want to say,' she said quietly.

He stopped, looking down into the depths of her eyes, and said quickly, 'There is nothing – nothing in particular. I – just wanted to – to talk to you. About – about what you will do, afterwards. You and Christopher. I would like to be able to see him. Often.'

She had withdrawn her hand and she did not answer him immediately. 'He is your son,' she said after a moment. 'It is only right that you should see him. I know he will miss you very much when – when this journey is over.'

Her voice had become suddenly husky, and he caught her by the shoulders, 'I shall miss him too, and you even more,' he said harshly. And then, his voice softening, deepening, 'Oh, if you only knew how much I shall miss you! My darling, darling girl!'

Her eyes flew to his. 'It's no use,' she whispered, 'can't you see that?' And with her words, even more than his, the weeks of careful distance were suddenly a forgotten memory.

'Because I have a wife?'

'Yes.'

'I don't love her. I never have.'

248

Her heart lifted, but she said quickly, 'You are still married.'

He dropped his hands from her shoulders, turning away. 'I know, and I would not put her away even if I could.'

'No man should do that – so why are we having this – this foolish conversation?'

'Because I *am* a fool, I suppose. And because I – have been hoping – that if I bought a house in London for you to live in, I could come and – and visit you there and – '

'Are you asking me to be your mistress?' She had to force herself to say the words.

'Don't call it that!' he begged.

'But is that what you mean?'

'I can't ask you to be my wife. I wish I could.'

'I don't want to be any man's mistress,' she said slowly.

'But I love you!' His voice had risen and the words seemed to echo and re-echo among the listening trees. 'I think I've loved you ever since you came out of that cursed fog!'

'And I you,' she whispered, 'since long before that!'

He took her in his arms then, and she came to him unresisting. He began to kiss her, gently at first, covering her face, her throat, with kisses until passion woke in both of them and she was clinging to him. 'Robert, oh Robert!' she whispered. He lifted her up and carried her deeper into the wood, where the grass was green and soft and thick, and laid her down and lay down himself beside her. The sun sent them its shafts of light between the leaves and high above the wood a lark began to sing. They undressed each other and made love, naked and beautiful, their passion like a flame in which they burned and died and lived again.

'I'll be careful,' he had whispered. 'I'll be very careful, this time,' and afterwards she lay beside him, drowsy with love, satiated with it. That is what love is, she thought. I know now. I know at last.

They slept for a little while, and when they woke they slipped through the trees like wood sprites and bathed in the little river that bordered the wood. When they got back and she began to put her clothes on again he tried to stop her.

'What's the hurry?' he said, laughing, trying to pull her down

249

on top of him, half in, half out of her shift, but guilt was hovering now, black and inescapable and she had suddenly realised how long they had been away.

'We must go,' she said. 'We have been away too long.' Once again it was as if the words had been put into her mind to say and she looked at him, her eyes wide with sudden fear.

'What is it?' he was frowning, but sitting up now himself, beginning to draw on his breeches. 'You look as if you have seen a ghost!'

She shook her head, trying to laugh. 'I – I don't know. I – just feel we should go back. Quickly.'

She was fumbling with the tiny buttons of her bodice and as she cursed them for being so small she told herself to be calm, that she was imagining things. What could possibly be wrong? Christopher had Brechtje and John to look after him, and as for the treasure, surely Frans was trustworthy. But as she finished dressing she knew that her earlier joy had faded, slipped away from her, leaving only its memory behind. She tried to grasp at it, to hold it to her and found herself looking stupidly at her empty hands.

'Come,' Robert said, putting an arm about her shoulders. 'The sooner we go back the sooner you will know that you are worrying needlessly.'

But when they came out of the wood Brechtje was running towards them, John lumbering behind. 'Oh, where have you been? We have been looking everywhere for you!' The girl's plump face was streaked with tears and her eyes were wild with fear.

'What is it, Brechtje?' Robert said harshly, standing in front of Isobel as though to shield her, but she pushed him aside. 'Has – has something happened to Christopher?' she said quietly. 'Tell me. Quickly.'

She saw John look over her head at Robert, and the girl said, seeming on the verge of hysteria, 'He's gone! Disappeared!'

Isobel took her soft, fleshy arm, gripping it hard. 'He can't have! Were you not with him?'

Brechtje hung her head. 'He was asleep, fast asleep where I'd put him – in the shade of the big tree – and – and – I was talking to Frans – just for a few minutes – I swear it was no more than that!' She began to cry.

'So you left him,' Robert said through his teeth. 'For how long? Five minutes, ten?'

'No more than that,' the girl whispered miserably. 'I could not believe it when I went back and – and he was not there.'

Isobel began to run, and found John beside her. 'He – he must have crawled into some hiding-place,' she panted. 'He *must* have!'

'We've looked everywhere, mistress,' he grunted.

'Then we'll look again!'

By now they had all reached the stony path that led up to the place where they had made their camp. Isobel ran to the tree and saw lying beneath it the old, shabby blanket that was Christopher's most precious possession. He would not go to sleep unless he had it clutched to him. When he was teething he had sucked it and it had seemed to calm him, and when the teeth had finally appeared he still sucked it sometimes. Now it lay forlornly on the grass.

'We'll divide the area among us,' Robert said beside her, 'and search it thoroughly.'

'I'll come with you,' she said quickly, but he hesitated.

'It would be better to stay here with Brechtje.'

But she shook her head. 'No! I can't just – just sit here and wait. I – I would – lose my mind!' Her voice had broken in spite of her and he put his arm around her and held her close to him for a second. 'We'll find him,' he said quietly. 'He can't have gone far.'

They set out then systematically to search, Isobel with Robert, Frans with Brechtje, calmer now that someone had taken command, while John remained behind to guard their camp and the horses. They looked under bushes, behind rocks, walked through long grass – and found nothing. They even went down the path, as far as the wood, but they stopped there, for it was nonsense to suggest that a baby could possibly have crawled so far.

They walked back in silence to where John waited for them impatiently. Robert shook his head when he came up to him and then said harshly, 'Are you sure Brechtje was no more than ten minutes talking to Frans? Did you see them?'

'Yes, I saw 'em,' John growled. 'They were here, just a few yards away from where we are now. I was mending tackle and I could hear them laughing and talking – bloody Dutch!' he added sourly, 'Seems all they ever do – But no more than ten minutes – '

'Well, in that time he can't have got very far,' Robert was frowning now and turned to Isobel standing white-faced, beside him. He took her by the arm and said gravely, 'I'm afraid we have to consider another possibility,' he said.

251

'That he has been stolen?' Her voice was even, almost calm and none of them could have guessed the effort it cost her not to give way to hysteria.

He nodded. 'It seems the only explanation.'

'But – is it possible?' she whispered. 'Could someone have crept up and – and taken him without anyone seeing it happen? Is it possible, John?' she said, turning to the big man.

He looked down at the ground for a second and then shrugged his massive shoulders. 'Aye, 'tis possible, mistress. It would only take a second or two – whoever it was could have hidden behind that tree and then made for the bushes behind. They would have had cover for a few yards – after that, there is a hollow in the ground and more bushes beyond that again. Aye, 'tis possible all right.'

'Gypsies!' Robert said, harshly. 'It must be gypsies! Come, John, Saddle up!' He turned to Isobel. 'I'll leave Frans with you and Brechtje.'

'Where – where are you going?' she asked. 'I saw no gypsy camps near here.'

'Nor I,' he said grimly, 'but we must look, all the same.'

A few minutes later Robert rode away with John. Isobel watched them go with a feeling of disbelief. It could not be true that Christopher had disappeared. Christopher who only a few hours ago had gurgled and laughed and thrown pebbles and pulled her hair –

The two Dutch servants were standing close together, watching her warily, Brechtje's tears dried now, a look of defiance on her broad face. Isobel knew that with Robert gone she would find her less respectful, less willing to take orders, for she herself was only the meneer's friend, not his wife and she could guess what they were thinking – that if she had not gone off with the meneer, Christopher would not have disappeared. It was *her* fault, not Brechtje's. It was as if they had shouted the words at her. And they are right, she thought, turning her back on them. It *is* my fault. She could see her nakedness again, and Robert's, and hear the lark's song of love, but the birdsong was so faint that she began to wonder if she had imagined it at the time and even the memory of happiness was gone.

She went slowly back to the tree, picking up Christopher's old blanket, and holding it to her cheek, bent over like an old, old woman. She tried to take in the fact that she might never see him again, but she couldn't. Any moment now she expected to hear his chuckle, see his arms reach out for her, or hear him crying because he could not have his own, stubborn little way. He would crawl out of that bush in front of her – or they would find him among the baggage – and at the thought of the baggage she jumped to her feet and ran over to where it lay piled up on the ground. But Brechtje came forward then and said sympathetically enough, 'We looked there, first thing.'

Even so Isobel turned over the sacks, seeing the treasure sack at the bottom, and covering it again slowly. She was wasting her time and she knew it. Yet she could not sit still. 'Come,' she said to the girl. 'Those bushes near the tree – perhaps we did not look carefully enough.' And the two women and Frans got down on their hands and knees to search again, until their clothes were muddied and their faces and hands scratched and bleeding, until they had covered all the immediate area round the camp. And still they found nothing.

It was late afternoon now and the heat had gone from the sun. 'You must eat,' Brechtje said at last. 'Otherwise you will be sick.' She led the way back and Isobel followed her, not wanting to eat but too exhausted to argue, and as they called to Frans, a young boy in ragged clothes ran into the clearing where they had set up camp. They were still yards away from him, but they saw him throw something down on the ground and then run off before anyone could stop him.

It was a letter that the boy had thrown down, with Robert's name written neatly on the outside above the seal, and as she turned it over and over in her hands Isobel wondered who it could be from. The inn in which they had stayed the previous night was only an hour's ride away – it must, she thought, have been sent on from there. But why had the boy run away? Surely it would have been more natural for him to have waited for a reward?

When Robert and John rode up the track shortly afterwards she had forgotten all about the letter as she ran to meet them. She had not really expected that they would have Christopher with them but she knew from their faces that they had nothing good to tell her. Robert slid down from his sweating horse, his face grave and almost old. 'We were told that there have been no gypsies about for weeks,' he said, 'and we saw no signs of them anywhere.' He

253

hesitated, and then went on slowly, 'But a farmer said that it might have been a – a wild animal.'

He had to put a hand out to save her from falling, as a wave of nausea washed over her. 'Surely, surely there would have been – blood – something?' she whispered.

'That is what I think, too,' he said quickly.

The nausea had receded, but her mind, her whole body seemed numb and John's heavy face behind Robert's shoulder was ashen grey. None of this is happening, she told herself. No one has really said that my Christopher could have been savaged, eaten alive. It's only a horrible dream and I shall wake up in a moment – but of course it was not a dream, and then she remembered at last the letter she had put into the pocket of her dress. 'This came for you while you were away,' she said dully. 'A young boy threw it down and then ran off.'

Robert took it from her, frowning, turning it over and over as she had done. 'You were not able to talk to him at all?'

She shook her head, but he was already breaking the seal and she watched him open up the single page, his face growing hard as stone as he read the few lines of writing.

'Read it,' he said briefly, after a moment, handing the letter to her.

The words seemed to leap up at her from the smooth, cream vellum.

'I have the child. Bring the Cîteaux treasure to the entrance of the old ruined church tomorrow at dawn. Come alone. Unarmed. On foot. The child will be returned to you alive if you obey my instructions. Otherwise he will die.' The signature was written with a flourish. *'Edward Dutton.'*

'Christopher is alive!' she breathed. 'Oh thank God! Thank *God*!' But Robert was cursing.

'He must have been behind us all the time! Christ! What a bloody fool I've been to have thought for one moment that he would have given up the search! He could have found out about Andrew easily enough and he must have been waiting all this time for me to leave England and then followed! I was sure it was all over, with Cromwell and the King so occupied – ' He began to stride up and down, seeming to be driven by a demon of rage and self condemnation, but as he came back to her again, in the middle of his feverish pacing he said more calmly, 'He must be quite near. We could find him – I'm sure of it! I've seen the church – it's the only ruin – the only church in fact – about a mile away.'

'Oh no, no!' She caught frantically at his arm. 'You must do exactly as he says. *Nothing* else! He is quite capable of killing a child. I know it! He's as much animal as man.'

'But I can't let him get away with it!' he said harshly. 'A jumped-up nobody! I can't let a fellow like that trick me into handing over a valuable treasure that a brave man has already given his life for – just so *he* can curry favour with the King – '

'They are only *things*!' she said desperately. 'But Christopher is – is my *son*! I have nothing else. It is different for you. You will have other children.'

He seemed to draw back from her. 'You are wrong,' he said quietly. 'It is not different for me. I care greatly about Christopher, and my wife cannot bear another child, ever.'

She looked at him for a few seconds without speaking, not taking in the full implications of what he had said, but there was a coldness suddenly in her mind for which she did not yet seek a cause – later there would be time for that. 'I am sorry,' she said slowly. 'I did not know.' But the distance between them still seemed to be there.

'Christopher's safety means as much to me as it does to you,' he said evenly, as if she had not spoken. 'I will meet Dutton and hand over the treasure. But once Christopher is safely back with us – ' He stopped, looking back over his shoulder and she saw him exchange glances with John.

'What will you do then?' she said quickly, although she had already guessed what his answer would be.

'Go after Dutton, of course.' His voice was still even, matter of fact. 'Get the treasure back, if I can.'

'He will be expecting something like that, surely? He will make sure you can't.' But she could see that it was useless to argue with him, useless to say, I love you and I don't want you to risk your life for any treasure, no matter how valuable, how old!

She walked slowly back to the tree and sat down where Christopher had lain asleep only a few hours before. She had put his old blanket away and she sat, staring into space, wondering if it was Edward Dutton himself who had hid his paunchy body behind the tree, seeing the soft, white hands again, the immaculate cuffs. She watched Robert as he talked now to the two Dutch servants and wondered what he was telling them, since he had never told them about the treasure – her mind, as always, coming back to Christopher. Would Edward Dutton keep his word? Would he hand over Christopher unharmed when the time came? Would this, would that – until Brechtje started to cook the evening meal and she dragged herself to her feet and went over to help her.

But when the food was ready at last she could not eat. After picking at her roast chicken she put the platter aside untouched and got to her feet, finding herself on the stony track, walking up and down as if she were back in the convent again, trying to pray, but no words, no images coming, as they had not come for a long time. Then she found Robert beside her. He took her by the arm and led her gently back, sitting down beside her, the distance that had been between them and that had seemed solid as a wall, gone as if it had never been. John had lit a fire and she could feel the heat of the flames on her face, but Robert put his half cloak round her and drew her to him. 'It will be all right,' he whispered. 'Don't fret, my love. Don't fret! I'll bring Christopher safely back to you!'

Sometimes he kissed her, murmuring endearments, but mostly they sat in silence, and under the cloak the warmth of their bodies was like a blessing and his strength became her strength, his courage her courage. *This* is what love is, she thought. This is what it *really* is.

She fell asleep at last and woke to find him on his feet, a rug thrown across her. It was that time before dawn when death seems everywhere and she threw back the rug, shivering, and stood with John watching as he went to the pile of baggage and drew out the treasure sack. The others were still asleep and she wanted to tell him to arm himself, to take John with him. She even wanted to go with him herself, but it was not possible. He picked up the sack then, and raising his hand in mock salute, turned and strode away.

She watched him go with an ache in her heart, wondering if she would ever see him alive again.

Chapter Thirty-Two

Edward Dutton stood inside the entrance of the old, ruined church watching the path that snaked its way up the bare hillside. He had been watching since the first hint of dawn and now his eyes were beginning to feel strained. Perhaps after all FitzHugh would not come, he thought. He had gambled on two things – that the fellow had the treasure and that the child was his own son. He himself was not a gambling man by nature, and the other two had told him he was going about things the wrong way – that they should have crept up under cover of darkness and taken the treasure by force, but then neither of them had wanted to kidnap the child.

The Dutchman, Klaas Groot had been particularly against it. He was from Amsterdam, about twenty-eight or thirty years of age, the son of an English mother by a Dutchman, and in London Edward Dutton had been told that he had studied for the church and then had left to become a merchant's factor for a time. But he was not one of the vast army of voluntary informers abroad, on whose information Lord Thomas Cromwell relied in his hunt for 'offenders', and who gave it out of malice, or a sense of duty, or in the hope of some reward. Klaas Groot was one of that rarer species, a paid 'espial' or spy, employed not only because of his linguistic skills, but also because of his ability to blend into his surroundings like a chameleon, so that Edward Dutton himself would have been hard put to it to describe his appearance other than to say he was of average height, not too heavy, not too thin.

Colby, on the other hand, was immensely tall and broad with

257

it, but as light as a dancer on his feet. Lord Thomas Cromwell's secretary had said that they had found him in Newark, and had recruited him with some misgivings, but that he had afterwards proved himself invaluable to King and country.

They were not an easy pair to handle and Edward Dutton was well aware that they disliked him, the Dutchman in particular. During the night, which they had spent in the woods, on the far side of the hill, when the child's crying had nearly torn his nerves to shreds, he had slapped it several times across the face to stop the hideous din. Colby had merely grunted and turned on his side but Klaas had actually caught his wrist and said coldly, 'He's hungry. You should have got proper food for him.'

'Well, I can't get it at this hour of the night!' he had snapped. 'Anyway, all that matters is that he should be alive when FitzHugh comes at dawn.'

'He won't be if you go on hitting him.'

He had had to let the Dutchman lift the child and try to get him to drink milk from a spoon. The child's vest and blanket were sodden and stained with vomit, and one side of his face was already beginning to swell. Edward Dutton had never liked children, not even his own daughter, the only one of his children to survive childbirth, and he disliked babies most of all. Dirty, puling, whining creatures he thought them, reminding him of pigs, and the fact that this was probably Robert FitzHugh's son had made him slap him all the harder.

Now the child lay at the back of the church, at the foot of the old stone altar that was covered with moss and lichen. He had tied the tope around him himself, taking a pleasure in the job, pulling the rope tighter than was necessary, listening to the whimpering grow steadily weaker until it became no more than the cry of a very young kitten. When the Dutchman was not looking he had given the child a kick in the side hoping to stop even that small sound, and it seemed that he had succeeded for he had heard nothing at all for some time now.

And then, at last, he saw the solitary figure of a man, walking steadily up the footpath that years before had served the local people on their way to Mass.

'He's coming!' he said to the others. 'Look!'

But they had seen him too and moved closer to the entrance, while behind the church their horses whinnied softly. Soon they

258

could see that he was carrying a sack, and Edward Dutton's heart lifted. He had been right after all. FitzHugh had had the treasure, or at least knowledge of its whereabouts and it no longer mattered whether the child was his or not, although it seemed as if he must be.

He was striding towards them now, the red of his doublet and breeches like a banner against the faded green of the summer grass. He was wearing no sword belt and yet Edward Dutton felt a savage jab of envy – he looked so handsome, so arrogant even in defeat.

'Kill him if he gives any trouble,' he said curtly, 'any trouble at all.'

'We should kill 'im anyway,' Colby growled, but Klaas shook his head emphatically. 'Not unless we have to. He will try to follow us afterwards but he won't find us. I know the area too well and there is to be no killing if it can be avoided. His wife is well connected and I told you already that there are rumours circulating in Rheims that Lord Thomas Cromwell has lost favour with the King and might even be hanged.'

'Aye, you did!' Edward Dutton snapped, 'and you know what I think of your damned rumours! It's not possible!'

'Don't be a fool, man! Of course it's possible!' Klaas said shortly. 'And if you find Thomas Cromwell is dead when you get back to England who knows how the wind will blow for you –'

The tall figure in red was half-way up the hill now but although Edward Dutton wanted Robert FitzHugh to die as painfully as possible, he needed the treasure, and he needed Klaas's help if he was to keep Colby's itchy fingers off it before he got back to England. 'All right,' he said grudgingly. 'But if he gives trouble – '

'In that case we kill him,' Klaas said impassively, his face without expression as always.

The church had never been more than a simple, stone building but now the roof had fallen in, although some of the walls with their slits of windows still stood. Robert could see the figure of a man inside the narrow entrance but he was much too far away to recognise him. As he came closer, however, the man stepped forward and he saw that it was Edward Dutton, dressed as always in sombre black. Two more men followed him from inside the church, one dwarfing him by his great size, the other young, nondescript, a Dutchman by the look of his high crowned hat and baggy breeches.

The big man moved with astonishing speed to stand behind Robert, running expert hands over his body, while the other stood back so that he could see both up and down hill. When the man behind him grunted and dropped his hands Edward Dutton came a little closer. 'I am glad that you seem to have been sensible,' he said.

'Sensible? Is that what you call it?' Robert's voice was as bleak as his own. 'I have brought the treasure. Now give me back my son.'

'In time, Master FitzHugh. In time. First, I must make sure that you have not cheated me.'

'You can look,' Robert said curtly. 'It is all there. But if you have harmed my son in any way – '

'You will do what? Kill me?' Edward Dutton laughed suddenly, a grotesquely, high-pitched sound more like a giggle than a laugh, that went oddly with the rest of him. 'You could not kill a fly at this moment! You could not even raise your hand to me!'

'I would not be too sure of that.' But even as he said the words Robert felt the edge of a knife blade against the back of his neck. What Edward Dutton had said was true and they both knew it.

It was growing lighter by the moment and he could see him more clearly now. The soft face seemed strangely altered, and the smooth, lardlike skin was covered by grey stubble. But more than anything else, there was something new in his expression that Robert could not put a name to, as if a wild animal lurking in undergrowth had shown itself at last.

'Where is my son?' he said again with growing uneasiness. 'I have kept my side of the bargain – '

'Down on your knees first and show the treasure to me!'

'I'm damned if I will!' Robert said coldly. 'Look for yourself, and tell your ape to take his knife off my neck!'

But the knife pressed so hard this time he could feel a trickle of blood run down between his shoulder blades, and Edward Dutton said very softly, 'I always knew you were a fool,

Robert FitzHugh! I can have your ears cut off, if I so wish, or your nose, or your private parts, of which you apparently make such good use. I can do the same for your son – or I can of course have you both killed. Now. This very minute. Is that really what you want?' And when Robert said nothing he added with sudden viciousness, as if he were speaking to a dog, '*Down*, I say! Down on your knees!'

The knife pressed again, more painfully this time and slowly, very slowly, Robert went down on one knee and then the other, telling himself through a red mist of rage that it was no shame, that he was doing it for Christopher; pulling the sack towards him and opening it; unwrapping the cowhide as he had done in Amsterdam and hearing the same stunned silence after he had done so.

The triumph in Edward Dutton's face was obscene as he bent and touched with loving, greedy fingers, the jewels, blazing like coloured fire, the gold, like captured sunlight against the rough grass. The man who had been watching and had taken off his conical hat, came forward a few paces, staring down, and the pressure of the knife against Robert's neck eased slightly. But only for a second it seemed. Even as he became aware of it, the knife pressed down again, and as he began to get to his feet Edward Dutton said sharply. 'Wrap them up and put them back in the sack!'

There was nothing for it but to do as he said, and Robert all but threw the sack then at Edward Dutton's feet. 'My son,' he said harshly, getting to his feet at last. 'Where is he?'

'He is in the church – ' Edward Dutton put up a hand as Robert moved forward. 'Not so fast! You can get him when I say so! Not before!'

'Damn you!' Robert shouted, lunging forward now, regardless of all else but the wish to smash in the face of his tormentor, but a mighty arm shot out from behind him and gripped him like a vice, holding him to a massive chest, the knife now against his throat.

'I do really advise you to be more patient,' Edward Dutton said and Robert watched helplessly as the other man went around the side of the church and a moment later led three horses forward. 'You'll find your brat inside,' the smooth unctuous voice had hardened, 'but he needs some attention, so

I suggest you give it to him before you make any attempt to follow us. You would in any case be wasting your time.'

'You filthy cur!' Robert gasped, 'What have you done to him?'

The blade cut him more deeply this time and blood trickled down the front of his shirt.

'I dislike babies,' Edward Dutton said in the same smooth voice, 'and your son most of all. But he is alive, and I daresay will do well enough.'

He mounted his horse then, the sack thrown across his saddle, the other man already on his horse beside him. 'Let's go, Colby,' he said, and with a grunt the man holding Robert released him, and swung himself into his own saddle in one, fluid movement.

But Robert did not wait to see them ride away, and for a second he stood in the entrance of the church, trying to see into the gloom – then, at the far end he saw something lying on the ground . . .

Christopher lay like a sacrificial offering at the foot of the altar, and Robert found himself staring disbelievingly at the rope that had been bound so tightly round his small body that there was congealed blood on his legs and arms. He wore only his vest and his eyes were closed. For a terrible second that seemed to last a lifetime Robert was sure he was dead, in spite of what Edward Dutton had said. But he was warm to the touch, and there was a pulse beating very faintly in his neck.

Robert broke his fingernails tearing at the knots, but at last he succeeded in opening them and when he pulled the ropes away Christopher's arms fell down limply as if he were indeed dead. He picked him up and held him to him, his little bare buttocks ice cold against his arm in spite of the faint warmth in the rest of his body. 'Oh Christopher, I'm so sorry!' he whispered against the matted hair. 'I should have taken better care of you! I'm sorry!' and the eyes that were so like his own opened at last and looked up at him dully, as if the mind behind them had broken.

He carried him out into the sunlight and began to walk back as fast as he dared, until he saw John and Isobel running down the track to meet him. 'He's alive,' he said quietly. 'He's – he's all right, I think.'

'Oh, thank God!' Isobel whispered, taking Christopher and holding him close. 'Thank God!'

And then she saw the blood on his own shirt. 'Are you hurt?' she said quickly. 'Oh, what have they done to you?'

'It's nothing. Just a scratch.'

'You're sure?'

When he nodded, she looked down at Christopher again, frowning. 'He's very quiet,' she said, 'and – and – look at his arms and his legs!'

'They tied him up,' he said heavily. When he saw her look of shock he put his arm around her shoulders and began to lead her gently back up the path. 'There seem to be no bones broken, no serious injury. I am quite sure he will get over it quickly – '

But she was running ahead and he followed her, feeling suddenly weary, a sense of failure settling on him like a black cloud.

While John attended to Robert's throat, Isobel, with Brechtje helping, bathed Christopher in heated water and put oil on his skin where the ropes had torn it. His body was badly bruised on one side and he whimpered when they touched it but, although his left cheek was swollen too, the shocked look in his eyes was no longer there. He had taken a little gruel, smiling at her afterwards for the first time, his eyes hazy with recognition and love, and she had caught him to her suddenly, covering his face with kisses. 'He's going to be all right, Brechtje!' she breathed over his head. 'When he has had a good sleep! He'll be himself again! You'll see!' And Brechtje's plump, pretty face had been wreathed in smiles, for she loved children and this one especially.

Robert came over to Isobel and sat down beside her, looking down at the gentle rise and fall of Christopher's chest under the blanket that she had wrapped him in. There was a little colour in his face now and he touched the cheek that was not swollen, gently with his knuckles. 'He's a good soldier,' he said smiling, and she nodded.

'I hope John has looked after you properly?'

'Just scratches, like I said.'

'Tell me about it.'

'The worst part was that I had to do as that animal told me.' When she said nothing, he went on slowly. 'He had two other men with him. One, a giant of a fellow, held a knife to my throat, while the other kept watch.' He plucked a blade of grass as if to chew it and then threw it away. 'He made me kneel!' he said with sudden bitterness. 'I will kill him for that one day.'

'You must just forget about it, about him,' she said quickly.

'I can't,' he said shortly, 'but you must not worry. Your job is to get Christopher well again, and mine is to go after Edward Dutton and get the treasure back.'

'Oh, no!' She put out a hand, as if to ward off a blow. 'You can't leave now. Not until we are sure that Christopher is really well again!'

'If I wait any longer I shall never catch them before they leave the country,' he said quietly. 'Once they get back to England, it's all over. I can't touch them there.'

'It's not worth it!' she said, her voice husky with unshed tears. 'You might be killed this time – '

'He made me kneel,' he said again, as if she had not spoken, his face, his voice grown hard, 'and the abbot gave his life. I can't leave things as they are. It's not possible.'

Christopher stirred in her arms, settling his head more comfortably against her breast. Perhaps he is right, she thought unwillingly, and surely Christopher will be strong again in a day or so. But he will be in such danger himself –

'I shall leave Brechtje with you,' he was saying, 'and Frans, but I shall have to take John with me.' He got to his feet. 'I shall take you back to the inn at St Auguste where we spent last night.' He was smiling now, but his smile did nothing to reassure her. 'The patron and his wife seem a kindly pair. They will look after you until I come back.'

'You may not be able to find Edward Dutton and the other two now,' she objected. 'They will have had a few hour's start of you, and they could hide anywhere for months.'

He shook his head. 'Dutton will want to get back to England as soon as possible and claim his reward, and he will go by Calais most likely. If necessary we will wait there for him, so I must make sure we travel faster!'

There was nothing more she could say, nothing she could do

264

to make him change his mind. She knew that from the obstinate set of his long jaw that, although she did not know it, was so like his grandfather's.

An hour later they rode into the courtyard of Les Trois Faisans to be welcomed profusely by the patron, Louis Maillard, small and pot-bellied, with shrewd, calculating eyes, and his big, good-natured wife Marie. Both of them were delighted that the so-generous English monsieur and madame had returned. Like the other innkeepers they had come across on the journey they took Isobel to be his wife. Since they had never stayed in any inn for longer than one night and had always asked for separate rooms because of Christopher, it had scarcely seemed to matter – certainly neither he nor she herself had ever alluded to it, even when speaking to one another, and now it seemed even less relevant in view of his impending departure.

She had lain Christopher down straightaway on the small mattress that Marie had given her for him and he was already fast asleep, his old blanket clutched tightly to him, his breathing regular and even, and leaving Brechtje with him, she went down to the dark room below, that smelt of garlic and the used up air of generations of customers, to find Robert talking to Louis. He walked with her then out into the blazing sunlight, as Louis hurried off to attend to new arrivals, and he lead her to a stone seat.

'I will be back as soon as possible,' he said quietly. 'But I will be back! And then we must talk about the future, yours and – and Christopher's.'

It was very hot, and she looked at the geraniums flowering in the pots set about the tiny, paved courtyard without really seeing them. 'You want to take him from me, don't you?' she said quietly, as if all that had happened in the past twenty-four hours had cleared her brain and at last she knew every-thing, or almost everything.

'Yes,' he said quietly. 'Now is not the time to talk about it, but I want to make him my legal heir. One day he would be Sir Christopher FitzHugh. Surely you would want that for him? And I would bring him to see you, as often as possible.'

'Why did you not tell me in the beginning?' she whispered. 'Why were you not honest with me?'

He looked away. 'I wanted to, but – I did not want to upset you, and we had only just met again – Try to understand.'

He was pleading with her, and she tried not to blame him. After all, should she not be glad for Christopher, glad that he would have all that he would never have otherwise, for what could she give him but love? And if without him she would have nothing, was it not only selfishness on her part to let herself think that?

He thrust his hand into a pocket and took out a bag of coins. 'You should have enough French francs here to pay for everything until I return,' he said, 'and – and for a journey to London, should that be necessary.'

'London?' she said, her heart missing a beat.

'If – anything should happen to me.' He hesitated, and then went on quickly, 'My grandfather wanted me to make Christopher my heir if I could find him.'

'So – so you came to Amsterdam to look for Christopher, not just on a visit?' She found herself looking at him as if suddenly he were a stranger, and he bit his lip.

'Yes,' he said shortly. 'I did.'

'I wish you'd told me then.' Her voice was toneless, dead, and he caught her arm as if he wanted to shake her. 'What difference does it make now? I've told you already why I didn't – surely you can understand – after all these weeks – being together – ' His voice had grown suddenly hoarse and when she said nothing his hand tightened on her arm. 'I've got to leave now,' he said, abruptly. 'Remember, if – if I don't return, you must go to my grandfather. His house is in Chelsea, on the river – you will find it easily enough. But he's a difficult old man – '

John had bandaged his throat but blood had seeped through the linen and she saw the weariness in his eyes, the sense of failure and she knew that she might never see him again. The cold reality of it struck her like a blow – everything else, his wanting Christopher, her own feelings paling into insignificance beside that reality. She tried to speak, to beg him once again to stay, but the words would not come. He had let go of her arm, but now he bent and kissed her, his lips cold and smooth against hers. He left her then, sitting alone on the stone seat in the hot, afternoon sun.

266

She watched him ride away from the inn a few moments later with John, thinking about that last kiss that had seemed only as if he were asking to be let go rather than saying goodbye. If he does not look back I shall die, she thought. But he did, and as she got to her feet and waved she saw him lift his velvet cap in the air while little clouds of dust rose behind the horses' hooves from the stony, twisting path. And then he was gone.

Chapter Thirty-Three

She went back up to the attic under the sloping roof where she and Brechtje were to sleep with Christopher, and sat beside the small box bed looking down at him. In two more days he would be one year old. He lay on his side, his precious blanket clutched tightly to him, the marks on his bare arm where the rope had bitten into his flesh red and angry looking. His face was flushed and his forehead felt hot to her touch, so that her old fears returned to torment her. She wondered again if he could have been injured internally in some way, although he did not cry when they lifted him, or if he might have caught a chill. Perhaps he had been left lying on the ground tied up all night? But she told herself that she was being foolish, giving way to irrational fears – Robert would not have left him if he had not believed him to be well, if he had not *been* well. 'But Robert is not a doctor,' a voice said inside her mind, 'and he was too concerned with getting the treasure back from Edward Dutton . . .'

She saw Edward Dutton's face, heard his voice, saw the treasure again as it had been that day in Amsterdam when Robert had shown it to herself and John. She remembered his hands unwrapping the cowhide, remembered the colours of the jewels, the gold against the polished wood, and the feeling of depression that had driven away her brief moment of happiness. Have I the gift of second sight, she wondered, not for the first time. 'Oh God! she prayed, putting her face in her hands, 'Don't let Robert be killed! Please, don't let him be killed!' And for a while she forgot her fears for

Christopher, until not long afterwards he woke, coughing, and she knew for sure now that he was running a fever.

She stayed up with him all that night. In the beginning, shortly after waking he had vomited, and vomited again and again after that, until there could have been nothing left to vomit. He took occasional sips of water but as morning came and she sat bleary-eyed and stiff beside him, he refused even to take water and his body seemed to burn, racked by a dry cough, his breathing shallow and laboured. In desperation she asked Louis to send to Dijon for a doctor. 'My servant Frans does not speak French,' she said frantically. 'Please, monsieur! It is not very far, and I am sure there is no doctor here.'

'There is not indeed, madame! But I cannot spare Jean!'

'Oh Pierre, for shame!' his wife Marie cried, hands on broad hips. 'Madame is beside herself, with the baby so ill! I shall help you until Jean returns!'

In the end Pierre had agreed and Jean, the youth who normally served his customers with the sour, local wine and helped Marie in the kitchen, was sent off to Dijon for the doctor. 'But he will not come immediately, madame. He is a very busy man, very important. It will be tomorrow before he arrives!'

There was no more she could do, but towards midday she and Brechtje bathed Christopher in cold water, and for a while he seemed easier, but a couple of hours later, his body began to twitch and jerk, his eyeballs rolled up and there was froth on his lips. She had never seen a child having convulsions before, but she remembered Dame Cecilia telling her what it was like and that she used to rub the sick child's limbs after dipping her hand in cold water, making sure it did not bite its tongue by slipping something into its mouth. But her own hands were shaking so much now and Christopher's jaws seemed so tightly clenched that she could not open his mouth and had to content herself only with rubbing his arms and legs with her cold, wet hands, wishing that the old nun was beside her now. After what seemed a lifetime the twitching stopped, his eyeballs rolled down and he lay quietly.

'It's over!' Brechtje whispered. 'He'll be all right now!'

But Brechtje was wrong. Isobel knew that as if someone had said the words aloud, and as the day wore on, although she

269

managed to force a dew drops of wine down his throat his body continued to burn, and there was a terrible, wheezing sound every time he tried to draw breath, that tore at her heart. She found herself cursing Edward Dutton with a depth of violence that frightened her and brought her no comfort, but she prayed now that Robert would find him and kill him, and at the same time found herself blaming Robert for not being there. But what could he have done, she would ask herself, that she had not done?

Jean was back by nightfall. 'The doctor will be here tomorrow, as early as possible,' he said, his young eyes sympathetic as he looked down at Christopher, the gold franc she had given him put away carefully in his breeches pocket. I should have sent for the doctor sooner, she thought dully as he clattered down the rickety, wooden ladder to the room below.

For the first time since she had got him back she faced the possibility that Christopher might die. To have lost him to Robert and his grandfather would have been bad enough, but to lose him in death – that would be to lose part of her own self. Surely she had not sinned so grievously that God would do that to her? She began to pray – wild, incoherent appeals for mercy, for forgiveness, on her knees beside the bed – until Brechtje came to her and put her arm around her and lead her downstairs to sit for a little while in front of a plate of untasted food, white-faced, shivering with cold in spite of the evening's heat.

She stayed up with him all of that night too while he turned and tossed, his breath coming in short gasps, coughing that dry, hard cough that seemed to tear at her body apart. She tried to get him to take honey from a spoon but he spat it out, gasping for air as if he could not breathe. Some time during the night, while Brechtje slept, she lifted him up and carried him outside, to sit on the stone seat where she and Robert had sat such a short while before, hoping that in the night air he might breathe more easily. But it seemed to make no difference at all and after a while she carried him back inside and put him in his bed again, sitting down on the stool beside him once more, trying to fight off the sleep that threatened to overcome her. In the end, in spite of herself she nodded off, but early the following morning Brechtje shook her awake again.

Christopher's breathing had become even more laboured and there was a bluish shadow about his mouth. His eyes were open, but he did not recognise her and she lifted him up and put him on her knee, holding him against her, rocking backwards and forwards, losing all sense of time or place, locked away in her grief.

After a time she was vaguely aware of heavy footsteps, and of another, strange presence beside her. She saw a man's hand reach out and touch Christopher, saw the black hairs on the back of that hand, and heard a harsh voice say in French, 'This child is dead! I have wasted a whole morning!'

'He can't be!' she whispered. 'He *can't* be dead! This is his birthday!'

Some time later they took Christopher's body away from her, led her downstairs and gave her wine to drink. She pushed it away untouched, and they stood around her in a circle, Brechtje, Frans, the Maillards, the doctor long gone, fat with importance and too much good food and wine, his fee put carefully away in his leather pouch, but still complaining about his wasted journey.

'Madame, you must rest,' Louis said kindly. 'Otherwise you will be ill. My wife and I will look after everything for you.'

Yet she could not cry. And she wanted to. Her grief tore at her, was destroying her slowly but she could not let it out, could hardly speak or move, could only sit, frozen, as if gradually her body was turning to stone.

'We – we shall arrange for the burial.' Louis bent his swarthy face to hers, speaking in a whisper. 'And my cousin will see to the coffin – he makes beautiful coffins – he is – '

He stuttered to a halt as his wife dug him in the ribs with a massive elbow, and Isobel got to her feet at last. 'You are very kind,' she said dully. 'Brechtje and I will wash my son and make him ready. If you will please tell the priest and – and your cousin – '

'Of course, madame! Of course!' Louis muttered. 'I shall call at Père Philippe's house at once myself, and – and – make all arrangements!'

271

She and Brechtje went up to the attic then and together they washed the small, still warm, body, combing back the thick, blond hair that always reminded her of ripening corn, for the last time. They put a white linen gown on Christopher and laid him gently back on the bed, and when Marie had brought a lighted candle and placed it beside the bed, the two women left Isobel alone with her dead.

The priest came first, an old, kindly man, his stole round his neck. 'If only I had known I'd have come sooner,' he whispered, and he began to pray aloud, raising his hand at the end in a final blessing.

'My deepest sympathy, madame,' he said to her then. 'It is sad to see so young a child die, but he is with the angels. You may be sure of that.'

She could only nod her head and he said, after a moment, 'Where is your husband, madame?'

'I have – no husband,' she whispered.

'But I thought – the Maillards said – '

'They do not know. But what does it matter, anyway?'

He pulled at his long nose, clearing his throat. 'Are you quite alone, now?'

'Yes.' But then she added quickly, 'My son's father is to come back here.'

'When, madame?'

'I – don't know. Soon, I hope.'

'I see.' He took off his stole and looked at it as if at a loss for words. 'Well, I shall see you later then, in the church. I have given instructions for the grave to be dug. It is better to have the funeral early tomorrow morning in view of the exceptionally hot weather – ' His voice trailed off in embarrassment and the words seemed to bounce off the walls.

It was a nightmare, she told herself, a horrible dream from which she would shortly waken. Christopher, her beautiful, laughing little boy was not really going to be put down into the cold earth, to be eaten by worms. It was not true! It could not be! She bent to touch his face and found to her horror that the warmth she had felt there earlier was already beginning to leave his body – that the blundering, well-meaning old priest had been speaking no less than the truth. Christopher was dead, as Cornelis van Ophoorn had been dead, and the smell

272

of death would soon be in this attic as it had been in the house in Amsterdam. She felt the room begin to swim before her eyes and heard the priest calling for help as he tried to catch her before she fell to the floor.

She came to a few minutes later, and they brought her downstairs again. She stayed there for as long as she could bear to be away from Christopher, but then she went back and sat down again beside the bed, until Louis and his cousin came at last. She watched as they lifted the body and put it into the small, oak coffin and carried it below, following behind them, her mind numb, her legs moving, it seemed, of their own accord.

The others walked with her behind the coffin to the church, Marie and Brechtje and Frans and Jean and some of the women from the cluster of small houses that called itself a village. When they got to the small, bare church Père Philippe was waiting for them, and the coffin was put on trestles in front of the altar. She did not know about that other altar in the old church on the hill, but even as the priest led his small congregation in a decade of the rosary she found herself cursing Edward Dutton again with that same cold venom that seemed to come from some secret part of her mind that she had not known was there.

She wanted to remain on afterwards in the church, but Père Philippe would not let her. 'You must go back to the inn and rest, my child,' he said kindly. 'Besides I must close the church now, but God and His angels will be close to your son.'

So she had gone back with the others and even tried to force herself to eat, and gone to bed later, to lie awake staring into the darkness. Brechtje had not yet come to bed and she knew that the girl was with big, good-looking Frans and she envied and pitied her at the same time. The attic room was very quiet, full of emptiness and she felt suspended in some kind of vacuum, as if Isobel Willis did not exist. But she fell asleep at last and when she woke next morning Brechtje was sound asleep beside her, exhausted after a night of love-making. She woke the girl, and together they got dressed and went below, and an hour later the others went with them to the funeral.

They buried Christopher in a cemetery behind the new church and Isobel knew that she would hear the sound of clay falling on the lid of the coffin for the rest of her life. Afterwards she walked away, ahead of the others, stoney faced and dry-eyed.

Chapter Thirty-Four

Robert was not a religious man or even a susperstitious one, but he had prayed for help in finding Edward Dutton, for the man and his two companions had had at least three hours' start when he and John set out at last from Les Trois Faisans, and it was already evening then.

Beyond his own firm belief that his quarry would make for Calais he had no clues as to where they might be and there were several tracks that led northwest from the village of St Auguste. In the end he chose the one that was easiest to follow and they camped out that night, setting out early next morning in the general direction of Troyes, climbing all the time.

It was already very hot and Robert's shirt clung wetly to his body while beside him John sweated like a pig. In the distant vineyards they could see men and women working, waving and shouting geetings they could not hear as they rode past, but Robert thought only of Christopher and Isobel, seeing the bloodied marks on the small, chubby arms and legs, the sadness in her face as he left her. One should not have to hurt those one loved, he thought, and wondered briefly at himself for accepting so easily that he loved her, as if it were a fact of life long established, indisputable. But what shall I do if I lose her, he thought, lose them both perhaps? What will be left then of any value? When he got back to her he would have to make her realise that by giving him Christopher and coming back herself to London with him, she would have more in the end than she would ever have had.

But could he honestly believe that, he asked himself as they reached more level ground and his horse lengthened his stride. Would it not be kinder to leave her free to find some other man who could marry her and give her children to take the place of Christopher? She was so beautiful now, surely there would be many men willing to do so? He should let her go – but he couldn't, any more than he could consider leaving Christopher with her.

They travelled fast, riding sometimes at night if the moon was full, the kilometres flying by under their galloping hooves for he no longer thought in miles, and his French had become quickly, strangely fluent, as though his short stay in France had revived a knowledge of the language handed down to him over the years by his French forbears. But despite this newly found fluency, though he asked at farms, in villages, at a remote, primitive inn – scarcely more than a hovel – no one, not even the occasional shepherd driving his flock of sheep before him, seemed to have heard or seen anyone answering to the description of Edward Dutton or his two companions. But then they could have been anywhere in the woods that covered the areas not cleared for sheep rearing – it was like looking for a needle in a vast hay-stack.

Until they came to the farm near Troyes, and, after buying milk and a dozen of their best brown eggs and a pair of fat chickens, he got into chat with the farmer's young daughter while her mother was busy in the dairy. As he put the coins down on the spotless kitchen table he asked his usual question.

'An Englishman?' she said. 'As good-looking as you, monsieur?' – her young mouth pouting, offering, her shoulders straightening so that her breasts showed high and pointed under her tight, black bodice.

He smiled in spite of himself. 'No! Much older, with a big stomach and wearing black – '

She frowned, perching herself on the side of the table, ignoring John who was glowering into his bowl of milk. 'There was one such here last night, looking for food.'

'Were there two others with him?' he said quickly.

She nodded. 'The one who spoke French was German, or Dutch perhaps, – but the second man with him was English like himself – I heard them talk together. He was very big, as big if not bigger than your friend.'

275

'Where were they going when they left you?'

She shrugged. 'I don't know, but I heard them ask my father afterwards for directions.'

'Is you father here now?'

'No, monsieur. He left for the market early this morning but I heard him tell them how to get to Lille, and there was some mention of Calais.'

Calais! Surely, surely, it must be Edward Dutton and the other two, Robert thought, turning to go.

'Is there anything else you need, monsieur?' she said hopefully.

But he shook his head, smiling again. 'Perhaps we shall be this way again.'

She gave him a quick sceptical look from dark eyes that he guessed had been able to read a man's face when she had been no higher than the table, and a few moments later he rode away with John.

Isobel found herself down by the river without having any recollection of leaving the cemetery or of how she had got there. She had put a black, silk, embroidered shawl, that had been one of Cornelis van Ophoorn's last gifts to her, over her gown, this being the nearest garment to mourning clothes that she possessed, and she looked down at it now in surprise, wondering why she was wearing it, for it was very hot. Then the dazed feeling left, suddenly, cruelly, and reality came flooding in so that she found her legs giving beneath her and had to crouch, like a wounded animal, staring down into the green, rushing water.

'Christopher is dead,' she said aloud. 'He is lying in his coffin and by now they will have filled in the grave. I shall never hold him again, never hear him speak. He will never grow up to be a man. All the suffering, even the moments of joy have been for nothing.' She thought of Robert then and his hopes for him, of the old man waiting in London, hoping most likely to see his grandchild before he died. But all she could feel for them was a kind of distant sympathy.

I have sinned, she told herself, closing her eyes. I have sinned and I have been punished, and rightly so. I broke my solemn

276

vows and I have drifted since, like a feather on the wind. Behind her closed eyelids she saw all that she had been – child, nun, mother, Andrew's cousin, Saskia's companion, Cornelis van Ophoorn's protegée, Robert's friend and lover – even that shadowy now, uncertain. And all the time I was nothing, she thought. I did not deserve to be given Christopher, and he has been taken from me because I am not worthy to be a mother. I should never have come away with Robert. I came only because I wanted to be with him. And with her new, terrible honesty she admitted to herself now that from the very beginning of the journey south she had hoped they would become lovers, and later had known that she would have gone back to London with him in the end, and become his mistress. Because she loved him, would love him until death and beyond, as in a different way she had loved Christopher.

Crouching there in the sun that was becoming hotter by the minute she remembered the day Andrew had read to her from the homily – 'love is a licking of honey off thorns.' She had burnt the manuscript in the convent parlour brazier when no one was about, not wanting to be reminded of what she already knew and feeling guilty as the flames consumed Andrew's beautifully painted flowers. But the thorns were deep in her now so that when she opened her eyes at last she half expected to see blood. Yet all she saw was the deep, green water. It drew her like a magnet and she got slowly to her feet, letting the shawl fall from her shoulders. She had bathed in this same river with Robert not so very long ago. She could only swim a few strokes but she had felt safe beside him then, the water cool against her nakedness. It would be cool now too, she thought, cool and full of peace. She took another step, feeling the river bank beginning to crumble under her foot, and heard Dame Cecilia's voice calling her.

'Isobel! Dame Isobel!'

She turned to look for the old nun but there was no one there, and as she felt the bank give way beneath her weight she threw herself backwards on the spiky grass. Had she imagined that calm, cheerful voice? Was she going mad? Maybe I am, she thought, but the water frightened her now, repelling her instead of drawing her to it. She turned on her side, the tears coming, her grief escaping at last in great racking sobs that seemed to

277

tear her apart, until, in the end, there were no more tears left and she lay, exhausted, and shivering. But as she got wearily to her feet she knew what she must do if she were ever to find peace for herself in this world.

Brechtje came for her soon afterwards and took her back to the inn. When she had eaten a little she went up to the attic. They had taken Christopher's small mattress away and she lay down on her own beside where it had been, still fully dressed and fell instantly asleep. She did not wake until nearly midday next day, and when she went down to the others she found a change in the Maillards' attitude towards her. They were as friendly, as sympathetic as ever, but there was an easy familiarity about them now, a look of speculation in the patron's eyes that she had seen before in other men's eyes. She guessed that either Brechtje or Frans, or perhaps the priest, had told them she was not Robert's wife – although it did not really matter, as so many other things did not matter now.

As the days drifted slowly past she found herself longing not only for Robert, but for the companionship of a woman, and remembered Saskia of whom she had not thought for a long time. She even found herself thinking of her step-mother Joan and her good-natured chatter. She never wanted to see her father again, but she wondered about the new baby which must have come long ago, and her two little step-brothers, re-membering that once she had hoped that they and Christopher might meet one day – And, as she always did now when her thoughts came full circle, she would force herself to think then of something else. But at night the same recurring dream haunted her – of herself alone, in a vast, grey wilderness, stumbling forward to nothingness, and she would wake with relief, listening to Brechtje's gentle breathing beside her. Sometimes Brechtje would not be there, however, but sleeping some place else with Frans, and once she had tried to scold her about it, feeling a hypocrite at the same time.

Brechtje had only laughed. 'We are to be married as soon as we return to Amsterdam,' she said happily, 'and I think I may be pregnant! Last year when my sister was married, the little one was peeping out from behind her skirts and the priest blessed the three of them!'

Isobel had felt old and withered, although she and Brechtje

278

were about the same age. She said no more about Frans and each day she visited Christopher's grave, praying for Robert's safety and for the strength to keep to her decision. But she could not bring herself to leave until she knew the outcome of his search for Edward Dutton.

Klaas Groot had been as good as his word, and he and Edward Dutton and Colby rode along the cliffs above Calais harbour not much more than three weeks later, having travelled by lonely, unfrequented ways known to the Dutchman, without ever having seen any sign of Robert FitzHugh. Edward Dutton's paunch had fallen in like his lard coloured cheeks, and there had been times when he had thought he would never reach Calais alive, for he suffered greatly from the heat – once they had had to rest for two whole days hidden deep in a wood until he recovered.

'He may be waiting for us down there,' Klaas said coldly now. 'We lost two days.'

Colby fingered his knife with blunt, loving fingers. ''E can't know for certain as we'd make for Calais,' he growled. 'There be other ports, surely?'

But Edward Dutton frowned, looking down at the crowded harbour. 'Something tells me that he's down there,' he muttered.

'Well then, you'd best say your prayers,' Klaas said grimly, gathering his reins. He led the way down the rutted path that led to the harbour and they followed him in single file, keeping close together. When they reached the crowd that was slowly gathering there they found that no boat had left for England for a whole week because of bad weather conditions, but today the wind had dropped and there was one leaving for Dover on the evening tide.

'Your prayers have been answered,' the Dutchman said to Edward Dutton with a cold smile.

But, although Edward Dutton was indeed relieved that he would soon be able to leave France, he was too busy searching the crowd for a tall figure with blond hair to bother to reply, and Klaas left him and Colby and did not return until fifteen minutes later. By then Edward Dutton was gibbering with fear and rage. 'Where the hell have you been?' he snarled. 'Anything might have happened!'

'I've been arranging for our passage and selling the horses,' Klaas said evenly, 'and he's not here – I told you that already. I've been up and down the length of the jetty and beyond it, and there's no sign of him. And he has not booked a passage on the boat. I asked.'

'When does the boat sail?' Colby grunted.

'In an hour's time.' The Dutchman looked behind them at the chattering crowd. 'No one else has gone on board yet, but I think we would be wise to do so now.'

Edward Dutton tightened his grip on the sack and was about to step forward when Klaas said quickly, 'Colby first, then you. I'll watch our rear.'

There were boatmen in long boots and canvas jackets with woollen caps pulled down on their ears talking and laughing on the boat deck and two more of them busy with ropes that tied the vessel to an iron post sunk in the stone jetty close by. As Colby started to walk across the narrow wooden plank that led onto the boat one of the boatmen, a fellow nearly as big as himself, moved forward in front of Edward Dutton and bent down. Edward Dutton saw the plank move and heard a terrified shout as Colby fell backwards into the deep water between the side of the boat and the jetty.

In the same instant, the boatman straightened and Edward Dutton found himself pushed backwards on top of Klaas. He saw the knife in Klaas's hand even as he fell and then Klaas's face, wearing a look of surprise as the handle of a knife protruded from his chest. He groped frantically for his own knife, but he was on his back now, the weight of Klaas's body across his legs and Robert FitzHugh's hands were at his throat, his boatman's cap fallen off, his blond hair like some terrible crown of victory. 'Don't kill me!' he gasped, thinking what blind fools they'd been. 'We can share – anything! – But please don't kill me!'

'You filthy cur!' Robert FitzHugh said through his teeth, 'Why should I spare you?' But the grip of his hands had relaxed for a second and Edward Dutton groped for his knife again. This time he found it and he drove upwards blindly, feeling it go into softness, hearing a grunt of pain, and then he

280

saw Robert FitzHugh's clenched fist raised. He turned his head sideways, but he was not quick enough to dodge the blow, and his head hit the stone of the jetty.

When Robert got slowly to his feet he found John looking down at the body of the man whom he had thought might be Dutch with a glazed look on his face. 'I never killed a man before,' he muttered. 'I never did.' And then he saw the blood seeping through the front of Robert's canvas jacket, Edward Dutton's bloodied knife in his hand. 'How bad is it?' he asked hoarsely.

'I'll live,' Robert said grimly. At their feet a pool of blood was spreading beneath Edward Dutton's head and when Robert put his hand to the thick neck he could feel no pulse. 'He's dead,' he muttered, 'but 'twas too easy a death for him.' They could hear the cries of the man who had fallen in the water above the chattering crowd, and one of the boatmen had thrown a rope over the side of the boat, but a sudden surge of water drove the vessel against the stone wall of the jetty. There was a single, high scream, and then silence as the water receded. The crowd surged forward to peer down into the narrow space and John took Robert by the arm. 'We'd best get out of here fast, or we may find ourselves in trouble!'

Robert picked up the sack that was spattered now with Edward Dutton's blood and they began to walk away, not daring to run. They had reached the end of the jetty when they saw two men hurrying towards them, a look of officialdom about them.

'Laugh!' Robert said through his teeth. 'Laugh, damn you!' He had stopped, and John was looking at him as if he had gone mad, but Robert began to speak in rapid French, laughing himself meanwhile and the two men stared at them both, frowning for a second or two, and then hurried on to see what was causing all the commotion further along the quay. As soon as they were safely past, Robert and John ran to their horses that they had left tied behind the jetty and rode as fast as they could up the path that led away from the harbour, and eventually brought them to the top of the cliffs.

Robert had been losing blood from the wound in his arm

281

and he was beginning to feel light-headed so that they had to dismount, while John tore a strip of linen from his shirt and bound the wound. 'You're lucky,' he said grimly. 'But you'll have a sore arm for a while, and if it gets infected – '

'I'll just have to see that it doesn't,' Robert said cheerfully enough. He thought again that Edward Dutton had died too easily, but the sack containing the treasure lay across his saddle – a quick look inside had confirmed that it was all there – and in a few weeks' time he would be with Isobel and Christopher again. The little fellow must be walking by now, he thought fondly, and saw John looking at him sourly. 'God in heaven man, does nothing ever please you?' he said irritably.

'I killed a man just now,' John said slowly. 'Maybe two – most certainly two.'

'They'd have killed *you* if you hadn't. Think on that.'

The massive shoulders straightened then and John looked far out to sea. 'You're right, Master Robert,' he said. 'O' course you're right.'

'Well, it's all over,' Robert said briskly. 'And we've a long way to go before we get back to London!'

A moment later they were cantering along the clifftop, the gentle wind cool and bracing and full of promise, and they began to ride back the way that had brought them to Calais a day before Edward Dutton and his two companions had got there – that precious twenty-four hours which had given them time in which to plan their strategy and buy their boatmen's clothes in the market stalls above the harbour.

Knowing the way, they travelled even faster on the return journey, but in Châtillon Robert met a merchant on his way to Dijon and Nancy, who told him that the way south from Dijon would be a hard ride for a woman and young child. So changing his plans, he asked the man if he would deliver a letter to Isobel on the way through St Auguste.

'But of course, monsieur! I shall be enchanted to do so!' the merchant said, smiling happily. 'Madame Maillard's cooking is renowned and there is no other comparable inn for miles once one has left Dijon! I shall be stopping there in any case!' His red face had beamed in anticipation of a splendid meal and a meeting with a no doubt charming Englishwoman.

They had ridden with him as far as Dijon where Robert had

given him the letter that had taken so long to write, and then they had parted company, turning south themselves, with the hills of the Côte d'Or on their right, until they came to the swampy valley of the Sâone and the abbey of Cîteaux, fourteen miles south of Dijon.

The abbey lay in the midst of thickly wooded country on the borders of Burgundy and Bresse, in the commune of St Nicholas and the parish of Villebichot. It must have been a lonely place indeed, Robert thought, when the monks first came there, but when he and John rode down the tree-lined avenue they were confronted at the end of it by a sprawl of fine stone buildings, far bigger and more magnificent then Wolden. They were brought immediately to the prior, Dom Gerard, in the absence of the newly elected abbot, Dom Jean Loysier, who apparently was still in Paris after his election in March, following the death of his predecessor, Dom Guillaume le Fauconnier. All this the prior told them before he discovered that they had brought back the Cîteaux treasure. Once he realised the reason for their visit his amazement and delight was like a child's, although he was close to sixty.

'I cannot believe it!' he gasped as Robert unwrapped the cowhide in his study. 'After so long! After all that has happened in your country and mine – to think that it is back here again, safe! The whole community, France itself, will be so grateful, *so* grateful – But it has grieved us very much that Dom Richard should have been executed,' he said, becoming suddenly grave. 'He was a brave, good man. It is terrible that such a thing should happen.'

'I wondered if you knew,' Robert said quietly.

'Oh, yes. A member of our community was in England at the time – and we have just heard that Lord Thomas Cromwell has been executed too.'

'Cromwell? *Executed?*' Robert said incredulously. 'I would never have believed it possible!'

'Nor I, as things seem to have been between him and King Henry, but I hear the King even married again on the same day!' The prior looked then more closely at Robert, his shrewd eyes uncomfortably perceptive. 'Has it been hard for you?'

'There were difficulties, mon père, but that is all in the past.'
Robert had been able to take the bandage off his arm, but he
did not want to talk about Edward Dutton. Above all he did
not want to talk about Christopher.

'I see.' The prior looked at John standing impassively on the
other side of the table, and then back at Robert. 'Well, I hope
you can stay with us for a few days? We will have a special
Mass said in thanksgiving for the safe return of the treasure.
The Bishop, I know, would like to be present and – '

But Robert interrupted him hastily. 'I must get back to
England as soon as possible. My grandfather has been ill for
some time and he will be anxious to have news of the treasure.'

Yet when the prior discovered that Robert was descended
from the Count of Beaune, who gave the treasure to the abbey
originally, it became very difficult to refuse to stay on for the
Mass. One by one the members of the community came to the
prior's study to admire and exclaim over the treasure, for Dom
Gerard had given permission for speech on such an important
occasion, and Robert was thanked and congratulated so many
times he felt he could not bear much more of it. After a
magnificent meal in the huge refectory he and John went
straight to the guest-house, where they fell asleep the moment
they lay down.

A few days later, during which time both of them were
treated as honoured guests, the bishop arrived with his entourage to celebrate a special Mass of thanksgiving. There
were six priests with him in richly coloured vestments of
embroidered silk on the high altar of the huge church that had
been built in the shape of a cross, with side altars everywhere
or so it seemed to Robert, and chapels opening off the nave. At
the Consecration, after he had consecrated the bread the
bishop bent low over the chalice that had been hidden for so
many months inside a canvas sack.

'This is my blood . . .' There was a hush throughout the
church as the bishop said the words. No one even coughed,
but Robert raised his head and looked at the white hands
holding the jewelled gold cup, thinking of another time,
another place when a young man who was soon to die had sat
with his twelve followers at a plain, wooden table and had said
the same words. Later, at Benediction, he saw those white

hands raise the monstrance high in all its glittering magnificence, lit by the flames of what seemed a thousand candles, while tall, painted statues looked on with blind eyes, and pungent waves of incense rose to the high, domed roof.

He did not know that King Henry had once dreamed of having the Cîteaux treasure on the altar for his marriage to Anne of Cleves, and he could not know, nor could anyone else in the church that day have known, that nearly one hundred years later the treasure would be stolen when imperial troops ransacked Cîteaux Abbey. It was not to be heard of again until the mob found the monstrance and chalice in the home of a French nobleman during the Revolution. Far into the future the chalice would be found by the Nazis when they occupied Paris during the Second World War, only to disappear into obscurity once more.

On that sunny morning of fifteen hundred and forty, Robert had done what he had set out to do and the treasure, it seemed, was safe now for ever. I should feel happy, or at least content, he told himself, but he felt neither, and as soon as Benediction was over he hurried outside, telling John to fetch their horses. But he could not leave yet. He had to be presented to the bishop. He had to kiss his lordship's ring and receive his blessing, and even then Dom Gerard did not want to let him go, insisting that he should stay to eat a splendid repast with them both that seemed to go on and on.

Finally in the late afternoon, he rode away with John, the two barrels of Clos Vougeot that the prior had given him hanging on either side of his pack horse, counting the hours when he would be with Isobel and Christopher again, and refusing to think about Beatrice.

Isobel did not open the letter immediately but sat on the stone seat outside the inn staring at the seal. Robert was alive and well, the man had said, and that for the moment was all that mattered. The man himself was inside eating one of Marie's veal pies, clearly disappointed that she herself would not eat with him, but she had forgotten his very existence from the moment he had handed her the letter and now she wondered what Robert could have to say to her, why he had not come himself instead of writing. The thought that perhaps he would never come and she might never see him again should have been a relief, for after all was that not what she wanted? But it wasn't, and she told herself angrily that she was weak, that she had no strength of purpose at all.

She broke the seal at last with fingers that trembled slightly and began to read the unfamiliar handwriting that sloped across the page as if he had written in a hurry, although the letters themselves were well-formed, heavily black against the parchment.

'*My dearest, dearest Isobel –* ' She caught her breath and then read on. '*Edward Dutton is dead and all is well. I am going on to Cîteaux with John as I am told the journey there would be too hard for you and Christopher, but I hope to be with you both very soon and I look forward to that time more than I can say, for I have missed you greatly. Until then, I send you all my love. Robert.*'

She read the letter over and over until tears blinded her eyes and she could no longer read it. *My dearest, dearest Isobel* – How can I leave him, she thought, how can I get through the rest of my life without him, without love? And Christopher – he is so sure he will see him again. His son. His heir to be. 'Oh Robert, my love,' she whispered aloud, 'I am so sorry I could not save him for you!'

She got stiffly to her feet, folding the letter carefully and putting it away in her pocket. She must leave before he came back. That much she was sure of now, for if the mere sight of his written words could do this to her, how could she keep to her resolution if he stood beside her, if he touched her? It was not possible, and as she stood there a party of travellers rode up to the inn – a French family on their way north. Mother. Father. Two noisy children. Their servants.

She went slowly inside after them and listened to them talking to Marie and Louis and when she had spoken to the mother she went up to her attic room and packed her baggage. When the French family had finished their meal, and she had said goodbye to Brechtje and the Maillards and Frans, she followed the family outside and rode away with them on their spare horse, turning her head as they passed the cemetery at the end of the village, her face wet with tears.

* * *

A week later, at the beginning of September, Beatrice FitzHugh, tired and irritable, arrived with her two servants at Les Trois Faisons, drawn by its attractive appearance and as usual, looking for Robert. She had discovered that he and the woman and child had stayed at several other inns at which she herself had stopped on her journey south, but she was always behind them by several weeks. At some of the inns where she had asked about Robert she had been told of an Englishman who was also looking for him, but the last time that had happened had been nearly a week before, and after she had talked in her schoolroom French for several minutes to Louis and Marie Maillard she followed Marie up to the attic that had been Isobel's bedchamber. When Marie had left she threw herself down on the hard mattress with a sigh.

'It's a pigsty,' she said peevishly to her maid Sarah, 'but it looks as if we shall have to stay here until my husband returns.' She smiled her cat's smile all the same for she had understood the Maillards to say that the nun slut had left Robert, and that the brat was dead of a lung illness. It all seemed too good to be true, but there it was! It seemed too that Robert had gone on to Cîteaux alone and would soon be returning, so perhaps the wretched treasure that he had thought so much of had been found.

More importantly, neither the patron nor his fat wife seemed to know anything at all about Walter. She wondered idly what had happened to him but it did not really matter now, and if he did show up later she would think of some story to explain his presence. All that mattered was that Robert would soon be hers again at last, and only hers.

Down below, in the busy kitchen of Les Trois Faisans that smelled of herbs and olive oil and tender, juicy, roasting meat, Louis Maillard muttered to Marie, 'Madame is not at all gentille! Poor Monsieur Robert!'

While Brechtje, with good, Dutch commonsense, said to Frans as they sat on the stone seat outside, 'It is as well that Madame Beatrice did not arrive a week earlier!' And none of them paid any attention to the small, dark bearded man who slipped through the open door of the inn shortly afterwards.

Chapter Thirty-Five

Walter Clifford sat alone at a small table at the back of the noisy room, his jug of wine in front of him. Les Trois Faisans was crowded, and the other customers, all men, cast an occasional glance at him over their shoulders before burying their faces in their own wine, but he had grown accustomed to being stared at, although recently, with his already sallow skin growing darker by the day in the heat of the sun, it was not until he spoke that people knew he was a foreigner.

But he was about to become a murderer and the thought filled him with terror. If he were found out he would hang for it, he knew that, and even if he were not found out, how much kindness would Beatrice show him, how much love, when he returned to England? He knew what she was like, how cold she could become the instant he had obeyed her commands. But how could he go back to her and tell her that he had succeeded in finding Robert, and that the woman was with him, but that he had lost courage and let her live – How could he bear her scorn? Her bitter rage?

But Robert was not here, although expected back soon apparently, and for some reason that he could not understand, for his French had not improved, the child was not here either. So perhaps he would not be found out. But the woman was certainly here. Femme meant woman – even *he* knew that. The patron had repeated it several times, putting his hands together under his cheek as he bent his head sideways miming someone asleep, and the fat creature who presumably was his wife, had jerked a dirty-nailed thumb towards the ceiling, smiling and saying 'en haut' several time too as if he himself were an imbecile. So what more did he need to know – since there was no doubt whatever about the name, although 'Monsieur Fitz'ugh' had a French sound to it? No, it was quite clear that the woman Isobel Willis was in a room above asleep, and soon Robert FitzHugh would be returning to join her, whatever about the child.

He put his hand into his pocket feeling the package of rat poison that he had got from the cook in London on Beatrice's instructions, telling the woman that rats were becoming a nuisance in his mistress's bedchamber. He was not even sure what the stuff was or how much it would take to kill a human being but Beatrice had assured him it would work – But, God in heaven, to kill a woman he had never even seen! To put her through agonies of pain probably before she died, how could he bring himself to do it? And in any case how could he possibly get close enough to her food to do it? It was crazy – the whole plan was insane! A few days before he had in fact turned back, but had lost his way only to find himself within a mile or two of St Auguste, heading for Dijon. It had seemed like a sign telling him that there was no escape, that he must do what Beatrice had told him to do, and he had gone on until he had seen Les Trois Faisans basking in the sun and been attracted to it, as was every traveller who came this way.

When he got to his feet a few minutes later he had decided that he would do nothing. He would pay for his wine and leave, and tell Beatrice on his return that it had not been possible to put her plan into action – he would think of something to pacify her. But when he came over to the table that served as a kind of counter there was no one there.

Walter could see the patron and the youth who helped him serve the customers busy on the other side of the room, and then the fat woman came out from the kitchen carrying a steaming bowl. She beamed at him. 'You are leaving so soon, monsieur? Will you not wait until Madame descends? See, I am bringing her up a bowl of broth!' She spoke very slowly so that he would understand her, for Marie had taken a liking to this strange little man who seemed so nervous of everything.

'This is for – for the Englishwoman?' he said slowly, staring down at the broth.

289

'Yes, monsieur!' Marie said gaily. 'It is very good! Everyone likes my broth!'

The devil has done this, Walter thought, and wanted to bless himself, but the woman was looking at him with her great cow's eyes and he dared not – If he had left a moment sooner or later this could not have happened. But the bowl of broth was there in front of him and all he had to do was to –

He took out the leather bag of money that he had in his other pocket and fumbled inside it, and when he gave her the money for his wine she took it from him and turned her back, bending down to put it in the box that was kept well out of reach of anyone on the other side of the counter. It did not take her long, but it was long enough for him to pull out the package of poison and empty the greyish-brown powder in the broth, stirring it quickly with his finger before she straightened and turned to face him again.

There had been no time to think about how much or how little he should put in and he was shaking slightly, but she seemed too concerned now about getting her precious broth up to her new visitor to notice and when he said that he could not wait she picked up the bowl with a brief, 'Bonjour, monsieur!'

He stood watching the sway of her red skirt over her great haunches as she climbed the wooden steps that apparently led to the next floor, paralysed for a few seconds by the realisation of what he had just done. Then he turned and walked out quickly into the autumn sunshine, getting on his horse and cantering away, not even sure if he was heading in the right direction, the dust rising in clouds behind him, the shirt under his shabby black doublet sticking to his thin, sweating body, not realising that he was being followed, galloping now down a track that although he did not know it, led only to a small, lonely lake.

The sound of his horse's hooves were still audible when Marie put the bowl of broth down on the rough, wooden chest that had to make do for a table since Beatrice had said she was too tired to eat below and visitors were not usually served meals anywhere else.

'I hope you enjoy it, madame!' But Marie's smile was forced for, like Louis, she had not taken to Robert's wife, and hoped she was not going to insist on having all her meals brought up to her.

Beatrice thanked her off-handedly, and sat down on the stool Sarah brought forward for her, spreading her skirts over the bare, wooden floor as if to emphasise that she was not accustomed to eating in such primitive surroundings. She had taken a spoonful of the broth, thinking that it was passable enough if a little more strongly flavoured than she was used to, even in France, when Marie stopped in the open doorway and said over her shoulder, 'There was a man, an Englishman I thin, asking for your husband just now.'

'An Englishman?' Beatrice frowned, putting down the spoon. 'Did he give his name?'

'No, madame.'

'What did he look like?'

Marie shrugged. 'Not tall, not handsome. But dark, and thin, with a beard.'

Beatrice put down her spoon and was getting to her feet. 'Where is he now?'

'Oh, he is gone, madame! I asked him to wait until you came below but he said he must go. He seems to speak only a few words of French, but I think he understood me. Do you know him madame?' Marie's large, round eyes were full of curiosity.

'I – I don't think so,' Beatrice said, but she was sure that the man had been Walter and she felt vaguely uneasy. Why had he not waited for her to come down if he knew that Robert was away? But perhaps he had not understood the woman – he could have no more than the merest smattering of French after all. Not for the first time she blessed her tutor who, among other things had taught her to speak French middling well, as she finished her broth slowly, enjoying the taste of it less and less with each spoonful.

'Go and fetch the rest,' she said irritably to Sarah. 'I don't want that woman up here again, breathing garlic all over me!'

But when Sarah brought up Marie's famous veal pie her mistress seemed suddenly to have lost her appetite, and Beatrice was already aware of a queasiness in her stomach by the time the two men who had seen Walter take his money pouch from his pocket and had followed him, finally caught up with him. They were rough looking fellows who made their living by what they could steal from travellers, and they had him off his horse in seconds. If he had not tried to draw his knife he might have lived. As it was, the bigger of the two men saw his hand move and drove his own knife deep into his chest.

They emptied his pockets, counting the gold coins in his money bag and laughing aloud with delight, for Beatrice had been generous. Then they stripped him and carried his naked body a few hundred yards further, throwing it into the lake before riding back down the track, until they came to the main road, where they turned left for Dijon and the pickings that promised to be even better –

And long, long before Walter's corpse had begun to grow cold, Beatrice was already ill, crying for water to relieve the terrible burning of her mouth and throat and then spitting it out, vomiting until there was nothing left to vomit, racked with pain that seemed to spread from her stomach through her whole body. It was as bad, worse than having a baby, she gasped to a frantic Sarah and a white-faced Marie, and while she screamed for a doctor all she could think of was the small dark man who had been in the inn earlier that day and to whom not so long ago she had given a packet of poison.

Robert came before the doctor, taking the steps two at a time and almost falling into the room. He had expected to see Isobel's face against the pillows, for Louis had been too distraught to make sense, and when Beatrice turned her head and looked at him from eyes that had sunk far back into her skull he was in terror that his relief had shown in his face. But he need not have worried. She was too near to death to notice, too happy to see him and he sank on his knees beside the bed, remorse, relief, and distress for her suffering tearing him apart.

'I'm sorry, Beatrice,' he whispered. 'I'm sorry! It must be something you ate – we – we will get you better. The doctor is coming!'

As he smoothed the thin hair, wet with sweat, back from her high forehead he wondered how she came to be here and where Isobel and Christopher were, but when she spoke he could scarcely make out what she said.

'I thought you would never come, Robert.'

'Well, I'm here now,' he said, trying to smile, 'and you must rest. When you have had a good sleep – '

But she shook her head very slowly. 'I'm not going to get better.'

'You must not say that!' He took her long, narrow hand in his and began to rub it gently.

'It's true.' Her voice seemed to have become stronger and she tried to raise herself off the pillows. 'I've been poisoned, Robert! I'm sure of it!'

'But – but who would want to do such a thing?' He still had her hand in his but he was no longer rubbing it and he looked down at her pityingly, thinking that illness had affected her mind, but she said slowly, her voice fading again to a whisper, 'Walter did it but – it – it was a stupid – mistake – He thought I was Isobel – '

Her voice died away and he realised to his horror that she knew what she was saying. Walter had set out to poison Isobel – *Isobel!* He had let go of her hand, unable to speak, but she was looking up at him now and as he forced himself to meet her eyes they became suddenly incandescent. 'I love you, Robert!' she whispered. 'Please hold me!'

He took her in his arms then and held her, her head against his shoulder and he tried not to think of the implications of what she had told him, to remember only that, if what she said was true, then she was indeed dying, and she clung to him like a child. 'I'm frightened,' she whispered once, 'so frightened!'

He kissed her then, very gently but her eyes were closed and when he looked down he saw that her face was a strange, blueish colour.

But she did not die immediately. She was unconscious but still alive when the doctor came, the same man that had come before to Christopher, and this time he said stiffly, 'There is nothing I can do for your wife, monsieur. From what I have been told about her symptoms it seems to me that she has been poisoned, but I cannot be sure. Perhaps you should tell the authorities.'

The doctor did not say that it had been a wasted journey like the other, but he wondered at the strangeness of this Englishman with the stone-hard face who paid him his fee with only the briefest of thanks, for Robert seemed in a world of his

293

own. Soon after Beatrice had lost consciousness they had told Robert of Christopher's death, and that Isobel had gone away a week before. Now he could find no words for anyone, least of all this doctor – a useless stranger. He had not yet been able to read Isobel's letter that Brechtje had given him, but when the doctor left he took it out of his pocket and read it, sitting beside Beatrice, in the candle-lit darkness, waiting for her to die.

'Dear Robert, by the time you read this you will know that our son is dead. I share your grief for him but it is better that we do not see each other ever again. Please do not try to find me. Isobel.'

He read the words over and over, branding them into his mind, and when he looked back at Beatrice he saw that she too was gone from him. I have lost everything, he thought dully. What I valued most and what I valued least of all.

Chapter Thirty-Six

On a blustery evening in late October Isobel stumbled along a lonely country road. The soles of her thin shoes had split across long since, letting in the wet, and she drew her cloak more closely about her – the long, velvet, sable-edged cloak that Cornelis van Ophoorn had had made for her, which was the only thing left to her now besides her gown and her shift and her shoes, for everything else had been stolen from her in the inn outside Selby. She had shared an attic room there with a woman and her daughter, thinking that they seemed honest enough and would give her protection from the men drinking below. But when she woke in the morning the two women had gone with what was left of her money and all her baggage.

York must be still a long way off, she thought now and she had seen no building, not even a barn, for miles. She shivered, and thought of the journey with the French family to Calais from St Auguste. It seemed a lifetime away – the quarrelling, spoiled children, their peevish mother, the father with his wandering hands and sly innuendos; creatures from another planet. Yet they had seen her safely to Calais, while they went on to Bruges where the father had business, and she owed them thanks for that.

The journey to London she had made on horseback, riding as far as the outskirts with half a dozen nuns from one of the last convents to be closed, but she had arrived in the city alone, and it had terrified her. The size of it. The crowds. The tall, old buildings. But at a livery stables she found a group of businessmen and their wives, hiring horses to travel north and she had gone with them as far as Doncaster. From there she had had to go on alone, but soon after she had left Selby she had found a farmer willing to let her sit beside him in his cart. He had put her off the cart a mile back, however, because she would not let him fondle her, and now the certainty that she would never reach York alive grew in her with each passing moment as the light began to fail.

When she heard the clip-clop of horses' hooves on the road behind her she did not turn her head, wanting only to hide even though the farmer and his cart were far ahead of her by now, but at this hour, on this lonely road any stranger could mean danger. It was too late to hide, however, and when the rider pulled up beside her his voice was gentle and educated.

'Good evening, mistress! And where in the name of God are you going alone at this hour?'

She looked up, and smiled with relief. He was a priest, not much older than herself, an itinerant Franciscan like others she had seen, wearing the brown habit of the Order, his sandalled feet big and ungainly against the shaggy sides of his cob. 'I'm going to York,' she replied.

'Then you'll not get there before dark!' he said cheerfully, dismounting and talking to her across the cob's broad back. 'Not unless you get up on my old friend here.' He patted the shaggy coat. 'I would not ask him to carry both of us!'

It seemed like a miracle. The warm, human voice. The offer of help. The old horse waiting patiently for her to mount, and when she did the warmth of its body spreading through hers like a blessing. 'Thank you, father,' she said. 'I am very grateful. I had not realised how tired I was.'

With the priest leading the horse they began to move on and after a moment he said, 'Have you come far?'

'From outside Selby.'

'You've had a long walk!'

'I did not walk all the way.' She hesitated for a second and then she said, 'Do you know the nuns' house in York? Could you direct me there?'

'I know it well! I shall bring you to the door!'

'Thank you.'

There was silence again until she said quietly, 'Would you hear my Confession, father?'

'Of course!'

She had surprised herself by asking and yet now that she had spoken the words she was glad, and she looked at the empty road ahead, trying to collect her thoughts. But in the end the words came easily. 'I was once a nun, father, and I broke my vows. I – I lay with a man and had a child by him. And after he married, I lay with him again.'

She waited for the storm of condemnation to break over her head, but all the gentle voice beside her said was, 'Did you love this man?'

'Yes.'

'Do you still love him?'

'Yes.'

'Have you anything else to tell me?'

She hesitated for a second and then said, 'No, father.'

'Then for your penance, say one Hail Mary.'

She was sure she had mis-heard him. '*One* Hail Mary, Father?'

'That's right, and now, an Act of Contrition – '

'But father – '

'Are you sorry for what you did?' he asked her quietly.

She thought about that for what seemed a long while, then she said at last, 'I can't say I am truly sorry. But I *want* to be sorry – '

'That is what matters,' he said gravely. 'To *want* to be sorry.' After a moment he looked up at her for the first time since she had begun her Confession. 'Where is the child now?'

'He's dead, father. I think that – that God took him from me in punishment for what I did.'

'No!' he said quickly, shaking his head, 'You must not think that. I cannot tell you why your son died, but I do know that God is not like a clerk in a counting house balancing his books, and your sin seems to me not to be in loving too much but in doubting His mercy.'

She thought about that as he began to say the words of Absolution and the old cob walked on, tired like herself and dreaming of a warm stable.

After a long time she said, 'Father, would you not like to ride now?'

But to her relief he only laughed. 'I'm glad to stretch my legs – I've been riding all day – but – forgive me – I am curious to know why you are going to the nuns' house?'

She did not really want to tell him and she was so weary now that even the effort of talking seemed too much. All she wanted was to lie down. To sleep. Not to eat – she was too tired now for that, although earlier her hunger had been like a pain. But this man had been kind to her and she said reluctantly, 'I want to enter religious life again, to renew my vows.'

'Do you mind if I ask you why?'

'There is no place in the world for me.'

'You cannot know that until you have looked. Have you looked?'

'I – I don't need to. I *know*.'

'I see. And would it be that you feel that by entering again you will make amends; atone for what has happened?'

'That is part of it.'

'Then I strongly advise you to wait at least a year before making a final decision.' His voice was brisk now, matter of fact. 'Were you a nun in St Mary's?'

'Yes.' She hoped she had not sounded curt, but she wished he would stop asking questions and giving her advice she did not want to hear.

'You realise that some of the good ladies may not be very sympathetic, to say the least of it?'

'Yes, I do. I – am prepared for that.' But was she really, she wondered, as they turned a corner and she saw in the distance the great town walls of York with their towers stark against the evening sky. Am I mad, she asked herself, but it was too late now to turn back and soon they were under the tall arch of one of the towers and into the streets beyond it, full of people hurrying home. They crossed a bridge over a river and there was a church on their right not long afterwards that the priest said was St Mary's, and then he was leading her down a narrow street lined with meat stalls that he called the Shambles, and at the end of the street they turned left and left again until he stopped before a modest looking timber house that leant crazily forward across the narrow street like its neighbours.

'Shall I go in with you?' he asked, as he helped her down off the horse.

But she shook her head. 'Thank you, but this is something I must do alone.'

'As you wish,' he said cheerfully, 'but I shall wait until the door opens.'

298

He got up on his cob then, gathering the reins in his hands and turning its head as she walked up the narrow path and knocked on the door. When she looked over her shoulder he was still there, but as the door started to open he raised his hand in a last blessing and began to ride away, and she knew, as she sometimes knew such things, that they would not meet again. And then she saw Dame Agatha's red face, her gooseberry coloured eyes staring up at her, saw the shock and then the malice in them as the nun recognised her.

The nuns were gathered around the glowing brazier as they used to be in St Mary's in winter time, but the parlour in this old house was tiny in comparison with the convent parlour. Even the brazier itself was smaller, and Dame Petronilla's hands were idle now, for her sight had failed so much she could no longer see to stitch even her little gifts. But her greatest cross was that Dame Agatha had come back. For although Dame Agatha had chosen to go to her relations when St Mary's had been closed, she had returned to the little house in York some months later. It appeared that, contrary to her expectations, her relations had not wanted her, and she had gone from house to house, staying for a shorter period each time until the day came when an irate cousin had thrown her out, bag and baggage.

'I was tact itself,' she told Dame Margaret on the evening of her return, her face redder than ever with self-righteous anger. 'I merely told my cousin, very gently, very *kindly*, that her housekeeping left much to be desired. Such ingratitude! Such *arrogance*!'

The abbess had had no choice but to make the best of it and tell the other nuns that they must accept Dame Agatha's return as their cross, and be as tolerant and forgiving as possible. 'Remember the Rule,' she said to each in turn. 'We must live together in peace and harmony.'

'But it is quite impossible to live harmoniously with Dame Agatha, my lady,' Dame Petronilla said, her voice still clear and almost young.

'Just do your best, then,' the abbess said wearily. That had been months ago, and in a few short days everyone in the house, especially Dame Petronilla, was conscious of the special kind of unease which Dame Agatha spread all round her.

There were, of course, other factors which made it difficult for some of them to adjust to their new surroundings. The prioress, Dame Helen, for example felt humiliated when her grand friends and relations came calling. Recently she had had to open the door herself to Lady Mary Percy! She sat opposite Dame Agatha now, thinking about the humiliation of it. Perhaps I should go home after all, she thought. I am not suited to this – this style of living. But her brother and his wife had not seemed at all anxious to have her back when she last raised the subject. She sighed, looking down at her worn shoes, at the careful darning in her one and only habit. The pension she had been given as prioress was slightly more than the others had received, although of course not as much as had been give to Dame Margaret, but really, it was *pitiably* small, she thought for the hundredth time, quite inadequate for the needs of someone as gently born as she was!

She stole a glance at the abbess for Dame Margaret shared the fire with the rest of the community now. She has aged, Dame Helen thought, not unkindly. She has aged more than any of us over the past year. But was it any wonder? She had had all the responsibility of the move from St Mary's – the awful journey to York with Dame Ita who had never stirred from the infirmary in five years, dying on the way, and the rain that had drenched them all to the bone – and then the settling-in, in this *wretched* little house – she had had far too much to carry on her shoulders! It was not right, not *just*. And the business about Isobel Willis had not helped either, Dame Helen thought, her small mouth tightening. She wondered where the girl was now and if she knew or cared about the worry and trouble she had caused – Dame Helen doubted it. The young were so selfish, so *unfeeling*.

The abbess herself, however, was thinking of none of these things. *She* had long ago adjusted to the move from St Mary's and Dame Agatha's return and, although she often thought of Isobel with an ache in her heart, she was not thinking of her this particular evening, but of Dame Cecilia, who should have been home hours before and had been called out to a dying mother. Since she had come to live in York the infirmarian had been giving more and more of her time to the sick poor of the town.

'You must not overdo things, Cecilia,' she had said to her the previous week, as sternly as she could. 'The poor need you but so do we, and if I lose you there is no one to take your place.'

300

'But my lady, there is such poverty! Such misery! And the doctor only goes to those who can pay.'

Dame Cecilia had been right, of course – sadly, everything these days seemed to come down to a question of money, or the lack of it. She looked across the brazier at Dame Katherine, who was staring into the fire and guessed that the cellarer was worrying about their stores. If the stall holders in the Shambles did not keep them supplied with free meat she did not know what they would have done. She would soon have to find someone who would charge less for their milk and eggs, and she would have to think of a tactful way of asking Dame Helen to drink less beer – She was lost in thought when there was a knock on the door. Thank God, she thought. It's Cecilia at last!

It was Dame Agatha's turn to be portress this week and she watched as the other nun got awkwardly to her feet and hurried out. She loves to be portress, she thought, she loves to know what is going on. She could hear a voice, a young voice, oddly familiar. There were footsteps, and then Dame Agatha was ushering a young woman in, a young woman in a long cloak, with curling, dark hair and a pale, tired face. The abbess put a hand to her heart, afraid she was going to faint, but in fact it was not she but the young woman who fell to the floor before anyone could catch her.

'It's Isobel Willis,' Dame Agatha said in her flat voice. 'She's come back!'

They had all got to their feet, too shocked to speak, when there was another knock on the door. 'Go and answer it,' the abbess whispered, and went down on her knees, cradling Isobel's head in her arms. Her eyes were closed and she did not seem to be breathing and for a terrible second Dame Margaret thought she was dead, but then she felt a hand on her shoulder and heard Dame Cecilia's voice. 'It's all right, my lady, I think she has only fainted, but we must give her air.'

She took Isobel from the abbess then, loosening the strings that tied her cloak so that it fell back off her shoulders, sitting her up and pushing her head down between her knees. In a moment or two Isobel was looking round her with a dazed expression on her face. 'What – what happened? I – I – '

'You fainted, child,' Dame Cecilia said, beginning to rub her hands that were cold as ice. 'Sit there quietly now. Don't try to talk.'

But Isobel insisted on getting to her feet. She was still very pale, and the infirmarian said quickly, 'My lady, she should lie down for a while. I shall take her to the bed beside the kitchen,' and without waiting for argument from anyone, least of all Isobel, she led her quickly out of the parlour and put her lying down in the box bed where the servant of the previous owner of the house used to sleep.

Back in the parlour the nuns had found their tongues, or at least Dame Agatha had.

'I wonder where she came from,' she said looking from one to the other of them. 'Did you see the state of her shoes?' When no one answered she picked up the cloak with an audible sniff, holding it well away from her. 'I wonder where *this* came from?' In the fire-light the sables were dark and sleek against the rich, plum-coloured velvet and Dame Agatha's voice hinted at a world of self-indulgence and dissipation. But the abbess seemed suddenly to come to life and she took the cloak quickly from her, draping it over her arm.

'Vespers will be late this evening I am afraid,' she said quietly, 'but you will please carry on without me.'

She waited while they left the parlour obediently, Dame Agatha trailing behind the others with obvious reluctance, and when they had all gone at last into the back parlour which she had had converted into a tiny chapel, then and only then did she go to Isobel and Dame Cecilia.

But Isobel was asleep, so deeply asleep that the abbess doubted if anything on earth would have wakened her, her lashes dark against the pallor of her skin, her hair spread in a tangled mass on the old straw mattress.

'She seems completely exhausted,' Dame Cecilia muttered. 'She just lay down and fell asleep, as if she had been given a potion.'

But both nuns knew what the other was thinking – Where was the child? Where was Andrew, or had she never been with him? Above all, why had she come back?

It was not until Isobel woke at noon the following day that any of their questions were answered.

'Are you feeling better, love? Would you like to eat now?' The infirmarian put her hand on Isobel's forehead, and was glad to find it cool to her touch.

'I – I feel – all – all right but I'm not – hungry.' It seemed to cost Isobel a great effort to speak, but there was one more question Dame Cecilia felt she had to ask, for she feared that the child might have been left somewhere with no one to look after him. 'Where is Christopher?' she said gently.

'He's dead,' Isobel whispered. 'And Andrew is dead too, and Saskia, and – and Pieter, and – Cornelis. They are all dead.' The tears began to slide down her cheeks and she did not even try to raise a hand to brush them away while the infirmarian looked down at her, horrified. What could have happened to Christopher, she wondered. He had seemed so strong that first night, so full of courage. 'My Christopher' she had always called him in her own mind, thanking God for having allowed her to help bring him into the world, hoping at one time that she would be able to see him grow into a sturdy boy at least, since she would be gone herself before he became a man. But he was dead. She tried to control her grief, to think instead of Isobel, of what it must have meant to her to lose him, and Andrew, and those others with the queer sounding names. Who were they, and what terrible things had happened to her after she had been sent away? I should have gone out to the farm to see her, she thought, no matter what Lady Abbess said. I should have disobeyed and gone.

But all she could say now was, 'I'm sorry. So sorry – ' She thought Isobel had fallen asleep again but she began to talk in a dull, flat voice as if all emotion had been drained from her, her eyes half closed as if she might indeed fall asleep at any moment, and Dame Cecilia listened, appalled, to what she had to say.

When she had finished the infirmarian said quietly, 'I prayed for you every day since you were sent away. I knew things would be hard for you but I never imagined, never guessed they would be so terrible.'

Isobel's eyes opened wide, holding hers. 'I know you prayed for me,' she said. 'One day in particular.'

Dame Cecilia wanted to ask what day that was, what had happened, but, like other questions she would like to have asked, she left the words unsaid, afraid Isobel would retreat into a silent, inner world of her own where no one could ever reach her again, as she had seen other women do. There was one thing, however, she had to know. 'Where is Robert FitzHugh now?' she said quietly.

'Back in England, I imagine,' and then Isobel added, her voice suddenly bleak, 'with his wife.'

She still loves him, Dame Cecilia thought, wondering what had happened this time between them, and why the Lord had brought them together again. She wanted desperately to ease Isobel's pain and did not know how to do it, for this was no woman crying because her drunken husband beat her or forced her to let him lie on her after giving birth, as some men did. She could try to heal those women's bodies with her nursing skill. She could lash their men with her tongue until they cringed like beaten curs, but no one could heal Isobel's wounds except Robert FitzHugh and it was not in his power to do so even if he had the will. But it seemed that he was not just the unprincipled philanderer she had first thought him to be, and what man did not want to have a son?

'Can I tell Lady Abbess what you have told me?' she said at last.

'Why not? And now I must get up – I can't lie here for ever.' Isobel started to sit up but the infirmarian pushed her gently back. 'Not until you have eaten.' She hesitated and then went on quickly. 'The gown you are wearing is torn at the hem and splattered with mud. I have found you another one, not so elegant I'm afraid, but it's woollen and you will be glad of that in this house – '

When Isobel had eaten a breakfast of sorts Dame Cecilia brought her an old-fashioned grey gown, not unlike the one Saskia had given her, and when she had taken off the tattered, mud-stained Dutch silk one, of which she had once been so proud, she found it fitted her well enough, and the shoes, which Dame Cecilia had bought for her in the market, were neat and comfortable. When she had combed her hair with the comb the infirmarian had also given her she sat down on the side of the bed waiting for her to return, knowing that soon she must meet Dame Margaret face to face.

But the infirmarian was still in the parlour with the abbess. She had told her Isobel's story and after she had finished Dame Margaret said nothing for several minutes. 'I wish – ' she began, and stopped. 'I wish I had done more to help her,' she said quietly. 'With hindsight I can see that I acted without charity. May God forgive me.'

'We can make up for it now,' the infirmarian said quickly.

'*We*?' The abbess's voice was very gentle. 'You have never acted without charity in all the time I have known you, Dame Cecilia. No, the sin is mine and mine only. And now will you ask her to come to me, please? I should like to talk to her alone.'

As Dame Cecilia stood up the abbess said quietly, 'The rest of the community need know only that Isobel left the country with her cousin, who was entrusted with the task of bringing the treasure back to Cîteaux; that he was hanged through a dreadful misunderstanding, and she was sheltered by a kind Dutch family, but Christopher became ill and died. And she has come back to us because she has nowhere else to go.'

The two nuns looked at each other and Dame Cecilia guessed that Dame Margaret was thinking as she had thought, as everyone would think if they knew the whole story – All that time together. Nearly the whole summer! She could actually hear Dame Agatha's voice saying it. 'But what about the treasure?' she said quickly.

'We shall say only that it has been safely returned to Cîteaux – that Isobel herself does not know the full details of the final handing over, which is the truth, is it not?'

Dame Cecilia nodded her head slowly, and Dame Margaret said with the ghost of a smile, 'Send her in to me now, please, before I begin to worry about sins of omission – '

Not long afterwards Isobel sat facing Dame Margaret as she had done so often in the parlour in St Mary's. She sat very straight as she had done then, but in other ways she had changed greatly since those early days. The look of happy, almost childish expectancy was gone completely. Her eyes now were the eyes of someone who has nothing more to fear because she has reached breaking point and has not broken, but who has nothing to hope for either. She had dark shadows under her eyes, the soft curve of her cheeks was gone, and she was very pale. But Dame Margaret realised with a shock of surprise, as Robert had done when he had seen her the first time in Amsterdam, that she had become beautiful, like a butterfly emerging from a chrysalis. It's going to be very difficult, the abbess thought with dismay. What on earth am I going to do with her?

But all she said very quietly, was, 'Dame Cecilia has told me everything that happened to you. I can only say that I am deeply sorry especially – especially about the loss of your son.' Faint colour had come into the abbess's face, and Isobel did not know that she was praying silently for the right words to use. After a moment, when Isobel said nothing, she went on slowly. 'Your mother was one of my dearest friends and she put you in my care, but I feel that I failed her.' She stopped to clear her throat for she had become suddenly husky. 'And now it seems that I have been in a way responsible for her grandson's death.'

'I have only myself to blame for all that has happened,' Isobel said quickly. 'That is why I have come back – not just for a roof over my head, but to atone. To give my life to God, this time in reparation.'

Dame Margaret sat back in her chair, frowning. 'You want to enter again?'

'I did until yesterday, my lady, but I met a priest on my way here and he advised me to wait for a while before finally making up my mind.'

'That was good advice, Isobel,' the abbess said slowly, 'and I doubt if you could enter again at the moment, as things are. It would be easier perhaps if you went to Spain and tried to enter there. This time, however, you must be *really* sure that that is what God wants for you. Meanwhile, you are welcome to stay with us for as long as you wish. Dame Cecilia badly needs help, and Dame Petronilla will welcome a young arm on her walks. Do you know she likes nothing better than to walk down the Shambles and listen to the women bargaining for meat?' The abbess was smiling now, beautiful in her relief that she had been given an opportunity to undo a wrong that she had once done. 'Perhaps later on you might also consider a position in a good family? I am sure it could be arranged.' She reached across and took Isobel's hands in hers. 'It won't be easy, any of it. But Dame Cecilia and I will tell only part of your story, and we will both be here when you need us.'

Yet, although the abbess's hands were warm on hers, the hurt would always be there. They both knew that, but when Isobel left the parlour shortly afterwards her face had lost some of its tension, and she went and sat on the side of her bed again, listening to the clatter of pots and pans from the kitchen close by and wondering where Dame Cecilia was, and if she would soon have to meet the rest of the community.

Dame Cecilia, however, was busy elsewhere and the others were waiting to see Dame Margaret. Dame Helen was the first to go in to her and when the abbess had finished speaking the prioress looked at her aghast.

'But you cannot – we cannot have her here,' she said, in tones of horror. 'Not after all that has happened! Beatrice FitzHugh is related to me! What would people say? Lady Mary – the countess – it would put me in an impossible position!'

'Isobel has nowhere else to go,' Dame Margaret said quietly. 'It may not be for very long, but meanwhile she will stay here and I hope I can count on your co-operation.'

The words were gently said but there was a hint of steel behind them.

'If you say so, mi'lady. But I really *must* protest!'

'I have noted what you have said,' Dame Margaret went on. 'And as prioress you of course have a say in all such matters, but I am afraid that this time I must over-ride your objections, and I would ask, beg of you, to treat the girl with kindness.'

Dame Helen left then, no longer protesting, but clearly still unhappy. She was followed by Dame Agatha and Dame Katherine. The cellarer spoke first, as Dame Agatha had decided to wait to see how the land lay before she opened her lips.

'We cannot afford to feed an extra mouth,' the cellarer said, 'but if I understood Dame Helen correctly – you intend to have Isobel Willis to stay for an indefinite period?'

'Yes. That is my intention,' the abbess said evenly. 'I am quite sure one more mouth to feed won't make all that difference.'

'Young girls eat a lot more than we do,' Dame Agatha said, speaking at last. 'And I remember when Isobel was in St Mary's – ' She stopped, her face turning crimson. 'Of course,' she added, looking down at the floor, 'there was a reason for *that*!'

'What is past is past,' the abbess said, her voice very cold. 'I presume Dame Cecilia has told you of what the poor girl has had to go through since?'

'Indeed she has!' Dame Agatha snapped. 'And there's a lot more to it than Isobel has told you, I daresay!'

Dame Margaret counted up to ten before speaking again, then she said very quietly, 'I would ask you to remember the Rule, you in particular, Dame Agatha, and to bear in mind that Isobel Willis has lost her child, to whom I am sure she had grown very attached. She has also lost her cousin and her Dutch friends who seem to have shown her great kindness.'

'We shall do what we can to help her,' Dame Katherine said quickly, 'and I am sorry for bringing up the matter of supplies. Of course we shall manage –'

But Dame Agatha was not finished yet, and her jealousy of Isobel was even more bitter now than ever, since the abbess had clearly forgiven her. 'May I ask, mi'lady,' she said with an attempt at humility, 'if the matter was put before the Council?'

'It was not,' Dame Margaret said, her voice grown sharp in spite of her determination not to lose her temper. 'The decision has been mine, but the circumstances are exceptional, and I have counted on the support and help of all members of our small community.'

Dame Petronilla's knock on the door came as a relief to the abbess, and apparently to the cellarer also, for she all but dragged Dame Agatha out of the parlour as the older nun hobbled in, leaning heavily on her stick.

Dame Margaret rubbed her forehead as she was wont to do under stress. 'Please sit down, Petronilla.'

'I want to talk to you about Isobel!' the old nun said briskly, settling herself as comfortably as she could on one of the stools. 'Poor child! She should never have gone off with that cousin of hers. Such a *dull* creature! But gifted in a small way, I believe – I met him once you know.' Dame Petronilla lowered her voice. 'That handsome young man I saw her with in the garden – Robert FitzHugh – He would have been far more suitable!' Recently she had become mildly confused and the abbess looked at her now, not knowing whether to laugh or cry.

'Isobel only went to Holland with Andrew Ellerton because she was unhappy at home,' she said, choosing her words with care, 'and Robert FitzHugh is now married to the niece of the Earl of Westmorland.'

308

'I know! I know!' Dame Petronilla sighed. 'A plain-looking girl, I'm told, and not at all a *nice* person! But of course, I must not gossip!'

The abbess tried to lead her back to the present. 'Isobel has had a hard time since she left us, but she would like to stay here for the present. I hope you will be kind to her?'

'Kind? But of course I will! I've always been very fond of the girl. We can go for walks together and she can tell me about her little boy. You know he is dead?'

The abbess could only nod her head.

'So sad! So very sad!' She leant across the table suddenly, lowering her voice. 'I must warn you that Agatha is – is – ' She seemed to have forgotten what she was going to say 'Do you think that *she* might return to her relations again?' she said instead.

'I'm afraid not,' the abbess said, and then corrected herself quickly. 'At least, I should say that she – does not appear to have any plans to leave.'

Dame Petronilla sighed. 'A great pity!'

Dame Margaret thought it wiser not to ask her why and with a gentle reminder about the Rule of Silence which Dame Petronilla tended to ignore, she let her go soon afterwards, no doubt looking forward to her next walk when she would have Isobel beside her once again to take her arm and see she did not fall. And Dame Margaret sat back in her abbess's chair and wondered how it was all going to work out and if she had been mad to act as she had done.

But surely I did the right thing, she told herself, thinking back to the day a few weeks ago when she had seen Giacomo Frescobaldi again. She and Dame Katherine had been coming back from the markets, their baskets on their arms, when he and his entourage had come riding down the narrow street. She had known him at once, even after more than twenty years, although his face, like his body, had grown heavy and his black hair that had been like a raven's wing was now silvery grey. But in his florid, Italian clothes, he looked as handsome as ever.

''Tis t'Italians coom to buy wool, bless 'em,' someone in the crowd shouted, but as he drew level with Dame Katherine and herself, a dog had run forward barking and snapping at his horse's feet and the horse had reared. She and Dame Katherine had had to step back so hastily that she had dropped her basket, and when he had steadied the animal he had slid off its back and bowed low to her in apology, velvet, bejewelled cap in hand. Then, while one of his servants hurried to pick up the carrots and onions strewn all over the muddy street, he had stood staring down at her, frowning. 'Surely – surely we have met before, madame?' he said, and his voice and his dark, liquid eyes were the same.

She had felt herself blushing like a young girl. 'A – a long time ago.'

'In the convent, yes? Of course!' She had seen in his face that look of sadness that comes when a kind and gallant man meets a woman after a long period of time and sees that she has aged, but he added quickly, 'I never forget a charming lady!'

'St Mary's has been closed,' she said hastily, aware of Dame Katherine standing beside her and aware that she herself had not only failed to observe proper custody of the eyes, but had actually broken silence without good cause.

'I know,' he said gravely. 'It is a terrible, *terrible* thing, and now you live here in the town, eh? You must permit me to have your purchases carried home for you.'

But she had shaken her head quickly. 'No, no! Thank you, but it is not necessary, Signor Frescobaldi!' She knew from the look of faint embarrassment in his eyes that he had forgotten her name.

He had straightened his shoulders, and said with a faint sigh, 'Very well, madame. May I wish you good fortune then, and go on my way?' He had taken her hand before she was aware of what he was about to do, and she had felt his lips brush across her skin like the touch of a butterfly's wings – and felt nothing more than that. I won't need to go to Confession this time, she had thought, as she watched him mount and ride away, remembering that first time when she had confessed afterwards to Father Francis. The old man had raved at her for nearly half an hour, and she often wondered if he had understood what she had been trying to tell him, or if he thought she had actually lain with a man.

It had all seemed of enormous importance at the time, and yet, when viewed against the realities of her life since, it seemed a small enough experience. But she had never been able to forget it and had never been able to understand why it had happened to her and so late in life. But she knew now that it had happened because of Isobel. That she had needed to have some inkling of what sexuality meant.

Yet for all that she had failed her. Well, now was her chance to make amends, and sitting there at her parlour table in her abbess's chair, she found herself, to her astonishment, wondering what Giacomo Frescobaldi would have said had she been able to tell him. Did men and women ever talk to each other freely about such things? How strange it must be if that were so! How – comforting! She smiled at her foolishness in thinking such thoughts at her age and got to her feet as the bell rang for dinner. Isobel would have to eat with the community and she must see to it that there was no awkwardness.

But for Isobel in the weeks that followed there was more than mere 'awkwardness'. The abbess and Dame Cecilia were unfailingly supportive, but Dame Helen kept a careful distance from her and in general treated her much as she would have treated a kitchenmaid who had been admitted to the parlour by mistake. The fact that the lay-sisters had all left and the nuns could not now afford any servants at all, except the woman as old as themselves who came by the day to cook for them, was beside the point. In any case, Isobel knew that the prioress had always regarded her as of lowly birth and no fit company for gentlewomen – and now of course in addition she had disgraced herself.

Dame Agatha, on the other hand, was forever at her side, avidly curious about her time 'away' as she called it, somehow implying that the time had been spent in disgraceful circumstances. If Isobel so much as broke a dish, for she helped in the kitchen as well as helping the infirmarian, it was immediately reported to the abbess by Dame Agatha. If she returned late with Dame Cecilia she reported that too, and if Isobel came back from her walks with Dame Petronilla looking, if not happy at least less miserable than usual, Dame Agatha would look at her suspiciously. Once Isobel had heard her whisper to Dame Katherine, 'Perhaps it is not wise to give the girl so much liberty – you *know* what I mean – ' and the cellarer had looked embarrassed but had remained silent.

The only person, apart from Dame Cecilia, with whom Isobel

311

felt really at ease now was Dame Petronilla. The old nun chatted to her on their walks as if she had never gone away, as if in fact the past year had never happened – and perhaps for Dame Petronilla it never had.

Yet she had a roof over her head and food to eat – Isobel would tell herself this as she lay in bed, afraid to go to sleep for fear her dream of wandering alone in the wilderness would come back to haunt her. The nuns slept upstairs and she would lie in the dark silence that was broken only by the nightwatchman calling the hour. Her need for Robert came then like an illness, and she tried instead to think of the poor in their hovels, or huddled against the town walls or lying on the steps of the Minster. She did what she could for them with Dame Cecilia but when she bent over a filthy mat and tried to force a few drops of milk into a tiny mouth crusted with sores, all she could see was a small grave in a French cemetery, as if her suffering was greater than anyone else's could ever be.

She knew that Dame Margaret was already making enquiries about a position for her as governess, but that when the families heard who she was, they remembered the trial and refused to take her. And when, at last, she would fall asleep, her last thoughts were not of Robert, but of a Spanish convent with high, stone walls.

Chapter Thirty-Seven

Beatrice FitzHugh was buried in the cemetery at St Auguste but
far away from the children's plot, and after the burial Robert
went alone to stand in front of his son's small grave. The
gravestone read simply, 'Christopher. Born xxth July 1538. Died
xxth July 1539' and among all the many regrets that crowded in
on him not the least was that, in the end, his son had died
without a name – and yet, he thought bitterly, Christopher was
more a FitzHugh than Beatrice could ever have been, but her
gravestone, after the stonemason had finished with it, would
carry the name of FitzHugh when he himself was dead and
gone.

He left the cemetery alone then, as Isobel had done weeks
before, but he did not go down to the river to grieve. Instead he
saddled his horse and waited for John, and when he came they
rode off together to continue their search for Walter. But
although they scoured the area for miles they could not find
him.

'I'll never know the whole truth, now,' Robert said bleakly.
They were riding back along the Dijon road and he could see
already the small cluster of houses that was the village of St
Auguste. 'People will say I poisoned her myself.'

'But how could you have? You weren't even here.'

'I was close enough – a few hours' ride away at most. By the
time the story reaches England I'll have been here all right! But
I'm sure from Marie's description of the man who was asking
for me that Walter *was* here, and somehow managed to slip
poison into Beatrice's food, thinking that it was for Isobel. But

313

unless I can find the little rat and beat the truth out of him I can prove nothing. Even the Maillards won't stand by me – Marie says he was here when she carried up the broth, but the last thing she'll admit is that he could have tampered with it behind her back – and yet he *must* have done!'

'Aye,' John agreed heavily, 'that must ha' been the way of it, God rot his soul! But it seems to me we should make for home.' The big man's voice sounded weary, and indeed he had not yet got over the shock of the two deaths and the manner of Beatrice's dying. But when Robert told him he intended to look for Isobel before leaving for England the weariness turned to anger.

'She could be anywhere,' John growled. 'No one knows where those French people were going, beyond that they were travelling north – For Christ's sake, man!' he went on, growing angrier by the second, 'you've been away from your grandfather for months! He's back there in London, lying in that bed fretting about you! You can't go off on a wild goose chase!'

'If I've not found her by the time we get to Calais you can go back to him and take Sarah with you, while I continue on to Amsterdam with the others.' Robert's voice had grown hard. 'It's possible she might have gone there. It will only mean a few more weeks, and you can tell my grandfather I shall soon be with him.'

They were outside the inn now and John shrugged his shoulders before he began to dismount. 'I'll say no more,' he grunted. 'But you're wasting your time searching for her in Holland. She'd more likely go back to England if she doesn't stay in France.'

Robert had dismounted himself and he looked at John across his horse's back, 'She always said she'd never go back to her father or the nuns again. And there seems to be no one else she could turn to.' But as he watched John lead the horses away without bothering to reply, he knew that it was very unlikely he would ever see Isobel again. But he had to try to find her – her letter had been so cold, so devoid of love or even affection. He could think of several reasons, but he had to hear her say the words. And he had to tell her that now he was free. That, most of all.

They left Les Trois Faisans early next morning with Sarah

and the two Dutch servants, to the obvious relief of the Maillards who were clearly worried that if they stayed a day longer their reputation would suffer even further. When Robert passed by the cemetery, however, at the end of the village there were no tears in his eyes as there had been in Isobel's when she left St Auguste, but he could hear her voice as clearly as if she stood beside him. *'They are only things.'*

The words stayed with him for a long time on the journey back to Calais and, although he asked at every inn on the way, he could find no one who remembered a French family who had an Englishwoman travelling with them. Nor did he have any better luck in Calais, and so when a boat left at last for England with a surly John on board, Sarah beside him tearfully making sure that her late mistress's belongings were all safely in their care, Robert remained ashore.

That same evening he, too, left Calais with Brechtje and Frans, and headed north for Amsterdam. But when at last they arrived he found, as John had predicted, that no one knew anything at all about Isobel – neither in his own house nor in Cornelis van Ophoorn's house, empty of servants now except for Griet and one old woman, the furniture dust-sheeted and the house itself to be sold. And, since there was no one else to ask and nowhere else he could look for her, he got on the next boat to England and arrived in London at last, the cold wet rain of an early December evening blowing in his face.

John opened the great oak door of the Chelsea house and as soon as he saw who it was he pulled him inside. 'Thank God you're back,' he growled, 'but keep your voice down!'

'What in heaven's name is going on?' Robert said impatiently and John's big hand tightened on his arm, drawing him into an alcove off the main hall.

'The King's men have been here looking for you several times,' he said. 'You've got to leave the country at once!'

'*Leave* – but I've only just arrived! And why, for God's sake?'

'Quiet! I beg you!' John was whispering. 'I don't trust anyone here! You're wanted for murder and for robbing the King! Treason they call it and you'll swing for it if they find you!'

'But my grandfather – I must see him – '

'He's been dead and buried this three weeks,' John said quietly.

'Grandfather is dead?' Robert felt a strange, cold feeling of shock even though he had been prepared for the old man's death for months. It did not seem possible that he would never hear that harsh voice again, never see those angry old eyes peering up at him.

'Aye,' John said. 'He died in his sleep. The young nurse girl found him – she was good to him, I'll say that for her.'

Three weeks, Robert thought. Only three weeks sooner and I'd have been in time. And as if John could read his mind he said shortly. 'He couldn't wait any longer, you see.'

Robert began to curse quietly and John said again after a moment, 'You must leave now, this very minute. It's not safe to be here.'

'But – but how did they *know*?' Robert said, trying to collect his thoughts. 'And Cromwell is dead – '

'Maybe the fellow we thought had drowned lived to tell a tale after all – they've not bothered with me so far except to pester me with questions as to where you were. But even if Lord Cromwell is dead 'tis said the King is like a new man since he married again.'

They could hear men's voices, and footsteps, as servants came into the hall to close the window shutters and light wall flares, and they waited in the alcove holding their breath until the men had gone. 'Has Walter Clifford come back?' Robert asked then, and when John shook his head, he said grimly, 'I'm not surprised, but I must first go to Raskelfe in case he has gone back there with some tale that lays the blame on me for Beatrice's death.'

''Tis not worth it,' John muttered. 'The Nevilles will believe what they want to believe anyway.'

'Maybe so, but still I have to tell them what happened, or as much as I know at least.' Robert said grimly. Afterwards I'll get a boat to Holland and stay there until all this has blown over, if it ever does – '

'Did you find Mistress Isobel?' John asked abruptly.

'No,' Robert said flatly, 'and I don't know where else to look.'

'Maybe 'tis as well.' John was muttering again and Robert felt a sudden, useless spurt of anger.

316

'I'll need a fresh horse,' he said coldly, 'and more money. Can you get whatever is left behind the panelling in my grandfather's bedchamber? I'll share it with you, for you'll need some meanwhile – '

'I'm coming with you! I'll tell them I'm going to Wales for you!'

Did John *really* want to come with him, Robert wondered as he reached out a hand and clapped the big shoulder he could only see in outline. 'I'll be glad to have you with me,' he said gruffly, 'but you don't have to come on my account.'

''Tis only the two of us are to know it, but your grandfather told me before he died that I was one of his bastards.' The rough voice had become almost gentle. 'So you see, I'm a kind of half uncle, and how could I let a nephew go off with no one to stand by him?'

Robert began to laugh quietly. 'I think I always knew it!' He laughed again. 'Well, I'll not say I won't be glad of your company!'

Twenty minutes later they were riding through the unlit, evil-smelling streets of London heading north, and as the horse that John had had waiting for him for days carried him by open sewers and picked its way among pot-holes and the refuse that lay everywhere, Robert thought grimly that he was *Sir* Robert now. That at last he was what he had dreamed of being for as long as he could remember. He owned the house he had just left, and Critley, and the land up there, and land over in Wales, besides what he owned in Holland, and there was no longer anyone to shout orders at him from a sick bed or tell him he was a fool. Yet he was on the run like a common thief, and if he was caught it would be no near-drowning in that hell hole in the Tower. This time it would be the block and his head rolling like all the others.

It seemed poor consolation now, that he had honoured his ancestors and the memory of Dom Richard, and gladdened the hearts of the monks of Cîteaux by restoring their treasure to them. Even the fact that in doing so he had triumphed over the King and Lord Thomas Cromwell and Edward Dutton seemed to have become less important, and he had an instant's piercing insight into Isobel's anguish when Christopher had been kidnapped, although in his arrogance he had thought he felt her

317

pain as if it were his own. He was suddenly bitterly ashamed that he had not immediately put Christopher's safety above all other considerations at the time, and he wished from the bottom of his heart that he could tell her so, but like all the other things he wanted to say to her it seemed that the words would remain unsaid for the rest of his life.

They had reached the meaner streets now and in spite of the watchman's cry of 'Hang out your lights!' there was scarcely a house that had a burning oil lamp above its door. John had not spoken for a long time but he rode alongside, solid and dependable, and they spent the night in an old, run-down inn on the outskirts of the city, using assumed names, as they were to do for the rest of the journey to Raskelfe.

Early next morning, just after dawn, they set off again – two men as different as it was possible to be, yet bound together by ties of blood and friendship. And, although there were as always moments of disagreement and even outright anger between them, they were still friends when they rode through the village of Raskelfe three weeks later, greatly relieved that in all that time they had seen no sign of the King's men or anything at all to suggest that Death was snapping at their heels.

The village was set in moorland where nothing seemed to grow but whins and ling, and when Robert and John rode past the cluster of houses they seemed to arouse little interest. Its few inhabitants were apparently well used to the sight of 'gentry' on their way to the castle – not that either Robert or John had the look of 'gentry' after nearly three weeks on the road and no change of clothes.

They passed the old stone church at the end of the village and followed the track north east of it. When they had crossed the double ditch they found themselves inside the park and rode on more slowly. The trees stood tall and straight, and small animals darted away through the undergrowth, but Robert noticed nothing, his whole mind concentrating on what he would soon have to say to the earl and his wife. So lost in thought was he that when they rode past a clump of bushes and came upon a group of men sitting round a smoking fire, the sight took him by surprise – he could not even remember having been conscious of the smell of smoke.

They were beggars by the look of them, some of the starving

318

thousands that were swarming all over England now, with no one to help them since the monasteries and convents had been closed. They wore the tattered remains of old cloaks over their rags of clothes and it was impossible to guess at the age of any of them, but when they turned their faces to stare at Robert and John there was the same gaunt look of hunger and dull resentment in all of them. Beyond, through the trees, Robert could see the outline of the castle with its high walls and turrets and many chimneys, and he had a sudden mental image of the tables in the great hall as he had seen them on his last visit, groaning under the weight of food, and the dogs lying on the rush-covered floor being given the leavings that would have been sufficient to feed these men for a week. On an impulse he took the sack of food that hung from his saddle and threw it to the man nearest to him. There were a few seconds of stunned silence and then with shouts of delight the rest of the beggars fell on the sack like starving animals, pulling out the two roasted chickens, the lump of ham, the bread, the cheese, the butter –

'Come on!' John growled, 'before they take our clothes off our backs!' But as they began to ride on, one of the beggars struggled to his feet, a chicken leg in his hand. He was young and tall with fiery red hair and he shouted after them, the burr of the border counties strong in his voice, 'God bless you, sir! And good luck to you!'

Robert had forgotten the incident by the time they reached the gatehouse of the castle. By then, too, John had stopped lecturing him about the folly of having anything to do with 'rascals who might have done them all kinds of mischief' and half an hour later, while John was still seeing to their horses, he faced the earl and countess in the earl's study and began to tell his story. They let him talk without interruption but when he had finished there was silence for what seemed a very long time.

''Tis a sorry tale from start to finish,' the earl said sombrely at last. 'My little niece buried in France and no one even sure how she died!'

'I told you – ' Robert began, but the earl interrupted him.

'Unless Walter Clifford can be found we shall never know what *really* happened.'

'I am very much aware of that – ' Robert's voice was even colder now than the earl's ' – and of the position in which I find

319

myself as a result. That is why I have searched everywhere for the fellow, why my first question as soon as I arrived here was to ask if he had returned.'

The earl drummed thick fingers on the polished wood of the table in front of him. 'If you'd come straight back to England with the child, instead of dashing off to France, Beatrice would still be alive,' he grated. 'You've been a poor kind of husband to her.'

'I had a duty to see the treasure safely back to Cîteaux, my lord,' Robert said stiffly. 'There was no one else who could have done so and how was I to know Beatrice would follow me?'

The countess, round-faced and sallow in an unbecoming yellow gown opened her mouth to say something and then closed it hastily as her husband barked, 'The girl was probably lonely, and she likely guessed you were with the bloody nun! What did you expect her to do?'

For the hundredth time Robert wished he could have left out all mention of Isobel and the treasure but it had to be the whole story or nothing and he tried not to lose his temper. 'Mistress Willis is no longer a nun,' he began, but before he could continue the earl interrupted him again.

'For God's sake, man, don't try to split hairs at a time like this! Nun – whore – what difference does it make now?' He was beginning to shout. 'My little niece, the girl I took into my care when her parents died – that I gave into *your* care – with a damned fine dowry – *that* girl is dead, dead by poisoning – lying in a foreign country – and – and you have the audacity to – to – '

He began to splutter and the countess got to her feet, putting a plump hand on his arm. 'My dear, you must not excite yourself so!'

The earl took a deep breath and his alarmingly high colour began to fade to a dull pink. 'We'll have a memorial service first thing in the morning,' he grated. 'You say the King's men are after you? Well, you're safe here for tonight, but after the service you leave, and I never want to set eyes on you again!'

'Nor I you, sir!' Robert said coldly, bowing to the countess who was looking down at her husband with a worried frown on her face. He turned on his heel and left the room, but as he strode away, still furiously angry he heard a door open and shut behind him and heard his name called. Looking over his shoulder he saw the countess hurrying towards him. She beckoned to him and drew him into a small parlour, closing the door quickly behind them.

'You must not take my husband's words too much to heart,' she said quickly, refusing a stool so that they remained standing, looking at each other warily. 'He always had a fondness for Beatrice, you see.' And then she added bitterly, 'He did not know the girl as well as I did.'

'No?' Robert said cautiously, not knowing how far he could trust this woman with the pale, anxious face and searching eyes.

'She was always a – a difficult girl,' the countess said, as if choosing her words now. 'She and Walter Clifford have always been *very* close. *Too* close.' She looked nervously at the door as if it might open at any moment and hurried on. 'It is *quite* conceivable that she might have put him up to some mischief in connection with Isobel Willis.'

'So at least *you* don't think I poisoned my wife!' Robert said with relief.

The countess shook her head, her greying curls bouncing with the vehemence of her denial. 'That is what I wanted to say to you. I've always liked you, Robert, even if we've never had much to say to one another and I've always thought Beatrice did better than she deserved in getting you for husband.' She hesitated and then went on slowly. 'She was two months pregnant when she married you. Did you know that?'

'No,' Robert said flatly, 'I did not. I was told the baby was premature. I never saw it.'

'It was Walter's, I think,' the countess said. 'I saw the two of them together, the night of our masked ball. Sarah, the maid – she knew she was pregnant. Everyone knew in the end except my husband – it's impossible to keep a secret in a place like this where there are so many gossiping women, but no one except myself seemed to suspect that it was Walter – '

Walter's child. And if it had lived – Robert felt faintly ill. What a fool he had been, he thought, and yet was it not what he deserved for letting himself be pushed into a marriage he did not want?

There was the sound of footsteps in the passage outside and the countess said quickly, 'I must go. But you must never tell anyone, especially not my husband, what I have said to you – '

321

'I won't,' Robert promised, and as he moved to open the door for her she whispered. 'We had a letter recently from my husband's cousin, Dame Helen Scrope – Isobel Willis has gone back to the nuns' house in York and is considering entering again!'

'Isobel is in *York?*' Robert's voice had risen with excitement in spite of himself and, with a sudden frightened look on her face, the countess almost ran from the room, out into the passage that was now empty and he watched her hurry away with a queer ache in his heart. He had found Isobel again when he least expected to, but it seemed as if he might be about to lose her again – and for the last time.

Chapter Thirty-Eight

Robert sat at the top table in the great hall that evening for supper, but as far away as possible from the earl and countess, and the countess's grandniece leaned forward across the long, narrow table to talk to him. She was young and virginal, but he could not have said whether she was pretty or not pretty, and he was not really listening to her. All he could see was Isobel. All he could hear was her voice. All he could think of was that she was in York, a mere day's ride away, but by now perhaps wearing, once again, the long, black habit that he had come to loathe. After a time the girl gave up in despair of catching the attention of the eligible young widower with the hard, bitter mouth and the brown eyes that looked at her as if she did not exist. She told herself that he was half-foreign anyway with his straw coloured hair and air of being 'different', even though she longed to run her fingers through that blond hair, and feel that mouth on hers. But a girl had her pride, and she turned her attentions reluctantly to the guffawing nonentity beside her who was unmistakeably English. He soon told the table at large that he was Francis Challoner and that his father, Sir Anthony, had just been granted Wolden Abbey and its land, and while the young girl began to give him the whole of her attention now that she had discovered he was also an 'eligible', Robert smiled into his wine for the first time that night. So much for Edward Dutton's dreams of grandeur, he thought, turning the stem of his goblet round and round with restless fingers, and as soon as the meal was over, even before the Fool came out, he looked for John sitting at a side table and the two of them slipped quietly away.

They went up to their bedchamber and when they had drawn a

chest across the door they lay down fully dressed, their swords beside them, as they had done for the whole of the journey north. But no one came to their door that night either, and after a hurried breakfast the next morning they took their places in the private chapel in the east wing for the memorial service. John was sulking, for Robert had told him earlier that he intended to call at York on their way to Kingston-upon-Hull.

'You're mad!' John grunted. 'You've been seen here in public by too many people. Someone will tell the King's men.'

'It's a risk I've got to take,' Robert said stubbornly. 'I must see Isobel again before I leave.'

John had shown no pleasure when he had heard that Isobel was in York and now he said with disgust, 'That woman will be the death of you yet!'

'You don't have to come with me! You can go ahead and we'll meet in Amsterdam!'

Robert did not know whether John was coming with him or not for he had not bothered to reply and strode off instead to fetch their horses from the stables and leave them tied outside the chapel, and now the two of them knelt side by side, not in the family pew but close behind.

The small chapel was crowded with house guests and servants as well as the immediate family, and the priest from the village church had been droning on for what seemed hours about the greatness of the Neville family and the sadness of the tragedy which had befallen Mistress FitzHugh in faraway France. But at last the good man came to an end with a final prayer and the congregation got to its feet with an audible sigh of relief. The earl and countess walked slowly down the aisle close-wrapped in heavy cloaks, and after a moment Robert pulled John by the sleeve and followed them. He was immediately conscious of all heads turning to stare, of the whispering all round him, like the rustling of dead leaves – ' . . . poisoned . . . always wild . . . bad end . . .' – and then the word he had been dreading, 'nun' – and the titters that followed.

His face was red with anger when he saw the soldiers standing just inside the door of the chapel, and a man beside them with a pale, soft face, staring at him as if hypnotised. *Edward Dutton!* Robert thought incedulously. But it can't be! He's *dead!* I'm imagining things – but the face was still there when he looked again, yellower than he remembered it, he realised now, but it was Edward Dutton's –

Robert turned even as he felt John's hand on his arm, and together they pushed their way back through the people behind them. There were angry mutters of 'Careful there! Damn you!' but they paid no heed, and pushed and shoved until they were in front of the altar and through the door behind it, and into the tiny room that served as a kind of sacristy where the priest was disrobing. He had just pulled his vestments over his head, and he stared at the two of them. 'What – what – ?'

'Forgive me, father – ' Robert did not wait to explain and he was through the far door, John on his heels, before the priest could say another word. And then they were outside, running for their horses, and as they mounted John gasped, 'How can the bastard be alive?'

'I don't know – I'd have *sworn* he was dead,' Robert said through his teeth. 'A curse on him anyway!'

They were riding towards the wood and he knew that they had no more than a few mintues' start, but the park to the right offered no cover of any kind. Even now he could hear the pounding of horses' hooves close behind, but soon they were among trees, riding along the track they had followed the previous evening, and suddenly it was very quiet. Robert wondered if by some miracle they could have lost their pursuers, but when they came at last to the far side of the wood they found them waiting for them – four soldiers with their pikes pointing straight at them, and Edward Dutton sitting on his horse beside them.

Even as Robert and John tried to turn and make a run for it one of the soldiers cried out, 'Halt in the King's name!' and the four began to advance until they were only feet away, Edward Dutton advancing with them.

'You thought I was dead, didn't you, FitzHugh?' he said softly. 'I am sorry to have disappointed you. And you thought you would not be seen and recognised returning to your own house and that your servants would not betray you!' His voice had begun to rise. 'You are stupid and arrogant like all your kind, and your man's a fool too! That ridiculous story about going to Wales! At this time of the year! Really, FitzHugh!'

'What do you want, Dutton?' he said harshly, wondering briefly which of the servants had betrayed them. 'I'll not say I'm not sorry to see you alive but your master, Lord Thomas Cromwell is dead and buried – and Wolden Abbey and its lands have been granted to Sir Anthony Challoner – '

'Lord Cromwell may be dead but there are others to take his place and to see that justice is done, FitzHugh! And it's your fault that I've been refused Wolden!' The malevolence in Edward Dutton's voice seemed to dribble from his lips like some visible, poisonous substance. 'I take my orders now from Sir Thomas Wriothesley, who is to be Ambassador to the Netherlands and *you* are wanted for robbing His Majesty of the Cîteaux treasure and for murdering two of his representatives! I have a warrant for your arrest!'

'The treasure belongs to the monks of Cîteaux Abbey,' Robert said shortly, 'and those two men were killed in self-defence – As for Wolden – '

But Edward Dutton did not let him finish. 'You can tell your story to the Judge,' he shouted, 'that is, if you live long enough to stand trial!'

He muttered something then over his shoulder and the soldiers began to move forward again, the one nearest to Robert lifting his pike an inch or two higher. But Robert drew out his sword and jerked on his reins at the same time so that his horse reared suddenly, pawing the air. The move took the soldier by surprise and his own horse became restless. Robert could see the others closing in, saw John with his sword out – thrust, and heard a blood-curdling yell. Then everything happened so quickly it became a blur.

The beggars came out from behind the trees like giant bats in their flapping cloaks, armed with iron bars and heavy stones, and Robert found himself on the ground, the soldier on top of him, the fellow's pike fallen from his hand as Robert's sword had done. They rolled over and over, snarling like fighting dogs, clawing and biting and kicking until Robert drove his fist into the face beneath him. The fellow lay still and he began to struggle to his feet, feeling sick and dizzy. He saw two soldiers slink off among the trees, limping and John sitting on the ground holding his head – and then Robert caught his breath.

The beggars had formed a circle and in the middle of the circle he could see the naked figure of Edward Dutton. They had stripped him of every shred of clothing and he stood with his hands clutched in front of him, covering himself as best he could. Robert could see his lips moving but could not hear what he was saying and then one of the beggars laughed and the others took up the laugh and the wood rang with the harsh, jeering sound. And Edward Dutton began to shout, to curse, to threaten. Even as Robert willed him not to be a fool he saw the arms raised, the iron bars, the stones.

'No!' he panted, trying to force his legs to move. 'Not that way! Leave him be!'

But he was wasting his breath. The pale, naked body disappeared from sight. There was a dreadful scream that Robert was to remember always, and then the arms fell, and lifted and fell again. He closed his eyes for what seemed only a second but when he opened them again, the beggars had disappeared, as swiftly as they had come – all but one, the tall, red-haired young fellow to whom he had thrown the bag of food the night before.

'We owed you a good turn,' he shouted, and then he disappeared too, and all that was left was the bloodied horror that had once been Edward Dutton and the limp bodies of two soldiers. One was dead, his head beaten to a pulp, but it would not be long before the other came to again.

Robert looked at John struggling to his feet, a dazed expression on his face. 'We'd best get out of here before the whole country is after us!' he said grimly, taking the older man by the arm.

First, however, they hid the two bodies in undergrowth as best they could, covering them with branches and handfuls of leaves, and then, just as the still unconscious soldier was beginning to groan, they mounted their horses and rode away, their swords back in their scabbards and the wind behind them.

'You'll swing before the night is out! You've lost what wits you had!' John shouted angrily as Robert announced that he was still determined to go to York before heading for the coast.

'Maybe!' Robert shouted back, thinking that it might have been his grandfather talking to him. 'But I'm going there! Meet me in Amsterdam!'

They had been riding towards Easingwold but as they came within sight of the first cottage he broke off, taking instead a track that led away from the village in a southerly direction. He turned to wave to John, only to find him still close behind.

'God's curse on you for a fool, but I'll come with you all the same!' John roared like an angry bull.

'It could cost you your life,' Robert said over his shoulder as he drew level. 'I don't want that on my conscience.'

But whatever John replied was lost on the wind and they rode together side by side in silence as mile after mile flew by and, although Robert in his turn cursed John for an obstinate fool, he was glad of the company, and he told himself that they had a couple of hours' start of whoever might come after them.

When he knocked on the door of the nuns' house in York just before dark the next day the door was opened by a red-faced nun with gooseberry-coloured eyes.

'May I speak to Mistress Isobel Willis?' he said, trying to sound confident.

'She is no longer here,' the portress said flatly.

'She has left?' He was unable to keep the bitter disappointment out of his voice and the nun nodded with the faintest of smiles on her red, bland face, looking over his shoulder at John who stood in the lane holding their two horses, his heavy shoulders drooping with fatigue, for they had ridden through the night.

'Where has she gone to?' His voice was harsh with sudden anger. But before the portress could reply, the little old nun whom he remembered seeing with Isobel hobbled forward, leaning on her stick.

'What *are* you saying, Dame Agatha?' she said in her clear voice. 'Isobel is still here! I have just been talking to her!' She peered up at Robert and said quickly before the other nun could reply, 'Why, you are the young man I saw in the garden!' Then she added graciously, while the portress still seemed to be struggling for words, 'Do come in! Isobel will be so pleased to see you!'

Not knowing which of them to believe, Robert followed the old nun down a narrow passage, and when they came to a door at the end of it she rapped imperiously on it with her stick. Robert could hear movement inside, and then the door opened and Isobel stood there.

Lady Isobel. The title would suit her, he thought, but there was so much to say and so little time in which to say it.